"Steven James has created a fast-moving thriller with psychological depth and gripping action. *Opening Moves* is a smart, taut, intense novel of suspense that reads like a cross between Michael Connelly and Thomas Harris . . . a blisteringly fast and riveting read."

—Mark Greaney, *New York Times* bestselling author of *Gunmetal Gray*

"[A] fast-moving, intense thriller that has as many demented twists and turns as the crimes themselves."

—Examiner.com

The Pawn

"Riveting."   —*Publishers Weekly*

"[An] exceptional psychological thriller."

—Armchair Reviews

EVERY WICKED MAN

THE BOWERS FILES

STEVEN JAMES

BERKLEY
New York

BERKLEY
An imprint of Penguin Random House LLC
375 Hudson Street, New York, New York 10014

ISBN: 9781101991596

First Edition: September 2018

Printed in the United States of America
3 5 7 9 10 8 6 4 2

Cover design by Jae Song
Cover photographs: Abandoned greenhouse by Gregory A.
Pozhvanov / Shutterstock; Silhouette of a man by Carlos G. Lopez / Shutterstock

For Ashley

"We are, I know not how, double in ourselves, so that what we believe we disbelieve, and cannot rid ourselves of what we condemn."

—PHILOSOPHER AND WRITER
MICHEL DE MONTAIGNE
(1533–1592)

"If we could see each other's thoughts, no one would be considered good."

—FROM *MAXIMS* BY ST. STEPHEN OF MURET
(1045–1124)

STAGE I

Denial

Camera angles. The observer.
There's a number for everyone.

1

"Have the nightmares been getting worse?"

Timothy Sabian didn't like being here at his psychiatrist's office, didn't like what it implied. "No. I mean, they're about the same."

"Well, that's good, then. I'm glad to hear that, Timothy—that they're not escalating in severity."

Sometimes they happen when I'm awake, Timothy thought, but kept that to himself.

Dr. Percival looked maybe fifty or so, and even though he was about the age Timothy's father would be, Timothy had never seen him as a father figure. This was a different kind of relationship.

"And the bugs?" the doctor asked.

"They're not real."

But even as he said the words, Timothy could feel the insects crawling across his abdomen.

In the literature, the feeling was described as "disturbing cutaneous sensations" rather than just saying that it felt like bugs crawling on you day and night. Then you had the constant itching, which doctors tried to make sound more scientific by naming it *pruritus.*

He didn't want to show Dr. Percival the scars on his arms from the scratching and from trying to use the

tweezers and the razor blade to dig out the bugs that burrowed into his skin. The bandage wrapped around his left
arm was keeping the fresh blood hidden today. That, and
the dark knit, long-sleeved sweater.

Yet still, Timothy felt the urge to scratch at them, to
swat at them, to make them somehow, somehow go away.

Somehow. Go.

Away.

But he did not. He just sat still instead and nodded
knowingly to his psychiatrist. "No bugs. That's just *delusional parasitosis.*"

"That's right," Dr. Percival said. "They're delusions."

But Timothy caught a hint of condescension, that sub-
tle shift in tone that meant the doctor had moved from
believing the patient to trying to understand what the patient believed.

He'd been through this before.

He'd seen how these things end.

It meant that empathy was on its way out and a diagnosis was on its way in. And at that point, it was just too hard
to go back. Once doubt crept in there, the more you
claimed you weren't mad, the more convinced they became that you were.

"We both know there aren't any bugs," Dr. Percival
went on, "but I'm more curious if they're still bothering you."

"All gone," Timothy said. "I'm not here today about
the nightmares or the bugs."

"Okay. Tell me why you're here today."

"How do you turn it off?"

"Turn what off?"

"The noise, the voices. Is it this way for everyone?"

"What do you mean?"

Since he didn't want his doctor to think he was crazy, Timothy hadn't brought this up before, but today, for some reason, he felt like he needed to talk about it, just to make sure, just to be certain that there wasn't anything seriously wrong with him.

"All the chatter, chatter, chatter," he said. "The words and the spiderweb connections, back and forth, all the time, touching each other. Intertwining, overlapping. Threading between things, around them. Is there a way to turn it off?"

"Tell me more about this chatter. About what it's like."

"I see a leaf on the ground and wonder about the tree that dropped it there, when it was planted, how long it's been growing, how many other trees its roots touch down there, deep underground. A server at a restaurant hands me a pen to sign my credit card receipt, and I think of all the other people who've ever held that pen—the dates they were on, the argument or lovemaking or chilled silence that might have followed later that evening after one of them signed the receipt and handed back the pen. I pass a girl on the street and see her smile after reading a text message, and I fill in what it was she might have read."

"That simply shows you have a vivid imagination."

"So you don't hear them?"

"I imagine different scenarios. Yes, of course. Different ways things might play out. Everyone does."

"There's something wrong with me."

Dr. Percival glanced at the clock on the wall, something they should teach psychiatrists never to do, for all that it communicates to their clients.

Still twenty minutes left in their session.

"I think it's natural to see connections between things," the doctor said, "to wonder about something's past, its origins, its future. I think it's a skill you've honed over time. Being a novelist, you've taught yourself to be observant and inquisitive. Your livelihood depends on it. Don't mistake creativity for mental illness. Your imagination is—"

"Overactive. That's what my fifth-grade teacher used to tell me: 'You have an overactive imagination.' Is that possible?"

"It's just a saying."

"How can an imagination be *over*active? Isn't there something wrong with it, then? I mean, if it's more active than it should be?"

"Timothy, most people's imaginations have been blunted by years of sensible thinking and—"

"Beveled dreams."

"Beveled dreams?"

"Dreams that have been chisel-wedge sharpened by the futility of slamming against an uncompromising reality."

Timothy caught himself scratching at his arm, at the bugs crawling out of the open sores he'd been so careful to bandage over, the bugs Dr. Percival assured him weren't real.

The doctor watched him carefully, then jotted something in his notebook—another therapist habit that silently spoke volumes.

Sometimes Timothy wondered if Dr. Percival was really writing things related to his case. Maybe he was scribbling out a shopping list. Maybe he was drawing farm animals. Maybe he was writing a letter to his daughter and he was going to mail it to her as soon as Timothy left for the—

Kill him.

"It's happening," Timothy whispered.

"What's happening?"

You see that letter opener on his desk? Pick it up.

"No." Timothy shook his head, tried to quiet the voice. "Make it stop, make it stop."

Pick up the letter opener.

Dr. Percival was watching him carefully. "Tell me what it's like right now, Timothy. What you're hearing."

"No. I can't."

Do it.

He had to make it stop. He had to had to had to had to. And there was only one way.

Timothy picked up the letter opener.

"What are you doing?"

Now drive it into his neck.

"No," Timothy yelled. "I won't!"

"You won't what?"

Lean across the desk, grab him by the collar to hold him in place, and then push it up into his throat. Just like the others.

No, no. There haven't been others. You're lying to me!

I'm not lying, Timothy. You know that—

"No!"

But yet he stood.

The psychiatrist eased back and reached for the button under his desk, the one he'd pressed eight months ago and Timothy knew was still there. He wasn't stupid, after all. He wasn't dangerous anymore. Not like he was back then.

He wasn't—no, of course he wasn't—or else he wouldn't be here today; he would be back at the White Shirts Place with all those people who needed to be locked away, the ones who were a danger to themselves or others.

The crazy ones.

The unstable ones.

You're unstable, Timothy. You're crazy.

"No, I'm not!"

"You need to put that down, Timothy."

But Timothy walked around the desk to where Dr. Percival was standing, and the doctor backed up even farther, until he was almost to the window.

Timothy felt his hands trembling. "You have to help me."

"Timothy, get back." The psychiatrist's voice caught with fear. "Now!"

You have a vivid imagination. Overactive. There's something wrong.

Beveled dreams.

Oh, beveled dreams.

Just like the others.

And then, Timothy Sabian shoved his psychiatrist fiercely against the wall and drove the letter opener into his own neck.

You're not supposed to survive something like that. Some people said he was lucky; others, that it was a miracle. Timothy just knew that he was in the hospital for a long time afterward. They kept his wrists and ankles strapped down so he couldn't move, so he couldn't hurt himself, and despite all the drugs they gave him and all the therapy they tried, the voices didn't go away.

And neither did the bugs.

He knew that too.

2

"C'mon," my stepdaughter begged me. "Just once more around the pumpkins. Seriously. I've got this."

It was our fourth visit to this parking lot since she'd turned sixteen a week and a half ago. Teaching a daughter to drive. A rite of passage for dads, and in this case, I was the closest thing she had to that.

"I need to get back, Tessa. I have to work tonight."

"It's that suicide, isn't it?"

"I can't tell you about the case."

"Thought so."

She shouldn't have known anything about what I was working on, but because of who was dead and what I do for a living, it hadn't been hard for her to deduce how I might be spending my evening.

But as bright as she was, she wasn't exactly a prodigy at driving a car.

Not having any traffic cones, I'd opted for the pumpkins, a good seasonal choice—and now deeply discounted after Halloween. The day after the holiday, the price dropped in half. Stores only decorate for upcoming holi-days, never the ones in the rearview mirror. They build up to a holiday for months and then, the moment it's over, start advertising for the next one.

People were already looking ahead to Thanksgiving. Always looking ahead. Frantically scrambling forward.

"I promise to be quick and not to squish any more of 'em," Tessa vowed with one hand raised in an earnest sa-lute. There she sat in the driver's seat. Inquisitive yet sad eyes. Light on the makeup—apart from the blood-dipped color of her fingernail polish. Dark, night-washed hair.

"You do know what those pumpkins represent, don't you?"

"Traffic cones."

"People."

"If they were people, they'd get outta my way."

We lived in New York City—not the ideal place to teach a teenager that it's not supposed to be the job of pedestri-ans to avoid getting run over.

"We don't want you smack-whamming the car into anything," I said, "let alone running over pedestrians."

She stared at me coolly.

"What?"

"Did you really just say 'smack-whamming'? Was that you trying to be hip?"

"It's just what came out. Why? Was it hip?"

"Um. No."

She'd flattened two of the eight pumpkins so far, and I wasn't holding my breath about the other six, especially if we went with the figure-eight pattern again rather than just practicing stopping in time without nudging the fruit, which she was a lot better at.

Earlier, I'd made the mistake of referring to the pumpkins as vegetables, but she was quick to correct me, informing me that, *of course*, they're fruit, that everybody knows *that*.

With her off-the-charts IQ, she would undoubtedly ace the written portion of the test, but the behind-the-wheel part was clearly going to be a challenge.

"Alright, let's see it." I pointed to her hands. "Remember, ten o'clock and two o'clock."

"I still can't believe you're stuck on analog," she complained wearily, but she did move her hands to the places I'd shown her earlier on the steering wheel. "It's so twentieth-century of you. You're showing your age."

"I'm thirty-five years old, Tessa."

"Uh-huh. And your point is?"

I indicated the line of pumpkins. "Let's see you do it this time all the way through. And watch out for pedestrians."

"Right."

"And remember, if you start to skid for whatever reason, it won't seem to make sense, but steer into the skid."

"Steer where you veer."

"Exactly."

She rounded the first pumpkin, then the second, and was confidently on her way to cruising past the third when she overcompensated the turn, cranking the wheel too far to the left. The bang and bump made it clear what'd just happened.

She cringed.

"Another fruitality," I sighed.

She eyed me.

"Come on, now," I said. "That was funny, right?"

"You're starting to scare me." Then she shook her head. "I wasn't gonna hit that pumpkin. I *swear*. Maybe it rolled in front of us because of the Coriolis effect."

"C'mon, let's pick them up and head home."

Lots of people in the city choose to go without personal vehicles—and I understood why. If it hadn't been necessary for my job at the Bureau, I might not have kept mine.

I aimed the car toward the parkway. From here, at this time of day, I expected we should be back to our apartment within the hour.

"So," she said. "I watched the video."

"The video?"

"The one with the senator's son."

"Tessa, I told you not—"

"I know, but it's in the news and . . . It was . . . I didn't like it. I didn't like seeing it."

"Of course you didn't." *It's not something anyone should like seeing*, I thought.

Our Cyber division was taking down the video wherever it popped up online, but that hadn't seemed to be doing a whole lot of good. It was out there. And once something's on the Internet, you're fighting a losing battle trying to contain it, even with the resources the Bureau has.

"How much did you watch?" I asked her.

"Enough." Then she added, "But if it's a suicide, why are you involved? I still don't get that."

I didn't mention my observation that someone else had been present when Jon Murray died. Only a few people knew, including Assistant Director DeYoung and the senator, who'd invited me to his estate tonight so I could have a look around. Otherwise, we hadn't released the information—I didn't want the media reporting it. Right now, we had an edge, however slight that might be, and I needed additional information before we released any more details to the public.

"I never said I was involved," I told Tessa evasively.

"Gotcha." She'd started chewing a glob of vegan-friendly gum—which I hadn't even known existed until I met her. "So what's your plan?"

"I can't discuss specifics of an investigation."

"But if you could?"

"Sorry."

"Broad strokes."

"My plan . . . Hmm . . . I'd have to say I have a plan so secret that even I don't know what it is."

She stopped chewing. "How long have you been waiting to use that line?"

"It is possible I've been saving it up for a while."

"Huh," she said in a tone that was hard to read.

Oh, this was going brilliantly.

Christie, my wife of less than two months, had told me not to try so hard to connect with Tessa—to just be myself—but I was still trying to figure out what that self looked like in the role of a stepfather. I'd never been a dad before, and I certainly didn't know the right things to say to a teenage girl.

Tessa was quiet, and I wasn't sure if I should try to find something to talk about or not. In the end, I said nothing.

Empathy has never been my strong suit, but I'd been doing my best to remain understanding with her. It'd been a tumultuous couple of weeks for this girl.

She'd had a foster sister for a few months, but now that

was over, and her mood swings had been more pronounced than usual as she processed being an only child again.

Azaliya Saleem was a fourteen-year-old girl who'd been staying with us through a special arrangement with social services. As it turned out, she was with us nine weeks, and then a relative of hers from her extended family in Kazakhstan agreed to care for her.

Azaliya's departure from our lives had happened abruptly and took Tessa by surprise. Honestly, it was affecting her more than I thought it would. I hadn't realized how much having a sister, even if it was only a foster sister, had meant to her.

"Can I ask you something, Patrick?" she said, drawing me out of my thoughts.

"Sure."

"Do you know why Mom's pissed at me?"

"What makes you think your mom is mad at you?"

A shrug.

Tessa and Christie were extremely close, and the girl could read my wife even better than I could. But then again, I'd only met Christie in the spring and, after a bit of a whirlwind romance, proposed—and, since we couldn't come up with any good reason to put off the wedding, had promptly tied the knot.

Neither of them spoke much about Tessa's biological father, but from what I'd gathered, he hadn't even stuck around long enough to be present for her birth.

"She just needed some time to herself this weekend," I explained.

"You mean time away from me."

From us, I thought.

"From everyone," I said.

"Yeah, but at a monastery?"

"They have a retreat center there. It's really not as weird as it sounds."

"Uh-huh. Well, it sounds pretty weird. I think she's upset about something, and I want to know what it is."

Christie, who somewhat enigmatically attended a fundamentalist Baptist church and was also a fan of the Catholic mystics and contemplatives, had taken the weekend to attend a silent retreat at the Abbey of Gethsemani in rural Kentucky. One of her favorite authors, Thomas Merton, had lived there as a hermit before his death in 1968.

Over the years, his books had sold hundreds of thousands—maybe millions—of copies, and since he'd taken a vow of poverty, the money from the royalties went back to the monastery. Using the funds, they'd built a retreat center beside their church. It was open to the public and, as long as you made a reservation, you could come and participate in a silent, unguided three- or four-day spiritual retreat.

Christie had been there once a few years ago and decided, somewhat on the spur of the moment on Tuesday night, that she wanted to return. As it turned out, they had a room available for this weekend, and she'd flown to Lexington this morning.

Getting back to Tessa's concern, I said, "Don't worry about your mom. I'm sure she's fine. It's good to give people a little space sometimes."

"Ha."

"Ha?"

"I see what you did there—first you said she needed *time*, then that we need to give people *space*. Time and space. This from Mr. Geospatial Investigator himself."

I hadn't even noticed. "Glad you caught that."

"You didn't even realize you said that, did you?"

"Don't be ridiculous."

She blew a bubble. "That's what I thought."

Time and space. She was right about that much.

I leave means, motive, and opportunity to my associates. I'm looking instead at context, timing, and location since they provide a much more reliable set of indicators on which to base an investigation. Searching for motives is simply a guessing game that we're not nearly as good at as television crime shows make us out to be.

People love to go motive hunting. They want to know why someone could do such and such a thing, the reason behind it all, and even what initiated the behavior in the first place. A clean-cut and forensic answer, something understandable and definable that they can put their finger on:

"Did you always like lighting fires?"

"No."

"When did you start?"

"After my mom died. Then everything changed."

Ah. Yes. So that was it. The loss of his mother. That explains things—that's the stressor, the psychological trigger we were looking for. Case closed.

It's somehow comforting to find that single event, that precipitating one, that explains the subsequent choices someone makes, to play pin the motive on the crime. A way to make sense of it all.

However, life isn't that simple and tidy. Although motives are always present, they can never be established with any degree of certainty. Because of that, the search for them is always a search for circumstantial evidence rather than hard facts, and I want my investigations to be built on facts rather than conjecture.

Normally, I'm only called in when we've finished a comparative case analysis, or CCA, and established a link between serial offenses. However, this time since the assistant director knew the senator, he'd asked me to look into things.

"You have a knack for seeing the connection beneath the connection," he'd told me. "I want you on this."

Tessa and I arrived at our apartment, I threw on some canned vegetable soup for dinner—a meal even I could prepare—and then, after we'd eaten, I made sure she was set for the evening and left for the senator's mansion.

It wasn't far outside the city, and I would be arriving at the same time of night that his son died two days ago, drowning in their heated outdoor pool.

Being there at the same time would allow me to evaluate any nearby lighting from the streetlights surrounding the estate and help me determine the most logical entrance and exit routes for the person who I believed stood by and watched that young man drown.

3

The video was troubling.

Two nights ago, Jon Murray had turned on his phone's camera and started live-streaming through a video app. He placed the phone on a deck table next to his father's swimming pool, then stepped out of the frame for a few minutes. When he returned, he was rolling the executive chair from his dad's home office.

Two pair of handcuffs waited on the seat of the chair. We still weren't certain where he'd obtained them from, but we were checking his credit cards for recent purchases.

It was nighttime, but lights from inside the pool and around the grounds gave enough light to see what was happening.

A hedge bordered one side of the pool. The L-shaped mansion lined two other sides of it. A guest house with no lights on sat beyond the pool's far end.

Jon returned to the camera and repositioned it so the office chair was centered in the screen. He walked over, picked up the handcuffs, and rolled the chair back another foot so that it was resting near the edge of the pool. Then he cuffed his left wrist to the left arm of the chair. The chair's arm formed a loop so he wouldn't be able to slide the cuff off.

If it wasn't clear before then what he was about to do, it was pretty evident at that point.

He turned his attention to the chair's other arm, locked one of the bracelets around it, then slipped his wrist into the remaining open cuff. He was able to snap it shut by nudging it with his leg. Even on the video, you could hear the ratcheting click as the handcuff closed.

He stared into the camera, tears in his eyes, and said four simple words: "This is for you." Then he scooted backward, rolling the chair to the lip of the pool. The wheels caught on the splash rim around the ridge.

For a moment, it seemed like he might change his mind, and he hesitated there, staring somewhere beyond the camera, but then, with one violent motion, he threw himself backward. The chair tilted and splashed in, although, with the limited perspective of the phone in that position, you couldn't see exactly what happened after Jon hit the water.

Yesterday, some of our analysts tested a similar chair, thinking that the cushioning would provide enough flotation, but Jon's weight and the weight of the base of the chair must've been enough to drag him under. Whether the chair flipped around, holding him facedown in the water, or sank right away, we'll never know. We just know that when his body was found, it was at the bottom of the pool, his wrists still cuffed to the arms of the chair.

The video was live-streamed through a link on the anonymous /b/ bulletin board on 4chan, but since no location or identification had been given at the beginning of it, even though it looked real, since it was Halloween night—the perfect time for a hoax like that—some viewers assumed the footage was faked and began a thread of comments, picking apart how tipping an office chair into a pool like that wouldn't kill you.

The video continued to feed through for the next three hours until someone who'd seen a picture from a dinner party that the senator's wife had hosted before she died last year recognized the pool, called it in, and officers responded, finding Jon dead in two meters of water.

This morning, I'd watched the first few minutes of the video over and over again, trying to see if there was anything we'd missed. Only on the ninth time through did I notice a reflection on a darkened window from the guest house just beyond the far end of the pool.

With no lights on behind them, the windows were black and reflective, and at first I thought that the image was just the lights from the mansion glimmering off the water and playing tricks on me. I paused the footage and zoomed in but wasn't able to make out anything for certain until one of the techs in our digital forensics unit enhanced the footage, which I could then see reflected this side of the pool, including the glass sliding doors behind the camera.

And the outline of someone standing in the living room.

I rewound it.

Watched it again.

Yes, the figure first appeared twenty-two seconds after Jon left to get the chair from his dad's office and finally disappeared only after the water in the pool was still and the young man was dead. Based on the broadness of the person's shoulders, I started with the working hypothesis that we were looking at a male rather than a female.

So if this was a suicide, someone watched it occur. That person could've stopped Jon, helped him, maybe even saved him after he was in the water, but he didn't. He didn't even call 911.

There's nothing illegal about watching someone die. In other words, although mental health officials must act if they feel someone is suicidal, the public has no legal obligation to stop a person from killing himself.

However, don't assist with someone's suicide or you might be in real trouble. Help her position the razor blade against her wrist and you could spend the rest of your life in prison, but stand aside and watch her do it and you'll be able to go on your way without any care or concern. You can even film her doing it and face no legal consequences.

It was the law. It might not be perfect, but it was what it was.

So, even if we could identify who the person was, it wouldn't make him guilty of homicide—unless he'd somehow coerced the young man into taking his own life or assisted him in some way. Maybe providing the handcuffs or helping Jon obtain that office chair? It was a stretch, but it was possible we could get a conviction based on that.

The senator had three security cameras positioned around his house, in addition to the ones monitoring the perimeter of his estate. Our team was analyzing the exterior feeds. I focused on the footage from the residence and saw no evidence that anyone else had been on the premises at the time of Jon's death.

And yet, there was that person in the living room behind the camera.

It was hard to get a good feel for the route someone would've needed to take through the mansion to avoid appearing in any of the CCTV footage and yet also be present there by that poolside door when Jon died.

The best way for me to figure out the route would be walking through the house myself.

A few phone calls later, I had the assistant director's approval and the senator's invitation: "My son wasn't suicidal," he told me. "I have no idea why he did this to himself. Anything I can do to figure out what happened here, I'm glad to do it."

"Thank you, Senator. I'd like to have a look around tonight, if possible."

"Of course."

I gave him a time, and he gave me the address.

"I'll be here," he said.

So that was all earlier today before I managed to slip away to work with Tessa on her driving. Now, I paused at the gated entrance to the senator's estate, showed my credentials to the guard posted out front, and then pulled forward onto the circular drive that terminated beside the residence's grand and sweeping front porch.

4

Senator Murray was waiting for me.

Despite the time of day, he still had on a tie, now loosened around his neck. Though lean and good-looking, he had the weary eyes of an old man. They seemed foreign and out of place on his forty-eight-year-old face. Grief might not scar the skin, but it leaves its marks all the same. And it doesn't always take its time doing so.

Some people recover; many never do, and their eyes are changed forever.

Senator Murray shook my hand firmly. "What can I do to help you, Agent Bowers?"

"First of all, let me say how sorry I am about your loss. My sincerest condolences."

"Thank you."

I wasn't exactly sure how to follow up on that—I never am—and a moment passed before he led us out of the silence. "So tonight, what do you have in mind?"

"Yes. If I can have access to the footage from the security cameras, that would be most helpful. In fact, if you could walk through the house using different routes while I watch the feed, that might work out even better."

A brisk nod. "Follow me. We can pull up the footage from the television in my office."

Jon had been the senator's only child and the house already felt lonely and way too vacant.

The office was a study in mahogany—from the matching bookshelves lined with thick law volumes to the broad desk and elegant end table. On his desk, the inbox had only four or five sheets of paper in it. The pencil holder, desk calendar, family photograph, and iMac were all positioned with careful precision, forming a semicircle that kept everything within easy reach.

Nothing in the office was out of place, except the conspicuously missing executive chair that'd been replaced with a kitchen chair that now sat behind his desk.

I briefly wondered how long he would go before replacing the rolling chair. Maybe never—it might be too emotionally difficult. We often act inexplicably in our grief, and survivor's guilt, if that was at play at all here, can make us do strange things for penance.

When he turned on the wall-mounted television, it was preset to Cable Broadcast News. I recognized the anchors from the instances when they brought on my mentor, Dr. Calvin Werjonic, as a guest criminology expert. He was in the city now, as a matter of fact, lecturing at Columbia University, and we were planning to meet for lunch on Monday.

The network mostly interviewed him during high-profile serial crime sprees—rape, arson, murder—to analyze the geospatial aspects of the crimes. Dr. Werjonic was nearly twice my age, and although he was still going strong, he'd recommended my name to the producers to replace him. However, I wasn't interested in a job like that. To put it mildly, working with the media did not thrill me. More often than not, they just get in the way and make it harder for law enforcement to do its job. I'd seen it happen all too often.

Senator Murray clicked through a password prompt and brought up his home security system's feed.

The live footage from eight surveillance cameras appeared in a grid on the television screen.

Five of them covered the estate's periphery. The first of the three monitoring the house was positioned at the front door above the porch and targeted the circular drive. On the footage from the night of Jon's death, there hadn't been any indication that another car had been on the drive or that anyone had left the house. The guard saw no one and hadn't opened the gate for any cars, except for Jon's.

The second residential camera covered most of the elegantly furnished living room and part of the kitchen.

The third was located out back and actually rotated to span both the pool area and the entrance to the guest house. From studying its footage earlier, I knew that from its vantage point you could see Jon positioning the chair, but no one else was visible outside, and the camera rotated before we could see exactly how Jon died.

"Senator," I said, "may I ask why you only have three cameras on the house itself and five around the edge of the property?"

"My wife's idea, before she passed. She didn't like cameras in the home and figured that if there was an intruder, he'd be picked up on the other footage before getting to the house, and the home's security system would take over from there."

"Tell me more about that. The security system."

He gave me the rundown—upon intrusion, the alarm

would go off, the guard out front would be notified, and a 911 call would automatically be placed.

"And you know that it's functioning properly?" I asked.

"Yes. We had it checked just last month, and then I rechecked it yesterday after . . . well . . . just to make sure."

"And Jon would have known the password?"

A slight pause. "Yes."

"Senator, who do you think Jon was talking about when he said, 'This is for you'?"

"I don't know."

"Did he have a girlfriend?"

"Not that I'm aware of."

"Any grudges with anyone? Any enemies?"

"No, of course not. Do you think it was a message for the viewers? The people watching online?"

"Perhaps. Or maybe the person most likely to find the phone?"

"Me?"

"I'm just wondering."

"No. That doesn't make any sense. He would never have killed himself for me. He was a vibrant, optimistic young man. I'm no perfect father, but we had a strong, loving relationship."

"Okay."

"Pete told me that you suspect someone else was here when Jon died. What makes you think that?"

It was unusual for me to hear someone refer to Assistant Director DeYoung by his first name, but there was no reason to think it odd that his friend would do so.

"There was an image reflected back in the guest house's window," I said.

"I watched that video. I didn't see anything."

"It's more visible when the resolution is enhanced. I'll show you."

Using my phone, I logged into my account on the Federal Digital Database and then pulled up the zoomed-in, digitally enhanced version of the video and showed it to him.

The senator watched the footage quietly.

When it was finished, I asked, "Do you have any idea who that might be?"

"No. No, I don't."

Since the person in question didn't appear in any of the CCTV footage either before or after Jon's death, he evidently knew the placement of the cameras. So, as I walked through the house and then directed the senator to take different pathways himself while I studied the feeds, I tried to discern the most likely path that the observer might have used to enter or exit the residence while avoiding detection.

After twenty minutes of trial and error, I came up with two possible routes.

One ended in the garage, the other at a window west of the front porch. Upon closer inspection, I found that the window was unlocked, something no one had noticed up until now, because no one was looking.

I called for the Bureau's Evidence Response Team to send someone over to check for prints and DNA near the window, then I returned to the pool, placed my phone where Jon's had been, and began recording.

Wearing gloves to avoid leaving prints, I tapped the garage door opener. Since both the click of the handcuffs and the splash of the chair into the pool were audible on Jon's video, I anticipated that we would be able to hear the sound of the garage door as well—if it was used while the young man's camera was filming.

When I checked, however, the rattle of it opening was clearly audible on my phone. The video Jon had recorded contained no sound of the door.

The garage's side door was wired to the alarm, so, for now, I went with the most likely scenario of the observer using the window to exit the premises and perhaps enter it as well.

The storms earlier this week would have left the soil outside the window damp, and I believed it was possible that we would find sole impressions.

Further scrutiny revealed a couple of partials near the flower bed. The lab could run them against our database and see if anything came up. I photographed them and sent the pictures to the online case file I'd started earlier today when I first identified the image of the person in the house.

Often in an investigation, you end up engaged in triaging evidence. You don't know what a clue is until you see that it's tied to the rest of the case. And sometimes what you think is a clue ends up being only a distraction.

The solution?

You keep your eyes and your options open as you move forward.

I made sure that the same combination of lights was on in the pool area, then stood where the chair had been when Jon tipped it backward into the water.

Based on the perspective, the person behind the sliding glass doors that led to the pool area would've been easily visible to Jon Murray while he sat there in front of the camera. Maybe that's what he was looking at right before he killed himself.

I faced the pool and stared at it. I wanted answers even though they touched on motives: What would drive a person to such an extreme act? Why was someone watching? Who was the "you" Jon had referred to when he said his final words?

Maybe he was speaking to the observer when he said, "This is for you."

And maybe not.

It's natural, I suppose, this curiosity regarding the *why*, but that's not what I was here for. I was here to figure out the truth, not guess what someone else may or may not have been thinking.

Who would know the precise placement of those three cameras? All three were positioned unobtrusively so if you weren't aware of their location, you wouldn't likely be able to find them—and you almost certainly wouldn't know with such accuracy exactly where they were aimed.

A family member? Someone from the senator's security team? The company that installed the cameras?

We would look into all of those possibilities.

Sometimes the most obvious answer isn't the first one you come up with because it's too self-evident, but certainly the senator would have known about the angles of the cameras.

Could he have been the person behind the glass?

That seemed incomprehensible to me. However, I wasn't going to count anything out at this point.

Also, Jon would've likely known the cameras' locations. He could have told the person who watched him die. He could've also been the one who unlocked the window so the observer could enter the residence.

Why didn't the observer help the young man?

Where did he go when he left?

The more I thought about the whole scenario, the more chilling it became to me, this idea of just standing by and watching someone kill himself. I've tracked some cold and remorseless killers over the years—first as a homicide detective in Milwaukee and more recently as an FBI agent—but there was a callousness to this act that unsettled me, even after all the things I've seen.

You can't work in a job like this and not ask questions about the evil we are capable of as a species, which, of course, means the evil we are capable of as individuals.

From all indications, people are born with the desire to do good but the penchant to do evil. This is part of the dichotomy at the heart of human nature. Psychologists studying children as young as three years old have found this—the child will refuse to push other children down when he's told to, but he'll do so when the other child has a toy that he wants.

In other words, he knows right from wrong but will go against his conscience when he wants something for himself.

And that's what happens when we grow up too. It's just that adults have different toys we're after.

And more permanent ways of pushing people down.

5

They told Timothy that the drugs would help, that they would make the bugs go away.

But that had not worked.

No, it had not.

The meds just made his thinking fuzzy and the nightmares more real, more vivid, more troubling. And so he'd stopped taking the drugs after he was released from Grand Haven two months ago.

It made things both easier and harder at the same time.

Now, as he sat in the restaurant finishing his dessert, the server was staring at him, and Timothy was certain that he must have been scratching his arm or his stomach without realizing it. Otherwise, why would the man be looking at him like that?

Get out and get home. Then you can take care of things. Then you can get rid of the bugs, and no one will know.

He laid a credit card on the table to signal that he was ready for his check.

When the server picked up the card, however, he paused, glanced at it somewhat nervously, and then said, "Excuse me, I don't know how to say this. I was wondering if it was you when I saw you earlier."

"If it was me?"

"Timothy Sabian."

"Yes. I'm Timothy."

You did something. Something wrong. He's not going to take your credit card. Maybe he's—

"I've read all your books, Mr. Sabian. I'm a huge fan. I loved *The Nesting Dolls*. Thought it was amazing."

Timothy heard the words, but they were distant. Fuzzy. Staticky. AM instead of FM. Coming from somewhere beyond where he was.

Do not scratch your arm. Don't do it. Not here. Not in front of him.

"Thank you," Timothy heard himself say.

Go. Get moving.

"I especially liked how, in that last scene, everything gets turned on its head and we find out the villain wasn't the person we thought it was all along." The man shook his head in sycophantic admiration. "I love twists like that."

"Okay."

"Do you ever do book signings?"

"I'm signing at the Mystorium on Monday night. It's a bookstore over in Manhattan."

"Wow. Yes. Of course. I'll be there. Um . . . Do you mind if I get a selfie with you?"

The bugs wouldn't leave him alone.

Would not.

Leave him.

Alone.

"No photographs, please. I was just on my way out."

"Oh, I'm sorry." The man already had his phone out. "I didn't mean to—"

Timothy pulled cash out of his wallet. The meal with

drinks and dessert had been less than forty dollars, but he laid down three twenties, retrieved his credit card, told the server to keep the change, and hustled out of the restaurant.

He didn't see the man snap the photo of him as he was hurrying out the door.

Rather than ride the A train, which would have taken as long as forty-five minutes depending on how the lines were running, Timothy flagged down a taxi to take him back to his place in Ozone Park.

Get home.

Just get home.

No one knew exactly what Morgellons syndrome was, and the first record of it was tough to pin down. Some epidemiologists believed it was first identified in France in 1674 when Sir Thomas Browne noticed inexplicable clumps of hair protruding from children. He described them as "endemial distemper of little children in Languedoc, called the *morgellons*, wherein they critically break out with harsh hairs on their backs."

Morgellons meant "black hairs."

Timothy knew all of this, had researched it years ago when he first started feeling the bugs crawling across his stomach and when the fibers first started protruding from the tender sores on his arm.

It wasn't clear if this was the same condition that Mary Leitao, a lab technician in Pennsylvania, came across in 2001, but she chose to use the same word as Dr. Browne to describe the odd, unidentifiable fibers growing from her two-year-old son's back when he complained of bugs crawling on him.

It certainly seemed to be the same condition.

Condition—was that even the right word for it?

Disease? Disorder?

The doctors weren't even sure how to classify it.

Was it bacterial? Viral? Fungal? Parasitic? Genetic?

Psychologists said it was dermatological, some sort of infection.

Dermatologists said it was psychosomatic, all in the patient's head.

Over the last decade, the CDC, four separate research universities, and the FBI lab had all studied the fibers, and no one had been able to identify them or understand exactly how they formed.

In the end, the CDC just indirectly acknowledged that they had no clue what they were dealing with, and rather than label it Morgellons, they'd started calling it "unexplained dermopathy." According to them, it was a cluster of symptoms, including sores, that resembled those from spider bites or chronic excoriations, delusional infestation, fatigue, depression, memory loss, muscle twitches, mental deterioration, and cognitive impairment.

At least Timothy hadn't suffered from those last two— no mental deterioration or cognitive impairment.

He hadn't lost the ability to concentrate.

To concentrate.

Yes.

He could concentrate.

And no one believes you when you tell them what's happening with you.

But he could do it. He could concentrate.

Foreign material (they called it "birefringent" as a way to sound more scientific, always trying to sound more scientific) was found in the sores. Most often it resembled cellulose similar to cotton fibers, but it wasn't cotton. In other cases, it contained DNA from other animals. It might be that there's some genetic reason that in certain people, their skin becomes a host for the parasites often found on plants or animals.

Timothy had seen the movie *Bug* with Ashley Judd and the very creepy character Peter Evans, played by Michael Shannon. It wasn't clear if the movie was meant to accurately portray Morgellons, but whether or not the writers had this specific condition in mind, they'd nailed some of the aspects of the disease: the bugs, the isolation you feel, the frenzy to stop it from happening, the extreme measures you'll take in order to quiet the symptoms and not let them take over your life.

The fibers are not from an external source. Somehow they materialize inside the body—perhaps from some sort of residue left over from an infection. There might be a neurotoxin or microorganism that accounts for the memory loss and muscle control problems. That seemed to be the current thinking, but no one really knew.

The doctors prescribed him medication that they used to treat Lyme disease—that was all they could come up with. "It helps some people who suffer from these symptoms," they told him a bit ambiguously. "It'll help you concentrate."

Some people who suffered from Morgellons treated it with oral and topical antibiotics, antifungals, or antiparasitics. You try them all, and you find that they don't work. The sores stay, the cluttered thinking gets worse.

At his house, Timothy hurried to the bathroom and opened the medicine cabinet, pulled out the tweezers and the magnifying glass.

Free.

He needed to be free.

He used the magnifying glass to study the sores covering his left arm. As he traced the scratch marks he'd made while trying to deal with the itching, he tried futilely to resist the urge to scratch at them again.

Some of the sores hadn't healed in more than a year, and their scabs were black and raw and came off with a tiny snag of irritation whenever he scraped them hard enough.

Which he did. Yes, he admitted it, he often did.

He clamped the tweezers onto a tuft of fibers protruding from the largest sore on his arm.

Maybe if he could pull them out, it would get better.

You've tried that before. It never works.

But something needs to work! Something will!

He dug at them, pried them loose, but the itching didn't stop.

No no no no. The tweezers weren't going to be enough.

You need something better. Something to get at the roots. A knife. Some sort of knife.

The X-ACTO knife on your desk.

Delusions? They were awfully real delusions. Just the fact that it could "all be in your head" was astonishing in and of itself. How could your mind decide to grow strange fibers from your body, fibers that have plant DNA in them? How could something like that even happen?

The doctors opted for the easy answer and claimed that the fibers were from clothing caught on the sores after you scratch them, but the fibers had been found on babies that couldn't scratch their sores and beneath smooth skin that surrounded the sores on adults.

How did they get there?

Timothy found the knife and returned to the bathroom.

Free.

Of course, there were the conspiracy theories about Morgellons. The most common one postulated that the condition was somehow linked to chemtrails, or contrails, from airplanes resulting from some sort of government test on the American population. Ridiculous, yes, of course it was ridiculous, but people often turn to the absurd when faced with the inexplicable.

But on the other hand, the government *would* keep it a secret if they were doing tests. It would make sense that they would.

Timothy angled the tip of the blade into position and began to carve as deeply into the flesh of his forearm as necessary to get the bugs out, using a washcloth to sop up the blood.

Then.

A nightmare.

The worst kind. The waking kind.

The fibers began twitching, began coming to life. Thin black worms wriggled from his skin, clusters of them that began growing fatter and fatter as they tugged free and then dropped, slimy and writhing, to the tiling.

They squiggled toward the baseboard near the sink, leaving lurid, bloody trails in their wake, and he stomped on them to make them go away, all go away!

Kill them, just like you killed those people.

"I haven't killed anyone."

Are you sure?

"Yes!"

How many has it been?

How many more will there be?

"There haven't been any. There won't be any!"

Timothy squashed the worms that he knew weren't real.

No one can find out what you're doing or how many there've been. Don't let anyone know the truth, Timothy.

"I need to know. I'm going to find out."

No, Timothy. If you poke around, the police will find you. They'll put you away, lock you away. That's not what you want.

"It's not what *you* want. If there've been any, any at all, then I need to know. I need to know the truth."

Even if it means being locked away?

"No matter what it means!"

He finished with the last of the worms, then stared at the clean tiling, spotted only with drops of blood from the weeping sores on his arm.

And so, Timothy Sabian made the decision to find out for sure how many people he had murdered. There was a number—of course, there was. After all, there's a number for everyone.

6

Killers tend to show up at the wakes and funerals of the people they've killed. I wondered if someone who'd witnessed a suicide would do the same.

Back at our apartment, I texted Assistant Director DeYoung, telling him that I wanted to attend Jon Murray's funeral tomorrow. Give me a call when you get a chance, I wrote.

I didn't have to wait long. As I was finishing getting ready for bed, the phone rang: DeYoung contacting me for a video call.

His haggard look, his sighs, and his head shakes were all evidence of the stress that was a constant companion in his job.

After a quick greeting, he said, "Senator Murray is on board with us surveilling the funeral tomorrow morning."

"Excellent." I filled him in on what I'd discovered at the senator's house earlier.

"But we still have no idea about the identity of the person in the window?"

"Not yet, sir. No."

"I want you to put everything else on hold for a couple days. Let's find out who was there, and let's find out why."

"I might be able to give you the who, but—"

"The why isn't in your wheelhouse."

"Right."

"Because it deals with motive."

"Yes."

"Yeah." He rubbed his forehead in that worrisome way of his.

"I'll see what I can do," I said. "Listen, I want a team looking over other suicides or homicides that've been posted live online, especially from any contacts from Jon Murray's social networking accounts or on sites he might've visited recently."

"What are you thinking?"

"We need to establish if this is an isolated incident."

"Hmm. So we're looking for footage in which someone else might have been present when the other deaths occurred?"

"Yes."

"Do you think the person at the senator's place wanted to leave you a clue that he was in the house? That he planned for his reflection to be visible?"

"That seems unlikely. There would've been much easier ways of letting us know he was there. Let's start with Jon's online interactions and Internet history, see where that takes us. Circle out from there."

"I'll get some people on it. I'm going to have Bill Greer join you tomorrow at the funeral."

Jodie Fleming, the agent I typically partnered with, was presenting at a criminology conference in Orlando this week, so it made sense that DeYoung would assign someone else for me to team up with.

I'd worked with Greer before on a couple of other high-profile cases. He specialized in homicides and had a good instinct for dealing with the media. Early fifties, experienced, dedicated. I liked him. Trusted him.

"I'll have him meet you there," DeYoung told me. "It's at that graveyard over near the East River Medical Center—Lancaster Cemetery."

"I know the place."

It was an expansive property, not as large as Green-Wood Cemetery in Brooklyn, but still substantial.

After our call, I wanted to touch base with Christie and make sure she wasn't angry at her daughter—or at me—for something, but earlier when she left, she'd told me that she wouldn't be turning on her phone while she was at the retreat center. "It's supposed to be a silent retreat. The monks don't even want us talking with the other people staying at the monastery. I'll be fine."

Off the grid for a weekend didn't sound all that bad to me.

After checking in on Tessa and finding her asleep, I lay in bed, computer on my lap, and studied the files until I must have dozed off because I awoke suddenly, jarring the laptop and barely catching it before it would have plummeted to the floor. I took that as a sign, closed it up, and went to sleep.

++++

"Kiss her."

"Her?"

"The lady."

"Honey"—the woman whom Blake Neeson had hired for the evening threw a hand to her hip—"that's not a lady. That's a *mannequin*. You want me to kiss a mannequin?"

Blake sipped at his whiskey and gave her a nod.

The mannequin was unclothed, perfect and smooth. She came from the most recent Russian shipment, and she contained the compound. This silent lady was one of the prototypes. The final products were already in Connecticut at the greenhouse. After they were treated, the distribution would begin early next week.

The escort glanced toward Blake's associate, Mannie, a giant of a man who hailed from the Gambia and now edged closer to the door, blocking her exit. He was tall enough and wide enough to cover nearly the entire doorway.

"And he's gonna watch?" the woman asked him.

"Call it a threesome—well, a foursome."

"Whatever turns you on," she muttered as she faced the mannequin. She caressed its cheek, closed her eyes, and leaned in close to give it a kiss.

Blake watched her for a few minutes. Even the moisture on her lips wasn't enough to affect the mannequin. Even—

Mannie's phone rang, interrupting his thoughts.

After answering it, Mannie said, "Looks like there's someone here to see you."

"Who knows we're here?"

"Just the men downstairs."

"Hmm."

"It's a woman. I don't recognize her."

Mannie showed his phone's screen to Blake, who studied the live footage.

Attractive. Late twenties. He was intrigued. "Have the boys show her up."

The woman from the escort agency was still making out with the mannequin.

"Keep kissing her," he told her quietly.

"It's your dime, sweetie."

The two guards led the visitor in. She wore a blouse that revealed a left arm that hadn't developed properly, leaving her with just one usable arm.

After Blake dismissed the men, he asked her, "Who are you?"

"My name is Julianne Springman. I worked with your brother."

"My brother? When?"

"In Detroit."

"And he told you about me? Is that how you found me?"

"He told me where to look."

"Detroit was last summer. You just found me now?"

"I just *showed up* now. That doesn't mean I just found you. You need to do a better job covering your tracks."

"My brother is dead."

"And I'm here to honor his life, to carry on his work."

"Justice."

"Yes."

He evaluated that as he took a sip of his drink.

Mannie gestured toward the escort. "Should I arrange a car for her?"

Blake understood it as Mannie's way of asking if he should get rid of her, which could have meant permanently or simply for the evening.

"Let her stay." Blake turned his attention back to the woman calling herself Julianne Springman. "And what brings you here tonight, Miss Springman?"

"I want to find someone like your brother. Someone with his interests."

Blake was quiet for a moment. "I see you've learned one of the early lessons."

"And that is?"

"It's difficult, once you get started, to turn it off."

"I don't want to turn it off."

"Huh." Blake walked to the window and peered out across the darkened city dotted with the confident lights of Manhattan's skyscrapers. "Let me tell you a story, Miss Springman."

"Julianne. Please."

"Alright. Julianne. This comes from Aesop. Do you know the fable about Bat and the Fight Between the Animals?"

"I don't think so. No."

"Long ago, there was a war between the birds and the beasts. Bat was fighting on the side of the birds, but it looked like they were going to be vanquished by the beasts, so in the middle of the night, he sneaks over to the other camp. Shocked to see him, all the beasts exclaim, 'What are you doing over here? You're a bird!'

"'No,' he tells them, 'I'm a beast just like you. Look, I have fur. No birds have fur. I'm a beast.'

"Well, the beasts talk it over and can't think of a way to refute that. They say to him, 'Okay, that is true. No birds have fur. You must be a beast. You can fight with us.'

"The war continues, and soon it looks like the birds are going to win, so Bat slips over into their camp at night, and they say, 'Hey! You were fighting with the beasts. What are you doing here?'

"'No, you're mistaken,' he explains. 'I'm a bird like you. Look, I have wings. No beasts have wings.'

"They couldn't argue with that, so they let him join them, but once more it looks like they might lose, so Bat goes over to the beasts' side once again.

"'We know you were fighting with the birds,' they tell him, but he just shakes his head. 'No, my friends. Look. I have teeth. No birds have teeth. I'm a beast just like you.'"

Blake paused momentarily to watch the escort kiss the mannequin. There still seemed to be no adverse effects—in either direction. Then he finished the story: "Eventually there was peace between the birds and the beasts, but they told Bat, 'From now on you must live by yourself in a cave in the dark, and you will be considered neither a bird nor a beast, for you could not decide which side you were fighting for.'"

++++

Julianne waited for more, but when it was clear that Blake was done with the story, she said, "There are consequences to switching sides—is that your point?"

"You must know who you are, which side you're fighting on. Most people could be either birds or beasts. I used to be a police officer—I'm sure my brother told you that. But then I chose my side and I never looked back."

Julianne had been a police officer herself, had worked on the CSI unit in Detroit, but this didn't seem like the right time to mention that. If Blake took it the wrong way, if he assumed she was here to betray him or turn him in, she didn't stand much of a chance of walking out of this room alive.

She had no weapon. Yes, she was strong in her one good arm—she'd had to compensate—but she was no hand-to-hand fighter and absolutely no match for Blake's enormous bodyguard, who might very well have been three times her size.

"Have you chosen your side?" Blake asked her.

"Yes. That's why I'm here."

"Did you love my brother, Julianne?"

"I didn't know him for long, but yes, I loved him."

"You're the one they never found, I mean, after he was killed. His partner."

"Yes."

"And you're telling me you want to find someone with his interests?" he said, circling back to what she'd told him earlier when she first came in.

"That's why I'm here. Yes."

"What makes you think I can help you with that?"

"You chose your side a long time ago. I'm newer at this. Besides, I believe that Dylan would have wanted it."

Blake considered that. "I can do some checking. Perhaps offer an introduction, but I can't make you any guarantees. The person might not be to your liking."

"A name is all I need."

"No doubt. And you might not be to his liking. Have you considered that?"

"I can take care of myself." She handed him her card. "My number."

He studied it. "Mourn in peace?"

"It's my website. Photographs. It's for mothers. Call me."

++++

Blake entrusted Mannie with leading Julianne Springman back downstairs.

She'd exhibited admirable initiative and courage showing up here tonight, and Blake respected her for that. He decided that if he could help her, he would, in honor of his brother and the love Dylan had apparently shared with her.

"That's enough," he said to the escort.

She compliantly stepped away from the mannequin and eyed him alluringly.

"Come here."

She sashayed toward him, took his hand, brought one of his fingers to her mouth, kissed it gently, and then traced his fingertip in a circle over her moist lips. Then she said softly, "Are you ready to get started now with just the two of us?"

"I'm ready."

"Well, then." She reached for his belt buckle. "Let the games begin."

STAGE II

Anger

Vapour. Photos of the dead.
Barbed wire. Julianne's proposal.

7

Nearly all of the trees at the graveyard had already turned, and most had bare branches. Now, in the wind, dried leaves skittered before me across the ground, creating an iconic Halloween-ish feel.

The sun, as if it were anxious for winter to arrive, was crouched low against the late-morning skyline, and cold shadows draped along the north side of the gravestones.

Our team checked Jon Murray's phone but found no indication that he was planning to meet anyone on the night he died. None of his friends knew of any plans he had to see anyone either. Over the summer he'd worked as an intern for a nearby office of the social networking and search engine giant Krazle, but no one from work was aware of him being depressed or suicidal. We were still looking into filmed suicides and homicides—ones he might have heard about or viewed online.

Bill Greer was fifty-two, but most people would've probably pegged him as a decade younger. With his bushy mustache and stocky frame, he'd always reminded me of the pictures I'd seen of boxers in the early twentieth century.

As we were getting our earpieces situated, he said, "You know how they sometimes talk about it being a cat-and-mouse game? Cops and criminals?"

"Yes."

"It's a misnomer."

"Why do you say that?"

"To the mouse, it's never just a game. If he loses, he dies. If he escapes, he's been traumatized."

"But if the cat loses, well, no big deal."

Greer nodded. "Exactly. He just walks away. Maybe hungry, maybe not—maybe he never even intended to eat the mouse anyway. Just terrorize it."

"You're saying it's really just a cat game."

"Yeah."

"So are we the cat here," I said, "or are we looking for him?"

"That is the question, isn't it?"

Because of who the victim was and since there'd been only a private viewing at the funeral home, a crowd of at least a hundred people, including the press, had already gathered near the gravesite, and more cars from the funeral procession were still arriving, pulling slowly and reverently to the curb so the mourners wouldn't have to walk far on the muddy ground, which was still recovering from this week's storms.

On a planet where death is a certainty, where it's never more than a heartbeat away, a person's passing might come to us as a surprise, but I don't think we should ever claim that it came out of the blue.

We're all on the train to the grave, and there's no getting off until that final stop. The timing of our death might be unexpected, but its inevitability is never in doubt. There's never a question mark there.

Only a period.

Or, perhaps, when it's a brutal or tragic end, as in this case, an exclamation point.

But it's never out of the blue.

They don't call this world a vale of tears for nothing.

I heard that a recent survey found that the percentage of the U.S. population who believe in God is the lowest it's been in seventy years, but more people believe in heaven than ever before. Of course, this makes no sense, but it goes to show how deeply addicted we are to hope: even if we conclude that there's no deity, we're still apt to cling to the belief that there must be more to existence than this.

Logically, if there's no God, there's no afterlife. No heaven. No hell. Nothing but nonexistence after death. After all, where would consciousness go? If it's simply the result of biological processes in a finite organism, then when that organism dies the consciousness dies with it.

Unless the unseen, the unprovable, the type of unconquerable life our hearts long for is as real as the physical world our senses tell us is here.

Is there really more to life than life?

Atheists sometimes point to the vast expanse of the universe in their quest to find hope—there must be life out there *somewhere*—or maybe there was, or maybe there will be. After all, the idea that God doesn't exist and that we're alone on an insignificant and dying planet in a vast, lifeless universe is existentially almost unthinkable.

We've been graced with life on this earth, a tiny speck of dust in an endless sea of stars. And we are slowly, or, if you believe the growing number of alarmed scientists and environmentalists, shockingly quickly, destroying our home.

And when we do, we'll have nowhere to go. An outpost on the moon or on Mars isn't going to sustain our race for the long haul. To think that it would isn't to embrace science or to believe in human potential but to live in denial.

We will die out.

And our planet will die as well.

Without the glorious intervention of a divine being, life will cease to be a meaningful word in the universe.

Regardless of what you think about God, from all the evidence astrophysicists have collected, it's clear that life is the exception in the universe, not the norm.

There's plenty of speculation that life outside our solar system exists, but no evidence that it does, and in my line of work, evidence is everything and speculation doesn't get you anywhere useful at all.

The Drake Equation, which proposes that with this many planets in the universe life elsewhere is a veritable certainty, is simply conjecture masquerading as science. However, people will cling to the merest thread of hope wherever they can find it. For some, that's God; for others, it's aliens. And for an increasing number of Americans, the artifice of a Godless heaven.

Someone once told me that people can live for a month without food, a week without water, four minutes without air, but not for one second without hope. From what I've seen, there's a lot of truth to that.

As people were gathering at the grave, among the members of the media and the other congressmen and dignitaries, I noticed Marcus Rockwell, the founder of Krazle, speaking with the senator.

Because of Jon's internship with his company, I wasn't

surprised that they knew each other, but I was impressed that Rockwell would come to the funeral, considering all the obligations he had leading an organization that daily served more people than the population of any country on earth.

The service began with the minister reciting a Bible verse about life's brevity. "Life is a mist," he said. "James 4:4 tells us, 'Whereas ye know not what shall be on the morrow. For what is your life? It is even a vapour, that appeareth for a little time, and then vanisheth away.'"

Life appears.

And then vanishes away.

Like it did for the young man lying in that casket today.

And he saw it vanish from the bottom of a swimming pool, handcuffed to the chair he used to kill himself.

As I scanned the area, I thought of the minister's words, and it made me think of a time when I was nine and I went hiking with my dad along Lake Superior's shoreline in Michigan's Upper Peninsula. It was early fall, and threads of mist were hanging across the water, lazy and white, tendriling their way onto land, all around us.

I kept reaching out to grab the mist, but I couldn't quite seem to touch it.

"I want to put it in my pocket," I told my dad.

"You can't hold on to mist, Pat. It's always going to be just out of reach."

Now, that's what I remembered. That's the image I was left with—trying to grasp those ghostlike vapors that floated so tantalizingly close to me but never being able to wrap my fingers around them.

Time wears a bandit's mask. It is so sly and so quick to steal away our moments, and all too often, the more we try to cling to life, the more we find it slipping right between our fingers.

"Does God even listen to our screams?" the minister asked us in what I took to be a rhetorical question. "How does a loving God remain quiet in the midst of so much pain? How is he silent in reply to the tragic wailing of so many broken hearts, the stinging despair of so many weeping children? He offers such a deafening silence. He is so conspicuously quiet for so long and in so many ways while his people suffer and beg him for relief. How could anyone consider that response to be one of love?"

Those were some pretty good questions, ones that I doubted he was going to be able to satisfactorily answer in a fifteen-minute graveside homily.

I studied the layout of the graveyard. Two hills north of me sloped down and flattened out into the area where the service was happening. Based on the time of day, I figured that the best vantage point would be on the rise to my left. "I'm going to head up to get a visual from the ridge," I told Greer through my earpiece.

"Right."

Easing back from the service, I made my way up the hill. When I reached the top, the force of the wind reminded me that it was November.

I zippered up my jacket and studied the area.

Greer's voice came through: "Nothing down here. What about you?"

"Not yet."

Apart from a swath of land southeast of me that was dedicated to soldiers and was laid out with uniform grave markers, the somewhat random positioning of the headstones throughout the rest of the property covered the gamut from small, almost indistinguishable markers to looming stones large enough for me to have hidden behind, even though I'm over six feet tall. In many cases, the tombstones were hunched over their graves like uneven teeth rising from the earth, revealing the age of the graveyard.

As I scrutinized the grounds, I saw her.

Approximately forty meters away, a figure crouched in the shadow cast by a substantial aging headstone that stood at an awkward angle from decades of leaning in settling soil. The woman was peering down at the service but was clearly trying to avoid being seen.

"I'm on the rise to the north," I told Greer. "Someone's up here. Keep this channel open."

I started to approach the gravestone but only made it a few steps before the woman turned and looked at me. I was still too far away to determine her age, but she was Caucasian. Small frame.

The moment she saw me, she leapt to her feet, but when I called out, asking to speak with her for a moment, she took off in the opposite direction from the funeral.

And so did I.

8

The woman was quick.

Despite being a runner myself, I had trouble keeping up with her.

"She's on the move," I said into my radio. "Get to Amber Road. If she goes through the woods, you should be able to catch up with her on the other side, over by the hospital."

The slick soles of my shoes weren't happy on the mud, and that wasn't helping me any. She made it to the eight-foot metal fence rimming the graveyard, clambered over it, and disappeared into the forest.

Glancing over my shoulder, I saw Greer's SUV leaving the graveside service. However, with the graveyard's meandering road layout and the only exit on the other side of the property, I knew it'd still be a few minutes before he could get up here. By then, she might very well escape down the other side into the neighborhood of brownstones, where it'd be easy for her to blend in, disappear, slip away.

Years of rock climbing were on my side, and I was able to scramble over the fence without any trouble. By the time I landed, I could see that I'd made up some ground on her. I called out and identified myself as a federal agent. "Ma'am, stop. I just want to talk with you."

She ignored me and darted farther into the woods.

If a police officer pulls you over or a federal agent asks to speak with you, there are three things that you just have to do: Follow orders, respect authority, and don't run. Never run. Don't disrespect law enforcement and don't act like you have something to hide.

And that's how she was acting right now.

Because of the time of year, most of the undergrowth was withered or dead, and I could track her progress as she scampered catlike between the trees.

Despite the uneven ground, I'd finally found my stride. I was within twenty-five meters of the woman, and closing.

Tumults of leaves flutter-wisped past me in the gusting air.

She became momentarily caught in a patch of persistent dried thistles that'd refused to die away after summer. I called to her again. She shouted for me to leave her alone, then tore herself free, abandoning her jacket in the thorny vines, and bolted forward.

On my way toward her, I flung a branch aside but stumbled over a hidden root and went down hard. On impact, my hands smeared out in front of me, wrenching my left wrist as my palm smacked into a rock.

Deal with it. Go.

Back on my feet, it took me a second to reorient myself and find her again. She was nearly to the road, and a silver sedan was on its way toward her.

"I'm with the FBI," I said. "Stop!"

The woman burst out of the forest and ran to the middle of the road to flag down the driver, but he must've been distracted, because he didn't slow until the last moment when he slammed on his brakes, narrowly missing her. He cranked the car to the right, flying off the shoulder and down a steep drop-off. The vehicle flipped over on its way down the embankment and came to a smoking crunch at the base of an ancient oak.

I yelled to the woman to stay where she was. She did but eyed the neighborhood across the road from where the car had crashed.

I rushed to the vehicle to assess the injuries of the driver and any passengers while shouting into my radio for Greer to inform dispatch that we had a 10-53 and needed an ambulance ASAP.

Because of the sloping ground, it wasn't easy to get down the bank.

Once at its base, I knelt and peered into the car.

The driver, the car's sole occupant, was conscious, pinned upside down, and when I asked if he was alright, he coughed out in a pained voice that he couldn't move his leg.

A piece of metal protruding from beneath the dash had pierced his left thigh, and based on the amount of blood already dampening his jeans, I guessed it might've severed an artery. If that was the case, it would almost certainly prove fatal within minutes—unless I could stop that bleeding.

The man started asking for help, but his voice faded as he drifted into unconsciousness.

I tried opening the door, but it was too mangled to move.

If I could have gotten something around his leg, I

might've been able to tighten a tourniquet above the wound, but the way he was positioned, that wasn't going to happen. I needed to get him out of that vehicle.

The smell of gasoline was not a good sign.

Normally, because of the possibility of a neck or back injury, after a crash you want to support the victim's neck and keep the spine aligned and immobilized until paramedics arrive, but in this case, the only way to save this man's life would be getting him out and stopping that bleeding.

I checked his pulse and found it thready and weak.

Gas was dripping down and pooling onto the interior of the car's roof.

You need to get this guy out now.

A hefty, guttural voice called out behind me: "Back away."

I turned, only to find Blake Neeson's hulking bodyguard towering over me. Blake was one of the most wanted men in the country. I'd been tracking them both since last summer, and I had absolutely no idea what Mannie was doing here right now.

"On your knees." I drew my weapon. "Now!"

He didn't move, just said, "You can arrest me after I get him out, but if you cuff me, the man in that car will bleed to death."

"Get down!"

"You're not listening. Do you want me in custody, or do you want him to survive? Because right now, you get to choose one or the other."

He's right. Don't stall.

I didn't like it, but time was definitely not on the side of this injured driver.

Mannie had me by at least a hundred and fifty pounds, and looking at him, I guessed nearly all of it was muscle.

"Can you get the door off the car?" I asked.

"I can try."

"Do it."

I moved aside and, somewhat hesitantly, holstered my weapon.

Mannie gripped the door.

I doubted that even my friend Ralph Hawkins, who was a former All-American high school wrestler and Army Ranger, would've had the strength to pry the door loose from the car, but Mannie was a human mountain, and though he strained mightily from the effort, he managed to twist it to the side and tilt it upward. Then he torqued it off the car and tossed it aside.

He was winded—even for him, it'd been a challenge.

I tried to get the driver free, but with the way the car was crushed, it wasn't going to happen.

"I'll lift it," Mannie said. "You slide him out."

"You're going to lift the car?"

"Yeah."

"You could try, but I'm not sure we—"

Before I could finish, another vehicle came screeching to a stop nearby, although it was out of sight from where we were in the ditch. I was hoping it was Greer, and I was relieved when he appeared at the roadside.

He identified Mannie and reached for his gun.

"Hold on," I said. With the two of them, they just might be able to pull it off. "C'mon down. If you two can lift the front, I think I can get the driver out."

Greer looked momentarily confused, but when I called

for him to hurry, the urgency in my voice registered, and he scurried down the embankment to join us.

I still didn't know where Mannie had come from or why he was here, but we could settle all that in a minute. Right now all I cared about was helping save the driver.

Greer and Mannie positioned themselves at the front of the car, and working together, they hefted the vehicle just high enough for me to slit the man's seat belt with my automatic knife, free his leg, and ease him out onto the ground.

I yanked the seat belt to get enough webbing, then cut off a length of it near the buckle and used it as a tourniquet while a spark started a fire somewhere in the engine, and smoke began curling out toward us.

Hurry, Pat.

An ambulance siren cycled through the late morning, coming our way from the hospital down the road. I figured that if we'd been any farther out, this guy's chances would be close to nil, but with the hospital this close, he just might make it.

While Greer supported his neck, Mannie and I carried the driver to a flat patch of ground about ten meters from the car.

Just after we set him down, his car erupted with a gash of fire slicing through the day, and I bent over his face and torso to protect him from the wave of heat. Then, while I did what I could to quell the bleeding in the driver's leg, Greer handcuffed Mannie, who didn't struggle or put up a fight.

What is going on with this guy? Is this a trap? Is Blake here somewhere?

I glanced around. The woman I'd been chasing was gone. No sign of Blake.

I attended to the injured man until the EMTs showed up and took over for me, quickly and efficiently fitting him with a cervical collar and getting him on a gurney and into the back of the ambulance.

Resuming my search for the woman, I scanned the forest, both sides of the road, and the path leading down to the brownstones, but there was no sign of her, so I returned to Greer's SUV, where he now had Mannie in the backseat. The behemoth filled most of it by himself.

Greer was leaning over the window, questioning him. "What are you doing here?"

Mannie didn't reply.

"Where's Blake?"

Silence.

"Mannie." I noticed how much of the driver's blood had gotten onto my hands, and I wiped them without much effect on my pants. "Thank you. For helping there."

He said nothing, but nodded.

I was no psychologist, but I did know something about human nature: wanted fugitives do not usually surrender themselves so promptly and without incident to law enforcement unless they feel their life is at risk. "You could've gotten away a few minutes ago. Whatever you were doing up here, you chose to stay and help that man, but you must know, based on what we have on you, that you could be facing decades in prison."

"I'm aware of that."

"Then why? Why did you stop?"

"Because he was dying and he didn't deserve to and I could do something about it."

I thought back to one of the first times I'd encountered this man. He'd helped save the life of a police officer even though he'd been shot himself in the process.

Was Mannie pure evil? Certainly not. This was at least the second time he'd saved someone's life when given the chance, and both times it had cost him dearly. However, he was no saint either. From what we could tell, he helped facilitate Blake's human trafficking and illegal arms deals. Motives are fibrous and tenuous things. And the human heart is all too often a contradiction to itself.

I first met up with Blake Neeson last summer during a missing person's investigation. Later, I discovered that he was a former undercover cop from L.A. who'd found his way into the criminal underground and become a kingpin in the dishearteningly lucrative world of smuggling both drugs and human beings into New York City.

Blake was now operating under a new name—Fayed Raabi'ah Bashir—but he would always be Blake Neeson in my book, and taking on the persona of an infamous terrorist wasn't going to intimidate me or dissuade me. Blake wasn't interested in fueling a movement, he was simply interested in benefiting from it.

His brother was a serial killer who'd murdered at least five people before being fatally wounded by a friend of mine and fellow FBI agent while she was attempting to apprehend him last summer.

"We'll work with you," I said to Mannie. "Give us Blake."

"Take me in." He eyed the blood that I'd wiped onto my pants. "Then we'll see what happens next."

Greer closed the door, and we stepped out of earshot of Mannie.

"What do you make of this?" he said.

"I'm not sure, but wherever Mannie is, Blake is probably somewhere close by. I say we have officers go door to door down in the neighborhood and maybe even set up a roadblock."

He shook his head. "I doubt that'll fly. Not with all the dignitaries at the funeral. The condos, maybe, but we can't check all of those cars as they're leaving."

"This is Blake Neeson we're talking about."

"Yeah." He considered that. "I'll call DeYoung, see what he thinks." Greer unpocketed his cell. "That woman you were chasing—do you think she's working with them?"

"Hard to say. Listen, I'll be right back. I need to go collect some evidence."

"What evidence is that?"

"Her jacket."

9

Christie Ellis knelt before the fourth Station of the Cross and brushed a strand of her blonde hair aside when it tipped across her face as she was repositioning her knees to avoid some rocks on the ground.

For a moment, she wondered what her Baptist friends from church would think if they saw her here at this monastery, on her knees in front of a statue. But she wasn't praying to a piece of metal or stone. She was praying to the one this statue represented. Besides, who cares what others might think. This was between her and God. The two of them had some things to sort out.

The rural Kentucky landscape surrounded the monastery—patches of farms and quiet woodlands interspersed with panfish ponds. The moist scent of leaf cover from the ground filled the monastery's walled-in courtyard around her.

Christie's parents were dead. She was an only child raising an only child.

But you won't be raising her for long. She's only sixteen, and you're almost done being a mom. You'll never see her graduate from high school or head off to college. You won't watch her get married. You'll never hold a grandchild in your arms.

And Pat. You finally found a man who treats you right, a man you could grow old loving, and you won't get to do that either.

The oncologist hadn't wanted to give her a time frame. "I've found that it's not helpful," he told her. "At least not this early."

"But you said we weren't catching it as early as you would've liked."

"I just mean, listing a time frame can cause unrealistic expectations."

"I don't want unrealistic ones, I want realistic ones. That's why I'm asking. That's what I want to know. Tell me the truth," she pressed him. "How much time do I have left?"

At first, he'd couched his answer in phrases like "aggressive treatment strategies" and "promising new drugs," and she'd listened, she had, but when he was done, she repeated her question again. "How long do I have, Doctor? Be honest."

"With this type of cancer, at this stage . . ."

She waited him out.

"Three to six months," he said at last, but his voice faltered a little. "But we can never tell for sure. Some people beat it and live a long and happy life."

"And some don't make it three months."

A long pause. "That's right. Some don't."

She hadn't told her husband yet, hadn't told her daughter. And now, as she looked at the statue of Christ carrying his cross, this man of God, this Savior, this one who she believed was both risen and here by her side, she did not feel his presence at all.

Christie believed in miracles, or at least she said that she did, she *thought* that she did, and so now, unless there was a miracle here, unless God healed her, she would die from this cancer that he had allowed to have free rein in her body.

How could he be so present and yet seem so distant? How could he be both so strikingly real and so glaringly absent? *My God, my God*, she thought, *why have you forsaken me?*

Jesus's words from the cross—

My God.

Cried out into the lonely day—

My God.

Uttered by a brutalized and dying man.

Why have you forsaken me?

And the Father refused to reply. There was no miracle that day, only death. Only grief. Only the power of the grave.

Sunday would see a resurrection, but Friday would leave a corpse in its wake.

Three to six months.

A corpse in its wake.

Why give God only one side of the equation? Could he heal her? Sure. Would he? Who knows? But why didn't he stop this from happening in the first place? Well, that was the question at the heart of all suffering, wasn't it?

Christie thought of Pat mourning her, of her daughter growing into adulthood without a mother. Pat was a man of passion and resolve, he had a good heart, but he often kept his emotions closed in, and she wasn't sure how well that heart would heal after it was broken, after it was pierced by her death. His work might consume him, and both he and Tessa would suffer the consequences.

Christie let the tears come and did not try to stop them. And there at the feet of her silent Savior, there at the feet of her slaughtered Lord, she buried her face in her hands and wept.

10

We came up empty in the neighborhood.

DeYoung had been on board with us searching the residences looking for Blake and the unidentified woman, but since we had no solid evidence that Blake was in the area, the assistant director didn't approve us setting up a roadblock or investigating vehicles leaving the funeral.

Which, honestly, despite my desire to bring Blake in, I understood.

I checked the woman's jacket for any identifying pocket litter and found a ring of four keys, a still-wrapped lemon cough drop, and a crumpled-up receipt from a parking garage less than two blocks from the federal building where the Field Office was located.

Okay. That was interesting.

My shirt was smeared with mud and my pants were ripped from when I'd fallen chasing the woman through the forest, not to mention the fact that I was splattered with the driver's blood. After we cleared the neighborhood, Greer, who'd taken Mannie in to be processed, called me and encouraged me rather bluntly to head out and change clothes.

"Mannie's not talking and there's nothing more for you

to do at the graveyard. I'll be in touch later this afternoon when I'm done with all this paperwork."

I thought about just buying some clothes somewhere, but the blood was another matter—I did need to get cleaned up. And icing that tweaked wrist would keep it from swelling up too much. The driver was in stable condition in the hospital—no neck or back injuries, and the doctors were able to treat his leg without the need for amputation.

The mystery of where the woman had gone and where Mannie had come from were still all too present, but at least it looked like that driver would recover from the crash.

There was no crime scene unit on-site, so in order to maintain the chain of evidence, I handed off the woman's jacket to one of the officers who'd responded and had an evidence bag large enough in his cruiser to hold it. Then I signed off on it so he could deliver it to our lab.

Back home again, I was hoping to slip into the shower and get changed before Tessa saw all the blood on my clothes, but she was in the living room reading when I came through the front door.

She stared at me.

"It's not my blood," I explained helpfully.

"Okay."

"The guy's doing alright. There was a car accident."

"Oh. Did you run him over?"

"No."

"'Cause if you did I'm gonna find someone else to teach me to drive."

"We're good. I'm going to get cleaned up. I'll catch up with you in a few minutes."

But before I could even make it to the hallway, she asked if I'd heard from her mom.

"She wasn't going to turn her phone on this weekend," I said.

"I know, but . . ."

"No, I haven't heard from her. But I'm sure she's fine."

++++

After the murders in Detroit, Julianne Springman had not bothered to change her name.

For a while, she'd toyed with the idea of taking on a new identity, but then she realized that if Julianne Springman suddenly disappeared it might seem suspicious since, as a CSI tech, she'd been on the team that was investigating the homicides in Detroit—and the authorities still hadn't identified who Dylan Neeson's partner had been.

Even though she'd been painstakingly careful to cover her tracks and mask her involvement with Dylan's crimes, no one catches everything, and it was best to simply merge into the background rather than draw any undue attention to herself by suddenly dropping off the radar screen.

In her exit interview and debrief with her lieutenant, he'd asked her the reason she was leaving the force. She told him truthfully that it was to pursue photography. She didn't tell him what kind of photography that would be, but at least she could answer the question without lying.

The other officers at her precinct had told her they'd miss her and wished her well and said they understood. She could infer, however, even in their well-wishing, that some of them were envious of her. With the amount of violence in Detroit—taking into account the high crime rate, the low clearance rate, and the average salary—being an officer there was not an ideal career choice for someone who's trying to move up in the world and stay alive doing it.

Anyway, that was over and done and she had moved on, camera in hand.

Now she repositioned it to better catch the light on the face of the young woman seated in the chair beside the hospital bed.

Mrs. Sheehan gently tucked one hand beneath her daughter's head and drew her closer.

The baby didn't coo or cry.

Of course she didn't. Julianne specialized in photographs like this, as a way of helping the mothers cope.

"My husband doesn't know I'm doing this," the woman told Julianne.

"I understand."

"He . . . When I told him about it, he got pretty upset. But this is for me. It's important."

"Maybe it's just harder for men to accept."

"Maybe."

Julianne's website was dedicated to photographs of mothers holding their stillborn or crib-death children, to help them find community and closure during the grieving process. To help them mourn in peace.

Some people might've called it macabre to photograph the living with the dead like that, but Julianne didn't look at things that way. To her, it was a service both to the surviving family members and to herself.

It helped the mothers remember the dead.

And, on a more personal level, it helped her think about what it might have been like to kill those children, to smother them while their mothers slept peacefully just a few feet away. She'd had the opportunity but had always refrained. She wasn't sure how long her self-control would hold up. It would have made for so much more of a meaningful photo if she'd played more of an active role in its genesis.

In time.

Time would tell.

Julianne was still waiting to hear from Blake regarding a potential partner to work with. She didn't know how long it would be but decided to give him another day or two before following up.

Right now, patience was her friend, and pressing the matter could easily backfire.

She turned her attention back to the grieving mother in front of her.

Knowing what mourning mothers need, Julianne refrained from speaking much in instances like this, except for offering a few gentle words of comfort and solace to the women.

She snapped several photos. From this position, there in the arms of her mother, the baby simply looked asleep. You couldn't even tell that the child was dead.

"I think I have what I need," Julianne said softly. "Do you want to be alone for a little while?"

"Actually, I'd like you to stay. If you don't mind."

"I'm glad to stay as long as you like."

++++

By the time I finished showering, getting dressed, putting my bloodstained and mud-covered clothes in the wash, icing my wrist, completing my report on what had happened at the graveyard, and touching base with Greer—

Mannie still wasn't talking and hadn't asked for a lawyer—it was time for dinner.

I asked Tessa, "Do you want me to whip up some soup?"

"You mean do you want me to hand you a can opener?"

"I can also make some sliced fruit."

"Slicing fruit doesn't count as *making* it." She sighed. "Alright, look, I'll fry some falafel burgers. You want one or are you gonna eat meat right in front of me even though you know I'm morally opposed to it and it grosses me out?"

"When you put it that way, it makes me seriously hungry for falafel."

"You're lying, but I don't care."

++++

Blake had not heard from Mannie since he'd checked in earlier that morning.

He'd sent him to the hilltop overlooking the funeral in order to keep an eye on things through the binoculars.

"What do you want me to look for?" Mannie had asked.

"Anyone we might recognize. And take note of whoever the senator talks to."

"Especially Reese?"

"Yes. I understand he's coming in from Phoenix for the funeral. See if you can confirm that."

"Also Rockwell?"

"Yes. It might be informative if the billionaire shows up."

"Alright."

Now Blake tried Mannie's phone again, but no one answered.

Though his thoughts were mainly on Mannie and the

arrival of the canisters within the next couple of days, he'd made a promise to Julianne Springman and he wasn't about to go back on his word. So he took a little time to review the material he'd gathered for her and then gave her a call.

"I have a name for you," he said. "All the information you need. I'll send you an encrypted file. Do you have a secure server?"

"I don't trust my network. We should meet in person." She gave him an address—a pub and pizzeria in Brooklyn.

"Why there?"

"I know the place. It doesn't have any working video cameras."

He decided that allowing her to choose the location was acceptable. "I can be there at eight."

"I'll see you then."

11

As we ate dinner, Tessa asked me about the case, as she was apt to do: "I know you can't tell me anything about your investigation, but if you could, what would you say?"

"Pass the ketchup."

"Right. So'd you find out about the cows?"

For some reason, earlier this week we'd gotten talking about what you call different groups of animals: a herd, flock, school, and so on. Neither of us knew off the top of our heads what you refer to a group of cows as. I'd had to look it up.

"The plural of cow is kine," I told her. "But actually, twelve or more cows is a flink, so that one's sort of arbitrary."

"Huh. Have you heard about crows? It's an appropriate one; fits in with your job."

That one I knew. "A murder of crows."

"Impressive."

"And a sleuth of bears," I said. "Another good one for my job."

"Hmm. Nice. Oh—there are some really good reptile ones: a quiver of cobras, a lounge of lizards, a rhumba of rattlesnakes."

"Are all the reptile ones alliterative?"

"A float of crocodiles isn't."

"I have to say, two of my favorites are still the ones you mentioned on Monday: a bloat of hippopotami and a fluther of jellyfish."

She took a bite of her falafel burger and hadn't quite finished chewing it when she went on. "You think those are good? There are some really weird ones that I found earlier today: a fesnying of ferrets, an implausibility of gnus, a deceit of lapwings, and a trip of dotterels."

"Are you making these up?"

She swallowed. "Totally true. I promise."

I'd heard of dotterels but couldn't place exactly what they were. "At the risk of sounding animal illiterate, what is a dotterel?"

"Find out. That's your assignment."

"Well, I guess that's why Al Gore invented the Internet."

"No. The Internet is for cat videos, celebrity death rumors, conspiracy theories, and dragging down the world's collective IQ a dozen points a year. No Googling dotterels. Too easy. You're Dr. Analog. Find another way."

"Fair enough."

Ralph Hawkins was leading the joint task force that was tracking down Blake, so after dinner I contacted him. Ralph was based at the National Center for the Analysis of Violent Crime near the Academy just outside D.C. Normally, his group focused on consultations between the Bureau and state and local law enforcement, but he'd been assigned a more active role in this case. Currently, he split his time between D.C. and New York City.

"You got word that we caught Mannie, right?" I said.

"I'm reviewing the files now. Is he talking?"

"Not yet."

"I'm coming up there tomorrow. There's a pile of paper-work staring me in the face here, but I'm about to flamethrow the whole freakin' thing and fly up to the city."

"Sounds good. By the way, 'freakin'?"

"Trying to clean up the language for Brineesha."

His wife must have finally put her foot down, and when she did that there was no moving it aside.

"Anyway," he went on, "I should be there tomorrow afternoon. Maybe Mannie will have decided to be a bit more cooperative by then. If not, maybe I can con-vince him."

"You can be quite persuasive when you need to be."

"Yes, I can."

++++

Julianne had ordered an appetizer of garlic knots and was finishing her second one when Blake arrived. He slid her a manila folder and she passed him the still-warm rolls. "Try one," she said. "They're to die for."

"I'm good. Thanks."

"Where's Goliath? I thought he'd be coming along. You two seemed quite close."

"He's occupied with other matters. I should tell you first of all that I'm not certain that the man whose name I'm giving you has committed any actual crimes—but there is strong evidence that he has."

"What kind of evidence?"

"Recordings of his meetings with his psychiatrist."

"How did you get those?"

"One of the doctors at the facility where he spent some time is a client of mine."

"A client?"

"A regular one, we'll leave it at that. Let me just say that from all I've been able to glean, the man I'm recommending to you has the potential to be, well, a fitting partner."

"Potential."

"As I told you yesterday—no guarantees."

She tapped the dossier. "And the information is in here?"

He nodded. "And I'd suggest you speak with him soon. Tonight if at all possible."

"Why?"

"Prudence," he said simply.

He pressed the garlic rolls aside with disgust as if he were nudging a slug across the table. "Now, I believe that our business in this matter is concluded. It isn't wise for either of us to spend any additional time together. Good-bye, Julianne."

"Good-bye, Blake," she said. *For now*, she thought. Because she had someone special in mind for her next photograph, and the irony that he had just given her the name of the man who was going to kill him was not lost on her.

++++

The ERT was able to pull some prints from the windowsill at the senator's house, but they turned out to be his son's. If someone else had entered the house through that window, he was being extra careful or wore gloves.

The sole impressions outside the house were Converse Chuck Taylor All-Stars, size eleven, men's. The shoes were popular with Tessa's generation, so I wasn't sure what to make of that. A classmate or intern coworker of Jon's? Perhaps.

Also, the team pulled some partials from the woman's jacket that I'd recovered from the thorn patch in the woods. The prints came up as "unavailable"—a rare category that meant the person had been printed, but then the fingerprints were expunged for some reason, maybe so that a confidential informant could remain confidential, maybe because a cop was working undercover.

Whatever it was, in this case, it added another layer of mystery to what was going on. I sent in a request for an expedited release of the name, but I didn't know when, or even if, I would get it.

Why did Jon take his life when he did? What clues from his travel patterns and his relationships might shed light on that? Did he intend to be home alone or not?

I decided to review the footage of the observer in Senator Murray's house to establish if I was perhaps wrong in postulating that the person was male. However, after studying it several times, I concluded that, based on height and build, this person was not the woman who'd fled from me in the graveyard, and Mannie, being black, was the wrong ethnicity.

I contacted Greer and learned that Mannie, apart from declaring that he would talk tomorrow, still hadn't spoken a word.

"Are you going into the office tomorrow?" Greer asked me.

"Yeah. At least in the afternoon."

Originally, I hadn't been scheduled to work, but in this job no matter how many hours you put in each week, there's always a reason to be at the office. I still hadn't figured out where to draw the line between personal responsibilities and work assignments. Full days off for me ended up being pretty few and far between—something I needed to sort out, now that I had a family.

"Bad guys don't take days off," Greer said, "so why should we?"

I couldn't tell if he was being reflective or sarcastic. "Right. What about you?"

"Mannie's not my case, and if he's not talking, there's nothing I can really do on that front. I'll probably tackle a few things here from home." Ever since moving from Chicago he'd lived in New Jersey and had an hour commute each way, so I understood. "But I'll come in if I need to. Let's see how things shake out."

He told me he would work with Public Affairs to develop a press release that stated we were still collecting more information about Jon Murray's death and asking the public for any facts they might have.

"Don't mention the observer," I said.

"We won't."

12

Tessa plugged in her earbuds and cranked the music from DeathNail 13.

Silence weirded her out, especially at night.

Well, that wasn't *completely* true.

When she was reading, silence was alright. But times like this, being here by herself, made her think too much, and right now she didn't want to do that. She didn't want to think about how mad her mom probably was at her, or why she suddenly took off for Kentucky this weekend. Or how lonely it was around here without Az staying with them.

She hadn't realized how much she liked having somebody her age around, a little sister, but whatever. That was over. Az was gone, back to Kazakhstan. Even though Tessa had tried emailing her a couple of times, she hadn't heard anything back. Which wasn't a hundred percent surprising. Az was probably just glad to be away from her.

A scrap of a poem came to her.

Tessa pulled out her journal and wrote:

i don't want to get too close to you
because i might get scratched by the barbed-wire
    necklace
you like to wear.

it is a deadly decoration that reminds me of the
   frontier.
and the slicing up of the land.

you've had it for so long that it's getting rusty.
it is a barbed-wire fence that surrounds your heart,
hanging delicately around your neck.

It wasn't super eloquent or memorable, but it felt real, and for right now that was enough.

Her mom wrote entirely different kinds of poems, more traditional and rhymy, but dabbling in poetry was something they actually had in common.

For Tessa, poems were a way to express emotions that couldn't be stated outright.

She'd tried explaining that to one of the girls at school once when she said she didn't "get" poetry. "Poetry isn't something you *get*," Tessa had told her. "It's something that quivers inside of you with truth that you can't quite articulate but that you feel."

"Poetry quivers?" Candice had said.

"Yeah. I mean, sort of. Reading a poem is like flirting with some cute guy, not like sitting in biology class. Or at least it shouldn't be."

"I have no idea what that means."

"Okay, well, did you ever have to dissect frogs in biology class?"

"Yeah." Candice squinched up her face in disgust. "Ew."

"Well, most English teachers treat poems like biology teachers treat frogs. They think that cutting them open, peeling them apart, probing into them, and identifying their different parts is the best way to understand them rather than watching them in the wild and marveling at how they move."

"Who marvels at a frog?"

"I'm just saying."

"Yeah, no. I get it. I guess."

Tessa continued. "They're like, 'See that simile there? The author is telling us he's really suicidal.' 'And here, we have Shakespeare writing in iambic pentameter. Let's take the next hour and totally cut the heart out of his work of art. It'll be so much fun.' Just like the biology teacher is doing when he hands out the dissection knives."

"Okay, I think that's enough with the whole dead-frog thing." Candice looked pale. "Get back to the cute-guy part."

"So when you see him, your heart races, right? You can't keep your eyes off him. And you don't want to take a knife or whatever and cut him open. You want to kiss him. To feel his lips against yours. To hold him in your arms."

A sly smile. "That's not all I want."

"My point is the only way to really write a poem is to stop thinking of it as a way of communicating an idea or getting a point across, but as a way of breathing life into words."

"Sorta like Frankenstein, making them alive?"

"Sort of."

"So give me an example. Not a dead-frog poem. A cute-guy-with-his-lips-against-mine poem."

"I have a gravity-laden heart," Tessa began. Then she let the words write themselves in her mind, and she spoke them softly as they did: "Dragging me deeper and deeper into myself. Only the orbit of a much greater sun could ever lift me high enough for me to breathe freedom air."

"How is that a poem? It doesn't even rhyme."

"You are so lame. Poems don't have to rhyme."

"Do one that rhymes."

"I don't want to."

"Ha. You can't think of one."

"I could if I wanted to."

"You're stalling."

As Tessa thought about it, words came to her: *Dark dreams awaken and rise in the night. What whips can tame them? What chains restrain them? What harness can rein them or quiet their bite?*

But she didn't say that to Candice. Instead, she just said, "You're right, I was stalling. I can't do it."

Now, Tessa looked at the words she'd just written about barbed wire and an isolated heart. Yeah, it could use some work, but it was enough for the moment.

She considered a title for it and ended up with a choice between "Loneliness" and "Love."

She decided to go with wishful thinking and chose "Love."

13

Julianne lit another cigarette and waited across the street from the address Blake had given her in Ozone Park, a neighborhood in Queens that she noticed contained mostly single-family households and not just condos or townhouses.

No lights were on in the man's home. Maybe he'd retired to bed early. Maybe he was out and would be returning later.

Blake had told her to contact him tonight. "Prudence," he'd said somewhat enigmatically, and she wasn't sure exactly what he was getting at, but she didn't want to miss her chance if tonight was the best time to connect with him.

She was betting on the fact that he was out and about. If he was in bed there was no rush. She could make her way up there and break into his condo if necessary anytime tonight.

Over the last year, she'd pretty much given up smoking, but there aren't too many reasons you can stand on a street corner in New York City and look around the neighborhood and not draw attention to yourself.

So, she revisited her old habit.

She hadn't been certain that she wanted to kill Blake

until she'd met up with him at the restaurant. He had a dismissive air about him that she did not like. Killing those whom she knew wasn't a moral dilemma for her. The first two people she'd murdered were both people she loved—her fiancé and her best friend, who he'd cheated on her with.

There was simply a moment when you realized that the person you were talking with or looking at needed to die. It wasn't helpful to question that feeling. It was simply a matter of a decision you made and then carried out.

Yes. Blake deserved the same fate as his brother.

There.

Done.

That's all there was to it.

Movement to her left caught her attention: two men approaching, hand in hand.

Was the gentleman she was tracking gay? She didn't know, but based on the physical description in the dossier that Blake had provided for her, it didn't look like either of these two men was the one she was here to meet.

She nodded cordially to them as they walked past.

She was still sorting out how she was going to ask him what she needed to—it's not a subject that a person would typically use to start a conversation with a stranger: "Listen, I've been following you. I think you might be a serial killer, and I'd like to help you with your next project. I'm good with photography. We could start an album."

Not a line they would teach you in a course on how to win friends and influence people.

A taxi rolled to a stop across the street from the house she was surveilling, and the man she was waiting for emerged.

A prototypical young artist—scruff that looked more like the result of just forgetting to shave for a week or two than an actual attempt at a beard. He was a slim man, wore glasses, dressed bohemian.

Was he really the kind of person who could kill another human being?

He looked remarkably harmless.

But then again, so did she.

From experience, she knew that killers could be unpredictable, so she'd brought a Beretta 92FS with her. Dylan had favored a blade, but since this man was likely a killer himself, she wasn't sure she wanted to get up close and personal like that.

Even the city that never sleeps does doze, and at this time of night in this part of town, there weren't many people out.

She snuffed out her cigarette and crossed the street.

The man did not head directly to the address she'd been given but instead crossed the sidewalk to a place where it passed beneath a leafless tree. A streetlight had burned out, leaving a gap of blackness in the neighborhood.

She eased her hand into her purse and slipped her fingers around the grip of her Beretta.

The shadows swallowed him, and she quickened her pace to try to catch him, but she'd only made it a few paces into the darkness when he reappeared, as if from nowhere, standing in the middle of the sidewalk, facing her, blocking her path.

He held what she at first thought was a knife but on second glance realized was a letter opener. Despite it not having a very imposing blade, it looked sharp enough to do some damage if it were used with any kind of practiced technique.

"Why are you following me?" His voice was soft and not necessarily accusatory, laced more with curiosity than a threat.

Why didn't he go directly into the house?

Did he see you waiting for him when he got out of the taxi?

"My name is Julianne Springman. I'd like to work with you."

He eyed her quizzically. "Work with me? I'm a novelist. I work alone."

"Not in that capacity."

"In what capacity, then?"

"Is there a better place—a more private place—we could talk?"

"Why would I want to do that? I told you I don't work with anyone else."

"You weren't careful, Mr. Sabian. I found you. And if I found you, there'll be others who'll find you as well. You could use some help. I used to work as a CSI tech back in Detroit. I know all about crime scenes. How to leave clean ones."

She glanced at the letter opener in his hand. "Would you really stab me with that? Do you really want to chance that I haven't told anyone else I was going to speak with you tonight?"

"What do you want from me?"

"Just a chance to explain myself."

He used the letter opener to scratch harshly at his arm. "My place is close. We can talk there."

++++

The falafel burger from earlier hadn't filled me up, and I slipped out of the bedroom to grab some leftover lasagna that Christie had made before she left. On the way down the hall, I noticed that Tessa's light was still on and I figured I would just tell her good night, but when I knocked and called to her she didn't reply.

I knocked again. "You alright?"

Nothing.

I wanted to respect her privacy, and she might just have her headphones on, so she was probably fine. But also I felt a thread of parental concern.

Privacy was a big deal to her, and even just opening her door could make her upset.

I knocked a little harder. "I just wanted to say good night."

I started to ease the door open, but she yelled, "Don't come in!"

Immediately, I closed it. "Are you okay?"

That's when I heard her sniffle.

"I'm fine. Leave me alone."

"Do you want to talk?"

"No."

"Was it me? Did I do something to upset you?"

"I said I don't wanna talk!" Her voice was cut through with pain.

I wished we weren't having this conversation through a closed door, but maybe, in a certain respect, it was better this way.

"Just leave me alone." More sobbing. "It's not you, okay?"

That worried her slightly.

She knew from the information Blake had given her that Timothy had some mental instability, but now a few questions fluttered through her mind, ones that she hadn't allowed herself to ask earlier: *Do you have the wrong man? Did Blake set you up here?*

"These photographs were a way of remembering the family members who'd passed away," she explained. "It was quite normal at the time to have pictures like that taken. When you see an old photo where one person isn't blurry but the rest are, well, that's a good indication that the person you can see with the most detail is dead."

++++

Timothy looked at the photographs.

Life after life.

Death.

After.

Death.

After death.

In each, the living were blurred by their breathing, while the dead sat as still as the staid, languid air in their lungs.

Then the woman clicked to another site.

A warning came up on the screen about the kinds of photographs this website contained, about how you needed to be eighteen in order to enter it, about how it was meant as a private page to help grieving mothers and not to go through the portal unless you agreed to the terms.

As if it's a true portal, as if you really enter anything. You're not entering a site, you're just moving a cursor and tapping a mouse button. Where did this idea ever come from

I stood there staring at her door, feeling helpless.

How do you help a girl who might very well need help but tells you that she doesn't?

It reminded me of a conversation I'd had with Christie one time when we were going through a rough spot in our relationship and I finally blurted out, "Listen, it seems like you don't want me to solve your problem—all you want me to do is sit here listening to you talk about it!"

"Exactly!" she'd exclaimed.

Women are a mystery I will never understand.

But in this case, Tessa didn't even want me to sit around listening to her talk about her problem, so where did that leave me?

I assured her that I was here if she needed anything, heard no response except the sound of more crying, and at last, unsure what else to do, I walked to my room and tried Christie's number. Not surprisingly, no one picked up. I left a message. "Hey, Tessa's feeling a little . . . well . . . out of sorts. If you get this, give me a call. I hope your retreat is going well." Then I added, "I love you."

And, of course, silence was all that I heard in reply.

14

Maybe it was just the recent studying she'd done on feng shui, trying to make sure the settings were as ideal as they could be when she took her photographs, but to Julianne, although nothing about Timothy Sabian's living room seemed unusual or out of the ordinary, nothing quite seemed in place either. It was an odd effect. The room wasn't in disarray, but something about the placement of the furniture and the arrangement of the room was off.

"Can I get you anything to drink?" he asked her as she followed him into the kitchen. "I don't have much—some vodka and vermouth."

She didn't anticipate being here long, but if she did accept a drink it might make it more awkward for him to ask her to leave before she was done explaining herself.

"Vodka," she said. "Thank you."

When he opened the freezer, she noticed that, apart from some ice, the vodka bottle, and two TV dinners, the freezer was empty.

Timothy poured a glass for each of them, then gestured toward the living room. Once they were both seated, he said, "Now, tell me what you're here about."

"Perhaps it would be best if I showed you." She took out her iPad. "Let me just pull up a site."

"What site is that?"

"You'll see."

She clicked to a website containing a series of black-and-white photographs that had been taken at the turn of the twentieth century.

She scrolled through half a dozen of them. "You see how in each of these, one person's face is clear and well-defined while the faces of everyone else are slightly blurry?"

In the first, a girl in a frilly dress who looked maybe five or six was holding a baby on her lap. The girl's face was blurry. The baby's was not.

The second photo contained two parents standing beside a chair where a young, smartly dressed man in his early twenties sat. His face and features were distinctly delineated while those of the couple weren't.

"What does that mean?" Timothy asked her. "The photos are faked? Altered in some way?"

"On the contrary, it's evidence that they're most likely authentic. Back in the days when these pictures were taken, the exposure took so long that, as the people tried to sit still, they couldn't help but move slightly while the photographs were being taken. That movement would cause the image to blur slightly."

"So, these people." He pointed. "The ones you can see clearly, they're especially good at sitting still?"

"That's one way to put it, but I wouldn't want to be in their place."

"Why is that?"

"They were dead when the photographs were taken."

"What? Really?"

She couldn't quite read his tone, but it sounded more shocked than intrigued.

that you can enter a site? You can't enter a book—there are just images and words. It's not something you go into, just something you look at. The Internet is the same. A website is a place you enter without going anywhere.

But then his thoughts were interrupted when Julianne showed him the photos she'd taken.

Babies. One after another. All dead. Most of them were in the arms of their mothers, some lay in cribs or hospital bassinets.

Stress made the bugs worse. And he felt more of them now than he'd felt all day.

Don't let her know. Don't let her see.

Don't let her find out about them.

He repositioned himself, but he did not did not did not did not scratch.

"It's a way for me to help mothers move through difficult times, to process grief," she said, then lingered over one of the photos. "This woman carried her baby for nine months. She loved him, she sang to him, she prayed for him, she painted a nursery, carefully chose his clothes, had a baby shower—and now he's gone forever. They call them stillborns, and it's a word that has two meanings. They were *still* when they were *born*, yes, but yet they were *still born* and they deserve to be remembered, to be grieved."

He couldn't tell how honest she was being. There was something about her explanation that didn't ring true to him.

"So you take pictures of women holding their stillborn children. I'm not sure what this has to do with me. I write novels. I don't write about dead babies."

"In our culture we hide our dead. We shield ourselves from the sting of death. In India when someone dies, the

newspapers will run a photograph of the person's face—
but not a recent smiling picture of them alive, but rather a
photo of the face of their corpse."

"I'm still not sure what you want from me, Miss
Springman."

"We start a new site. A photo album for people with
similar interests to the ones we have."

"And those interests would be?"

++++

Alright, just get it out there, she thought. *Just say it.*

"You kill people, Mr. Sabian. Here's what I propose:
you kill them, I photograph them, and I help you clean up
the scene. Neither one of us wants to get caught. I'll make
sure we don't."

He was quiet for a moment, then scratched fiercely at
the side of his abdomen. "You worked in law enforcement?" he said.

"Yes."

"Can you help me solve a murder?"

"Whose?"

"I don't know."

"You don't know?"

"I need to make sure."

"What do you need to make sure of?"

"That I didn't kill anyone. There are a couple of people
that I know who've gone missing, and I want to make sure
I wasn't the one who killed them."

"You don't remember?"

He shook his head. "The voices tell me I have, but I
don't know."

Julianne wondered what to do. She could shoot him

here, now, and walk away. But she doubted Blake would give her another name.

Test the waters, and if necessary, take him out. You can always kill Blake yourself as well. It'll be easy to pin his death on a guy who's this unstable.

"Okay," she said. "I'm in. How do you suggest we proceed?"

"Miranda Walsh. See what you can find out about her death. Take until tomorrow night. I'll meet you at nine. I know a good place by the river."

"Alright. Tell me everything you can about this Miranda Walsh."

++++

The person who'd paid the server to fawn over Timothy Sabian at the restaurant last night downloaded the photograph that the man had taken of the troubled novelist as he walked out the restaurant door.

Timothy's career had taken off several years ago, and it hadn't been difficult to find him and to keep tabs on him. However, it'd also presented a dilemma—introduce himself or stay away?

His job made it relatively easy to acquire a camera small enough and surreptitious enough to hide in the author's home. In the end, he'd entered the house under the guise of upgrading the television's cable connection and planted the camera in the living room.

Just as he'd expected, Timothy had not recognized him.

He'd felt strangely nostalgic being there with him like that, standing in the same room.

Now, he watched Timothy through the video feed and listened to him speaking with this woman.

It was quite a conversation.

And the implications of it were intriguing. The two of them were planning to meet again tomorrow night at nine.

Well then.

It was time to clear his schedule.

STAGE III

Bargaining

Torn hope. Shards of glass.
A missing wallet. Emily's hiding place.

15

I got up before dawn to look over the case files and spend some time evaluating what we knew about Jon Murray's suicide.

I didn't want to discount the fact that Mannie had been present near the graveyard during the young man's funeral. With Mannie there, it seemed like too much of a coincidence for the cases of Jon's death and Mannie's work to be unrelated. However, at the moment, I couldn't put my finger on the connection between them.

Jon's dad had ordered an autopsy, and it'd revealed no trace of alcohol in his system, but there was evidence of a synthetic drug called Selzucaine. Though I'd heard of it, I wasn't too familiar with its effects. However, a little research told me that it was a party drug with the street name of Silver High. It lowered inhibition and made you more open to suggestion. Though having similar effects to cocaine, it was more of a hallucinogenic and more difficult to detect in the field and at border crossings, tougher even for drug dogs to sniff out.

Being under the influence of the drug could've accounted for Jon's inexplicable behavior but not the methodical way he went about his suicide, why he filmed it, or who the observer was.

I had my notes spread across the kitchen table when Tessa appeared in the hallway. I quickly slid them into a single pile and flipped it over so she wouldn't see anything related to the investigation.

She'd been crying the last time I spoke with her. At least today she didn't look upset.

"Morning," I said.

"You know how sometimes you wake up with eye scabs?" she replied sleepily. She was wearing gray sweatpants and her favorite lounge-around-the-apartment T-shirt of House of Blood, one of her go-to screamer bands.

"I don't think they're called eye scabs."

"Gritties? Crunchies?"

"Crunchies?"

"I'm just saying." She yawned.

"I think most people just call it getting sand in your eyes."

"It's not sand, though. I mean, did you ever taste 'em?"

"You—wait. You ate eye scabs?"

"I thought they weren't called that?"

"We'll go with it for now. You *ate* them?"

"Back when I was a kid, sure. Kids eat boogers too. What's worse—nose boogers or eye scabs?"

Now that was a question I never would've thought I'd be asked.

"Well?" she said.

"I have a strict policy never to eat anything that comes out of my body."

"Probably a good idea." She yawned again. "So are we gonna go to church?"

"Do you want to go to church?"

"No."

"Okay."

"But Mom would want me to."

"Is that your way of asking me to take you?"

"No."

"So you don't want to go and you're not asking me to take you."

"Uh-huh."

"Okay."

"Well?"

"Well what?"

"Are we gonna go?"

I looked at her over the screen of my laptop. "Listen, there's a lot going on with this case right now. I have nothing against you going—us going—but it shouldn't be just because someone else wants us to."

"She's my mom. She's your wife."

I almost asked Tessa if maybe she could just read the Bible a little here at home or listen to a podcast of a sermon, but that didn't seem to be a very understanding response.

I'd gotten some solid work in already, and without Mannie talking and the team still searching for any additional videos of suicides, I probably could spare an hour for church with my stepdaughter who was so troubled last night that she was in tears.

Folding up my computer, I said, "We should go."

"I just told you I didn't want to. I hate it when Mom takes me."

"Do you promise to hate it just as much if I take you?"

"Yes."

"Are you going to complain if I take you to church?"

"Obviously."

"Would you complain if I didn't?"

"Yeah."

"Okay. Let's get changed."

She was quiet for a few seconds, then said, "Can I drive?"

"That would be a no."

++++

Blake knew something was wrong.

Mannie never would have gone this long without checking in if he could help it.

Considering that he was such a high-profile suspect, Blake thought it likely that if he'd been apprehended, word would've hit the cable news cycle or the wire, but so far there hadn't been anything about his arrest or any homicides of John Does fitting his description. But then again, the news couldn't always be trusted.

Additionally, the timing of his disappearance was not ideal, not with the distribution happening on Tuesday and all that needed to be done before then.

One of his men, Aaron Jasper, had been siphoning money into his own accounts and, if the intel Blake had received was accurate, Aaron had been to see the Matchmaker—something that was strictly off-limits for Blake's employees.

It was time to make an example of Mr. Jasper and to have a word with Ibrahim, who seemed to be keeping a few too many secrets himself—both situations that Mannie was typically more adept at handling than Blake was.

Until last summer, Blake would have leveraged his two

contacts in the FBI for information about Mannie's possible apprehension, but since then, one had been killed by terrorists and the other had been arrested, severely hampering the amount of intel he was able to get from the Bureau.

However, he still had a compromised NSA employee that he could contact, and now he reached out to him to see if he could find out what'd happened to his most trusted associate.

16

Knowing how conservative Christie's church was, I went with a tie, which Tessa smirked at when she saw me.

On the way out the door, she asked, "So did you find out what a dotterel is yet?"

"Actually, that sort of slipped off my radar screen."

"I'll give you a hint—it's a *trip* of dotterels, remember? That's a huge clue."

"A trip. Okay, got it. I'll look into it."

Christie attended a small storefront church, which, on a good Sunday, might have sixty people in attendance.

Apparently, this was not a good Sunday.

When the service started, twenty-five people were there, including the pastor and the young dreadlocked woman who was working at the sound board. I knew the number of people because Tessa chose seats in the back of the room, which was fine by me because in settings like this, I liked to draw as little attention to myself as possible.

As a kid, I'd grown up going to church with my parents but fell out of the habit as an adult until I met up with Christie. This weekend, her pastor had swapped pulpits with Dr. Trayvon Williams, a semiretired black preacher who'd grown up in the south and had only moved to New

York City a couple of years ago. Though I hadn't met him in person, I'd heard him once when I'd come with Christie, and she'd filled me in about his background.

I liked his interactive preaching style a lot more than the droning litanies of the usual pastor.

So at least that was in our favor this morning.

After a few songs, Dr. Williams took the pulpit and gave a couple of opening remarks, including welcoming "any and all visitors who might be with us here on this fine Lord's Day."

Then, after a reminder about an upcoming Thanksgiving meal for the homeless, he launched right into his sermon. "Are you weary, brothers and sisters?" he asked us. "Can I hear an amen if you know what it's like to feel weary in this weariful world?"

The congregation gave him an "Amen."

"Is anyone heavy-laden with cares and fears and worry from the drain of everyday life? Is anyone here heavy-laden today? Amen?"

They amened him.

"Jesus said that you could come to him for rest. His yoke is *what*?"

This time not everyone seemed to know the answer, but three enthusiastic Amen-ers from the front shouted, "Easy!"

"And his burden is *what*?"

"Light!" More people joined in this time.

It went on from there—Dr. Williams encouraging us to bring our burdens to Jesus, to cast them upon him, for he cares for us, and that "a bruised reed shall he not break, and smoking flax shall he not quench."

I took that to mean that even if someone's faith was

weak, Jesus would accept them; that even if their soul was bruised, he wouldn't reject them.

That message carried encouragement with it.

And yet, throughout the sermon, I kept thinking of what else Jesus had said: that those who follow him must take up their cross to do so. I knew those words referred to the disciples' willingness to be persecuted and even crucified, but how is carrying a cross to your own crucifixion an easy yoke and a light burden? Does Jesus take your cares or add to them?

It seemed like such an obvious contradiction that I figured I was missing something in the way the two teachings fit together.

"The Spirit itself maketh intercession for us with groanings which cannot be uttered," Dr. Williams declared. "This means, brothers and sisters, that some grief is so heavy and some sorrow so deep and some pain so raw that no words in any language that exists now, no language that has ever existed, no language that ever will exist, can truly express it. But God's Spirit can, amen?"

"Amen," came the reply, a bit more solemn this time, reflecting the more serious mood of his statement.

"Those emotions, those questions, your hurts and your heartache—the Spirit of God is aware of your suffering and prays to the Father to ask him to remove it, to heal it, to unknot it from your heart. That's the intercession that the Spirit gives. Those are the groans which cannot be uttered by human lips, the ones the Spirit of the Lord specializes in."

While there are certain teachings of Christianity that remained inexplicable to me—the cross-carrying, burden-lifting paradox, for instance—what Dr. Williams was saying about groans that words could not express, that I could relate to.

I'd felt groans like that arise from my own heart. I'd searched futilely for the words to express my heartache but found only the glaring ineloquence of pain.

Was it possible that God's Spirit understood me so well that he knew even better than I did how to express the hidden, thorny terrors rooted in my soul? If so, that was the kind of God I needed. That was the kind of God I could love.

After the service, while Tessa and I were on our way to the door, Dr. Williams made his way over, somewhat enthusiastically, to greet us.

"Good to see you, Tessa," he said.

"Yeah," she said noncommittally.

He looked at me with a touch of warmth and curiosity, then extended his hand. "I'm Dr. Williams."

I was about to shake his hand and introduce myself, but before I could do either, Tessa said, "That's Dr. Bowers."

The PhD in geospatial investigation didn't come up much in my job and I tended not to mention it.

"He's my stepdad," she added.

A wide grin. "Ah, so you're the lucky man who married Christie."

"I am." We shook hands. "I appreciated your sermon."

"But?"

"But?"

"Was that hesitation I heard in your voice a moment ago? You appreciated my sermon . . . but . . ."

This guy was better at reading people than half of the profilers at Quantico. I didn't really want to question him or put him on the spot, so I simply said, "It was thought-provoking, what you said about Jesus wanting to carry our burdens for us."

"We all have burdens."

"Yes, we do."

Though he waited for me to go on, I didn't.

"Well, if God's word spoke to you today, then praise the Lord. And where is Christie on this blessed day?"

"She's at a monastery," Tessa said.

That took him aback. "A monastery?"

"Yeah. One with, like, real monks. Nighttime chanting. Weird haircuts. The whole deal."

"It's a spiritual retreat," I explained. "Don't worry, she's not planning to join up."

"Or become a nun," Tessa inserted.

"Yes, yes, of course," Dr. Williams said. "Well, say hello to her when you see her and be sure to greet her in the glorious name of Jesus."

When Tessa and I were outside, I asked if she'd enjoyed the service.

"No. I told you I didn't want to come."

"You're welcome." My phone vibrated with an incoming text. "But are you glad we came?"

"Absolutely not."

"Perfect." I unpocketed my cell and looked at the screen. The text was from the assistant director: Call me. Mannie wants to talk.

"Tessa, can you wait for me in the car? I need to make a quick call."

She walked off, folding up the church bulletin and stuffing it into her back pocket.

I put the call through to DeYoung. "What do we know?"

"Mannie says he'll talk, but only to you."

"What? Why me?"

"Your guess is as good as mine. He gave us ninety minutes, said that after that he's gonna ask for a lawyer. I need you here ASAP."

"I have my stepdaughter with me." I was thinking aloud. I knew that with a time window that tight, it would be tough to drop her off at home, which was in the opposite direction.

For a moment, I contemplated hailing a cab or having her take the subway—she was certainly used to getting around the city that way—but decided that, considering how upset she'd been last night, I didn't want to send her home alone. She could wait for me in the lobby at the Field Office—she was always bugging me to let her see the place anyway. She might even think it was cool to hang out there.

I figured we could grab a late lunch after I spoke with Mannie. At least if I brought her with me she would know I cared about her. Last night there wasn't much I could do to encourage her and let her know that I was here for her, but this morning there was.

"Patrick? You were saying? Your stepdaughter?"

"Never mind. From here, I'm guessing it'll take me thirty to thirty-five minutes to get to the Field Office."

"Cut that in half. I want you here ten minutes ago."

17

Christie made her way through the woods, following the trail that skirted along the edge of one of the ponds on the monastery's property. Today, the water looked deep and dark, like the surface of some vast obsidian ocean, though she guessed that, based on the size of the pond, it was probably no more than eight or ten feet deep at the most.

In the rippling wind, the water had a troubled, leathery look to it, almost like a bat's wings. Nervous waves splashed impatiently against the shore.

An old ladder, rickety and slick with moss, had been rigged up against the hill's abutment to help hikers climb up to where the trail continued twelve feet or so above her.

The rain began as she was ascending the ladder. Large, random drops of water that splattered dime-sized onto her arms and her back as she climbed. She had to pay careful attention to her feet to keep them from sliding off the rungs.

The mud at the ladder's top was worn smooth from pilgrims who'd ventured to see the statues of the Virgin Mary, the disciples, and Jesus, but with the help of a nearby branch, Christie managed to get past the slick spot without sliding back down the hillside.

As the rain picked up, she tucked her hands into her pockets and felt the note she'd written just a few weeks ago, the poem that she'd jotted down at church when the pastor's sermon wandered, as it was apt to do, into the subject of abstaining from alcohol.

The fact that Jesus had turned dozens of gallons of water into wine just to keep the party going—and *good* wine, to keep the people *drinking*—seemed to be lost on him. And by her minister's ample size, it was clear that gluttony didn't figure into his list of deadly sins, although drinking a beer or sipping a glass of wine—which Christie tended to enjoy with dinner—topped his list.

And so, as his sermon detoured, so did her attention, and she'd written a short poem, one that she hadn't shared with anyone yet. But it'd meant something to her, and she'd intended to pass it along to a friend who had pneumonia. In the end, though, her healing had come before Christie could send the poem and she'd never gotten around to typing it up or mailing it.

She saw several statues ahead of her in the forest, and it didn't take long for her to traverse the trail and come to Mary.

Previous retreatants had left flowers at Mary's feet, some had even slipped notes into the envelopes the monastery provided at the front desk and had placed them under rocks near the base of the statue.

Though she was momentarily tempted to read what others had left here, Christie held back, reminding herself that those notes were for the Lord or his mother, and not for her.

The now-constant tapping of rain across the forest accompanied her, but here beside the statues, enough branches spread above her that she was protected somewhat from the coming storm.

She removed the poem and read it silently.

God can handle all your needs,
mend the heart that hurts and bleeds,
give the lonely something true
that changes lives and makes them new.

Jesus heals the fractured soul,
makes it breathe,
makes it whole,
gives us hope when hope is gone,
breaks the darkness, offers dawn,
to all who follow, all who dare—
the door is open, love is there.

She tucked it inside the envelope she'd brought with her and sealed it shut.

And stared at the envelope.

But was it true?

Did God handle all our needs?

Though it might have been too hard for her to admit to anyone else, she honestly wasn't sure anymore.

So many needs for so many people seemed unmet—the comfort for her friend Angie, a divorcée who was sliding deeper by the day into clinical depression. Drugs might handle her needs, but it sure didn't seem like God was. Or the needs of millions in Africa for clean water—where was God when it came to helping them? Or those who'd been given the diagnosis that changes everything—how was Jesus healing them?

Her.

How was he healing her?

She found a rock that had no note beneath it and was about to place her envelope with the others there at the statue's base, but stopped.

Truthfully, where was God?

Was he really anywhere at all?

She looked up at the lifeless statue, shiny with rain, then let go of the rock and let it splat into the mud beside her foot.

Then, Christie ripped up the envelope and the poem inside it and let the pieces of paper fall unceremoniously to the ground, where they would eventually rot and turn to soil whether there was a benevolent God watching over them or not.

18

"You know how fast I drove on the way over here?" I said to Tessa as we pulled into the parking garage beneath the Jacob K. Javits Federal Building.

"And how you ignored half the traffic laws in the city?"

"Yeah." I found a spot. Parked. "Don't drive like that. Consider that trip a teachable moment."

"Do as you say, not as you do."

"Right."

"Stellar parenting technique there."

"Thanks."

We exited the car.

"I still don't get it," she said. "What am I supposed to do while you're in there? Can't I wait in your office or something?"

"When you become an FBI agent, then you can come see my office."

"Ha. Don't they ever have, like, a 'bring your daughter to work day' or something?"

It struck me that she'd said "daughter" instead of "step-daughter."

"I don't think I'll be much more than an hour, but there is a possibility it could be longer. If you'd rather go home, you can take the subway or I'll pay for a taxi. Otherwise you can stay here in the lobby."

"You'd pay for a taxi?"

"If that's what you want."

She reflected on that, then said, "Naw. I'll wait."

"Alright, come on. Let's get you set."

After navigating through security and situating Tessa on a bench in the lobby, I took the elevator to the fourth floor, where we processed and interviewed offenders.

The joint task force tracking Blake consisted of half a dozen different alphabet soup law enforcement agencies including ICE, the DEA, and the NYPD, but we were lead on this, so the interview would take place here rather than at one of the NYPD precincts.

DeYoung was waiting for me.

"Does Greer know that Mannie agreed to talk?" I asked as he briskly led me down the hall toward the interview room where Mannie was being held.

"I contacted him. He's working from home today. But I'm sure if we need him to come in, he'll make the trip."

"And Mannie said he'll only speak to me?"

"Yes. What are you going to say to him?"

"Whatever I need to in order to convince him to give us Blake."

"Before you offer him any deals, run them by me so I can have our lawyers approve them."

"Right."

He put his hand on my shoulder. "No, I'm serious, Pat."

"I hear you." But I also knew that I couldn't let legal wrangling get in the way of us bringing in a guy on our Ten Most Wanted list.

"I'll have another agent join you in the interview room," DeYoung offered, removing his hand.

"No." I shook my head. "Mannie said he only wants to speak with me, right?"

"Yes, but—"

"Then I go in alone so we don't short-circuit getting the info we need. I'll be fine."

"It's standard operating procedure in a situation like this to have a secondary—"

"This is not a standard suspect."

DeYoung sighed. "Alright." He glanced at his watch. "He calls his lawyer in an hour. Let's see what you can find out before then."

I passed through the observation room where DeYoung and one of the Bureau's lawyers would be watching from the other side of the two-way mirror.

A computer tech I didn't know was seated at a console managing the video feed, and as I walked past, I could see Mannie through the glass, waiting in the adjacent room, seated behind a formidable steel table, with each wrist separately manacled and chained to a metal loop on the top of it, all of which made sense to me. If he was strong enough to wrench a car door off a chassis, I imagined he was also strong enough to escape from a pair of standard handcuffs.

Despite what you might hear, even with a restrained suspect, you don't typically take a gun into an interview room. The chance that he could get free and acquire your weapon in an enclosed area such as that is deemed too great, but in this case, DeYoung said, "Don't go in there unarmed."

"No, it's alright." I handed my .357 SIG P229 to him. "I'll be okay."

"You sure?"

"If Mannie wanted to harm me, he had his chance yesterday out on the road. If he wanted to get away, he could have fled then. He wants something else, and I'm going to find out what it is."

I located a legal pad and pen, and then the agent seated at the control panel pressed a button to unlock the interview room's door. I passed through the hallway, entered the room where Mannie was, and then closed the door behind me. Its tight metallic click indicated to me that it had locked.

I took a seat across the table from him. He looked at me, then at the video camera tucked up in the ceiling's corner. Finally, he gazed at the two-way mirror.

"They're watching us," he said, more as an observation than as a question.

"Always."

"Alright, then. Let's get started."

19

Interviewing a suspect usually takes more patience and subtlety than I'm known for, so it's not exactly my specialty. However, I did know three things.

First, showing interest rather than making threats is the best way to get someone to talk.

Second, the best questions are always follow-up questions. People lie themselves into corners all the time.

And third, when someone is confronted, he'll typically do whatever he needs to in the interest of self-preservation. Lying is a natural, primal reaction. Nearly everyone who's guilty lies at first. Law enforcement officers know they do, judges know they do, lawyers know they do. The secret is finding ways to help the person understand that telling the truth, not the lie, is the true act of self-preservation.

I set the notepad out of his reach on the table. "I was told you wanted to speak with me."

"I do."

"I don't know your background, Mannie, but I'm guessing you're familiar with how this works."

"Establish rapport. Find common ground. Build trust. Empathize with the subject. Leverage the relationship for information."

"Right from the manual. And I'm also guessing that

neither one of us is interested in any games or in wasting time here today, so what do you say we skip that chapter?"

Maybe it wasn't the ideal angle, but I figured it was worth a shot.

"I never was much for games."

"Why did you ask for me?"

"I trust you. You'll do what needs to be done."

"In what way? What does that mean?"

"You'll know. When the time is right."

"Why now? Why did you decide to talk today? The ninety-minute window?"

"Timing always matters. Isn't that your area of expertise?"

He apparently knew more about me than I thought. Maybe he'd read my book. *Understanding Crime and Space* hadn't hit any bestseller lists, but it was out there, and he wouldn't have been the first criminal to research a book like that in order to identify weaknesses in an investigator's approach.

"Mannie, what were you doing on Amber Road yesterday?"

"Keeping an eye on the funeral."

"Why?"

"I wanted to see who spoke with Senator Murray."

"And?"

"I wasn't able to confirm what I was hoping to."

"What do you know about Jon Murray's death?"

"I know that he didn't want to kill himself."

"How do you know that?"

"I saw the video. He was crying when he tipped the chair backward."

I wasn't sure how far to pursue this line of questioning,

but I decided that it might help me land on what DeYoung had brought me in to discern: "the connection beneath the connection," as he put it.

"If he didn't want to commit suicide, why did he do it?"

"The tox screen came back positive, didn't it? Selzucaine?"

I wanted to find out if he knew who was present in the senator's living room when Jon died, but I didn't want to give away any information he might not already know.

"What else?"

"Do you know what percentage of cases actually go to trial, Agent Bowers?"

"Less than ten. What do you know about the Selzucaine?"

"Just three percent. The rest are pled out—ninety-seven percent. Don't you find that astonishing?"

It wasn't at all how the system was intended to work. In one of the greatest failures of our judicial system, plea bargaining has become the norm rather than the exception. It's simply a way of saving money and resources by having fewer cases brought to trial, but it in no way serves the greater good or the cause of justice.

No legislator wants to be seen as "soft on crime." So with the increase in drug-related violent crimes during the seventies and eighties, a lot of mandatory minimum sentencing laws were put in place. As a result, some offenders, even today, faced decades in prison for minor or nonviolent drug offenses, and rather than go to trial and chance being found guilty, they pled out.

"What is the role of our justice system?" Mannie asked me.

Though I wanted to focus on Jon's death and the drug

connection, I figured as long as Mannie was talking I didn't want to shut things down, so rather than change the subject, I said, "The official answer would be that punishment serves four roles: rehabilitation, retribution, and general and specific deterrence. If the plea deal can promote one of those, it's usually offered."

"Innocent people will accept plea bargains. Why?"

"Are you wanting to work out a plea bargain?"

"Why do innocent people accept them, Agent Bowers?"

"Fear," I said. "People are afraid that if they take their chances with a trial they'll end up serving more time."

"And do you know the percentage of people who plead out but are really innocent of the crime?"

To plead guilty or not guilty has little to do with whether or not you committed the crime and more to do with how you want to be treated by the judicial system in regard to the crime. Someone who pleads guilty will almost always receive a lighter sentence than someone who pleads not guilty but is found to be guilty.

"It should be zero," I said, "but some studies put the number at eight to fifteen percent."

"It's tragic when the innocent are so afraid of a miscarriage of justice that they admit to crimes they didn't commit and then end up in prison. Sometimes for a decade or more."

Where is he going with all this?

"You mentioned the Selzucaine," I said. "Do you know where Jon obtained it from?"

"Follow it back to the source."

"What does that mean?"

He was quiet.

"Why are you so faithful to Blake?" I asked him. "What does he have on you?"

Mannie's gaze shifted to the video camera and then back to me. "Do you have any idea what he has planned?"

"Tell me."

He pointed at the legal pad and I handed it, along with the pen, to him.

"Mannie, do you know who Jon was speaking to when he said, 'This is for you'?"

"His father."

"How do you know that?"

"Let's just say the walls have ears."

He began to draw on the paper—a combination of dots, some within boxes, others with partial boxes drawn around them. It might have been a form of Morse code or Braille, but I didn't recognize it. I'd never seen anything quite like it before.

"This may take a few minutes," he said softly.

"Take your time."

20

Tessa hated reading books on e-readers or on her phone—for some reason she just liked the feel of an actual *book* book in her hands.

She usually kept one in the satchel she used as a purse just in case she got stuck somewhere and needed to read, but today she hadn't bothered since they were just supposed to be going to church.

Which only left her phone.

Not gonna happen.

A sign near the door to the elevators announced that anyone from the public needed to leave behind their PEDs. With advances in technology, personal electronic devices can be nearly anywhere and can record nearly anything.

It listed restrictions on smart watches, smart shoes, phones, any recording devices, even portable USB thumb drives.

Smart *shoes*?

Whatever.

Before her mom married Patrick, Tessa hadn't had any idea that the FBI had their own police force. Now, she walked to the officer who was manning the metal detector in the lobby. "Is there, like, a cafeteria or something here where I can get something to eat?"

"There's another level of security you'll have to pass through, but you'll need to be escorted by a credentialed employee." He pointed. "That visitor's pass of yours will only get you so far."

"How far?"

"Here."

"Vending machines? Anything?"

"Sorry."

Wonderful.

She pointed at the building's front doors. "And if I go outside, I'm guessing you'll check me again on the way back in?"

"Why? What are you planning to bring in?" Any warmth that might have been present at first had drained out of his voice. "Exactly?"

"Nothing, I mean, I just want a sandwich. I just—forget it. Never mind."

Tessa debated whether or not to leave. Who knew how long Patrick was gonna be—and what was she supposed to do in the meantime? Just sit around here doing nothing?

She could at least grab some lunch and then, if she had any trouble getting back into the building, she could just text him to come down to help her get past security again.

Even though she knew that her mom wasn't using her phone this weekend, Tessa checked her messages, just in case, to see if she'd sent any updates.

Nope.

Nothing.

She headed outside to find some food so she wouldn't starve to death by the time Patrick finally decided to return.

++++

Mannie set down the pen and slid the notepad to me.

"That'll get you started," he said.

I looked it over.

"And the key to decoding it?"

"Remember death."

"Death? How does that—?"

"Now, I recommend that you get out of the way."

"Why?"

"Trust me, Agent Bowers. Move back."

In an attempt to keep everything out of his hands, I quickly retrieved the pen. "Don't try anything, Mannie."

He rose to his feet, clutched the chains, and leaned backward.

At first I thought he was trying to pull free from the chains, but then I realized he wasn't trying to pull the chains free from the table—he was trying to pull the table free from the floor.

He heaved mightily until, all at once, a screeching groan cut through the room as the bolts gave way and the table tore loose.

Grasping the chains, he swung it toward the two-way mirror.

The glass, as thick as it was, managed to withstand the force of impact, but a web of cracks appeared.

"Put it down!" I shouted. "There's no way you're getting out of here."

Mannie ignored me and swung the table again. This time, when the legs of the table struck the glass, the mirror gave way and burst apart, raining shattered glass shards into the observation room.

Then, Mannie tugged his hands to the side, parallel to the top of the table, and, seemingly with no effort at all, snapped the manacles free from the chains.

With impressive grace, he vaulted through the opening and into the adjoining room. The agent who'd been seated at the control panel drew his Glock, but Mannie responded by simply yanking and twisting the man's forearm and relieving him of his weapon.

I heard the crack of bones and the agent cried out in pain and clutched his arm.

I followed Mannie through the empty pane and positioned myself between him and the door to the hallway. "You're not leaving here, Mannie."

I'd left my gun with DeYoung, but he wasn't taking any aggressive action with it.

"Drop that gun, Mannie," I said.

"That's not going to happen." Mannie pointed with the barrel. "Back up and no one gets hurt, no one dies. But if you try to stop me, it's gonna get messy."

"You don't want to do this."

"It's already done."

The agent whose arm hung limp and useless clenched his teeth in pain. The spiral fracture in his forearm had left his broken radius protruding cruelly through the skin.

Instead of aiming the agent's gun at me, Mannie targeted the man with the broken arm. "Maybe you don't care if *you* die, Agent Bowers," he said to me. "But do you care if *he* does? Get out of my way, or I squeeze the trigger."

I stood my ground. "You're never going to make it out of this building."

"Then you have nothing to worry about. Phones and weapons on the floor in front of me. Now."

When I was slow in complying, he slid his finger to the trigger. "Do it."

"Please," the agent begged. "Don't let him kill me."

I set down my phone and nudged it toward Mannie. DeYoung gave up the weapons, and he and the lawyer kicked their phones to him as well. I kept my automatic knife in my pocket.

"Collect the phones," Mannie said to the man he had the gun pointed at. "I want yours too."

With his foot, Mannie slid the guns out of reach beneath the console, then stuffed the phones into his pants pockets, tore the landline phone off the wall, backed up to the hallway door, and opened it.

Holding the gun steady in his right hand, he swung his left wrist mightily down, smashing the manacle that still encircled it against the doorknob with enough force to rip the knob from the door. Then he ducked into the hall and closed the door behind him, sealing us inside.

I rushed forward. I'm pretty good with locks, but since there was no doorknob left, when I stuck my knife blade in to try to jimmy the latch, it didn't help. I would've tried kicking it open, but the hinges were on our side of the door. However, the hinges for the door in the interview room were on the outside, so I could get out through there.

The lawyer was on his hands and knees reaching for the guns. He came up with my SIG, which he handed to me. Hastily, I returned to the interview room, positioned myself in front of the door, and kicked, planting my heel firmly beside the doorknob. The door was reinforced and it took three kicks before it flew open.

As I burst into the hallway, I called to DeYoung, "Have Cyber wipe those phones so he can't access them!"

Mannie was a human battering ram, and I found one agent unconscious in the hallway and another groaning on the floor near where the hall ended in a T.

"Where'd he go?" I said. "Which way?"

He pointed left.

I darted in that direction, evaluating the layout of the building with respect to the route Mannie had chosen. It made sense if he was heading for the parking garage. *How does he know where to go? Did he study the schematics of this building? Has he been in here before?*

I hadn't gone far before the lockdown alarm went off, and I knew we were talking about a total shutdown of exterior doors. If Mannie was still in this building—and based on the amount of ground he would've needed to cover to get out, I guessed that he was—we should be good.

My next thought went to my stepdaughter. I didn't know her well enough to guess how she would respond to the alarms, but I didn't want her to be afraid. However, I had no phone to call her, and the lobby wasn't close by. I figured we had enough agents to sweep through the parking garage looking for Mannie. I wanted to make sure nothing happened to her.

A security team of three agents came sprinting up to me.

"Check the garage," I said. "Every car, every trunk. And no one leaves or enters the front gate." I turned to the lead agent. "Let me have your phone."

"But I—"

"Now."

He unlocked the screen and handed it over. Tessa normally didn't answer phone calls—just texts. So I sent her a text to stay where she was in the lobby and not to worry about the alarms, that she was safe.

When I returned to the agent who'd told me where Mannie had headed, I asked him what his name was.

"Jason Thurman."

"Are you okay?"

"Yeah, yeah. I'm fine."

"What happened?"

"He got my phone and my wallet."

"He—wait. What? Your wallet?"

Thurman bit his lip nervously.

I'd seen this tactic before—an offender gets a guy's wallet, which has his home address in it, then he threatens the man's family to procure his help.

"Are you married?" I asked. "Do you have kids?"

"Yeah." The man was shaking. "I—"

"Did Mannie threaten your family?"

A tear formed in his eye. "I didn't want to—"

"Where did he go?" I demanded. "Tell me the truth."

Thurman pointed down the other hallway.

I cursed under my breath.

I gave him the phone I'd just acquired. "Call your family. Get them someplace safe."

Then I ran down the hall Mannie had actually used, thought through the routes he might have chosen to get out of the building, and remembered that there was a little-used tunnel that ran from the federal building on this side of Duane Street to the Ted Weiss Federal Building on the other.

I couldn't come up with any other scenarios that saw Mannie escaping this building.

In the past, Blake and his team had been able to access the Federal Digital Database, so they might have obtained the building's blueprints.

Is this part of their plan? Did Mannie want to get caught?

I descended the stairs and made my way to the tunnel that led under the street. Taking a deep breath, I opened the door.

The cramped corridor was less than two meters wide and had only sporadic fluorescent lights, leaving plenty of shadowy recesses. A network of pipes leading from one building to the other obstructed the view even more.

"Mannie!" My voice echoed thinly and sharply through the corridor.

No reply.

Alright, let's do this.

Quickly, but cautiously, and with the gun in the high ready position, I proceeded into the tunnel.

21

Shadow to light.

I moved forward.

The pulsing emergency lights and the glaring alarm weren't in sync with each other and it created a disorienting, vertiginous effect.

I'd never been in this corridor before, and I didn't know exactly where it opened up in the other building.

However, the farther I went into the tunnel, the more convinced I became that Mannie would not have holed up in here but would have bolted through to the other side.

Ten more meters.

The alarm kept cycling.

Then five.

Then two.

And then I was there.

Bracing myself, I threw open the door and entered a small, empty room that had a freight elevator on the right, a stairwell on the left.

I punched the elevator's up button, then opened the stairwell door while I waited for the elevator doors to open.

Gun raised, I studied the steps above me but saw no one, heard no one.

Back in front of the elevator, I leveled my SIG as the doors parted.

Empty.

If Mannie had used the elevator, he could have exited onto any floor in the building. Since I had no way to tell if that's what he'd done, I turned my attention to the stairwell.

I took the steps two at a time, crossed a short hallway, and found an exit door that was now lying on the pavement outside, either kicked down or torn free.

Busting down the door would've set off an alarm, but since one was already sounding, nobody would've necessarily noticed the difference or paid specific attention to it.

Not a bad strategy for getting out.

I scanned the street.

You'd think that someone Mannie's size would be visible a mile away, but I saw no sign of him outside the building. Even when I ran down the street to the corner, I came up with nothing.

He was gone.

But then another thought: *Or maybe he isn't. Just because the door is broken down doesn't mean he went through it.*

It was true, he could still be in the building somewhere.

When Ralph and I were working on a case in Detroit last summer, we'd found it necessary at one point to disable the GPS tracking on our phones. I wasn't sure if Mannie would know how to do that. Right now, our fugitive had five phones that we knew of. Certainly, we would be able to track one of them to locate him.

Even with the remote data wipe that I'd asked DeYoung to order, the GPS should still be traceable.

Back in the building, I flagged down an agent from a security team sweeping the hallway, told her to guard the doorway and make sure no one went in or out, then ran upstairs to our computer forensics suite on the third level to Agent Vanessa Collins, the woman who'd enhanced the footage of Jon Murray's suicide video for me. "I need you to track some phones," I said.

"Whose?"

"Everyone's."

"What are you talking about?"

"Ping the phones of any employees on the surrounding streets or in any vehicles leaving the area. Start with De-Young's, Thurman's, and mine. Then, find out the name of the lawyer and the attending agent who were stationed in interview room 422 across the street until about five minutes ago. Move out from there."

"I'm on it."

++++

"What are you doing, sweetie?" the escort asked him.

"Just getting everything ready," Blake replied.

He unfolded the plastic tarp in the middle of the room and began to meticulously spread it out across the carpet.

"Ready for what?"

"A chat."

He'd enjoyed Sasha so much Friday night that he'd brought her back now, during the day. A lesson he'd learned a long time ago: all of the pleasures of the evening do not need to wait for darkness to be enjoyed.

The NSA employee whom he'd contacted earlier hadn't been able to tell him much, other than that Mannie had been picked up by the FBI and was being held somewhere, but he didn't know where. "They're playing this one really close to the vest," the guy had said.

"I imagine they are."

Now, Sasha pointed. "But I don't get it. What's the plastic for?"

"Easier cleanup."

"But—"

"Trust me, my dear. The less you know, the better."

As he was setting a chair in the middle of the tarp, his encrypted phone rang, and when he answered it, Mannie's voice came on: "I'm out. I'm free. The Feds had me at the Field Office."

"What happened?"

"Picked me up on Amber Road. I'll fill you in when I see you."

"Where are you?"

"On my way to Kingsbridge Heights. The reservoir."

Blake knew the place. One of their prearranged meeting locations.

"I'll send a car to pick you up," Blake said.

"Don't worry. I didn't tell them anything."

Blake smoothed out the few remaining wrinkles in the plastic. "The thought never crossed my mind."

++++

Collins was good.

It took her less than four minutes to tag the phones. All five of them were traveling in different routes and at different speeds along nearby streets. One dot on the map might have been our suspect, but all of them clearly were not.

Mannie passed the phones out. He gave them away.

Not bad. That's what I would have done.

Over the next few minutes, we checked our external CCTV cameras to no avail and tracked down all the people carrying the missing phones. However, even when the agents or NYPD officers caught up with them and asked where the big guy who'd handed them the phone had gone, none of them could tell us anything helpful.

The fact that Mannie was able to elude detection on the street and avoid being captured on any exterior cameras made me think again of how the observer in the senator's house was able to avoid being seen on the security cameras at the residence.

I still hadn't spoken with Tessa, which concerned me, so, before regrouping with DeYoung, I headed to the lobby to touch base with her.

When I arrived, she wasn't there. I asked the FBI Police officer assigned to the metal detector if he knew where she was, and he told me simply that she'd left.

"Do you know where she went?"

"Nope. She was worried about coming back through again, though. Said something about getting a sandwich."

I felt a flood of frustration that quickly turned to worry.

"Was she alone?"

"Yeah."

"And you don't know where she might have gone?"

"I already told you that I don't."

This guy was irritating me. "Right."

I went outside and scanned the street but didn't see her.

Back in the lobby, I used the phone at the front desk and tried her number, but she didn't pick up. I told myself that it was maybe because I kept calling from all these different numbers rather than my own.

This time, I left a voicemail for her to give me a call—the Cyber team was doing a restore on my phone and I would have it back in a few minutes.

Of course, it was unlikely that something might've happened to Tessa with regard to Mannie's escape, but still, I was worried. From my encounters with Blake last summer, I knew that he was aware of Tessa and Christie and how much they meant to me, and right now that did not reassure me.

A rush of fierce protectiveness triggered inside me, something that felt both foreign and also somehow, at the same time, natural. Maybe it was how a dad was supposed to feel. I liked it even though it scared me. I never would've thought I would be this worried about someone else's daughter.

She's not just someone else's. Not anymore.

I knew that DeYoung wanted to see me again, but before I left for his office I put another call through, this time to Agent Collins. "Listen, there's one more phone I need you to track."

"Whose is that?"

"My stepdaughter's. She's going to hate me for this, but could you locate her cell?"

"You sure? My nephew, he's a teenager; if I did something like that with him, well . . ."

"Yeah, no, I hear what you're saying, but right now I just need to know that she's safe."

I gave her Tessa's number and headed to the conference room adjacent to DeYoung's office to debrief Mannie's escape.

22

DeYoung informed the receptionist that he didn't want to be disturbed, then tugged the door shut.

A television screen stared at us from one wall, a speaker's lectern sat on the other side of the room. We gathered around the mammoth table that barely fit between them.

DeYoung and I were joined by the lawyer, who I learned was named Vincent Ashworth and who was still shaking, and Agent Thurman, whose wallet had been taken. The young man whose arm Mannie had broken had been taken to the hospital.

"So what do we know?" DeYoung said. "Where are we at?"

"Blake is still on the loose," Ashworth muttered. "Mannie's gone. And we don't know anything more than we did before he escaped."

That wasn't quite true, but I didn't correct him. I was still processing everything Mannie had said to me.

DeYoung flopped the legal pad Mannie had used onto the table. "And what does this mean, Pat? This cipher?"

"I'm not familiar with it. He told me that remembering death was the key. I'm not sure if he was referring to any specific death—Jon Murray's, for instance—or just death in general."

"We can analyze it, though, right?" Thurman said to me. "Have our team decode it?"

"We can try."

DeYoung looked at me curiously. "What was all that about plea bargaining?"

"I don't know. I've been trying to figure that out myself."

A knock on the door. When DeYoung answered it, Collins appeared with our phones in hand.

As she was passing them out, she said, "Pat, your latest backup on the system was twenty-four hours ago, so we don't have your most up-to-date messages."

"Okay. And the other matter?"

"Renaldo's. Just down the street. A coffee shop."

I knew the place.

I gave her a description of Tessa and what she was wearing. "Do me a favor. Call the manager and confirm that a girl fitting that description is in there. And that she's alone."

"Done."

Collins told us to contact her if we needed to, then slipped into the hallway again.

Once she was gone, I said to DeYoung, "There are five things we need to do."

"Go on."

I ticked them off on my fingers as I listed them. "First, provide protection for Agent Thurman's family. If Mannie and Blake know where they live and decide to make a move on them, I want them safe and agents waiting in the house instead."

"Good call," DeYoung told me. "I'll get a team over there."

Thurman nodded, looking relieved.

"Second," I said, "contact Ralph Hawkins. He told me last night that he was planning to fly up here today. He needs to know that Mannie escaped. Third, let's see if Ralph has any information in his case files that might give us a bead on where Mannie might have gone. Fourth, check traffic cameras and exterior CCTV cameras from the surrounding blocks to see if we can catch sight of Mannie."

He was taking notes. "And number five?"

"Mannie told me to follow the Selzucaine back to the source. Let's work our CIs to find out all we can about the drug's dealers and distributors."

"Thurman, that's you," DeYoung said. "You handle high-level confidential informants, don't you?"

"I do. I'm on it," he said.

As DeYoung put things into play, I stepped aside and texted Tessa again, this time from my own phone, asking her one more time to call me as soon as possible.

I was considering how to gracefully make an exit so I could follow up with Collins and confirm Tessa's location when DeYoung's receptionist knocked once on the door and then pressed it open before waiting for him to invite her in.

"Annalise, I told you I didn't want to be disturbed."

"I know, sir. I'm sorry. This is important. I thought you might want to know. It's the senator. He's about to do a press conference."

"What?"

"Senator Murray. Public Affairs just gave me a call, wondered who was behind green-lighting it."

DeYoung clicked on the television. "What channel?"

"CBN."

He flipped to Cable Broadcast News.

"Is this about his son?" I asked Annalise.

"That's what the anchors are saying."

"You need to call him, sir," I told DeYoung. "Stop him."

He already had his phone out and was speed-dialing the senator.

"I should speak to him," I said. "I was there at his house the other night. I'm the closest to all of this."

Annalise left us alone, and while DeYoung put the call through, I thought about the possible fallout if the senator gave too much away about the investigation.

Once it became public knowledge that there was someone else present at his son's suicide, things with the media could easily spin out of control—especially if we ended up with a person of interest. The court of public opinion convicts all too many people long before the actual courts ever try them—if it even comes to that. Innocent people get mired in and permanently affected by issues like this all the time.

Cable news shows aren't so much reporters of the news as they are vendors of it. They package up and sell what they believe their viewers want to consume—even if it doesn't contain any truth at all.

DeYoung reached the senator.

I could only hear the assistant director's side of the conversation. "I know, Senator . . . He just needs to speak with you for a moment . . . Of course . . ." DeYoung glanced at me, but said to the senator, "Yes. I promise. He'll be quick."

He handed me the phone.

"Hello, Senator," I said. "You're holding a press conference?"

"Yes. There was someone else there when my son died. We can't keep it from the media any longer."

"Keeping that to ourselves right now is the best call."

"Where has that gotten you? Are you any closer to finding this person who was at the house when Jon died than you were on Friday?"

"We're looking for related cases that might contain—"

"This is my son we're talking about. My *dead* son. I'm not going to sit by and do nothing when I can get the public out there on our side, get them searching for whoever was there. I'm guessing that somebody knows something, and I'm going to offer a twenty-thousand-dollar reward as an incentive to help jog people's memories. Finding that person is the only way to get answers regarding what happened to Jon."

"Senator, this is not the appropriate time to—"

"Do you have any children, Agent Bowers?"

"I have a stepdaughter."

"And what would you do if you thought she might be in danger? Or if, God forbid, she was dead and someone else might've been responsible."

"I would do anything for her."

"Then do not judge me."

"I'm not judging you, sir. We both want the same thing here. I'm just trying to find out the truth of what happened, and the timing of bringing the public in on this isn't right yet."

"That's your opinion. My opinion is that if your team was doing its job we would know the identity of this person by now."

Something was definitely off here. The senator wasn't acting anything like he had the other night when he'd been so patient and helpful. It might have just been that the stress of what'd happened was getting to him, but I wondered if someone might have contacted him, maybe pressured or threatened him in some way.

"Listen," I said, "we'll—"

"I need to go," he told me bluntly. "I have a press conference to give."

End call.

"Well?" DeYoung asked me.

"He's not going to be dissuaded."

"This doesn't seem like the man I know," DeYoung said.

"Or the man I met."

Collins called and assured me that Tessa was at Renaldo's and was fine. "The manager said she's just sitting there writing in a journal and having a piece of pie."

DeYoung was staring at the television where the senator appeared on the screen and walked up to the lectern.

Alright.

Here we go.

23

"Thank you all for being here today," Senator Murray began. "And I'd like to also extend a special thanks to the many people I've heard from all over this great state and beyond who've shared their condolences with me for the loss of my son."

He paused for a moment and scanned the crowd. Although he had notes in front of him, it looked like he wasn't reading from a prepared statement but was speaking off the cuff.

"There is some important information that I need to share with you. The night Jon died, another person was present at the house. We don't know who it was, but we are seeking information about that person's identity. I'm personally offering a reward of twenty thousand dollars for information that leads to the positive identification of that individual. I need to emphasize that he is not a suspect, nor is he being accused of anything. He is simply someone who, as the last person to see my son alive, law enforcement would like to speak with. I'm asking you, the public, for help because I trust you and we all deserve answers about what really happened when my son died."

Why did he have to offer a twenty-thousand-dollar reward? Did he have any idea how many people were going to claim to have been there at the house? Or how much work it would be for our team to vet and follow up on them all?

He gave a hotline number that I didn't recognize, and I guessed he must have set it up without Bureau authorization.

What in the world is going on here?

After he finished, the reporters peppered him with questions: "Are the police and the FBI looking into this?" "Is there any reason to believe that the person is complicit somehow in Jon's death?" "Why haven't we heard about this before now?"

While I listened to him offer his responses, I watched DeYoung rub his forehead in exasperation. The buttons on the phone in front of him were already starting to light up. I guessed that the director would be one of the people calling. Probably Public Affairs. Maybe the governor. What a mess.

It was probably best to let DeYoung tackle those calls on his own, so I signaled to him that I was leaving. He wearily waved for me to go, and I slipped into the hallway. The rest of the team followed after me.

The press would undoubtedly want an official statement from the Bureau, and I was just glad that providing one didn't fall under my job description.

Today DeYoung looked even more worn out than usual.

I didn't know too much about his past, just that he was single and had been with the Bureau for nearly twenty years. Came from Cincinnati. He moved up through the ranks on the fast track to AD. He didn't keep family photos on his office wall or his desk, and we didn't discuss our personal lives much. I didn't even know if he'd ever been married or had any kids, but that wasn't too unusual.

Many of the people who work for the Bureau do all they can to separate home life and work life.

While I was on my way back to the lobby, I finally heard from Tessa.

"What's with all the messages you keep leaving me?" she complained.

"Why didn't you reply earlier?"

"What—am I supposed to walk around staring at my phone's screen every second? What's wrong? What's going on?"

"I've been looking for you. I was worried about you."

"I'm fine. I'm at this coffee shop down the street. Renaldo's. I can be back in, like, two minutes."

I debated giving away that I already knew she was there but decided against it.

"I thought I told you to wait in the lobby?"

"You said I could *stay* there. But I don't recall it as an official *order*."

"Listen, Tessa. I'm not trying to order you around. I just want to make sure you're safe. I went to find you in the lobby and you weren't there."

Her voice stiffened. "You've still got a lot of work to do on this whole stepdad thing. You can't freak out every time I'm not exactly where you want me to be."

I was about to counter that she had a lot of work to do herself in the role of being a stepdaughter, but I managed to hold back and said instead, "I'll meet you where you are." It wouldn't have been protocol to tell her that a prisoner had escaped. "Have you eaten lunch?"

"Got distracted by dessert."

And in that way she took after her mother—opting to eat dessert first.

"Okay, listen. There's a Thai place just another block or so from you down the street from that one bookstore. They have a ton of vegetarian items on the menu. I'll catch up with you at Renaldo's. We can walk down from there. Give me a few minutes to wrap things up here."

She hung up, which I took as her way of agreeing to the plan.

24

Julianne rang the doorbell and waited for the woman to open the door.

She'd spent most of the day looking into the disappearance of Miranda Walsh, a graduate student who'd attended one of Timothy's book signings and then went missing later that night. No one had seen or heard from her in six months.

There weren't any security cameras at the bookstore or videos of the signing, but Julianne had called in a favor with a former Detroit cop whom she'd worked with before he moved to New York City when his wife got a new job. He was with the force up here now, and he'd passed along some details about the case.

"So, we're square?" he'd said.

"We're square."

The favor was Julianne not telling his wife about the affair they'd had two years ago.

A middle-aged woman with frothy, gray-tainted hair answered the door.

"Hello. Mrs. Walsh?"

"Yes?" She studied Julianne somewhat suspiciously. "Can I help you?"

Julianne still had her Detroit Police Department badge

and now held it up just long enough to allow Mrs. Walsh to see that it was a legitimate police ID. "I'm Detective Springman. I'm wondering if I could ask you a few questions about your daughter, Miranda."

"My daughter?"

"I know she's missing. We're following up on some—"

"Do you know where she is?" The woman gasped. "Did you find her?"

"I'm afraid not, ma'am. We're just verifying some facts. May I come in?"

"Um. Yes. Of course."

Inside the house, Mrs. Walsh offered her "coffee or tea or anything," but Julianne declined. She knew there was no Mr. Walsh—he'd passed away a year ago. Heart attack. "I understand that Miranda was studying at NYU but that she still had some of her belongings here?"

"Yes. In her room. I haven't moved anything. It's just the way she left it. I mean, except for the boxes of things from her dorm room. I haven't even opened them up yet. It's just too . . . well . . ."

"I understand. It can be difficult. May I have a look?"

"Yes."

Mrs. Walsh directed Julianne to the stairs and led her up, somewhat slowly, as she favored a creaking right knee. A variety of angel paintings hung on the walls.

"Can you tell me about Miranda's interest in that author in particular?" Julianne asked.

"Author?"

"The one whose book signing she attended on the night she disappeared. Timothy Sabian."

"Oh, I don't know anything much about that. She

mentioned that she was going to it: the Mystorium. It's a bookstore that specializes in crime books."

"Yes," Julianne said.

"That's about all I know."

"Had she ever met him before?"

"I really couldn't say. Is he a suspect?"

"No. Not at this time."

Mrs. Walsh paused at the second room on the left and eased the door open but did not step inside. "It's all in there. The boxes are in the corner. That's all of her things from the dorm."

"Thank you."

"Do you need anything else?"

"No. I shouldn't be more than a few minutes."

After Mrs. Walsh left, Julianne started with the dresser drawers.

It felt a bit invasive to be looking through a dead girl's dresser—if Miranda really was dead, which certainly appeared to be the most likely scenario.

The young woman's body had never been found, but there was no reason to believe that she would have run away. Neither her phone nor credit cards had been used since she disappeared.

The girl was close to Julianne's size and she was tempted by a certain blouse, but in the end she left it behind, expecting it might be difficult to secrete it past the girl's mother. However, Julianne did help herself to a pair of frilly panties and a pearl necklace that Miranda would no longer be needing and tucked them into her pocket.

From her inquiries, it didn't seem like Timothy had ever been on the suspect list, hadn't even been questioned.

The officers had focused on an ex-boyfriend of Miranda's—arrested him, even—but then had to cut him loose because of lack of evidence.

The case hadn't gone anywhere.

Julianne turned her attention to the bookshelf but saw no books by Timothy.

However, when she opened the first box of items from Miranda's dorm, she found copies of all six of his novels that had been released prior to her disappearance. All hardback. All first editions.

She paged through them.

Dog-eared pages, underlining. Highlighting. This girl was really into his writing.

And all six books were signed but, interestingly enough, not with the same pen. Timothy had personalized them and written different inscriptions. So, it certainly looked like she'd run into him numerous times rather than bringing all of her books to that one final signing.

Interesting.

Julianne made a note to look at Timothy's website to see where else he'd lectured or held book signings over the last eighteen months.

It would probably have been asking too much to find a day planner or diary, and Julianne found neither. If Miranda had kept them, they would have been collected by the police and put into evidence, which, despite her NYPD contact, she did not have access to.

The final boxes contained an assortment of clothes and books but nothing of note.

Julianne carried the edition of *Cold Clay*, the volume that Timothy had been signing on the night Miranda disappeared, with her downstairs.

"Do you mind if I hold on to this?" she asked Mrs. Walsh. "I'd like to look into a few things. I can get it back to you later if you'd like."

"No, no. Please. Feel free to keep it if it'll help you in any way."

"It might." Julianne pointed to the two ceramic angels that Mrs. Walsh had on an end table near the sofa. "Don't give up hope, Mrs. Walsh. Don't ever give up hope. If you're a religious person, keep praying. You never know what'll turn up, and at the station, we can use all the help we can get."

"I believe in angels, Detective. And I don't believe my Miranda is one of them yet."

"Well, if it makes you feel any better, neither do I."

The woman began to tear up, and Julianne took her in her arms to comfort her. "It'll be alright, ma'am. You just need to have faith that things will work out the way they're supposed to."

25

"Why do serial killers always listen to classical music?" Tessa asked as we were finishing our lunch. "I mean, the slimeball ones don't—it's grunge or something. But the ones who're supposed to really creep us out are always into Mozart, and they sort of stand there entranced with their eyes closed, directing the music with their finger."

"I think that's just in the movies."

"So, what do serial killers in real life listen to?"

"It varies." I left our bill along with some cash and a tip on the table, and we rose to leave. "Just like with everyone, I suppose. It's really hard to make generalizations about serial killers."

"Except that they kill people. I mean, I'm not trying to be insensitive or anything, but, well, they are murderers."

"Yes." Outside, we passed into what was becoming a crisp autumn afternoon. "That is true."

"And fire-starting, torturing animals, and bedwetting—what is it about those three things and serial killers, anyway?"

"No one really knows. And by the way, how did you know about the Macdonald triad?"

She shrugged. "Dunno. Do you think I'm a psychopath, Patrick?"

"Do you close your eyes and direct Mozart with your finger?"

"No."

"Grunge?"

"Death metal, maybe. But I sorta direct it with my head instead of my finger."

"Then no. I think you're safe. I don't think you're a psychopath."

"I don't think you're one either."

"Well, then."

"I mean, for what it's worth."

"Thanks."

I doubted other stepdads had conversations like this with their teenage daughters, but then again, you never know.

As long as things seemed to be in a good place between us, in the service of honesty I decided to be up front about tracing her location through her phone.

"Hey, listen, I knew you were at Renaldo's before you told me you were there."

"What do you mean? How could you have known that?"

"I actually had someone in our Cyber unit track your phone."

She stopped walking. "What?"

"I was worried. We had a . . . well, a situation at the federal building, and I—"

"You tracked my phone?"

"Yes."

"Is that even legal?"

"It's not exactly protocol, but you're a minor. It's completely—"

"And you did it *why?*"

"I was worried about you."

"But why?"

"Because you're my stepdaughter."

"And?"

"I care about what happens to you."

She said nothing.

And I would never let anything bad happen to you or your mother, I thought. *Never.*

"Don't do that again. Don't do that *ever* again."

"Tessa, I can't promise you anything like that. If I'm ever afraid for your safety, I'll do whatever I have to in order to make sure you're alright."

"I'm not sure if I should be pissed off at you right now or feel thankful."

At this point, everything that I needed to take care of could be done online. I didn't necessarily need to be at my desk at the Field Office. Also, since Mannie had apparently threatened one agent's family, I didn't like the idea of leaving Tessa alone tonight, not with him free again.

"Listen," I said to her, "let's head home. I have some work to do, but I think I can do it there as well as anywhere."

"Okay. But it's only fair if I drive."

"How is that fair?"

"It's the least you can do for going all NSA on me. You need to make it up to me."

"Nice try." I gazed at the small indie bookstore across the street not far from us and had an idea. "Do you have any homework?"

"None that I really need to do. Most of my classes are mind-numbingly easy anyway."

I rarely saw her studying—reading, yes. Just not doing homework per se.

"Then how about I make it up to you by buying you a book."

"A book?"

"Sure. You like to read, don't you? Let's get you something you normally wouldn't buy. Most of the books you buy are used. We'll get you something new so you don't have to sit around with nothing to do the next time I bring you to the Field Office."

"You'll bring me again?"

"Someday. So, do you want one?"

She thought about it. "Well . . . you know that bookstore I'm always hanging out in?"

"The Mystorium?"

"Yeah. There's this author who's doing a signing there tomorrow night. I normally never go to book signings because the people I read are usually way dead by the time I read their books, but this guy is actually still alive."

"Okay, great." I led her toward the bookstore. "You know his name?"

"Timothy Sabian. He's good. A little out there, but good."

26

Christie tried attending the afternoon prayer time with the monks, but the service was in Latin and she didn't understand any of it. Tessa had studied Latin last year in school, so at least she would've had some idea what the monks were saying, but Christie was lost—she hadn't picked up any of it, even while her daughter was taking the class.

Thinking of Tessa made Christie worry again about how to tell her and Pat about the cancer.

Quietly, she slipped out of the church and went to her room to work on the letters she was hoping to give to the two of them. When she'd started writing them, she'd thought that by doing it this way she could really get the words right, but it just wasn't happening.

No.

Words on a page would never be enough. She finally had to acknowledge that.

This was something a note couldn't handle. Not to people this close to her. She needed to tell them in person, even though she had no idea how to actually pull that off.

The Bible says that in marriage the two shall become one, so even though she was close to Tessa, it felt right to tell her soul mate first before telling her daughter.

Tomorrow's schedule: breakfast, Mass, and then—and she could hardly believe she was going to do this—confession.

Evidently, one of the monks was a priest—she wasn't entirely sure how that worked—but he offered confession and, as uncomfortable as it made her feel, she decided that as long as she was here at the monastery she would take advantage of it.

Yes. For the first time in her life, she was going to confess her sins to a priest. Who knows? It couldn't hurt.

Then afterward she would drive to the airport, return the rental car, and catch the one-thirty flight back home.

Where she would tell her husband and her daughter that she was dying.

++++

"Sasha, I want you to watch. This is what happens to someone when he betrays me."

"Who betrayed you?"

"A man named Aaron Jasper."

"What did he do?"

"He's been stealing from me, my dear. And then he also broke one of my cardinal rules: those who work with me do not visit the Matchmaker."

"The Matchmaker? Who's that?"

"Someone you don't need to concern yourself with."

Blake's security team led two people into the room. Mannie still hadn't arrived, and even though it might have made sense to wait for him, with Aaron and Ibrahim here now, Blake decided to move forward without his associate.

He greeted the two men who'd been led in. "Ibrahim. Aaron."

"Hello, Fayed," Ibrahim said.

"Oh, let's keep it as Blake today. Less formality." He gestured toward the chair. "Have a seat, Aaron."

Somewhat hesitantly, he obeyed. "Good afternoon, Blake."

"Good afternoon. We have a few things to discuss here today." Then Blake addressed Sasha again. "Loyalty is important to me. I need the people I work with, the people who work for me, I need them to be loyal. That's not too much to ask, is it?"

"I don't think so," she said. "It's good to be able to trust people."

"I agree, Sasha."

Aaron eyed the tarp and swallowed uneasily.

Blake turned to him. "I have reason to believe that someone in my organization has been taking things that aren't theirs. Do you know who that might be?"

"Taking things?"

"Sticky fingers. Stealing. Purloining."

"No, sir."

"Are you sure? You look nervous. Are you nervous?"

"No, I just . . ." He gulped. "I'm good. I'm fine."

"And visiting the Matchmaker. Do you have any idea who I'm talking about?"

"No, I—"

"Aaron, you spoke with the Matchmaker. How could that've possibly seemed like a good idea to you?"

Blake drew his 1911 MC Operator .45ACP. "Ibrahim, I want you to watch. This is important."

"Blake," Aaron said. "You have to understand, I—"

"You know how, in the movies," Blake continued, "when someone is threatening to shoot someone else in order to get information, perhaps to try to get him to confess to something or to give up his secrets, whatever it might be— my point is—he has the gun near that man, but as the scene escalates, he brings it closer and closer to frighten or intimidate the person even more. Sort of like this."

He aimed the gun at Aaron.

And began to walk toward him.

"Please," Aaron begged. "I didn't do anything."

"See?" Blake said. "Amazing. That's exactly how it works in the movies. Then the person starts sweating and worrying, just like Aaron here is. They get more and more unsettled the closer the gun comes, until at last, the end of the barrel is pressed right up against the person's forehead—like this . . ." He demonstrated. "Or even angled up into his mouth. It's time, Aaron."

"No. I'm begging you!"

"Honey," Sasha said. "You made your point. Don't hurt him."

"It's okay. It's okay." Then to Aaron: "Open up."

"I'm sorry, I—"

"You're sorry?"

"I heard about the Matchmaker. I just wanted to find out for myself. I was just curious. I didn't pay anything. I didn't see anything."

"You wanted to watch."

"I . . . Yes, but—"

"Open up, now. Go on." Blake eased the barrel into Aaron's mouth, and the man began to tremble. A tear squeezed out of his left eye.

Sasha took Blake's arm. "He's scared. You're scaring him."

"It's alright, sweetheart." Blake held her hand reassuringly for a moment, then lifted it aside. "It isn't any more dangerous, any more deadly, than being shot from six inches away or a foot away or even five feet away. It's silly, really, when you think about it—this whole bit with getting the gun closer, insinuating that it's more of a threat. But I suppose that's what you have to do in a film to make things more dramatic."

He carefully removed the gun barrel from the man's mouth and backed up.

Aaron let out a huge breath of relief. "You'll see. I'll fix things. I'll—"

"I mean, watch." Then, without another word, Blake shot Aaron Jasper directly in the forehead.

Aaron's head snapped back, and the momentum carried the chair backward. It crashed heavily to the floor, where his body slumped limply across it, a dark, seeping circle indicating where the bullet had entered his skull, no doubt a larger, more pronounced hole in the back where it had exited.

Eyes and mouth open in surprise.

Everlasting surprise.

Sasha stared aghast at the body, hands clamped over her mouth.

"See, Ibrahim?" Blake nudged the corpse's leg with the toe of his shoe. "Just as dead as he would've been if I'd held the gun pressed up to his forehead or kept the barrel between his teeth. It might be less dramatic to shoot someone from five feet away, but it's just as effective, so why should the potential victim be any less scared?"

"You killed him," Sasha muttered in disbelief. "You killed him. You killed a man. You killed him."

"It's okay," Blake assured her. "He deserved it. You see? If someone deserves to die, then there's nothing to be sad about. It's justice. That's all. Isn't that right, Ibrahim?"

"Yes, sir," he said softly, staring at the corpse. Then he muttered a quiet prayer in Arabic.

Blake turned to his men. "Clear the chair. Let's let Ibrahim have his turn. Keep the plastic where it is."

"Oh, no, no, no," Ibrahim begged. "Please, sir—"

But Blake quieted him by patting him on the shoulder. "I'll be right back."

Sasha's eyes widened. "Sweetie, you're not—"

He put a gentle finger to her lips. "Shh."

She looked like she was losing her balance so he supported her, helping her to the bed in the adjoining room. "Take a little time. Lie down. I know watching that was hard."

"You're not gonna kill me too, are you?" she gasped.

"Why would I kill you? You haven't betrayed me." He kissed her forehead tenderly, the way a father might treat his daughter. "I'll be back to check on you later. I want you to stay here with me today. Don't worry. I'll pay you double for your time." He eyed the two mannequins standing nearby in the room. "I have something for you, something special to help you forget what you just saw in there."

"What is it?"

"A treat, darling. One to carry you away."

Then, he returned to the plastic tarp and directed the gun at Ibrahim. "Now, we could do this Hollywood style, up close and personal, but that isn't really necessary, is it?"

"No, no, Fayed."

"Like I said, we're just going with Blake today. Now.

You were responsible for getting the Tranadyl to the greenhouse and, as far as I've heard, the canisters have not yet been shipped."

"I've been trying to arrange things."

"Trying to. Are you keeping any secrets from me?"

"No, sir."

"Are the canisters on their way?"

"That's what I needed to tell you. The chemist. He's not cooperating."

"The one in Phoenix."

"Yes."

"Reese."

"Right. Yes. Reese."

"He was your responsibility."

"I know. But he wants to pull out. I had nothing to do with that. I swear!"

"We need his product shipped and ready to go by Tuesday morning."

"That's what I told him. He is aware of the deadline."

Blake knew some people in Phoenix. They were experts at smuggling people across the border. But they also had other skills.

"And you had nothing to do with it? With his hesitation to cooperate?"

"I swear it by my mother's grave!"

"Well then, let's resolve this. Do you have his authorization code?"

Ibrahim's voice was tremulous and faltering. "Get a pen. It's long. You'll want to write this down."

"I'll remember it. Go ahead. Tell me."

27

It was going to be a tough night.

The team had found five other suicide videos along with half a dozen live-streamed homicides that had taken place over the last few months that had the possibility of being related to the video Jon had made of his death. One of them had been aired live on YouTube, the others on the social networking giants Facebook and Krazle. And tonight, I got to study them all.

After putting on some coffee, I set up shop at the kitchen table facing the living room where Tessa was reading the Timothy Sabian novel *The Nesting Dolls* that I'd bought for her.

Feeling parentally solicitous, I was concerned for her not bursting into tears again. By using my headphones out here, I could watch the videos and also keep an eye on her to make sure she was doing alright, and I could do it much better than if I were sequestered working in my bedroom.

Next to my laptop, I placed a photocopy of the cryptogram Mannie had written down. I decided that in between watching the videos I would try my hand at cracking the code.

Normally, I study victimology—the links that victims of crime sprees have with one another. When you're tracking serial offenders, the better you understand the victims, the better you'll understand the offender. Then you can focus on why he was there at the times when the crimes occurred, and maybe discern where he might have gone when he left the scenes.

In this instance, however, I didn't know if or how the victims were linked to each other.

Time to find out.

Headphones on so that Tessa wouldn't hear any of the sounds from the footage, I cued up the first suicide video and pressed play.

++++

Sasha was on the veranda grabbing a smoke when Mannie arrived.

Through the window, she watched nervously as he spoke with Blake inside the condo. Although she couldn't hear them, it looked like their conversation was cordial enough.

The night had turned cold, and she was wearing a wool shawl over her shoulders. The tapped ashes from her cigarette glowed and curled their way downward, becoming dark, forgotten cinders as they descended from the fortieth-floor balcony and were swallowed by the night.

Inside the room, the plastic tarp was gone. At least Blake hadn't killed that second man. At least there was that.

She took a long drag from her cigarette and used it to try to calm her shaken nerves as she stared out across Manhattan.

Mannie slid the French doors open when she was nearly ready to snub out the cigarette.

"Hello, Sasha."

"Hey."

"How long have you been out here?"

She shrugged. "A while. I couldn't stop him."

"Stop him?"

"From shooting that man."

"No one could have."

She'd been crying. She couldn't help it. And now Mannie was looking at her tear-streaked face.

"Don't stare." She wiped a finger across her eye. "It's not polite."

"You're right. I'm sorry."

She scoffed lightly. "Did you come out here to throw me off the balcony?"

"Not at all."

"Where've you been? I figured you'd be in there helping him kill people."

"Are you okay?"

She shrugged again, dropped the butt beside her foot, and rubbed the life out of it with the toe of her shoe.

Mannie slid the door shut, isolating the two of them. She eased away from him as far as the railing would allow.

"I saw you there on Amber Road," he said. "Yesterday morning during the funeral. What were you doing out by the graveyard?"

"Keeping an eye on a client of mine."

"Who?"

"The senator."

He considered her words.

She gazed back inside at Blake, who was standing beside one of the mannequins, softly caressing her chin and then trailing his finger down her neckline.

She turned to face Mannie. "What does he want with me?"

"I'm not entirely sure." She heard something in his voice. It might have been concern.

"Blake told me he was gonna give me a treat to carry me away. Do you know what that is?"

"It has to do with his silent ladies."

"You don't mean . . . what—the mannequins?"

"Yes. But you're not going to want to accept that gift." He reached into his jacket, and she tensed, expecting him to pull out a gun or a knife or something, but instead he produced a roll of hundred-dollar bills.

"Come up with an excuse to leave—a family emergency, a health issue, it doesn't matter, just make it convincing. Get out of here and don't come back. I'll take care of things with him. I don't want to see you again."

She eyed him suspiciously. "Why are you helping me?"

"Because I can."

++++

It didn't take me long to realize that the homicide videos weren't going to be helpful. In nearly all of the cases, the offenders had eventually been apprehended, and there was no sign of a surreptitious observer. So instead I focused on the suicides.

They ran the gamut.

One young man hanged himself from the roof of his house, tying one end of the rope around the chimney and cinching the other end around his neck.

He found a way to level his phone on the rooftop and then stepped off the edge. Although you couldn't see him die, you could see the downward sloping rope snap taut as it caught him when he fell.

A twenty-two-year-old woman sat cross-legged in a tire, drenched herself and the tire with gasoline, and then set herself on fire. A teenage girl stabbed herself in the brain with a foot-long screwdriver jammed in through her left nostril. A grandfather poured bleach into his eyes and then down his throat. A mother of two overdosed on sleeping pills. Although less viscerally disturbing, that was actually the hardest to watch because her four-year-old daughter showed up and must have thought her mother was asleep because she tried in vain shaking her to wake her up.

Then the girl turned and stared out the window momentarily before leaving to watch the cartoons that were playing on a television at the far side of the room.

I paused the video.

Rewound it to the spot where she looked out the window.

Zoomed in.

Yes, it was indistinct. Yes, it was tough to see.

But yes, someone was there.

Because of the faintness of the image, it was impossible to verify, but the person appeared to be of a similar build to the man who'd watched Jon Murray die. Without granting too much credence to speculation, I started with the premise that it was the same person.

Whoever it was, he'd waited out the woman's death and stood by watching that little girl try to awaken her dead mother.

I felt a cable of rage tighten inside me.

I was going to find this man and I was going to make him answer for what he was doing.

But first, to track him down, I needed to discern how the young mother's death and Jon's suicide were related to each other.

Victimology was once again the vital artery that connected the different aspects of the case. I just needed to figure out what these people—who didn't appear to have anything in common—had in common.

I went back over the previous videos and found that, yes, there was a window visible in the background in two more of them—the hanging and the death by bleach. And behind the glass, in each video, an observer stood. In the case of the man who hanged himself, the outline of the figure was evident in a house across the street.

DeYoung had asked me if the observer might have intended to get captured on the video of Jon's death, and I'd expressed my doubt about that. Now, I realized that his intuition might have been correct.

I began pulling up everything I could on the suicide victims who'd died under the indurate eye of this nameless observer.

28

"My mommy and daddy, they hurt people."

"They hurt people?"

"Yes."

"How do they hurt people, Emily?"

Silence.

"Emily, why would you say your mommy and daddy hurt people?"

"'Cause I seen 'em. In the basement. That's where they take 'em. That's where they do things to 'em."

Timothy still had another forty-five minutes or so before he needed to leave to meet up with Julianne at the river.

In truth, he was nervous about finding out from her if he might have been responsible for Miranda Walsh's disappearance—well, her *murder*—and he needed something to distract himself from thinking about all that. So he looked again at the opening scene of his work in progress.

Since he wrote intuitively, allowing the narrative to unfurl as he was writing it rather than trying to storyboard it or plot it out beforehand, he wasn't exactly sure where the story was heading.

For him, part of the adventure of writing a novel was seeing the new directions that the story took as it emerged, and then following the twists and turns to their logical conclusion—even if that ended up being a place you never would've anticipated the book would go when you first set out to write it.

Which was what almost always happened with him.

As Robert Frost wrote, "No tears in the writer, no tears in the reader. No surprise in the writer, no surprise in the reader."

So it was for the poet.

So it was for the novelist.

Timothy liked that opening line: *"My mommy and daddy, they hurt people."*

But where would it lead? Where would it take him?

He often found that writing freehand in a journal rather than typing helped him uncover the story, one word leading him to the next.

And so now, that was what he did.

Detective Gary Hendrix shifted in his seat and watched the tawny-haired eight-year-old girl sitting across the table from him.

"Tell me what you saw, Emily. Tell me what happened."

"They bring the people in the side door. Over by the garage. Daddy carries 'em. Mommy holds the door. Then they go downstairs."

"You've seen them do this?"

Emily nodded. "Sometimes I play down there. One time I

was there the whole time when it happened, and they didn't even know."

Gary felt his heart squeezing tightly in his chest. "You were in the basement?"

Emily nodded again. "Under the steps. Back in the corner. That's how I seen 'em bring the boy down without anyone knowing."

Every one of the victims had been drugged before they were killed. Muscle relaxants, not enough to stop their hearts. No, the victims were conscious when it happened, they just couldn't move. Couldn't try to get free.

"Can you tell me what happened that day? What you saw?"

Emily was quiet for a long time before she finally said, "They hurt him."

Gary wasn't sure he should be pursuing this line of questioning without a child psychologist in the room. No, no, of course he shouldn't. But, although they had Emily's mother in custody, her father was still at large. The psychologist was on her way, but this was time-sensitive, and he didn't want to wait any longer unless absolutely necessary.

"How did they hurt him, Emily?"

She stared at the table. "Daddy used the hammer."

That was consistent with the wounds found on the body.

"Did you see your mommy and daddy bring someone to the basement earlier tonight? Before the police brought you here?"

Emily rubbed her fingers up and down the sweating Coke can that sat in front of her, the one Gary had gotten for her when they first came into the room, the soda that she hadn't tasted yet.

"It's cold."

"It was in the machine."

"Yes."

"Yes?"

"They brought her down."

"What happened then?"

"I was hiding. I'm a good hider."

"I'm sure you are."

Emily took a drink of her soda, then set the can down slowly.

"Daddy got out his hammer. When they weren't looking, I snuck upstairs. That's when I called the number."

"911."

Emily nodded. "Mm-hmm."

"And why did you call the number?"

"'Cause I like Elena. She's nice."

"You're a very brave little girl, Emily."

"Is she okay? Is Elena okay?"

A squad had been in the neighborhood and had made it to the house less than four minutes after the call came in. But it hadn't been soon enough.

Gary couldn't bring himself to tell Emily. He searched for a way out of the question.

"She's dead," Emily said. "Isn't she? Like the others?"

Okay, definitely out of his league. He needed that child psychologist here before he went any further in this direction, but he needed to be honest. He needed to tell Emily the truth.

"Yes," he said. "Your babysitter is dead."

And so, that's how it was so often when Timothy was working on a book: the characters would speak to him.

Listening to voices.

It was how he made a living.

It's how you make a killing.

"No," he said. "That wasn't funny."

It's how you ended up in the White Shirts Place.

Timothy wasn't sure how much of the material for his novels came from his imagination and how much came from his memory.

Who is Elena?

Who is Emily?

Who are you?

"I'm no one." Cognitive impairment was one of the symptoms of Morgellons, but he reminded himself that he had not suffered from that. "I'm not in the story. I'm the one making it up. I'm in the real world."

The real world is a comfortable illusion.

Life imitates art.

No. Art imitates life.

Well, either way, fiction and reality—they were not such distant cousins.

A car. A house. A garage. A basement. Most people in New York City didn't have them, but his books had sold well enough for him to live nearly the same as he would have if his home were in the suburbs somewhere.

And yet, Timothy almost never went into his basement. He avoided it just as much in real life as Emily did in his imagination. She chose never to go downstairs ever again. He ventured down only when absolutely necessary.

You are Emily.

"No no no no. I'm a man. She's a girl."

You were a child once.

"A boy."

That doesn't matter.

Yes, it did. It did matter.

And so, since Timothy was who he was, a man who'd been a boy and not a girl, he could write about a boy coming home to his father after a fight at school, about a boy whose dad told him he needed to grow up and not be a pansy, needed to learn to fight back.

It didn't mean it was real. It didn't mean it'd ever happened.

He could write about that.

Or about how a father slapped his son and kept doing it harder and harder in order To Teach Him a Lesson, and how the boy didn't want to fight back and also didn't want to turn away because it was his dad and he wanted to be brave and not let him down.

Or about the tears that the boy cried when he was alone in his room, and about how badly he wanted to make his father proud and wanted to love him and wanted to run away from him and never ever ever ever see him again, all at the same time.

Or about how his dad hurt his mom. About him punching her in the face and then laughing at the way she would cower when he raised his fist again. He could write about that. Or about how the boy wanted to hurt him for that, and especially for making her do those things with him in the basement.

And that's what you did.

"No."

You wanted to hurt him. Wanted to kill him because—

"No!"

Yes. You killed him that day when you two were out on the river. You pushed him over the side of that rowboat, and when he tried to get back into it, you hit him in the head with the oar. You had to do it three times before he finally stopped trying, stopped moving. And then he went under the water and didn't come up again. He was your first one.

"That isn't true," Timothy protested. He was shaking his head defiantly. "That's just a scene from one of my novels. That's from *Cold Clay*."

Life and art.

Art and life.

Imitating, becoming each other.

As far as Timothy knew, he hadn't seen his dad since he was seven, ever since that day when the police came to the house. Ever since they started asking the questions. Ever since his mom was arrested and taken away.

He had no idea if his dad was alive or dead, now, all these years later.

An overactive imagination. That's what you have, Timothy. An overactive imagination.

But how much of it was memory and how much of it was just a writer's vivid imaginings?

But maybe it's not overactive after all. Maybe your mind thinks about what you do in real life and then separates it from what you imagine just enough so you can't tell what's real and what's not anymore.

"Julianne is real. She's going to help me."

Help you what? Help you kill? That's what she offered to do, right?

"She said she would help me find out the truth."

But only if she could watch you kill, photograph the bodies.

"You'll see. It's going to be different now, now that she's helping me."

Hemingway once said that writers should write what they know, and since then, books on writing and the instructors at writers' conferences had been parroting back the same advice.

On the one hand, it made sense since you have to tap into your own experiences, at least somewhat, in order to tell a story, in order to make one up. How else could you do it? How else could you possibly make it work?

Writing what you know lends a certain authenticity to your writing, but on the other hand, you also have to branch out, enter the world you haven't yet experienced for yourself, or your work will read tame and fenced in and small.

Your dad is gone. He's dead and gone. You took care of him, alright. You taught good ol' Dad a thing or two. You learned your lesson about how to fight back, learned that lesson really well. You're an apt student, Timothy. As it turns out, you learned an awful lot from your father.

Then came the foster families, and by the time his mother was eventually released from prison, he was twenty years old and she had no desire to see him again.

And that was okay with him.

Because of the things he knew.

She was found in a bathtub with her wrists slit two weeks after she got out on parole, and he always wondered if she just hadn't been able to figure out a way to kill herself in prison, or if maybe she found that being out of prison was too terrifying or overwhelming.

Or maybe his dad had tracked her down and made it look like a suicide.

Timothy put his writing aside and looked at the clock. 8:12.

He was supposed to meet Julianne at nine. That gave him nearly fifty minutes to get to the dock where he'd arranged to see her, where he would find out if he was guilty of the things he knew he was capable of.

Even with traffic, leaving within the next ten minutes or so should give him enough time to make it.

He would see what she had to say and then decide what to do.

With her. What to do with her. You'll need to decide what to do with Julianne Springman.

"I won't do anything."

She's dangerous. Take a knife. Just in case you need it. Or better yet, a letter opener.

Timothy wasn't going to, but when he went to get his car keys, he noticed the steel letter opener on his desk and slipped it into his jacket pocket before he left to speak with the woman who photographed the dead.

29

After nearly an hour, I still had nothing specific to link the suicide victims, even after carefully comparing their locations and the dates and times of their deaths.

Three states. Nothing, as far as I could see, that the victims had in common.

Though the face was indistinguishable, upon further investigation I noticed him scratch his jaw with his left hand at least once in each video—a mannerism that, although by no means definitive, was distinctive.

Mannie had said to remember death, and in this investigation, that was all too easy to do. Did he say that because that's what these videos were a way of doing? Were the deaths related to him and his escape?

I wanted to know more about his background.

It took a little work, but I was able to dig up that he was from the Gambia. Apparently, he'd traveled to the United States a week before an African warlord attacked his village. The villagers held them off with arms and mercenaries provided from one of Blake's front companies.

Mannie's wife was saved.

Her name was Hope.

However, later, according to the information we had,

on the way to the airport to flee to the States, she was killed.

So maybe that's why he was so committed to helping Blake—a sense of thankfulness or indebtedness for the weaponry and manpower that had helped to initially protect his wife.

Although that seemed like a possibility, it was in the realm of motives and there was no way to verify it. Still, it was helpful background information to give us the context to understand Mannie's past and his loyalties.

Whatever Mannie's involvement and motivation, this was clearly a lot bigger than just the senator and his son. From all indications, someone was convincing men and women to kill themselves in graphic and disturbing ways and then standing by and watching it happen.

Why these people?

Why were they chosen?

And, of course, who was this observer?

Unless they weren't chosen. Unless they did the choosing. Maybe he didn't find them. Maybe they found him—or them. Maybe there's more than one observer after all.

We needed a tox screen from each of these victims.

I put a request through to learn if there was Selzucaine in any of their autopsies, then contacted DeYoung to see if I could get more agents on the case. I tried Greer's number, but he didn't pick up. I'd left him a voice message earlier, so I decided not to leave another one now.

I returned to the videos, but watching the people die over and over again was emotionally devastating.

At last, I took a deep breath, paused the current video, and rubbed my forehead.

In order to get a break from watching people take their own lives, I turned my attention to the code and jotted *Remember death* on the top of the page, then searched online for cryptography programs and for codes with dashes and dots, but Braille and Morse code were the two that kept popping up.

As I was trying to figure out my next step, I heard from Ralph. "Made it up here. I'm in the city."

"Excellent. Your flight?"

"Choppy. I'm alive, but just barely."

In my job, I rarely have the luxury of focusing my attention on only one case at a time. Most often it's a balancing act that I never quite get balanced. Even though I was investigating Jon Murray's death, I was also entangled in this business with Mannie. And the longer I worked on each case, the more convinced I became that they were somehow interconnected.

"By the way," Ralph said, "you ever hear of a zedonk?"

"A zedonk?"

"On the plane, I was flipping through a magazine someone left on the seat beside me, and there was this article about zedonks."

"I'm guessing that's a mixture of a zebra and a donkey?"

"Yeah. Which is odd enough in itself, but I kept thinking about how at least it's better than the alternative."

"The alternative?"

"A donkbra."

"Um, yeah. I would say so."

"Other combinations wouldn't be much better either."

"Other combinations?"

"A hippopotabra. A chiwawabra. A crocabra. A German shepabra."

"Ralph, it sounds like you've been spending time with my stepdaughter. I could hear her saying that."

She looked at me questioningly from where she sat on the couch.

"Speaking of her," Ralph said, "how's it going this weekend? Christie still gone?"

"It's going well. She flies back tomorrow afternoon. Tessa keeps asking me to let her drive even though she doesn't have her license yet. Is that normal?" I was speaking lightheartedly and loud enough for her to hear.

"Yes," she said.

"Asking the wrong guy," Ralph replied. "But I *can* say that teen girls tend to have a love-hate relationship with their dads. Stepfamilies just add another monkey wrench to the works."

"Hey, by the way, you wouldn't by any chance know what a dotterel is?"

"That's cheating," Tessa told me.

"They're kinda like sandpipers," he said. "Shore birds, you know. I think they stay mostly in coastal areas, sandy beaches, that sort of thing."

Ah. That's why a group of them is called a "trip." Because you would trip over them. Tessa was right—that was a big clue.

"Why?" he asked.

"Oh, it's . . . I was just curious."

"Anyway," he said, "I gotta go. I'll see you in the morning at the Field Office."

"Sounds good."

After the call, I told Tessa, "So, dotterels are shore birds similar to sandpipers. I think they're usually found in coastal areas and on sandy beaches."

"That was too easy. You just asked your friend."

"If I can't use the Internet, I need some source of information. Ralph works."

"Ralph. Is that Agent Hawkins?"

"Yes."

"Is he the guy who looks like he just might decide to eat you for dinner?"

"He does a good job of hiding it, but there's a teddy bear nestled in there somewhere under that Kodiak fur. By the way, you ever hear of zedonks?"

She eyeball-rolled me. "I heard your whole side of the conversation."

"Oh. Right. A chiwawabra—ever hear of that?"

"An annoying miniature dog and a zebra."

"Very good."

"Uh-huh."

As she passed by to get a glass of water from the kitchen, I folded up my laptop so she wouldn't see the images of the suicide video I'd been watching. However, the cryptogram was still beside me on the table and it caught her attention.

"What's that?" She pointed to the words that I'd scrawled on the top of the page. "'Remember death'?"

"Oh, it has to do with—"

"Memento mori."

"What?"

"It's this saying in Latin. Means 'Remember that you have to die.' So 'Remember death' would just be another way to translate it."

"How do you know all that?"

"You're always asking me how I know stuff. I just *do*. I learn something and then I remember it. It's not that hard."

"Gotcha. Sorry. So what else do you know about *Memento mori*?"

"The ascetics especially would use the phrase to remind themselves of the brevity of life and to help them refocus on the stuff that really mattered. Kind of like *Carpe diem*. You know, 'Seize the day,' except from the opposite perspective." She pointed at the photocopy of Mannie's cryptogram. "What's the rest of that?"

"Some sort of cipher."

"You don't know how to decode it?"

"Not yet. No."

"So . . . 'Remember death,'" she said reflectively, "and you've got this code?"

"Yeah. Why? Does that mean something to you?"

"I don't know . . . Maybe . . . There's this guy buried here in New York City and on his gravestone are all these weird markings, some sort of code, right? For, like, a hundred years no one knew what it meant—maybe nothing— so then one day, someone at a newspaper solved the riddle and decoded it."

"What did it say?"

"'*Memento mori*.' Or maybe it was 'Remember death,' I'm not certain. It was one of the two. I just heard about the story one time. We should look it up."

"*I* should look it up."

"Okay, *you* should, sure, but either you let me do it with you or I'll go back to my room and do it myself where you can't supervise my online activity. And I might go to a site that's not appropriate and you wouldn't know about it. Let me help you."

I was about to reply, but she kept going. "Besides, if you say no, I might be tempted to pout, and you'll eventually get tired of trying to get me to snap out of it and just give up and let me have my way. And don't even try to argue with me about that 'cause I'm more stubborn than you are."

"No, you're not."

"Oh yes, I am."

I folded my arms. "I'm thirty-five years old. I have nineteen more years of experience at being stubborn than you do. You're no match for me."

"Oh yeah? Well, I'm so stubborn I'm gonna let you have the last word."

I opened my mouth, then closed it as she tilted her head and smiled. She waited for me to speak, watching me with wide, expectant eyes.

"Don't even try that puppy-dog look with me," I said.

"You know how I feel about dogs. That wasn't very nice."

"Nice is not on the menu for today."

"I like that. For you, that was definitely A-list material."

"What's the deal with you and dogs, anyway?"

"Don't get me started."

"I thought you loved animals."

"I do. Dogs don't count. Any animal that can smell sixty thousand times better than human beings can and spends its time smelling people's shoes and other animals' butts is not on my list of most beloved animals."

"Did you get bitten by a dog once?"

"What are you, a psychologist now?"

"I'm just trying to figure out why you hate them so much."

"Who ever said that dog-loving should be the default setting for life? No, I wasn't bitten, but half a million people in North America are, *every year*. Imagine if that was the same with any other animal. Think about the public outcry. Sharks. Snakes. Raccoons. Armadillos."

"Armadillos? Really?"

"Half a million people," she reiterated, ignoring my comment. "But when it comes to dogs you don't even hear the stats reported on the news. But it makes sense that they bite—I mean, what do dogs eat? I'll tell you what they eat—meat and bones. What does it look like I'm made out of, broccoli and falafel? So, what about helping you?"

I sighed. "Alright. You can help me look at the cipher. But that's all. Once we figure out how to decode it, that's it. Do you know the name of the guy with the encrypted gravestone?"

"No." She took a seat beside me. "But let's find out."

++++

Dark water lapped at the pier.

The icy wind skidding across the river left no doubt that winter was on its way.

Julianne studied the road paralleling the shoreline but didn't see Timothy's car.

Though it was nighttime, there were sporadic exterior lights on the warehouses and dock buildings near her that illuminated small sections of the parking area, the boat ramps, and the pier. She waited in a pool of light so that he could see her, just in case he walked rather than drove.

To get to know him better and to study his methods, she'd spent most of the day perusing excerpts of his writing online, the book she'd gotten from Miranda's bedroom, and a copy of *The Nesting Dolls*, the book that'd come out since the young woman's disappearance.

And she wasn't sure what to make of what she read.

When Timothy had suggested this location, he'd said that he knew "a good place by the river" for them to meet. Now she wondered why he'd phrased it like that—said it was "a good place"—and if he'd been here before, maybe with Miranda.

It was the same phrase Lonnie Stillman, one of the killers in *The Nesting Dolls*, had used.

She made sure she had a round chambered in her gun as she waited for Timothy's arrival.

30

It took a little time, but eventually we tracked down what we were looking for.

James Leeson's tombstone in Trinity Church Cemetery was located near the intersection of Wall Street and Broadway. He died in 1794 and was buried there on the north end of the graveyard near a soldier's memorial monument.

However, it wasn't until 1889 that the *Trinity Record* newspaper printed the solution to the cryptogram:

Once you saw the way to decode the cipher, it was relatively easy to visualize since it was based on a tic-tac-toe board's layout.

The letters A through J contained one dot with the corresponding parts of the tic-tac-toe grid drawn around them. The letters K through S had two dots along with their corresponding lines, and the remaining letters only contained the lines with no dots.

Tessa had been right. Encoded on James Leeson's gravestone were the words "REMEMBER DEATH."

A •	B •	C •
D •	E •	F •
G •	H •	I/J •

K ••	L ••	M ••
N ••	O ••	P ••
Q ••	R ••	S ••

T	U	V
W	X	Y
Z		

"Why are the *i* and the *j* in the same square?" she asked me.

"I think that in the colonial days they used an abbreviated alphabet."

"How do you know that?"

"High school history class. So be sure to pay attention in school."

"Ha." She studied Mannie's cipher. "So now, we need to decode this message."

Having no idea what Mannie might have written, I said to Tessa, "This part I need to do alone. It might have to do with blood."

Despite her affinity for gothic horror stories and death metal music, she was as fond of blood as I was of needles.

"Ew. Really?"

"Maybe."

Though she grumbled, she gave in and left for the couch to read her new Sabian novel but kept looking up from it as if she were hoping that I would change my mind.

I set about decoding the message Mannie had left me, and it didn't take long before I'd figured it out.

TEN TONIGHT LEESONS
GRAVE GO ALONE

I stared at the words.

Evidently, Mannie had a lot of confidence that I would solve his cryptogram—and do so before this evening.

I took the laptop and the code to my bedroom, put through a call to dispatch, collected my SIG, and returned to the living room. "I have to go, Tessa. Lock the door behind me. Don't open it for anyone except me. Do you understand?"

"What's going on?"

"I just need to take care of something."

"You're scaring me. What did the message say?"

"Don't be scared. I should be back in an hour or so."

"What if you're not?"

"I will be. I promise."

"How long should I wait until I call the cops to find out if you're dead?"

"Don't worry about that, trust me."

I almost gave her a light forehead kiss, but after a short hesitation I just awkwardly patted her shoulder instead.

Once outside, I waited for the officers from the cruiser I'd called for while I was in the bedroom and told them to keep a close eye on the building. "No one enters our apartment. Got it?"

"Loud and clear."

Then I left for Trinity Church Cemetery to search out James Leeson's grave.

31

Julianne saw a pair of headlights slicing through the night toward her along the road hugging the riverbank.

While she was more than capable of killing on her own, she'd decided that she wanted a partner just as she'd had with Dylan. It was more satisfying to her, maybe because of the shared secret, maybe because of the shared danger. Whatever it was, she wanted to kill with someone, but she needed someone she could trust.

And she wasn't convinced that Timothy Sabian was that person.

The car pulled to a stop five yards in front of her, and Timothy stepped out, joining her in the wash of light from the nearby warehouse while that cold wind swept over them from across the water and up the boat ramp.

"Did you learn anything about Miranda?" Timothy asked as he approached her.

"All the arrows point to you, Timothy."

"Are you sure? What arrows?"

He really doesn't know. He really has no idea.

"Did you bury her in the woods up in the Adirondacks, or dump her body in the river here, at this dock? You used both methods in your books."

"But those things aren't real. They didn't happen."

"I can't work with someone I don't trust, and I can't trust someone who's unbalanced."

She tossed the folder that Blake had given her to the ground at Timothy's feet.

He bent and flipped it open, then thumbed through the papers. "Where did you get these reports?"

"From a friend."

"Who?"

"You were careless, Timothy."

"Who gave you this information on me? Dr. Percival?"

"It doesn't matter. What matters is what you did."

"So did I do it? Did I kill Miranda?"

"Were you sleeping with her?"

"What?"

"Were you involved in a romantic relationship with that young woman? You knew her before that final book signing, didn't you?"

"Why do you say that?"

"You used different pens to inscribe her books."

Timothy was quiet.

Julianne unpocketed the necklace that she'd helped herself to in Miranda's room. "And this? In your latest book, the killer gives his lover a pearl necklace."

He continued to stare at her without speaking.

"You gave it to her, didn't you?" Julianne said. "You gave it to Miranda. Just like Lonnie did in your novel before he killed Rose."

Timothy scratched at the base of his neck, leaving bloodied fingernail streaks behind.

Julianne held up the copy of his latest novel. "Why didn't you tell me you two were lovers?"

"What does it matter? I wanted to know if I—"

"If you killed her."

"Right. Yes. If I did."

"I'm going to read you something, Timothy." She flipped to a bookmarked page. "'Lonnie kept squeezing and squeezing and squeezing. He was strong, yes, he knew he was strong, but he was also scared. Even after the woman stopped moving, even then he kept squeezing her throat, hands tight around it, fingers clenched, arms trembling with the exertion. Even then. That was the fear part. It wouldn't let him stop, wouldn't let him let go.' Does that sound familiar, Timothy?"

"I wrote that, yes, but why are you—"

"You wrote it. You *lived* it!" She read the next paragraph: "'Finally, when the tears came, he was able to release his grip and step back. He tried to wake her, but she lay still and refused to move, even just a little, even just a secret little bit in her fingers or her toes or her eyelids or *anything*.'"

"Stop reading!"

But Julianne didn't stop. "'And no matter how much he shouted for her to stop playing games like that, she didn't sit up. She didn't start breathing again. When he shook her, she flopped around like she wasn't made of anything solid at all, and when he didn't, she just lay there. So still. So so so disobediently still.'"

"I said stop reading!"

Enough. Take care of this. You can't trust him.

Movement drew her attention away from Timothy.

A set of headlights appeared on the road he'd driven up. Another car, still in the distance, but coming their direction. This was a relatively isolated spot, and Julianne wondered if maybe it was a cop patrolling the riverfront. That might work to her advantage—or it might not, depending on how she handled things.

Or could it be someone Timothy asked to come and help? You didn't work alone when you were with Dylan in Detroit. Maybe Timothy isn't working alone here.

That was something she hadn't considered.

Timothy took a step forward, and she dropped the book and whipped out her Beretta. "Stay where you are, Timothy."

He stopped and slowly held his hands out to his sides.

"Here's what's going to happen," she said. "You're going to pop the back of your trunk. And then you're going to hand me the keys."

"I'm not going—"

"Do it!"

Timothy scratched at his stomach.

"Now!" She cocked the hammer.

++++

Timothy thought and thought hard.

Bugs swarming over him. Nervous nervous nervous. It always got worse always got worse when he was nervous.

He popped the trunk.

She motioned with the gun. "Now get inside."

You can't get in there. You can't let her do this. You have to stop her. You have to kill her.

"No. I won't do it."

"Yes." She came closer. "You will. But you get to decide if you'll do it with a bullet in your stomach or not." She took careful aim. "Which do you choose?"

Though still a hundred yards away, the approaching car must have hit a pothole because the lights suddenly tilted up into her eyes. As she winced, Timothy threw his keys at her face. Instinctively, she flinched, and when she did, he lunged at her. The gun went off. He didn't feel any pain, but adrenaline might have been masking it if he were hit.

You're shot. You're shot. You're shot.

Maybe. Maybe not.

Then he was fighting her and the gun was on the ground. She had only one arm to use, but her muscles were cable tight and her grip was unrelenting.

As the car neared them, Timothy grabbed Julianne's shoulders and threw her to the road. She clawed at his face, but he pushed her back down, hard. The crack of her skull on the pavement was thick and moist and sickening.

She won't fight so much now.

Her eyes rolled back, and she went limp.

You did it. You killed her.

"No, no, no. I didn't want to. I wasn't trying to."

But you did.

"Maybe she's not dead. Maybe she's not."

Make sure. Use the gun. Or the letter opener.

"No!"

Timothy patted himself down, looking for blood, for an entry wound, but found none.

That car. Hurry. You need to hide her . . .

He quickly dragged her body behind his car to get her out of sight. Part of him wanted to feel her pulse to see if she was alive; part of him didn't want to, just in case she wasn't.

He retrieved the gun and hurried back to the trunk to close it before the other car stopped, but he was too late.

With the headlights on and glaring in Timothy's eyes, the driver's face was obscured. "You okay?" the man called.

"Yeah."

"I thought I heard a gunshot."

Timothy might have heard that voice before, but he couldn't be sure. Nerves. "No, no. Nothing like that. I'm fine."

Julianne moaned softly, and Timothy's heart jackrabbited in his chest.

"You hear something?" the man said.

"Just the wind."

A pause. "Got a flat?"

"A flat?"

"Your trunk there."

Behind the open trunk, Timothy held the gun in his left hand, the letter opener in his right.

"All good. All fine. I'm sure."

Another pause, longer this time. "Alright," the man replied. "If you're sure."

At last, he pulled forward, and Timothy let out a deep breath and slid the gun beneath his belt.

As he watched the car drive away, he tried to read the license plate, but the numbers had been covered with duct tape, which he found both surprising and, obviously, suspicious.

Just get out of here.

He walked to Julianne's body.

She was bleeding from her head. Fresh blood.

Her heart's still beating. And she groaned a moment ago. She's still alive.

"But that's good, though, right?"

Now what are you going to do? You have to take care of this. You have to solve this, before someone else comes along.

"I could just leave her here. No one would suspect me. Why would anyone suspect me?"

That man saw you, Timothy. You have to get her out of here. When she's found, he'll know you did it. He saw your car. He might've seen the plates. He'll send the police. They'll come looking for you.

Timothy wished he were Lonnie from his novel. Lonnie always knew how to take care of things. He always knew the best thing to do.

For a moment, Timothy considered dumping Julianne into the river, but eventually she would be found. Conversely, the cold water might just revive her, wake her up, and then what would he do?

He glanced at the open trunk, then down at her body.

Use the letter opener. It's just what you need.

But this time he resisted the voice.

He knew what he needed to do instead. He would take care of things. Just like Lonnie would've done if he were here.

He is here, Timothy. Lonnie has never been far at all from your side.

++++

I could see that the Trinity Church Cemetery was surrounded by a sturdy, metal, spear-topped fence two meters high.

Bare-limbed trees protruded from the manicured gardens, now withered and dried out in summer's wake.

In the daylight, the cemetery might have been a tranquil and peaceful place, but there in the nighttime, it had a foreboding feel.

The church was closed and so was the cemetery entrance, so I scaled the fence and dropped to my feet on the other side.

Here I was, on my second visit to a graveyard in as many days.

Tired, brown grass covered most of the property wherever there wasn't a walking path or flowerbed. By the looks of the ancient, weathered headstones, I doubted that anyone had been buried here in decades.

I wasn't sure which gravestone was Leeson's, but from what Tessa and I had been able to uncover online about the stone, it would be located somewhere near the Soldier's Monument that rose grandly in the northeast corner of the cemetery near where Pine Street intersected with Broadway.

Crunching across the frozen grass, I angled my Mini Maglite down and began inspecting the area, looking for the grave.

32

It didn't take me long to find it.

Yes, it was near the monument and approximately five meters from the perimeter fence.

At first, James Leeson's gravestone didn't jump out as distinctive in any way from the other old headstones in the cemetery, and I guessed that most people would just walk right past it, oblivious to its historical significance.

However, at the top of the granite were the enigmatic carvings of the cryptogram Mannie had used. A wavering crack and chipped section across the headstone obscured any images that might have been engraved on the bottom third, but the symbols near the top were still clearly visible, even after all these years.

Below the code were three additional carvings—a winged hourglass, a smoking urn, and two overlaid symbols of the Freemasons.

I figured that the hourglass with the wings symbolized how time flies. The urn, I wasn't so sure about. Though I wasn't a Mason, the compass and the level and plumb line were common enough symbols for me to recognize.

As I scanned the area, the light from my Maglite glinted off something that lay nearly hidden under a mound of freshly overturned dirt roughly the size of a human head. A white glimmer. Shiny and smooth, like clean, sun-bleached bone.

I expected it to be a skull, but when I knelt and carefully brushed away the soil, I found that it was the head of a mannequin. It'd been detached from the rest of the body and now stared up at me with its blank, unblinking eyes.

Blake and his silent ladies.

Mannie directing me to a grave that had a mannequin's head beside it couldn't be simply a coincidence.

It wasn't unusual for Blake to have female mannequins stationed around him where he worked—or where he played. Often they were dressed in lingerie. A psychologist would've probably had a field day analyzing him and his fixation with them.

Memento mori.

Remember death.

Yes.

But what significance did it carry?

I tilted the mannequin's head in my hand. Hollow. Clean and unblemished. Mimetic. How did this fit in with the rest of the case?

After setting it down, I began scouring the area for any other body parts from mannequins and any observers in the shadows, then called for a forensics unit to analyze the soil and the head. Thankfully, the nearest NYPD precinct had a CSI team, and they told me to plan on a six-minute arrival time.

I checked my watch.

9:56.

Okay, well, if ten o'clock was significant in any way, then it looked like I would be here in the graveyard when the team arrived.

Then a thought struck me—maybe there wasn't someone waiting here for me, but maybe this was a tactic to get me out of the apartment and away from Tessa at a specific time so Mannie or Blake could make a move on her there.

With haste, I called the officers who were stationed outside our building and told them to go in, and to proceed with caution. "Make sure the girl is okay and no one else is there. I told her not to open the door for anyone. You'll need to show her your badges."

I texted Tessa that two cops were on their way up and to open the door for them. She replied: What?!

Just let them in, I typed back. I'll be home soon.

I kept a close watch on the graveyard but saw no one. Less than two minutes later, a call came back from one of the officers at our apartment. "The place is clear. You want us to stay here?"

"Just wait outside the door. I'll be there as soon as I can."

"The girl was not happy."

"I expect not."

Rather than call Tessa, I decided I would clear things up with her when I got back home.

As I was keeping watch on the graveyard, I caught sight of a person approaching from the other side of the cemetery. Male. About my size.

When I angled my light toward him, he bolted before I could see his face.

I took off after him, calling for him to stop.

He made it to the street before I did and was already on his way down the block toward the Wall Street Station subway stop for the 4 and 5 lines.

He descended into it.

I followed.

He launched himself over the turnstile ahead of me, and by the time I was past it as well, he'd jumped down from the platform toward the track and, avoiding the third rail, started sprinting into the darkness.

I made the leap as well.

A greasy smell tinged the air. With my flashlight, I caught sight of him, maybe twenty-five or thirty meters ahead of me, running with a harsh limp on his left leg. Calling out, I identified myself as a federal agent and shouted for him to stop.

It reminded me of my chase yesterday morning through the graveyard trying to catch that woman, although this guy wasn't nearly as fast as she was and I was gaining on him rapidly. But a light beyond him and a rattling on the tracks told me that a train was coming.

I studied the tunnel. It didn't look like there was enough room on either side to flatten myself against the wall and avoid getting hit. Or, if there was, it was going to be close.

Close worked.

Glancing behind me, I doubted I'd be able to make it back to the platform either. I debated for a second which direction to go—back or forward.

But only for a second, then I decided.

Forward.

The man I was chasing disappeared to the left, and I

realized there must be a connecting tunnel or walkway. With the train closing in on me, I picked up my speed, darting toward it.

As the train rocketed closer, time seemed to slow, and even the roaring clatter of its approach was slower and more drawn out than it should have been.

The pathway the man had found was close.

Another few strides and I leapt to the side. Only a moment later, the train careened past, the rush of air whooshing over me.

The rattle-clack of the tracks became deafening. The rock and drift and sway of the train sailing by so close to me made me feel off balance.

As I was dialing my light deeper into the tunnel that the limping man had escaped into, he grabbed my arm from where he'd apparently been waiting for me. And now, with the train racing past less than a meter behind my back, he slammed my hand against the wall to knock the light free. I would've reached for my gun, but with the way he had my arm twisted, that wasn't going to happen.

In the flickering, pulsing darkness, I still couldn't get a good look at his face.

I tried to push forward to get away from the train, but he held his ground. As I twisted to yank my arm free, he drew a gun, but rather than firing at me, he swung the butt of it toward my head.

Impact.

A burst of stars.

Then darkness.

33

I woke up alone in the tunnel, my head throbbing. I had no idea how much time had passed while I'd lain there in the dark.

My flashlight was still on, its light skewing off to the side across the ground in front of me. I snatched it up and searched the area, but the man who'd knocked me out was nowhere to be seen.

Checking the time, I realized I'd only been out a minute or so, but it'd been long enough for him to get away.

The train had passed, and silence loomed around me. I swept the light through the main tunnel, saw no one, and quickly returned to the subway platform.

By the time I made it back to the cemetery, the CSI unit was arriving.

I passed the mannequin's head along to them so they could check it for prints, then directed them to sort through the top layer of dirt surrounding the grave to search for other body parts from mannequins. "Let me know if you find anything."

"Yes, sir."

Maybe I should've been checked out at the hospital, but I'd been clonked on the head more than my fair share of times over the years, and once I felt regrouped and clear-headed, I left for home.

During the drive, I considered what Mannie might have been trying to communicate to me by pointing me to that specific grave. Was he the one who left the head there? If so, when? It seemed extraordinary for him to have written me that cipher, and then, trusting that I would decode it in time, traveled here to bury the head. However, if he'd placed it here prior to his apprehension, then did it mean he'd gotten himself arrested on purpose?

And why ten o'clock? Did the time carry any significance to what was happening?

And who was that man I'd chased?

At this point, there were simply too many questions and not enough information to bring me closure, not enough "routes to the truth, paved with the facts," as my mentor, Dr. Calvin Werjonic, sometimes said.

Once again I was reminded of my lunch with him tomorrow.

Well, it would be good to see him. Maybe I could even kick some ideas around with him on how to approach this investigation.

Back home, I found one officer waiting outside the building and the other upstairs in the hallway leading to our door.

I asked him if he'd seen anything.

"Nope. After we cleared your apartment, there hasn't been a peep from inside. No one else has been up here except for an elderly couple heading down to their place at the end of the hall."

"Alright. Thanks."

"That's a feisty girl you've got in there."

"Yeah."

I dismissed him, took a deep breath, and entered our apartment.

"Tessa?"

She was standing beside the couch, hands on her hips.

"You alright?" I asked.

"I'm *fine*. You told me not to open the door for anyone."

"I know."

"What the hell—and I almost said something a lot worse than hell—is going on?"

"I'm just trying to do all I can to keep you safe."

"And why would I be in any danger?"

"You're not. I mean . . . Maybe I'm just being a little paranoid."

"A *little*? You sent two cops in here to check on me! One of 'em went in my room, looked in my closet, under my bed. That is *a complete invasion of my privacy*. You do understand that, right?"

"It's been a long day, Tessa. Why don't you head to bed. We can talk about this more tomorrow."

She shook her head in exasperation and stomped off to her room.

Man, it was going to be good to have Christie home again tomorrow night.

I processed what was happening as I iced the side of my head and then tried to get some sleep, but whenever I closed my eyes, I saw that mannequin head staring at me and then winking. Then her lips curved into a sly smile and she mouthed words to me, but despite how hard I tried to concentrate on my dream, I couldn't decipher what the decapitated head was trying to tell me.

34

Julianne Springman felt consciousness returning to her slowly.

At first, she thought she was at home in her own bed, but it was cold, and she was going to pull the covers up but found that she couldn't move her one good arm. It seemed strange and part of a dream, unable to move.

Perhaps it was just a nightmare. She'd heard about lucid dreams and wondered if she could change the direction of this one. Once, she'd fallen asleep beside a floor lamp that came on with a timer every night. In her dream, the sun was glaring in her eyes, forcing her to try to turn away. Only after she woke up did she realize that what was happening around her in the real world was seeping down, impacting the dream she'd been a part of.

The cold didn't go away, so she tried to move again, and this time she found herself on the verge of waking up. *Why can't I move?*

Julianne blinked and attempted to focus, but everything was dim and indistinct. A faint smear of light was crawling over her shoulder but hardly illuminated anything around her. The musty smell of rain-dampened carpet tinged with the reek of oil and grease surrounded her.

Her right arm was drawn back behind her and somehow

secured in place with a rope that'd been tied off around her waist. Although her left arm was free, since it'd never developed properly, it was of no use to her at the moment.

Her legs were also bound, and now that she began to get her bearings, she realized that she was in the trunk of a car. "Timothy," she called angrily. "Let me out!"

First, she twisted onto her stomach and futilely kicked her legs up against the trunk's hood.

Then, although it was awkward and uncomfortable with her right arm torqued back the way it was, she turned onto her back and tried. Despite her best efforts, though, she could tell almost immediately that she wasn't going to be able to free herself, so she shouted again for him to let her out, then heard a garage door closing.

"Timothy, whatever you're thinking of doing, you better think again. There's a man who gave me your name, and if he finds out anything happened to me, he'll come after you. He will not stop, and he's not someone you want to be on the wrong side of."

No one replied, but she could hear someone outside the car and it sounded like the person was going through a pile of tools.

"Timothy!" she hollered. "Untie me!"

"You don't deserve to live." The voice sounded coarse and deep. She couldn't tell if it was Timothy or not. She already doubted his sanity and wondered if he might have different personalities that came out, especially when he was perpetrating his crimes or speaking to his victims.

Victim. No. Not a victim. You're going to get out of this.

Turning to the side again, she tried to maneuver her arm free but couldn't quite decipher how it was tied. When she attempted to move her legs, it became clear that she wasn't going to be able to untie herself until she had the use of that right hand.

Assets, Julianne. What are your assets? What can you use to get free?

The light that came through a rusted-out section of the car near the lock didn't reveal much. She tried to focus on what lay inside the trunk with her: a pile of rags, a first aid kit, a tire iron, so—

Wait. The first aid kit. Maybe there's a scissors or a blade of some type in it.

The man outside the car began to mutter to himself, something about how this one was different from the rest, how this one was special.

She scooted over as far as she could, and it took three tries and tremendous effort, but finally she was able to nudge the first aid kit to her good hand.

Working with her arm behind her, she managed to wedge the kit in place and pop it open. She felt her way past some bandages, a roll of gauze, some first aid tape, and then—yes. Her fingers closed around the blade of a scissors.

By the size and shape, she guessed it was a fabric scissors, the kind paramedics use.

From outside the trunk, she heard more muttering and then footsteps and a door—but not the rattling garage door—creak open and then close.

Do it now. You have to do it now. You have to get free.

She managed to turn the scissors so that the blades angled against the rope. It was too thick for her to close the blades, so she worked them back and forth to try sawing through it.

A few moments later, the man returned, the door closing creakily behind him.

Julianne felt her heartbeat skidding forward, faster and faster.

The strident footsteps approached the car, and then he threw the trunk open.

She was on her side, and before she could turn to see him, he placed a strong hand on her shoulder, holding her firmly in place.

"Look at you," he said in that odd, indistinguishable voice. "What have you found?"

He roughly tore the scissors from her hand. When she pulled on the rope, she realized she hadn't been able to sever it.

"I don't think it would be fair of me to take these from you, as clever as you were getting them out of that kit there. So here you go." He tucked the scissors under the rope around her thigh, out of reach from either of her hands. "I'll leave these here for you, sweetie, as a little reminder of how close you came to getting away."

"I'm going to kill you," she seethed. "You are not going to get away with—"

Letting go of her, he picked up one of the oily rags and stuffed it into her mouth as she tried to wrench herself away from him.

He tied another rag around the first one to hold it in place. Despite how desperately she attempted to pull free and see his face, she wasn't able to do either.

Once she was securely gagged, he said to her, "Some of the newer cars—they just don't work as well for this. But with the older ones, you can be pretty sure that the carbon monoxide will build up in a space this small pretty fast. I know how much you like photography. I promise to take a picture of you when it's all over. For posterity."

With that, he closed the trunk, and as she tried futilely to cry out, he started the engine. Less than five seconds later, she heard the car door close and then the house door as he left her alone in the garage to die.

STAGE IV

Depression

Silent ladies. Hot car deaths.
Turtles struggling toward shore. The Matchmaker's lair.

35

Monday, November 5

My head was still throbbing a bit, but it wasn't anything a few Advil couldn't handle.

Greer called me while I was collecting my notes for work. It was the first time we'd spoken since Saturday, and there was a lot to catch up on.

I told him what I'd found at James Leeson's gravestone last night.

"The silent ladies," he muttered.

"Yeah."

"And you don't have any idea who you chased?"

"No. I'm seeing if we can pull up videos from the subway station."

"Okay."

"Mannie said that he chose to talk with me because I would do what needed to be done when the time was right."

"What was he referring to?"

"I don't know. He also told me to follow the Selzucaine back to the source and that Jon killed himself for his father. I'm still not sure how that fits in with what we know or exactly what it all means."

"Huh."

"And, oh—Ralph Hawkins is in the city. He'll be coming in to the federal building this morning."

"Know him by reputation only. Never actually met him. From what I understand, though, he gets the job done."

"He does."

"And nothing more on Mannie's whereabouts?"

"No. Not yet."

"But he's the one who left that mannequin head for you to find?"

"There's no way to be certain at this point if it was him. It's possible it was the person I chased instead. We're running prints."

A short pause. "Good. Maybe that'll give us something useful." He asked me if I'd seen the senator's press conference.

"I did. I tried to talk him out of it, but he was hell-bent on going through with it."

"Something's up."

"Yes."

He sighed, and I could hear a head shake in his voice. "Do you know how many people have already claimed to be there at the house, hoping to get that twenty-thousand-dollar reward? Last I heard there were close to a hundred."

"I'm surprised it's not more."

"I'm wondering if we should take a closer look at the senator's life," he said.

"What are you thinking?"

"Maybe he was pressured to make that offer. Compromised in some way."

"Blackmail?"

"Possibly."

"If we start poking around, we'll need to tread softly. He is a ranking member of Congress."

"Not to mention a good friend of the assistant director," he noted.

"Yes."

"I'll put some feelers out. I can be a soft treader when I need to be."

I was filling him in on the suicide videos when he yawned and then apologized. "Sorry. It's not you. I didn't get much sleep last night."

"That makes two of us." I thought of that living mannequin head I'd envisioned, like a death mask that was trying to tell me something important through its bloodless lips, something I wasn't able to understand. "The more I have on my mind, the less sleep I tend to get."

"You must not get much sleep at all then, brother."

"Admittedly, there are times when it's a bit slim."

"So what's the plan for today?"

"I'm going to check on the receipt I found in that woman's jacket—the parking lot receipt from the garage over near the federal building. At least it gives us a time and a place to work from."

"Besides, most people in Manhattan don't even own a car. And with what it costs to park in the city, we should be looking for someone on the high end of the socioeconomic scale. That narrows things down."

"If the driver was even from New York City at all," I reminded him.

"Be careful with assumptions, right?"

"Always. Oh, and I'm planning to have lunch with Dr. Werjonic."

"*The* Dr. Werjonic?"

"Yes. He was my advisor for my postgrad studies. He's lecturing here in the city this week."

"That guy's a living legend."

"I'm hoping to be able to pick his brain a little. Maybe get some inspiration or direction related to the case."

"Sounds good. Alright. Talk to you soon."

After the call, I found myself caught up thinking about the implications of the senator's press conference until Tessa joined me in the kitchen.

"Okay," she said. "So with Mom at that monastery, I've been thinking about monks and nuns and stuff. For some reason that got me thinking about Easter."

"Alright."

"You ever been to an Easter egg hunt?"

"When I was a kid."

"Well, they're from the devil. They never end well. There's always at least one kid in tears. Always. I'm pretty sure Easter egg hunts were invented by the same people who decided clowns would be fun for kids."

"You don't think clowns are funny?"

"Clowns are to funny what Cheetos are to health food."

"That is . . . so true."

She sighed. "I hope when Mom comes back she doesn't have a monk haircut."

"I don't think you need to worry about that."

++++

Tessa was heading toward the door to go to school when Patrick suggested dropping her off on his way to work.

"I can walk. I do it every day."

"It's cold out there this morning."

"Not any colder than usual."

"It's not a problem. Really."

She looked at him curiously. "Are you being for real here? I'm not in the first grade."

"No, I know. I'm just trying to be helpful. It's no problem, really. I'll grab my things."

Just to get going, she gave in. "Whatever."

Five minutes later when she was getting out of the car, he said, "Have a good day at school."

"Now there's a contradiction in terms."

++++

Though I was feeling a little overly protective of my stepdaughter, I hoped she wasn't intuiting the extent of my concern. With Mannie on the loose and Christie not back yet, I couldn't help but have the girl's well-being on my mind.

I called in to see if the lab was able to pull any prints from the mannequin head I'd found last night. The technician I spoke with told me that so far they'd only found Mannie's and Blake's prints—and mine, from when I'd picked it up.

"Alright. Listen, I've been thinking: I want you to look for DNA as well."

"DNA?"

"Is it too late to do that?"

"At this point it's not ideal, but we can give it a shot. It would probably be contaminated. Why?"

"In the past, there were instances when Blake made his prostitutes kiss the mannequins that he had."

"You want us to look for the DNA of a *fille de joie* on this mannequin head?"

"Anyone's DNA, but yeah. On the lips, particularly. Let me know what you find."

Earlier, I'd sent an expedited request through to find out whose prints had been on the jacket the woman left in the woods beside the graveyard, but when I checked my messages, I found that the request had been denied, leaving the lingering question of whose prints those were.

And the even more baffling mystery of why I wasn't being told her identity.

At the parking garage, I reviewed the security footage at the time listed on the receipt and found that a late-model black Ford Focus with New Jersey plates had come through. However, when I ran the tags, I discovered they were actually registered to the Jeep Cherokee of a man in Newark.

Evidently, someone had switched the plates, which meant I needed another way to identify this car.

When I zoomed in and studied the vehicle closely for any unique markings, I noticed a broken front passenger-side headlight from some sort of fender bender. It was a long shot, but I wondered if this car had ever been pulled over for a missing headlight or if it'd been written up as part of an accident report.

I put a call through to Greer to have him check with local and state law enforcement in New York and New Jersey, then I continued studying the footage to see if I could catch sight of who left the car, but I came up empty. As I was getting ready to leave the garage, Greer called back.

"We've got nothing on the subway video of the guy you chased, but I do have a name with regard to the car," he said.

"Who is it?"

"Sasha Daye. She's registered with an escort agency in Manhattan. Upscale. High-end clients."

"Do you have an address?"

"Yeah. She's got a place in Brooklyn over near Prospect Park."

"Text it to me." I was already on my way to my car. "I'll meet you there."

36

Christie entered the confession booth.

The cramped quarters smelled of dried leather and the stale taint of body odor. A screened partition separated her from the man waiting to hear her confess her sins.

"I don't know how to do this." Christie wasn't sure how loudly to speak and had the sense that she was probably talking too softly. "I've never been to confession before."

"Okay. And you may speak up. No one else will hear you, I assure you."

She raised her voice a notch. "I'm not Catholic."

"Have you been baptized?"

"Yes. I'm a Baptist, actually." Irony. He said nothing. She went on, "Do I call you Father?"

"Not if it makes you uncomfortable. Does it make you uncomfortable?"

"I don't know."

She wasn't sure which of the monks was on the other side of the confessional, but his voice was raspy and weathered, as if he'd spent a lifetime at sea rather than singing and chanting here at the monastery. Maybe a life bereft of small talk and chatter did that to someone's voice.

"Just tell me what's on your heart, my child. Something brought you here today. What is it?"

"I believe I may be living in the worst kind of sin."

"And what sin is that?"

"The greatest commandment is to love God, so the greatest sin is to fail to love him. Right?"

"Or to blaspheme him, perhaps. But you are correct. Failing to love God is a mortal sin. Do you believe in God?"

"Yes. I do believe in him, but I'm afraid I've stopped loving him."

"And to your understanding, what is the cause of this loss of love?"

She hesitated but then plowed forward. "I have cancer. It's bad. I'm dying. Even though I want to believe God will heal me, I find myself doubting that he will. My love feels like only a dry husk of what it used to be. It's hard to put into words."

"Sometimes belief and unbelief can both be fruit that hang from the same vine. When a man came to Jesus to have him cast a demon out of his son and Jesus told him that all things are possible if only you will believe, the man cried out, 'I do believe, help my unbelief!' So in this instance, the man held both belief and unbelief in Jesus in his heart at the same time, perhaps even to equal degrees."

Christie knew the story but had never quite looked at it like that. "Are you saying that doubt isn't wrong?"

"Sometimes doubt is simply a stepping-stone on the journey toward a deeper faith. You don't need to understand God to love him. In fact, if you make understanding him a prerequisite for loving him, you'll always be disappointed."

"How can I fall in love with God again?"

"Through obedience, my child."

"Obedience?"

"First John, five, verse three: 'This is what loving God is—keeping his commandments.' Have you heard that verse before?"

"Yes." She'd memorized it many years before but in a different translation. She knew that John never separated obedience from love, but still, this idea of obedience as a way of expressing love for God was a tough one to grasp. "Father, our church teaches grace—God's undeserved love for us—and salvation through faith rather than works."

"Are you married?"

"Yes."

"And you love your husband?"

"Yes, of course."

"You cannot show your husband how much you love him by committing adultery. And so it is with God. We cannot express our love and devotion to him by running after other lovers."

"Idols."

"Yes. Or anything that we place between ourselves and the Lord Jesus Christ. Even demons believe in God, but they do not love him. They tremble. Love must lie at the heart of any person's relationship with God or that relationship means nothing, and the only way to show love to God is through obedience. Even in Protestant circles, faith is not recognized as enough. 'And though I have all the faith necessary to move mountains—if I am without love, I am nothing.'"

"First Corinthians thirteen."

"Very good. Perhaps you haven't lost your love. Perhaps you've simply lost your bearings."

She knew she could never obey her way into heaven, that it was a gift offered to her, but she could at least understand where the priest was coming from. And he did have a point.

"What else should I do?"

"I would give you penance, but would you do it?" he asked somewhat skeptically.

"I'm . . . I've never done penance. I've always been taught that Jesus provided all the penance we need."

"And that is a good Baptist answer." From someone else, the words might have come across as sarcastic or judgmental, but from this old priest, it sounded to Christie more like a compliment than anything else. "Obey the Lord," he told her. "Trying to feel more love toward God is not the pathway to a deeper love. Obedience is. God has heard your confession. He loves you. He forgives you. He awaits you."

She had another question that she didn't necessarily think he would be able to answer but wondered if he just might, if the Lord might have revealed something to him. "Will God heal me?"

"Perhaps it is not your body that is the most in need of healing. Perhaps you need to tell God, 'I do love, help my lack of love.' Go in peace."

He spoke a few words over her in Latin, and though she didn't understand them, she took them to be a blessing and thanked him before she left the confessional.

And though she was glad to have had the chance to speak with him and share what was on her heart, she did

not feel peace as she walked away. Instead, she felt fear—
fear that she would never regain the warm love that she
used to have for God. And also, fear that she might decide
she didn't even want to love a silent God who left her alone
to suffer.

37

Sasha Daye rented a townhouse with a back door that exited to a fire escape. I waited there, around back, while Greer took the front door.

The footprint of the building was minimal, so from where I was, I could hear him identify himself as a federal agent as he knocked on the door, asking for Miss Daye.

But then, rather than hear a door opening, I caught the sound of hurried footsteps inside the house, coming my direction. A moment later, the back door flew open, and even though I was ready for her, she nearly managed to get past me.

"Hold on, Miss Daye." I snagged her shoulder. "Stand still, or I'm going to have to—"

But she didn't stand still. Instead, she stomped severely on my left foot and tugged to get free. Pain shot up my leg, but I didn't let go. Instead, I twisted her wrist around and drove her to her knees.

"Easy."

"You can't do this," she gasped.

As elusive and agile as she'd been while fleeing from me at the cemetery, I didn't want to take the chance that she would rabbit again, so I cuffed and frisked her. She had no weapons, but she was carrying a hefty roll of hundred-dollar bills.

By the time I was hauling her to her feet to take her back into her townhouse so we could chat, Greer had made it around to my side of the building.

Together, we led her inside.

"Listen to me," she fumed once the door was closed behind us. "I'm DEA."

"What are you talking about?" Greer asked.

"Deep UC. And you two idiots might've just blown my cover."

"You have your credentials?"

"Of course not. What do you think? If Blake found out I was a federal agent, I'd be dead within the hour. Call my supervisor."

"Blake?" I tried to piece together her involvement with him. "Is he why you were at Jon's funeral?"

"Blake's the reason for all of this." She gave us a name and a number and Greer put the call through.

While he waited to get transferred, Sasha glared at me. "You have no idea how much of my work you just put at risk."

"Tell me about the money." I kept one eye on her as I studied the inside of the townhouse. Her place was simply furnished but had a touch of class and expensive-looking, somewhat erotic artwork that might well fit for a high-end escort. Maybe she was lying about being an undercover agent.

"Evidence," she replied tersely. "I'll need it back."

After Greer spoke with someone on the phone, he informed us, "They're transferring me now."

Sasha gave him an alphanumeric authorization code,

and he repeated it to the person on the other end of the line.

Well, if she wasn't an agent, she certainly knew an awful lot more than she should have.

At last, when the verification was complete, Greer listened for a moment, and then said to Sasha, "Your boss wants to talk to you."

She shook her head in aggravation, then turned to the side and held out her wrists to remind us that they were cuffed. "Well, bring it here."

Greer passed his cell to me, and I held it up to Sasha's ear.

"Yes," she said into the phone. "They just showed up here. No, it's . . . I will . . . I don't know. I hope not . . . Okay, yeah. I understand."

She nodded to me that she was done, and I ended the call.

"Satisfied?" she asked us.

Greer indicated to me that he was. I was on the same page. I returned his phone to him.

If she was a deep-undercover DEA agent, then it certainly explained why her prints came up as unavailable when I sent them through the system.

"Well," Sasha said impatiently, "can you please get these cuffs off me and save me the trouble of having to pick them?"

I removed the handcuffs, and she rubbed her wrists in annoyance.

"This is called a *joint* task force for a reason," Greer noted, a bit abrasively. "We weren't notified that the DEA was running a side op on this."

"Why do you think Blake is always one step ahead of

us? In the past he's compromised two people from the FBI—two *that we know of.*" She laid a heavy emphasis on those last four words.

It was true that Blake had gotten to an FBI SWAT member and one of the lawyers from our Office of Professional Responsibility. However, now she was dead and the SWAT guy was in prison.

She informed us that her last name wasn't Daye after all, but MacIntyre. Her first name actually was Sasha, a technique undercover agents sometimes use so they respond instinctively when their name is spoken rather than hesitating as they evaluate whether or not the person is addressing them. That momentary hesitation can sometimes be the difference between being made and staying alive.

Sasha went on. "My supervisor decided we couldn't wait around and let Blake continue to import drugs and expand his human trafficking network while he got all the information he needed from inside sources."

"Alright," I said. "I hear you. Tell us what you know."

"He's smuggling in a new synthetic. It's a drug similar to cocaine in the way it affects the brain. It's even more addictive, though, and can cause a person to be less inhibited and more aggressive. Like cocaine, it's a benzoic acid ester. The chemical structure is similar to cocaine but has an extra carboxyl group on the tropane ring and they're adding to the fluoride—".

"Hang on," Greer said. "In English?"

"Basically, it's found as a white powder just like cocaine. You can snort it or shoot it up. But it can be synthesized and molded into different shapes that hold their form until they're powdered once again."

"Selzucaine?" I asked.

"You know about it?"

"It was found in Jon Murray's system."

"Interesting. I didn't know that."

"Sasha," I said, "why'd you run from me at the cemetery?"

"In case they were watching—especially after you identified yourself to me as a federal agent. You didn't leave me any choice."

"And why were you there in the first place?"

"Looking for Reese."

"Reese?"

"A chemist from Phoenix. Works for a pharmaceutical firm down there. I don't know exactly how he's connected to Blake, but we think it has to do with synthesizing or distributing the Selzucaine. Blake has someone named Ibrahim who's working with Reese. I'm not certain what they have planned, but from what I was able to overhear, it's going down this week."

"If Reese is developing the Selzucaine, that would explain his connection to Blake." I was processing everything in reference to what Mannie had told me yesterday. "But why would he attend the funeral?"

"I'm still working on that."

"Maybe our senator here has his hands in the drug-smuggling business?" Greer suggested.

"It's possible," she acknowledged. "I expected that either Blake or Mannie would be keeping an eye on things—I just didn't know that Mannie would show up there on Amber Road. And then there was that accident. I just thank God the driver is recovering." She sighed heavily. "I witnessed Blake kill a man. Aaron Jasper. Blake shot him in the head because he was stealing from him and because he'd contacted someone called the Matchmaker."

"The Matchmaker?" I said. "Who's that?"

"Don't know. We don't have any files on anyone using that name, and looking online hasn't helped any—there are just too many search results for the word 'matchmaker.' Believe me. I've got nothing, and I've been at it for two hours already this morning."

"And Blake killed Jasper for contacting him?"

"And for not being faithful. He did it before I could stop him. I'm sure Jasper was no Boy Scout, but Blake played judge, jury, and executioner. No matter how corrupt the guy was, he deserved better than that."

"Why didn't you arrest Blake at that point?" Greer asked.

"The opportunity didn't present itself," she said somewhat evasively.

"Do you have any idea where Blake is right now?"

"He has a condo he uses, but he moves around a lot. Besides, it's not just about locating him, it's about getting access to his contacts, to his accounts. We bring him in now, we shut down his business for a couple of days or maybe a week or two. And then the people he works with just regroup and go at it again, as strong as ever. He's being financed from somewhere. That's who we want. Whoever's at the top of the food chain."

From our research, we knew that after Blake took on the persona of an infamous terrorist named Fayed Raabi'ah Bashir, founder of The Brigade of the Prophet's Sword, he started to receive funding from terrorist organizations. At times, it seemed like he was playing one side against the other, getting money from the jihadists and also benefit-

ing from arms sales to private security firms contracted by
the military to fight extremism.

But some of his money also appeared to flow in from
the tech sector. Murky ties. Offshore accounts. Nothing
solid.

If there's a lot on the table, you can be pretty sure that
there's also a lot going on under the table. All too often
where you find money you find corruption. It's as if the
two things are joined at the hip. It may take some time,
but dig deep enough into one and you'll most likely find
ligaments connecting it to the other.

"Listen," I said to Sasha. "I know you have orders to
wait so you can try to track down Blake's associates, but if
you have any idea where he is, we need to move on him—
especially now that Mannie is free. If we can get both of
them, I think Mannie might work with us and give up the
contacts you're looking for."

She didn't respond.

"Can you get us to Blake?"

Though she took her time answering, at last she did.
"Yeah. I think so."

While she pulled up the material we needed, Greer
spoke with DeYoung about getting an FBI SWAT team
dispatched, and I phoned Ralph to fill him in on what
we'd learned.

Once we had DeYoung's approval and the address from
Sasha, I realized that, despite how badly I wanted to be on
the incursion team, the location wasn't anywhere near us.
SWAT would get there long before we would—and this
was time-sensitive. If Blake was there, we needed to move
on him right away before he fled or changed locations
again.

"I'm not going to make it there in time," I told Ralph.

"We'll go in heavy. We'll get this done."

"Right. If possible, get me an eye on things. Have one of the SWAT guys send a video feed to my FDD account either from his body camera or helmet cam. We'll watch things go down from here."

"Roger that."

"This is the best shot we've had in a long time. Good luck."

I logged into my Federal Digital Database account and waited for the live footage to come through.

Finding Sasha this morning might've just been the break we'd been waiting for.

38

Timothy Sabian had a restless night, and when he finally rolled out of bed, it was nearly ten o'clock. He wandered into the kitchen to get some breakfast and saw the type-written note waiting on the table: *Look downstairs*.

His heart clenched. Someone had been in here. Someone had left that note for him.

That's not true, Timothy. You know that's not true. You left this note here yourself.

"No. I didn't. I wouldn't have."

But you did.

"I don't go in the basement. Just like Emily didn't after that night when Elena was killed."

You haven't even written the end of Emily's story yet. Go and see. Go and see what's in the basement.

The wiring downstairs had never been completed. The floor had never been poured. The ceiling panels had never been put up. The walls were still rough, unpainted cinder blocks. Although there was one bulb above the stairwell and one at the base of it, Timothy grabbed a flashlight from the drawer just in case he needed the extra light.

He eased the door open and flicked the switch. Yellow, jaundiced light fell across him and washed faintly through the stairwell. His breathing was quick and tense as he took the steps one at a time deeper into The Place He Did Not Want To Go.

He wasn't sure what to expect or what he might find, but even when he got to the base of the stairs and looked around, he saw nothing out of the ordinary—just piles of boxes, half a dozen crates of discarded books, a broken chair, an old table, and a dust-covered filing cabinet filled with notes of research for his novels.

Everything where it should be.

Nothing that didn't belong.

Except.

There.

A shape in the far corner of the basement near the old furnace that had never worked since the day he moved in here.

He targeted the form with his flashlight.

A body. A woman. She was lying on her side facing the wall and wore the same clothes Julianne had been wearing last night when she was at the pier.

And so.

But what had happened after that, after their encounter by the docks?

You put her in the trunk, Timothy. You brought her back here.

"Miss Springman?" he said softly.

She didn't move.

"Julianne." Timothy edged closer. "Are you alright?"

The woman didn't stir.

He approached her warily, then knelt beside her and rested a hand on her shoulder. Gently, he rolled her onto her back so he could see her face.

Oh yes. It was her.

And yes, she was dead. Her discolored skin left no doubt about that.

You did this, Timothy. You killed her.

"No, I wouldn't have. She was going to help me. I would never have hurt her."

And yet here she is. Now what are you going to do?

He couldn't leave her down here. He couldn't keep her here. He had to get rid of her.

"I'll call the police. I'll explain everything. I'll tell them that someone left her here, that someone is trying to set me up."

No one will believe that. Not with your history of mental illness. You've been violent in the past. You can't tell anyone. If the police find out what you did here, they'll send you to prison. Or back to the White Shirts Place. Lock you away there forever.

Even though Julianne appeared to most certainly be dead, Timothy felt for a pulse, then leaned close to see if she was breathing, just to be absolutely sure.

No response.

"I'll wrap her up in a blanket. I'll take her somewhere."

No, you'll leave prints. You'll leave DNA. You can't take that chance. You need to put her someplace where she'll never be found.

He thought through the possibilities—placing her in the river, burying her in the woods somewhere. The Adirondacks? He really had no idea. How do you get rid of a body?

Lonnie would know. If only he were—

Maybe it'd be best not to move her anywhere. Leave her down here. Bury her here.

"But this is my house. This is where I live. I could never stay here knowing she's down in the basement."

You can't move her out of here. What if you aren't careful enough? Bury her here, then make sure you haven't left any evidence that you two ever met. Nothing in your house, nothing in your car.

Timothy took a deep breath, let it out slowly, and then scratched at the bugs that were crawling incessantly across his arm.

It was as if his skin were giving birth to them. Always always always more and more and more.

He knew that if he buried her in his basement and anyone found out, they would most certainly think that he had done something bad to her, that *he* was the one who'd killed her.

He scratched again and finally decided that the safest thing, the best thing right now, was to listen to the voice and just make sure no one ever, ever found out that she was here.

Timothy Sabian headed to the garage to get a shovel.

39

The feed came on.

An FBI SWAT unit was outside Blake's condo and the team was coordinating its incursion.

Agent Raudsepp had the camera that was mounted to his helmet turned on, and I watched as he hustled up the stairs behind his team leader, watched as they positioned themselves outside the door, as they shouted, as they broke it down, as they rushed in and began to clear the condo. Shouts. Flashes of movement. Agents flaring off to each side as Raudsepp moved swiftly to the bedroom. It looked empty. He searched under the bed. In the closet. Nothing. Called out, "Clear!" and a few seconds later, returned to the living room where the rest of the team was assembling.

Greer and Sasha stood behind me as I sat at her kitchen table and watched things go down.

"It doesn't make sense," Sasha whispered. "I wonder if Blake cleared out because he somehow learned that you found me."

I didn't want to speculate on that either way but turned on the audio feed to Raudsepp and asked him to return to the bedroom. "Take us on a tour." Then I said to Sasha, "Watch carefully. Let me know if you see anything out of the ordinary."

As Raudsepp walked through the condo, starting in the bedroom, she occasionally asked him to pause, turn right or left, and walk closer to certain items.

"What do you see?" Greer asked her.

"It's what I don't see. The mannequins. They're all gone."

I had a thought, and if I was right, we wouldn't see Blake or his men removing the mannequins on any of the security cameras in the building.

Through the audio feed, I asked to be transferred to Ralph, and a moment later, his voice came on. "What is it?"

"Check the bathroom," I said. "And review the building's surveillance camera footage. See if you can catch sight of anyone leaving the ground floor."

"We're already on the CCTV cameras. What do you want me to look for in the bathroom?"

"Powder around the drain. I'm wondering if Blake might've taken a shower with his silent ladies."

"What are you talking about?"

"Sasha told us that Blake is trafficking a synthetic drug that's close in its chemical composition to cocaine but can be molded into different shapes. I'm wondering if the mannequins aren't what they appear to be."

"You're saying they're made of the stuff?"

"They might be." I looked to Sasha for confirmation.

"It's possible," she admitted, "if it was mixed with some sort of starch to give it enough solidity. It would certainly explain a few things—especially Blake's fascination with them and why he always has them around."

"It's called Selzucaine," I told Ralph. "Let's see where this takes us."

I hung up, and Sasha called the lab to have them analyze the composition of the mannequin head to see if it
might have been made out of the drug.

Then we waited for word on the security footage and
the findings from Ralph.

++++

Timothy heard the words from his novel *The Nesting
Dolls*, a refrain that came up several times in the book:
"Gone is gone is gone. Dead is dead is dead is dead."

Julianne had read from that book last night before the
man in the car drove up.

*But was that man even real? Did anyone else besides Ju-
lianne actually show up?*

Honestly, Timothy couldn't be sure.

"His car had duct tape over the license plate," he said,
trying to convince himself. "It was real!"

*But why would someone do that? Isn't it too much of a
coincidence that he just happened to show up while you were
talking to her? Right when she was telling you to get in the
trunk?*

Yes, it did seem too coincidental—unless someone had
known they were going to be meeting out there at that
time.

Did Julianne tell him? Was he working with her?

Timothy realized that right now he had no way of
knowing. He could figure all that out later—if the guy
really had been there. Right now, here in the basement, he
had to take care of this body at his feet.

Before beginning to dig, Timothy rested the shovel on
the ground and crouched by Julianne's side. "Why did you

have to die?" he asked her softly. "Things are going to be different now. You shouldn't have died."

He nudged her shoulder. Not hard. Not hard enough to leave a bruise. Just like you might do with a friend you're messing around with.

And then he heard her response: *"I would have stayed alive if you would've let me. I'd still be here, if only you would've stepped back, not held on to my neck so long."*

"But I didn't. I—"

"Yes, you did. Why did you hold on? Even when you could see it was hurting me?"

"I don't remember holding you. I don't remember any of that."

"You choked me just like Lonnie choked Rose. It was just like in your novel."

"No."

"Yes."

Timothy took her hand in his. Her dead, flaccid hand.

He was shaking as he tenderly kissed her wrist, but it wasn't like in the fairy tales. She didn't come back to life. She didn't magically awaken.

"What am I supposed to do now?" Though he spoke the words aloud, his voice was pained and quiet, a child speaking.

"I can't help you clean this up," Julianne told him. He was surprised at how clearly she spoke without ever moving her lips. She just lay there and didn't open her eyes and didn't move her jaw, but yet he heard her as clear as day. *"You've made a mess of things. You'll have to take care of it yourself."*

"Alright, Julianne. Alright, I will."

He found a freshly washed bedsheet and laid it over her so she wouldn't get dirty while he was digging and so he wouldn't have to look at her looking at him as he worked.

Then he drove the shovel into the dirt floor and began to dig Julianne Springman's grave.

40

We convened at the Field Office for a briefing.

Sasha rode with Greer, Ralph met us there, and after introductions, the four of us headed down the hall toward DeYoung's office.

On the way, Greer slipped off to the restroom, and a few moments later I received a call from Christie. Although I kept walking, I hung back from the team to answer it.

"Hey," I said warmly. "How are you?"

"Good. I'm good."

"And your weekend? Do you feel refreshed?"

"I think so. Refocused, at least."

"That's what you wanted, right?"

A pause. "Yes. Listen, is Tessa okay? I just listened to the message you left the other night. You mentioned she was upset?"

"I think she's alright. I heard her crying in her bedroom on Saturday, but she's seemed fine since then."

"Do you know what was wrong?"

"On Friday, she said that she thought you were angry at her. Also, I think she's still lonely from Azaliya leaving. I'm guessing it might've been a combination of the two things."

"Did she say why she thought I was mad at her?"

"No. It was just the way you took off, I think. Kind of abrupt. And you were more quiet, more reserved than usual before you left."

"I'm not angry. It's not that."

"Okay. I told her you weren't, but you should probably talk with her when you get back."

"Yes. Of course."

++++

Christie knew that Tessa's school didn't allow cell phone use during class, but she figured that her daughter would be checking her messages during lunch, so she decided to text her as soon as she was off the line with Pat.

"My flight is delayed," she told him, "but I should get to LaGuardia around three. When are you off work?"

"Probably not until six or so. The case has taken a few turns I didn't expect."

"Let's meet somewhere nice for dinner. Just the two of us."

"Great. Do you have a place in mind?"

"No. Surprise me."

"Hmm. Alright. I'll see what I can do. Maybe try to snag a seven o'clock reservation. That sound good?"

"Perfect. It's a date."

"Try 'extinct insects,'" he said.

She loved tongue twisters, and he was always searching for one that would stump her. She tried this insect twister five times fast and did pretty well until the fourth time through when she caught herself saying, "extinct inks-tects."

"I like it. You try."

"I think I'll sneak in a little more practice first. I'll give it a shot when I see you tonight."

"Deal. I'll try to come up with one for you by then."

"I love you, Christie."

"I love you too."

After their good-byes, she texted her daughter, asking her to call when she had a chance, then she left the monastery and headed for the airport.

++++

After I was off the phone, I heard Ralph confirming to Sasha that his team had indeed found Selzucaine residue around the drain. "It looks like the mannequins aren't being used as vessels to smuggle the drug inside of them," he said, "they *are* the drug. And hot water disintegrated them? Or do you think they needed another chemical to do it?"

"I kissed a mannequin and it didn't dissolve. But enough pressure, enough water, if it was hot enough, based on its chemical structure it's possible that could have been all that was needed."

Talking drugs and the next step for the task force, the two of them went on ahead. Greer caught up with me.

"He's a big fella," he said.

"Who's that?"

"Ralph."

"Toughest guy I know."

"I'd hate to have to fight him."

"So would I."

Greer was single and in the dating scene, so as we started toward the briefing room, I asked if he had any suggestions for a good place for a romantic dinner.

"Romantic, huh? So something beyond your typical pub and grub?"

"Yeah. Somewhere special."

"Giuseppe's in the Village. I was there last week. The place is amazing. That's where you need to take your woman. When are you wanting to go?"

"That's the thing. It's a bit last-minute. Tonight. You think it's too late to get a reservation?"

He scoffed lightly. "There, you'd be lucky to get one a month out. But I know someone who knows the manager. Maybe I can call in a favor."

"Not if it's any trouble."

"No trouble at all. What time?"

"Seven. A reservation for two."

"Don't worry, Pat." He congenially slugged my arm. "We'll get you two taken care of."

41

Blake stared at the email.

It was a photograph of Julianne Springman, the young woman who'd come to him the other night asking for his help, asking if he knew someone she could work with. Now, in this picture, she was in the trunk of a car, and based on the color of her skin, she was deceased.

The reddish tinge spoke to carboxyhemoglobin, which might come from carbon monoxide poisoning, or possibly, smoke inhalation.

Okay.

Interesting.

There was a message typed beneath the photo: I'd like to speak with you.

Was this the work of Timothy Sabian? Was that possible? How else would she suddenly show up dead right after having his name passed along to her?

Although it wasn't by any means conclusive, the timing certainly spoke to a connection.

It appeared that Mr. Sabian was mentally deranged and of murderous intent after all.

Well, you did warn Julianne. You did do that.

But how did Sabian get this email address? And why

would he have sent this photo? What was the point? Was it meant to be a threat?

Blake couldn't come up with any good reason why the psychotic novelist would've sent him a photograph of Julianne Springman's dead body. If it was a taunt, it was not well-advised.

Over the last eighteen months, Mannie and his hacker friends had proven to be invaluable to Blake, so now he called him into the room and showed him the picture. "I want to know where this email originated from. Can you figure that out for me?"

"I can."

"Do it. Whoever sent this deserves a little visit."

Mannie left for his workstation.

Blake had moved his team to the old greenhouse facility just over the line in Connecticut.

The Eastern Bay Greenhouse had closed three years ago, and no one had taken care of the plants inside it when the owners shuttered its doors. Consequently, the plants had continued to grow unchecked. Of course, over time, they'd all eventually died and dried out. Now, the brown stalks and intertwined vines tentacled up to the ceiling, nearly filling some of the glassed-in enclosures. When you looked at them, it brought a touch of cognitive dissonance: the buildings are greenhouses; you expect green life. Here, you found only brown death.

Six structures stood on the property: five sprawling, abandoned greenhouses that'd been built decades ago, and one recently renovated office building that was finished not long before the business closed its doors for good.

Despite their age, each of the tent-shaped, thick-glassed

greenhouses still had its ventilation fans. Three still had their climate control units in place. Garden tools, scattered pots for the plants, and stacks of replacement windows lay stored at the end of one of the greenhouses.

In some cases, the buildings' glass panes had shattered and fallen in, and wedge-shaped shards of glass were still embedded in the soil of the dead plants that'd climbed and entwined their clinging death grip on the tall wooden stakes meant to guide their growth.

No one ventured onto the deserted, fenced-in property anymore. Six months ago, Blake had purchased it and found it a useful place to regroup when the heat was on inside the city.

Also, this was the location where the mannequins would be treated, as soon as the shipment of chemicals arrived from Phoenix. It'd taken some work, but the sprinkler system in one of the greenhouses had been reconfigured and retrofitted so that it could be used to spray down and prepare the silent ladies for shipment.

A group of eighty of them stood in two obedient lines, patiently awaiting their turn beneath the sprinklers. With a street value north of thirty grand per kilo, it was a sizable stash of Selzucaine.

More than enough to do the trick.

On its own, Selzucaine gave a powerful short-term high. But when it was treated with Tranadyl, things took a turn in a more permanent direction.

It was similar to when a chemist in the 1970s tried to create synthetic heroin and contaminated it with 1-methyl-4-phenyl-1,2,3,6-tetrahydropyridine, otherwise known as MPTP. It crossed the blood-brain barrier and metabolized into 1-methyl-4-phenylpyridinium, or MPP+, which caused the user to develop a severe form of Parkinson's disease. Victims were completely conscious but unable to move. The user was trapped inside himself and was left knowing that he had imprisoned himself by his own decision.

Terrifying.

In this case, the user wouldn't experience that specific result but, because of the interaction of the two drugs, would very likely slip into a coma. Or, the drug cocktail would prove fatal.

Tranadyl was a synthetic derivative of Fentanyl. With its Fentanyl base, it was arguably more potent than either heroin or morphine, and if you mismanaged its dosage, just like China White, you could be in serious trouble.

People on the street knew not to mix Selzucaine and Tranadyl, so the key was not letting them know that the two drugs had been combined.

Designer drugs were being created on an almost daily basis. The DEA determined which drugs were illegal, but there was virtually no way for them to keep up with what was happening on the streets and in private labs across the country. So by manipulating synthetics, you could stay one step ahead of the law.

Earlier, Blake had received word from his NSA contact that the Feds were planning to raid his condo in Manhattan. He'd taken care of the silent ladies he'd had with him there before leaving, so he wasn't worried about them providing any evidence, but he was curious who'd betrayed him and leaked the location.

Ibrahim came to mind first.

After watching what'd happened to Jasper, it was quite

possible that the Syrian had gotten cold feet in moving forward with everything, and that did not bode well for the timing of treating the mannequins and getting them onto the streets.

And it did not bode well for Ibrahim.

The man's connections to extremist groups were vital to Blake's plan. To make things play out like he envisioned, it was crucial that Ibrahim stayed on task, at least for the next thirty-six hours. Then, it wouldn't matter whose side he was on, or which side he thought he was on. He would be revealed for who he truly was and would either spend the rest of his life in prison or die at the hands of law enforcement while being apprehended.

Or suicide.

That was possible.

He might take his own life.

Considering his religious devotion and his reticence to getting caught, that seemed like a legitimate possibility.

Of course, if necessary, Blake would be glad to take care of his demise personally—if things came to that. The office building was wooden and, with a fire started in the right place on the first floor or in the basement, the whole building would go up quite quickly.

A contingency plan. Just in case.

And after the mannequins were distributed and the jihadist was out of the way, public sentiment would be on Blake's side.

A puzzle slowly piecing itself together.

However, the betrayer wasn't *necessarily* Ibrahim, and Blake reminded himself to hold back from making unjustified assumptions.

After positioning his men throughout the grounds and telling them to contact him if there was any movement, he called Ibrahim and asked him to come to the facility. "I have some things to go over with you, and I think it would be best if we discussed them in person."

42

Briefings almost always go on too long, people are rarely as prepared as they should be, and the whole affair ultimately ends up wasting time that could've been better spent actually looking for the offender or actively tracking down suspects.

My philosophy? Have a meeting when absolutely necessary. Send a memo when a memo will do.

However, in this case, a memo wouldn't cover it—even I had to acknowledge that. Too much happening, too many connections, and too much at stake.

We had people committing suicide and posting their deaths online as they happened, all while someone was present watching them and refraining from stopping them. There was the drug connection. The Matchmaker, whoever that was. Blake and his team. The silent ladies and the chemist. Somehow all of those things were interrelated.

Our team was present, along with Collins, the cyber expert, and Jason Thurman, the agent whose wallet Mannie had procured during his escape and who worked with handling confidential informants when he wasn't being accosted by fleeing fugitives.

DeYoung got things rolling, and after we'd made introductions all around, he wasted no time in telling Sasha that he was going to have a long talk with his counterpart at the DEA. "We need this task force to be coordinated and not splintered off with each agency doing its own thing."

"I'll let you discuss that with him," she said in a clipped voice. "I'm just here to find Blake. Knowing his interests, going undercover as an escort was the best way we could come up with to get close to him."

Sasha received permission from her supervisor at the DEA to update us on everything she'd discovered so far. After filling in DeYoung about her work, she mentioned that she'd overheard a woman who was visiting Blake on Saturday night say that she was the one who'd worked with Blake's brother, Dylan.

"Wait," I said. "Dylan's partner showed up?"

Sasha nodded. "A woman named Julianne Springman."

"Springman was a CSI tech in Detroit," I told them. "I met her last summer when we were tracking Dylan Neeson." I could hardly believe she was the one who'd partnered with a serial killer to help him commit his crimes, but I trusted what Sasha was telling us. Julianne's apparent involvement just went to show how little you can actually know people or guess the evil they're ultimately capable of.

We all have a wicked streak, even though we might normally keep it in check.

DeYoung asked Sasha, "Do you know where she is?"

"No. She was looking for someone with similar interests here in New York City."

"Similar interests?"

"Someone to kill with."

I processed that. "Did Blake give her a name?"

"He said he was going to, but I don't know if he did or

who it might've been. If he did pass along someone's name, it was while I wasn't there with him."

"We need to put out a BOLO for Springman," Thurman said, stating the obvious. "We find her, she might be able to lead us to Blake."

Ralph put a call through.

"While we're on it," I said, "we should try to find this guy, Reese, in Phoenix. Let's send a couple of agents over to have a word with him. If he is connected to Blake's people, maybe he can give us the intel we need to locate him."

Greer let us know that he used to work with an agent who was stationed down there. "I'll contact her, put it into play."

Sasha asked, "What's the purpose of the observer if the suicides are being recorded anyway?"

"There's a lot bigger thrill to being present when someone dies than there is to simply watching it online like any other casual observer might do," Thurman explained.

DeYoung was going about things old school and laying out what we knew on a whiteboard, complete with arrows, boxes, and a slew of sticky notes. He included names as we discussed the known relationships between them: Blake, Reese, Ibrahim, Aaron Jasper, Mannie. Then Jon Murray, Senator Murray, Julianne Springman. He repeatedly peeled off and restuck the stickies as the briefing moved forward.

It might have been helpful for visual learners, but to me it ended up looking like a tangled mess of spaghetti with yellow square meatballs splayed throughout it.

Finally, he drew three empty boxes and labeled them

(1) *Julianne's new partner?* (2) *The Matchmaker?* and (3) *The Observer?*

"Thoughts on the next step?" he said.

"I want to know about the tox screenings from the previous suicides," I told him. "I still haven't heard the results."

He jotted that down on a legal pad.

"Did Jon leave a suicide note?" Thurman asked.

"Not that we're aware of," I said.

"What about the other suicides?"

"In two of the cases, yes. But there was no indication in them that someone was going to be present to watch the deaths."

DeYoung gave a heavy sigh. "Where does that leave us?"

"Victimology," I replied. "What do the other suicide victims have in common with Jon Murray? From what the team has pulled up so far, it's not past residences or schools attended. Not employment. There's no evidence they ever called, contacted, or even met each other. Nothing in credit card receipts that match up with each other."

"If they were all Selzucaine users, it might be their dealer," Sasha suggested.

I wasn't ready to make that leap. "Maybe a dealer, yes. Maybe someone else. Let's take a step back and do a deep dive into people close to the victims: Relatives. Friends. Work associates. Social networking connections. Anything. It might not be that they have a connection to each other but a connection to an individual who hasn't appeared on our radar screen yet. We find that link—"

"We find the Matchmaker," Greer said.

"Yes. Possibly."

I offered to look more closely at the victimology. Sasha agreed to leverage her resources at the DEA to find out more about the Selzucaine, ways to mold it for shipment and where else Blake's mannequins might have been shipped around the country.

DeYoung spoke up. "Counting Jon Murray, we have four known interrelated instances of someone videotaping their own suicide while someone else is present. If that person was influencing them, how do you talk someone into doing something like that? How do you convince a person to take his own life, especially in such shocking ways?"

"Choices are rational," Ralph noted, "not random. Even if people aren't consciously aware of it, they're always evaluating the cost-benefit ratio before they commit a crime: how badly do I want this thing? And usually—although not with suicide—how can I get away with this action without getting caught?"

"So, make him a promise or make him a threat," Greer suggested. "If you're trying to get someone to do something that drastic, you'd have to make a promise or threat big enough to convince him that it's something worth dying for."

DeYoung returned to his whiteboard. "Okay, let's play this out. Jon Murray is approached by someone who promises to reward him in some way or threatens to harm a person he loves. In order to find out why Jon might've killed himself or why the victims in the other videos might have done so, we need to find out who they loved the most—or anyone who might've benefited from their death or somehow been protected because of it."

"I'll take that," Greer offered.

"Also, let's see if the senator has any legislation before

him right now that has to do with the pharmaceutical industry or laws related to regulating Selzucaine. That could be the connection with the guy in Phoenix."

"On it," Ralph said.

After the briefing, I glanced at my watch and decided it would probably still work for me to meet Calvin at noon for lunch, as long as we could get together close to the Field Office. Just to make sure, I cleared things with DeYoung to confirm that he was on board with me brainstorming some investigative avenues with the famed environmental criminologist.

"Werjonic's worked with us before," DeYoung told me. "I trust him. If he can be of any help, I'm open to bringing him on as a consultant."

"I'll let him know."

Tessa had mentioned that Timothy Sabian was doing a book signing at the Mystorium tonight. The bookstore wasn't too far from the Field Office, their deli sandwiches were pretty good, and so was their coffee. Also, they had a broad selection of teas that would appeal to Calvin. I figured that if he was anywhere in the vicinity, lunch there might be a good choice.

Calvin wasn't a fan of texting, so I left him a voicemail asking if the Mystorium would work with his schedule. Then, while I waited for a reply, I began examining the lives of the people who'd killed themselves, looking for any connection they might have had with each other in ways that I hadn't yet considered.

++++

Although Timothy Sabian hadn't expected it to be easy, digging the hole in the basement's hard-packed dirt floor was even more work than he had anticipated, and listening to Julianne the whole time was difficult—listening to her ask him why he hadn't stopped, why he'd done this to her, why he'd killed her.

Muscle spasms and fatigue were common for someone who suffered from Timothy's condition, and he had to stop and rest a number of times to keep from collapsing from the effort.

Once he'd burrowed out a space large enough to hold her, he carefully lifted her body and nestled her into the hole. There was barely enough room—he had to force her right arm over her chest so she would fit.

There.

Still covered with the sheet.

The bugs that burrowed under his skin chose to scuttle out from the cuts and sores and descend onto Julianne's corpse. Timothy knew it was a hallucination, but that didn't make it any less terrifying. He didn't like the idea that he was seeing things, so rather than call it a hallucination, he called it a nightmare.

A waking one.

The kind he'd been having all too often lately.

When he began to fill in the dirt, he started with her face. That way, he wouldn't have to think about her staring up through the sheet at him while he shoveled dirt over the rest of her body.

However, covering her face with the soil didn't make her stop talking to him. She told him it was cold and that she didn't want to be left here alone, left here in the basement with all these bugs. She asked if he could take her upstairs, let her lie on something soft and comfortable.

"No. Absolutely not."

A bed.

"No!"

His bed.

"Why? Why are you asking me to do that?"

"Emily wouldn't want you to leave me here, would she?" Julianne said.

"Emily's not real."

He stopped putting the dirt on Julianne's body and listened to the other voice, the one that never left him alone.

You have the hole. You can bring her down here anytime. If it'll make her stop talking to you, then take her upstairs. When she quiets down, you can bring her back down. You can bury her then.

"But what if someone finds her upstairs? What if someone comes looking?"

Just take this one step at a time. Make sure nothing else points to you. Be careful. Just like Lonnie would be.

It was getting harder and harder to sift through the real from the imaginary.

At last, Timothy eased the sheet off her, tipping the dirt that was on top of it aside.

Even though he was careful, some of the soil spilled onto Julianne's face. He brushed it away, then gently blew the remaining granules of dirt off her cheeks and her eyelashes and her lips.

Finally, he lifted her, and she thanked him thanked him thanked him as he carried her up the stairs to his bedroom.

43

During her classes, Tessa kept the Timothy Sabian novel that Patrick had bought for her open on her desk but hidden under other papers or inside the textbook she was supposed to be reading. She wanted to get through as much of it as she could before tonight, so she spent each class venturing further and further into Timothy Sabian's imagination.

At times it was illuminating.

At times devastating.

The lyrical call of darkness was his friend, the shackled dreams of the world his canvas.

There are so many ways to feel pain as a teenager, so many ways to be lured into loneliness, so many places to look and find only darkness. She was lonely for her foster sister, missing her mom, and wondering what to make of Patrick, and so she read. Some people sneer and call reading an "escape"—as if that's a bad thing. But since when is it a bad thing to try to escape pain?

She didn't delve much into fantasy, but she'd looked over some of J.R.R. Tolkien's essays. In "On Fairy Stories," he explained why he wrote what he did. Whatever else might have been true about him, the man had no patience with people who derisively labeled some genres of literature "escapist." As he wrote, "Why should a man be scorned if, finding himself in prison, he tries to get out and go home?"

Yeah.

That was a good question.

This world is full of prisons that bear all sorts of names, and the most sensible response is to try to escape them— why should that be mocked, ridiculed, or looked down on?

Seeking escape is the most rational pursuit of all.

Like that guy last week. The senator's son. The final escape, the final choice. And he filmed it for all the world to see.

Sabian seemed to understand that. The necessity of escape, the stifling nature of life's many prisons.

Tessa read, and every word was a way for her to put more distance between her feelings and her awareness of her feelings, as if maybe, just maybe, by gorging herself on a story, by swallowing it whole, all the squibbles and frozen black letters would quiet the nameless ache inside of her.

The bell rang, and everyone shuffled out of the room toward the cafeteria.

"Watch out," she said as a boy brushed past her.

"You okay?" Candice asked her.

"Yeah. It's just that I suffer from triptostupophobia."

"What's that?"

"The fear of stupid people tripping and falling on me."

"I don't think that's a real fear."

"It should be. I'm scared of it."

"No, you're not."

"Whatever."

On her way to the caf, Tessa checked her messages and found a text from her mom asking her to give her a call.

She felt her chest tighten. Her mom knew all about the no-cell-phone policy at school, and she wouldn't have left a message like that unless something was up.

When Tessa tried the number, no one answered. She couldn't remember exactly when her mom's flight was supposed to take off, but she figured that she was probably either in the car on her way to the airport or in the air somewhere, so she left a text rather than a voicemail telling her that she'd talk with her later, as soon as school was done.

And then, as she ate by herself in the back of the caf, she again turned her attention to the novel and the welcome, necessary escape offered to her in the delicate, haunted prose of Timothy Sabian, a man troubled so much by looking without flinching at the truth of the world that his words veritably shuddered with despair and with the desperate wish that somewhere out there, there was hope.

Yeah, this guy really seemed to understand the need for escape.

The need to leave this world behind.

And to unchain yourself from the glaring, intractable pain of daily life.

44

Half an hour ago, I'd heard back from Calvin that noon at the Mystorium would work for him, and now I arrived five minutes early.

Over the course of the morning, the lab had confirmed that the head of the mannequin was formed out of Selzucaine along with a cellulose-based starch to help it keep its shape.

The team didn't find any more mannequin body parts at or near the grave of James Leeson.

I hadn't been able to locate the connection between the victims on any deeper levels.

I wondered how Mannie might be connected to Jon's death, or if perhaps there was more of a connection with the senator himself. In either case, it justified taking a closer look at the other people who'd attended the funeral and their relationship with the senator.

The Mystorium specialized in first-edition and out-of-print crime novels, and there was a certain allure about the place. A rarely explored, dusty-volumed, hidden-troved mystique.

I recognized the young woman behind the counter. Rebekah had hit it off with Tessa when they first met, and from what I understood, she was majoring in English lit at Brooklyn College. They shared a penchant for Edgar Allan Poe's writings, and today, almost serendipitously, she was serving Raven's Brew coffee, which I was glad to see. The roaster from Washington had become more popular in the last few years, although I'd been drinking them for the last decade. They were famous for their strong brews, and I tended to gravitate toward Dead Man's Reach.

A fitting brew for a crime bookstore.

And for a man in my profession.

Also, the company name reminded me of Tessa, whom I'd started calling Raven at times, in part because of her love of Poe, in part because of her untamable spirit.

I ordered a large coffee for here—java always tastes better in an actual mug than in a to-go cup—then added a hint of honey and cream and found a seat at one of the tables near the true crime section and began to think about what questions to ask Calvin.

Mannie's escape from the Field Office bothered me.

On Saturday evening, Greer had offhandedly remarked that bad guys don't take days off. It made me think of who *did* take time off on Sunday during Mannie's escape, and who was on duty at the Field Office. While it was possible that Mannie was able, on his own, to discern how to get out, the more I thought about it, the more likely it seemed to me that he might have had some inside help.

Two things to analyze—the work rosters for who was on duty when he escaped, and the CCTV footage of him moving through the hallways. I wanted to see if he lingered anywhere, spoke to anyone.

I put the request through.

I wondered if phone records would allow us to identify if the previous suicide victims had all visited the same location, even if it wasn't at the same time.

As I was reflecting on that, movement at the door caught my attention, and Calvin swooshed in, his iconic London Fog trench coat curling around him almost like the cape of a superhero in a comic book. It only took him a moment to find me. He smiled and called, "Patrick, my boy!" his distinctive English accent already evident in just those three words.

I rose to greet him. "Calvin, it's good to see you."

His handshake was brisk and pronounced, just like everything he did.

"Can I buy you lunch?" I asked.

"That you can. How did the briefing go?"

"Better than most. No chairs thrown this time."

He blinked. "And in the past?"

"Once or twice."

"Yes, yes, of course," he said good-naturedly as if he appreciated the joke that wasn't actually a joke.

For his drink, Calvin chose Earl Grey tea, which didn't surprise me, and after we'd both ordered a sandwich, we found our way through the stacks to the table where I'd been sitting and where my coffee mug awaited me. He shed his overcoat and folded it neatly and precisely over the back of the chair beside him.

"Before we speak of anything related to the case," he said with a mischievous twinkle in his eye, "I must ask you, how is married life treating you?"

"Very well, as a matter of fact."

"I'm sorry I couldn't make it to your wedding."

"It's no problem. Really."

"So you're happy?"

"Yes. Truthfully, I can't imagine ever being single again."

"Brilliant." He rapped the table definitively. "And now. The case—and before you say a word, you know how this works. Discuss only what you feel comfortable addressing, and I will only offer you my take on things if you wish."

"I spoke with the assistant director. He gave me the go-ahead to ask you to consult on this if it sparks your interest."

"It already has."

"You know what case I'm talking about?"

"The senator's son."

I eyed him. "How did you know that?"

"Timing of the crime and of your call. I'm hypothesizing that it's not an isolated case."

"It's not."

I told him we were looking for an individual who was apparently watching others die while their suicides were fed live over the Internet. "Some of the videos had thousands of views while it was happening," I added.

"It is our world. I hasten not to judge it for I am a part of it."

I had the sense that I should have known where that dictum came from, but maybe it was just something I'd heard him say before. "We also have Blake Neeson back on our radar screen," I said, "and, well . . . in your investigations and consultations with law enforcement, have you ever heard of someone known as the Matchmaker?"

"Have you been able to link the suicide victims?" he asked, which didn't seem in any way to be an answer to my question.

"No. Not apart from the fact that their deaths were broadcast online as they happened and that someone was present watching the deaths occur."

"The same person in each instance?"

"I can't be certain, but it appears so. Why? Do you think that's the Matchmaker? Have you run into him before?"

"Hmm . . ." He looked around curiously. "I wonder if they have Vidocq."

"Vidocq?"

"Yes, and let us hope they have the condensed version— *The Personal Memoirs of the First Great Detective*. Edwin Gile Rich edited and translated a copy of Vidocq's memoirs from the French back in 1935. A good thing too. The original was four volumes and more than three hundred fifty thousand words. At least Rich gave us a manageable size to work with."

Before I could even suggest that we talk with Rebekah, Calvin was already on his feet and on his way to inquiring of the young barista if they had a copy of Rich's translation.

"Not many people ask about Vidocq," she said.

"I would suspect not."

"Which might work out well for you."

She typed the name into her computer to search the inventory, and then her eyes lit up. "Follow me, sir. I think I might be able to help you out."

It took her less than a minute to locate the well-worn

volume on a shelf near the small cluttered office beside the hallway that led to the rear exit.

Calvin thanked her and purchased it before returning to the table. "We must frequent local bookstores to keep them in business," he said diplomatically.

"And we appreciate that," Rebekah replied.

Once the two of us were seated again, I asked Calvin to tell me about Vidocq.

"Eugène François Vidocq. Born in 1775. Worked as a pioneering detective in Paris. After spending a good deal of his early life as a bit of a ruffian who was repeatedly in and out of prison, he offered to work for the police as a spy—what we might today call an undercover officer. Eventually, he became a detective in Paris. Overall, Vidocq spent more than twenty-five years working with the police. Some criminologists claim that he was the father of many modern investigative techniques and also the father of the detective novel itself."

"You'd think I would've heard more about him."

"He's not as well-known here in the States as he is in Europe," Calvin said offhandedly. He paged to the end of the foreword and tapped the book. "As Rich points out, the memoirs of Vidocq inspired *Les Misérables* and Balzac's Vautrin character, as well as Charles Dickens when he wrote *Great Expectations*. Even the classic detective stories of Doyle and Poe owe credit to Vidocq. Though no one would ever accuse Vidocq of being too modest—and that has caused him to be disregarded in some circles—he was certainly clever, a master of disguise, and, as a former convict himself, he could think like the criminals he was tracking."

Calvin's passion for his work came through loud and clear.

"You know a lot about him," I said.

An earnest nod. "It was while I was reading him that I came up with the Investigative Triumvirate."

"Don't trust your gut," I recounted from memory, "trust the evidence. Don't trust your instinct—trust the context. Don't trust your experience—trust the facts."

He smiled. "Either you're a good student or I'm a good teacher."

"Let's go with you being a good teacher."

Calvin rubbed his thumb fondly along the book's spine. "Vidocq was quite a raconteur. For instance . . ." He flipped through the pages, muttering to himself. "Let's see if I can find an example . . ." Then he paused. "Ah. Yes. Here. Page thirty-one: 'I spare details, but it is sufficient to say that I was arrested dressed in women's clothes as I was fleeing from the wrath of a jealous husband.' Now that's a great line."

"That is a great line."

"Yes, and regarding his investigative approach, he blazed new trails in working undercover, which is what got me thinking of him in the first place when you were telling me about the case."

"About the Matchmaker?"

"Yes."

Calvin still hadn't told me if he'd heard of the Matchmaker before, but I trusted that this discussion of Vidocq's techniques was not a rabbit trail.

"How, specifically, was Vidocq a pioneer in undercover work?" I asked.

"In ways that today might seem self-evident but weren't typically practiced by law enforcement in those days: Change your name; go where the criminals are; disguise yourself, your posture, your voice, your appearance."

"Makes sense."

"Yes. And it's best to go in alone. The more people you try to take into a den of thieves, the more things may go wrong. And when that happens, it puts everyone in more danger and jeopardizes the investigation."

Although we typically strive for overwhelming force when we confront suspects, undercover work was different.

"That makes sense too," I said.

"Regarding the forensic aspects of a case, Vidocq analyzed pieces of clothing and bits of paper for trace evidence and studied sole impressions in mud to deduce who committed a crime. He even noted that those who serve time and return to their life of crime do so 'with all the advantages of prison experience.'"

"All too often, prison serves as an advanced class in how to get away with murder."

"Precisely. Also, he noted that the guilty tend to fall into one of two extremes—they become either quiet or overly talkative. Or, as he put it, they exhibit 'a dreary silence or an unendurable volubility.'"

"I need to read Vidocq."

He passed the book to me. "And that is why I purchased it for you."

"Really, Calvin, you don't need to do that. I can pay you for—"

He emphatically waved off my offer. "His memoir is undoubtedly a mixture of fact and myth, and it's somewhat difficult to discern at what points he's recounting history and at what points he's embellishing it in his favor. Nevertheless, it is worth a read."

Rebekah delivered our sandwiches to our table, and once she'd left for the register again, I said, "Calvin, back to the Matchmaker. What do you know about him?"

"I can only tell you that you'll need to be on your toes, my boy. The person you're looking for is extremely dangerous. I've only heard rumors, but if they're true, the Matchmaker operates out of the Bronx and coordinates what might be described as a suicide club."

"Where did you hear these rumors, Calvin? I need to find him. He's one of the cogs in this investigation, and I think if we locate him, we might be able to track down Blake."

Calvin looked at me intensely, then said, "Let me do some digging this afternoon. I'll see what I can find out for you. But you have to promise me, Patrick, that you will be sagacious as you move forward. From what I understand, this person has, in the past, convinced a blogger who located him to take his own life that very night. And that blogger was a good man."

"You knew him?"

He was slow in replying. "We met shortly before his death." Calvin checked the time and then stood brusquely. "I must go. I will be in touch with you soon. You have my word."

He took his food to go and whisked out the door.

Calvin's behavior left me scratching my head. Clearly, he knew more than he was saying, and I couldn't guess why he hadn't been more forthcoming about the Matchmaker, unless he was worried that what'd happened to that blogger might also happen to me.

I downed my coffee and finished my sandwich, and

then, taking the copy of Vidocq with me, I returned to the Field Office to fill in the team on what I'd learned from my conversation with Calvin, which admittedly, wasn't much.

I decided it might be prudent to look for recent suicides of bloggers, especially those who might've been posting stories on suicides, or on the Matchmaker himself.

45

The blast of air conditioning felt good on Jake Reese's face as he entered through the front door of Plixon Pharmaceuticals' office complex.

Not even ten o'clock yet, but the Phoenix day was already gearing up to be one for the record books.

Plixon's parking lot had been full, forcing Jake to park on the street, which caused him to be even later getting into the building. And, of course, that meant he would need to feed the stupid meter within the next couple of hours or chance getting another ticket.

Just another thing to keep track of.

And right now, there were too many of those.

By the time he made it inside, he felt a ring of sweat soaking his collar just from hustling across the lot.

To put it mildly, it'd already been a hectic morning.

He still had some tests to run by noon or else Chapman would be all over his butt. He'd been planning to head in to the lab earlier but had overslept, and Heather had only decided to wake him up fifteen minutes before she left, so as he'd rushed to get Toby ready for day care, he'd been thinking the whole time about the situation with Ibrahim and also how mad he was at Heather—well, at himself for not getting up, but *also* at Heather for not waking him up earlier, when she could have.

Okay, yeah, he knew it wasn't fair to blame her, but his natural inclination to do so was just another example of how out of sync they'd been with each other lately.

But even their marriage problems weren't the primary thing on his mind. It was getting out of what he'd agreed to do for the Arab. Lately, everything had been spinning out of control. He felt like he'd made a deal with the devil—sold his soul, so to speak. He was in way over his head, and he was clueless about how to swim to the surface and shake himself free from the things he had done—and had agreed to do.

So then, on top of everything else, on the way here to the office he'd hit rush-hour traffic, and there'd been an accident on the freeway, which slowed things down even more. He nearly rear-ended a car that slammed on its brakes right in front of him and—

"Mornin', Jake." Gracie, the receptionist, gave him a friendly nod as he neared her desk.

"Morning."

Jake took a deep breath. Yeah, the air conditioning did feel good.

"You alright?" she asked.

"Sure. Yes." He must have looked as frazzled-distracted-stressed as he felt. "Just a lot popping."

"The tests?"

"Yeah."

And things at home.

And things with Ibrahim and—

"Chapman's in." She made a face that was more of a grimace than anything else to show her impression of their boss's mood for the day.

"Gotcha."

Jake started down the hall, but she said, "Call came in for you. Someone named Ibrahim. He left a voicemail."

"Thanks."

He should know better than to call you here! You were very clear about that!

Even more agitated now, Jake passed through the hall to his office to drop off his computer bag before heading to the lab. He dialed the window shades closed to keep the sunlight that was roasting the city from slanting in and glaring off his computer screen.

When he saw the phone on his desk, he decided he wasn't going to call Ibrahim. No, he was done with all that. Giving them the chemicals that they wanted wasn't going to serve anyone's best interests. And the money they'd paid him up until now—well, he would pay it back. He would find a way. He was out. For the sake of his family, he was done.

Jake muted his cell, went to the lab, and spent the next hour and a half diving into his work, lost in thought, or at least trying to lose himself in thought.

As he was finishing up, two FBI agents showed up and grilled him about Ibrahim and Blake, but he denied any knowledge of what the agents were asking about. He told them he would be glad to help if he could, but that he was sorry he knew nothing about those men. "Never heard of them."

"What about Fayed Raabi'ah Bashir?"

"Isn't he that terrorist?"

"What do you know about that?"

"Nothing. Just what's in the news. They say he's in the country. Is that true?"

"What have you heard, specifically, in the news?"

The female agent asked all the questions while the other agent, a guy who looked to be a tired forty, silently took notes in his journal. They'd introduced themselves when they first arrived, but Jake had been too nervous to catch either agent's name.

"Sir?" she said. "What have you heard?"

"I just . . . That he was responsible for that attack in Detroit last summer and other bombings somewhere in the Middle East. That's it."

"Mr. Reese, did you fly to New York City last weekend to attend the funeral of Jon Murray?"

"I know the senator. I served on an advisory committee during some congressional hearings."

"And that was enough to justify a flight up there to attend the young man's funeral?"

"I wanted to show my support for the senator. Listen, I haven't done anything. I don't know anything. If I hear of any terrorist activity, I'll call you, okay? Now, if you'll excuse me, I have some very important work that's waiting for me."

The two agents exchanged glances, and then the one who'd been taking notes closed up his notepad while the woman handed Jake her card.

"Call me if you think of anything."

"Okay."

Finally, when they left, Jake hastily returned to his office, only to find a note on his desk from Gracie: *Ibrahim called again. Sounded urgent. He didn't leave a message. What do you want me to do if he calls back?*

He wanted nothing more to do with this.

He left Gracie a message not to accept any more calls from Ibrahim and, hands shaking, shredded the note and deleted the voice message waiting for him without listening to it.

His concern sent his thoughts spinning off sideways to home, to his wife, to his son, to Heather rushing out, to getting Toby ready, to changing the boy's clothes after he'd spilled juice on his shirt. Then positioning him in the car seat, buckling him in, almost getting into that fender bender—

Sometimes riding in the car helped Toby fall asleep. Heather and he would take turns driving the boy around when he got fussy just to get him to go to sleep, and then—

Focus.

Think.

Asleep.

Wait.

Day care.

The next thought came at him fully formed, and as it did the bottom dropped out of the moment as if he were plunging down a roller coaster, as if he were caught in that hover-quiver breath-holding gasp of time when you know you're about to plummet three hundred feet after just a few more slim clicks of that chain on the track beneath you, but you haven't quite started the descent yet.

But then you do.

You were supposed to drop Toby off at day care. You were supposed to—

The descent.

One heading straight for hell.

You never swung by the center. You never dropped him off.

Your son is in the car. Toby's still in the car.

It'd been over two hours already, and with today's heat, that was probably more than enough time to—

"Oh my God."

The chain clicked.

The plunge.

The descent had come.

Jake Reese bolted for the door.

46

Jake seemed to have no strength in his legs as he rounded Gracie's desk, her questioning look and the words, "Is everything okay?" hardly registering as he whipped past her.

Every parent's worst nightmare.

Please, God.

Oh please.

He threw the outside door open and the wall of heat met him like a thick, living thing, oppressive and grim and stifling.

All Jake could think of were the news stories that came out each year about the hot car deaths of young children, about how quickly vehicles can heat up and the insane temperatures they can reach in just fifteen or twenty minutes. A distracted mom or dad forgets their baby in the car. Maybe Mom goes shopping or Dad goes to the golf course and the child dies of—

No.

A distracted parent goes to work.

Like you.

No.

And the child succumbs to heatstroke and—

No!

As he darted through the parking lot, a driver who was backing out of his spot smacked into Jake hard enough to send him careening into a parked minivan six feet away.

The driver jumped out and shouted about *What was he doing?* and *Was he okay?* and how *He needed to look out for cars in a parking lot like this,* but Jake ignored him, ignored it all, found his footing and sprinted toward the street, disregarding the throbbing pain in his leg.

He imagined what it would be like for a child—*for Toby!*—to be in his car seat, strapped in, getting hotter and hotter, sweating, crying, screaming, helpless and trapped and dying alone.

A child being roasted alive.

Oh, God.

Jake tugged his keys out of his pocket.

He came to the street and punched the unlock button on the key fob.

A different car was parked where his had been.

And his sedan was gone.

++++

Blake heard from his contact: "It's done."

"The boy?"

"Yes. I think we have Mr. Reese's attention."

"And you're confident he won't contact the authorities?"

"Not if he wants his son back alive. And not if he wants to stay out of prison for his role in all this. We made that crystal clear in the voicemail we left for him."

"Don't trust a voicemail. Call him. Don't leave anything to chance."

"Yes, sir."

++++

Jake's phone rang.

Ibrahim's number.

He stared at the screen, trying to decide if he should reach out to the federal agents he'd just met or contact the police . . . Or if he should answer this call from the man who'd gotten him involved in all this in the first place.

The earlier calls that'd come in for him were on his mind.

His gut knotted up with apprehension as he accepted the call.

"Hello, Mr. Reese." It wasn't Ibrahim but another man, a voice Jake didn't recognize.

"What have you done?"

"I might ask you the same question. Leaving your kid alone like that in the car?"

"Where is he? Is he safe? I swear to God, if you hurt him, if you even—"

"Oh, he's not hurt. Yet. We were going to pay Toby a visit at his day care center, but imagine our surprise when you didn't even drop him off. You must have a lot on your mind, Mr. Reese, to be so distracted. What will your wife say when she finds out what you did? When she receives the video we took of that little boy in the car and—"

"Let me talk to him."

"Unless you did it on purpose. Did you do it on—"

"Let me talk to him!"

Jake heard crying in the background. It became louder as the man brought the phone closer to his son. Jake spoke reassuringly to Toby, and then, when he heard him say, "Dada!" it was all he could do to keep from crying himself.

"Dada's here. I'm coming to see you. I love you."

"Love you, Dada!"

Under his breath, Jake cursed the man who'd taken his son, but he stilled his tongue so he wouldn't upset Toby's captors and put the boy in any more danger than he was already in.

The man came back on the line. "You have something that we need shipped. Once you've delivered the canisters to our people at the airport, we'll deliver your son to you. Don't call the authorities. If you want to see Toby alive again, you know what you need to do. We want the canisters there within the next two hours."

"I don't have a car! I couldn't help you even if I wanted to!"

"Use the car that's parked in the spot where yours was. It's unlocked. The keys are under the driver's seat. Make the delivery. You do, and little Toby will be fine. You don't, and we'll park your car somewhere in the desert where no one would think to look, and we'll leave him inside it, strapped in that car seat just like he was when you left him to die. In fact, we might be on our way to doing that right now. Time is ticking, Jake. You have two hours and not a minute more."

++++

It took me a while, but I found a story about the death of a blogger from Baltimore named Thomas Kewley.

He died two months ago, chewing on razor blades until he bled to death. I couldn't find any evidence that his death had been broadcast live online when he died. There was no suicide note.

Kewley was found at home, and I added the location of

his residence to the case files. Perhaps analyzing the location and timing in connection with the other suicides would be enough to discern something about the travel routes of the observer who was present during the deaths.

If it was even the same person in each instance.

And if he was even there at Kewley's place.

It was worth a closer look.

So, mobile phone records.

Your cell phone is constantly tracking you as it looks for greater signal strength—and that means it's searching for and connecting with different cell towers. The resultant data is used by phone companies to help them develop their networks. Subpoenaing those records is common for law enforcement. Yes, there has been pushback from privacy rights and civil liberties groups that have brought lawsuits regarding when and how we use that information, but so far the Bureau has managed to justify the searches and they've remained legal.

All that—not to mention what NSA does on the books and off them—provides us with robust resources for tracking the pathways of mobile phones and smart device locations. Between the phone companies and NSA, tracing where a person has been is not nearly as difficult or implausible as it was just five years ago.

To better identify any connection between the suicides, I sent in a request to Cyber for the phone records of the previous victims. Incoming calls, outgoing ones, locations, anything. Since they were suicides and not homicides, I was notified that it might take twenty-four to forty-eight hours to get the data.

"I'll take it as soon as I can get it," I said.

Sasha had mentioned that Blake had killed a man

named Aaron Jasper and had brought up the Matchmaker in relationship to him. We had Aaron's prints on file, but they didn't match any prints found at the senator's house.

Maybe the Matchmaker was the person watching the suicides. If so, what, if anything, did that have to do with the death of the blogger Thomas Kewley?

I didn't know.

Then, thinking of what Greer had said about convincing someone to harm himself, I tried following up with Ralph, who was looking for people who might've benefited from the suicide victims' deaths, but he didn't pick up.

I spent some time reviewing the security footage of Mannie's escape. He didn't appear to speak with anyone. The fight with Thurman was brief and it didn't look like words were exchanged. DeYoung still needed to give me approval for the work records of the staff who were on duty when Mannie fled.

Alright.

Back to the suicides.

Timing and location.

Somewhere there was a link between these victims. I just needed to figure out what it was.

47

Blake evaluated things.

Within the hour he would know about the canisters, and Reese's little boy would either be returned to his daddy or would be on his way to experiencing a tragic and rather frightful end.

So that was one thing on his mind.

Then there was the matter of the email with the picture of Julianne Springman's corpse—who'd sent it and why—and the information he was expecting on the quantum encryption findings. It would provide more security for his transactions overseas, especially with the arms dealers he was in communication with.

And, of course, who was the person who gave up the location of the condo? After meeting with Ibrahim at the greenhouse, Blake had become convinced that the jihadist was not the leak.

He was thinking that through when Mannie returned.

"I found the origin of the email with the photograph of Miss Springman," Mannie told him. "Or, at least I believe I have."

"Tell me."

"The routing bounced around, pinballed across the globe through half a dozen countries, but from what I can tell, it looks like it originated from a computer in the Jacob K. Javits Federal Building downtown."

"What?"

"I know."

"You're saying it was from the FBI?"

"It could've been, yes. Or the postal service or the U.S. Army Corps of Engineers. They have offices in that building as well."

As far as Blake knew, Timothy Sabian wouldn't have clearance or access to any of those computers. So then, who would have sent it? Someone in the Bureau? But that didn't make sense. How would an agent have gotten ahold of that photo? Was it faked? And again, why was it sent— and how would the sender have gotten this email address in the first place?

The materials you gave Julianne? Maybe Timothy got your information from that—or he may have gotten it from her before killing her.

"What's your take on this?" he asked Mannie.

"For a novelist, Mr. Sabian is either a lot more skilled at hacking or a lot more connected than I would have guessed."

"Or it wasn't him."

"Yes."

Although Blake didn't want to get distracted by this, he did want some answers. "Mannie, it's time we find out more about that young man and what he's truly capable of."

"And Reese? The canisters?"

"It's being handled by the team in Phoenix."

"What about his son?"

"We'll have to see how things go."

Mannie hesitated slightly. "Alright."

After his associate stepped away, Blake thought of one other place where the leak might have originated. He put through a call to the escort. "Sasha, it's me."

"Hey."

"I'd like to see you."

"I'd like to see you too."

"You snuck out on me last night."

"I have . . . There are other clients that I work with."

"Of course. Are you free today?"

"When?"

"What about right now?"

"I'm free."

"Where are you? I'll send a car to pick you up."

"I can come to where you are."

"It's not a problem, Sasha. I'll send someone for you."

"Alright." She told him a location on the Lower East Side. "I'll be waiting."

++++

Sasha hung up.

She had to decide whether or not to tell anyone that Blake had just contacted her. On the one hand, she wanted to keep it to herself to avoid alerting any personnel who might have been compromised from finding out. However, on the other hand, she knew that since she was working with the Bureau now, transparency was important.

Greer was in the office with her and must have noticed how conflicted she looked because he said to her, "You alright?"

"Yeah."

So, fill him in or not?

Do it.

Cooperate with the Bureau.

She told him what was going on. "Do you think I should go? If we arrest the driver, that'll undoubtedly spook Blake, and if he's in the wind, we might have lost our chance of tracking him down. And his men are good. I'm afraid that whoever Blake sends will be able to make us if we have a team waiting."

Greer nodded in agreement. "Let's keep this under wraps. Right now we don't know who you can trust. I'll back you up. Take a tracking device. When they pick you up, we'll be one step ahead of them. I'll follow you and call your DEA supervisor to get a support team in place as soon as we've confirmed a location. Blake is ours."

++++

"Hello?" Christie stepped through the front door of their apartment and tugged her luggage inside. "Tessa? Are you here?"

"Hey, Mom." The voice came from her daughter's bedroom. "I'll be right there."

Christie closed the door behind her and noticed five pumpkins on the kitchen counter just as Tessa came down the hallway.

"Pumpkins?" Christie asked curiously.

"Patrick's been teaching me to drive. Those are the pedestrians. How was your trip?"

"It was good. The pedestrians?"

"I'm not supposed to run 'em over. You need a hand?"

"Yeah, but first a hug."

Tessa was not a hugger, but Christie was glad that today she at least put up with a brief one before helping to navigate the luggage down the hall toward the master bedroom.

"What'd you pack in this thing?" Tessa grunted. "Bricks?"

"Books. Plus I bought a few at the gift shop."

"A monastery with a gift shop. Sure, why not?"

They made it to the room. "So have you hit any yet?" Christie asked.

"Hit any?"

"Pedestrians."

"We might have started with a couple more, I guess, but I'm getting better. He won't let me drive on actual roads yet, just the parking lot."

"One step at a time. You need that license first."

"Yeah, but it sucks. Oh, we went to church yesterday."

"And how was that?"

"Boring."

"Okay."

Christie unzipped her suitcase and handed a shirt that she hadn't worn to Tessa to hang in the closet.

"The pastor told Patrick and me that we're supposed to greet you in the glorious name of Jesus. So consider yourself gloriously greeted."

"Ah. So it was Dr. Williams."

"Amazing deduction there."

"What was the sermon about?"

"Something about God. Oh, and Patrick tracked my cell phone. Can you believe that?"

"What do you mean?" Christie was working her way through her suitcase, sorting out the clean clothes from the ones she'd worn. "What happened?"

"I was waiting for him in the lobby of the federal building—he had some sort of meeting and brought me along—but I can't really complain 'cause I always ask him to take me there anyway—but the point is, it was taking him forever, so I went to get something to eat and he freaked out."

"He was probably just worried."

"Yeah, but I was only, like, a block away."

"Well, he loves you. He's concerned about you."

"He—wait. What did you say?"

"Patrick. He's concerned for you."

"No. Before that."

"He loves you."

"Do you really think so?"

"Yes. But he doesn't know how to show it yet. Give it some time. He's still new at this stepdad thing."

Tessa was quiet.

Christie tossed her dirty clothes into the hamper, then handed Tessa three books to place on the shelf: *The Cloud of Unknowing*, *Dark Night of the Soul*, and *The Way of a Pilgrim*.

"So really, though," Tessa said, "how was your weekend?"

"Nice. Quiet. Reflective. Gave me a place to think some things through."

"Like what?"

"Oh, some personal things."

"Okay."

"I'm not trying to be overly secretive. I just needed some time to myself."

"Was it me?"

"You?"

"Yeah. Did I do something?"

"Oh. No. Absolutely not. It's me. It's just me."

"You sure it wasn't me?"

"I'm positive."

"Okay," Tessa said, but not right away. "Gotcha."

++++

It wasn't unusual for me to lose myself in my work, and when I checked the time at last, I saw that it was almost four o'clock.

The agents who spoke with Reese in Phoenix hadn't found out anything—though they did note that he seemed a little less than forthcoming.

Calvin had promised to contact me, but I still hadn't heard from him. There was some paperwork for him to fill out if he was going to be officially brought in to consult on this case and, before we went any further with discussing things, I needed him to complete those forms, but he didn't answer when I tried his cell.

It's common to do a tox screen after a suicide to see if there were any contributing factors—alcohol, illegal drugs, prescription meds that might cause suicidal tendencies—so we had the results from the other deaths. They confirmed that each of the people had Selzucaine in their systems.

If we could discover where they got the drug, then finding their dealer might be the way for us to track down Blake or the Matchmaker.

However, since the suicides were in three different states, I anticipated that it would be unlikely that the victims all purchased drugs from the same person.

Also, if we could match the shipping locations of the

silent ladies with known drug distributors in the cities in which the victims lived, it might lead us somewhere helpful.

Maybe that's what Mannie meant when he said to follow the Selzucaine back to the source.

I sent an email to Sasha and cc'd Ralph requesting more info on Selzucaine trafficking and known dealers.

I thought that since the videos were posted live online there must be some way for the potential victims to contact the observer who was there when they died. So I studied the Internet histories of the victims and found that they all frequented the same chat room. It didn't appear to be a suicide club, as Calvin had mentioned, but rather a dating site.

The Matchmaker.

Oh. Okay. If that was the case, then it fit in a grisly way: he was setting up the victims with the person who would watch them die.

Too many investigators come up with a theory and then try to prove it. Calvin taught me to do the opposite—to hypothesize and then try to find flaws in the theory. "The truth will withstand all inquiries," he told me once. "Vigorously try to disprove yourself. When you can no longer do so, you are finally on the pathway towards a valid deduction regarding the case."

Never assume. Hypothesize, test, revise.

I passed the information along to Cyber to analyze and to see if they could trace the location of the site's administrator.

Greer had come through for me and gotten a reservation tonight at seven at Giuseppe's, and I'd sent a text to Christie that I would meet her there. Now I heard back from her, letting me know that she was home from the airport and was looking forward to seeing me at the restaurant.

Pumpkins, huh? she texted.

Cheaper than hiring agile pedestrians.

I'll meet you at 7.

See you in a couple hours.

++++

Timothy considered canceling tonight's book signing.

No, no, no. You can't. You have to go. People might get suspicious. If they get suspicious, they might come looking. And if they come looking, they'll find out what you did to Julianne.

He wanted to tell the voice that he hadn't done anything to Julianne, but there she was, dead and cold upstairs in his bedroom.

Resting in his bed.

He said nothing.

Alright.

He would go to the signing, and afterward he would figure out what to do with the body. Something permanent. Something that wasn't going to bring any suspicion onto him.

Thinking about her caused him to be distracted and made it hard to decide what section of his book to read at the signing. His muscles were aching, one of the symptoms of his condition—exacerbated, no doubt, from the fatigue of shoveling out that hole earlier in the day—and he felt like he had no energy, like he was spiraling down and down and down, deeper into some sort of obsidian sadness. He didn't like the word "depression," had never liked it. He wondered if he should start taking his meds again.

No, the drugs take too long to work anyway, and remember how they dull everything? Muting the good, the bad, making you live in a living fog? Don't take the meds. You can handle this on your own.

Timothy paged through the novel Julianne had read to him when he met her at the waterfront, and then reviewed the next chapter. Maybe this was what he was looking for. Maybe this was the section to read tonight at the bookstore.

Maybe maybe maybe maybe.

48

Deer Valley Airport
Phoenix, Arizona

Jake Reese swallowed tightly and stared across the steaming tarmac at the private jet thirty yards away. Three men stood next to it. One of them set Toby's car seat beside him on the ground; the other two flanked him and held some sort of assault rifles.

Toby was quiet. Not a peep from the car seat.

Jake was terrified. From where he stood, he couldn't tell if his son was alive or not.

"Is he okay?" he called to them.

"Sleeping," the man in the middle replied. "Do you have the canisters?"

"I'm not giving you anything until I know he's okay!"

"Do you want me to shake him? Pinch him? Make him cry?"

Jake worked his jaw back and forth. "Don't touch him. What you want is in the trunk of my car. Come and get it."

"You try anything, your son dies."

"I understand."

The man in charge of the car seat nodded to one of his associates, who strode forward to look in Jake's car.

Jake unlocked it, popped the trunk, and stepped back.

Somewhat cautiously, the guy peered inside, then inspected the two sizable canisters and announced, "They're here. We're good."

"They're sealed?"

"They're sealed."

The man looming over Toby nodded toward Jake, who immediately rushed forward, trembling, to get his boy.

Toby was still quiet.

Jake dropped to his knees. "Toby?" he gasped. "Dada's here."

The child didn't stir.

Jake unbuckled him, eased him from the car seat, and lifted him gently toward his chest.

"Toby, oh my Toby." His words became a desperate plea to the God he wasn't even sure he believed in. "You're okay, I know you're okay."

Finally, Toby sniffled and opened his eyes. He threw his arms around his father's neck and made no sound but just held on, clinging to him, loving him, this man who'd accidentally left him behind in their car to die.

"Our business here is concluded," the man who'd brought Toby said. "If you try anything, if you tell anyone what you've done or the research you were involved in for us, we know where you live. And we will find you if you try to run."

"I won't try to run."

"Alright."

"Are you the real Ibrahim?"

"That's no concern of yours."

"Are you Fayed Raabi'ah Bashir?"

"Keep asking questions you don't need to know the

answer to and see how well that works out for your family. How long will it take to synthesize?"

"You don't want to mix those two chemicals early. They're inert when separate—ideal for shipping. But they'll become potent when mixed together. Wait until you land in New York. Remember that once they're mixed, they'll reach their prime potency in four to five hours. Give it five to be safe."

"And the effects?"

"When snorted with the Selzucaine . . . Well, I guarantee you'll get the results you're hoping for."

Mixing a stimulant hallucinogenic, like Selzucaine, with an anesthetic analgesic depressant, like Tranadyl, would produce a similar effect to a speedball, when you shoot up heroin and cocaine.

A potent drug interaction that led to waves of euphoria and then a crash.

And then euphoria again.

Quite a ride, until you die of an arrhythmia or you bottom out into a coma.

Yes, he had sold his soul to the devil. But at least he'd saved his son. The brain-muddled addicts would eventually shoot up or snort their way into the grave anyway— they were just getting what they deserved.

No. No one deserves that.

Jake did his best to quiet his conscience, to beat it down with his well-rehearsed rationalizations.

"Five hours," the man said. "Alright. I understand."

Then Jake took his son home to spend as much time with him as he could before his past found him out and caught up with him for good, which he was becoming more and more convinced would eventually occur.

49

I finished skimming Vidocq, still unsure what specifically Calvin wanted me to glean from the memoirs of the pioneering detective.

However, I did take away a few of Vidocq's hints: Go where the criminals are, gain their confidence, and get them to respect you, to like you, even. Use subterfuge whenever necessary.

Good advice, reinforced by my own personal experiences.

It was just after six, and I started gathering my things to head out for my dinner date with Christie when Ralph stopped by my office to tell me that Senator Murray had gambling debts that he was keeping quiet.

"How do we know this?"

"Greer sent me a memo. I'll forward it to you. He said it took some digging."

"Well, if Murray does have debts and his son knew about them, it's possible that he really was speaking to his father when he said, 'This is for you,' just as Mannie claimed."

"You think someone paid to cover his dad's debts and then watched him commit suicide in return?"

"I'm not sure what I think, but that's a possibility."

I knew we were drifting into speculation, but when you're working a case with so many variables, sometimes it's helpful to just throw ideas out there and see where they lead.

"Is this you looking for motive?" Ralph asked me.

"It's me looking for answers."

Ten years ago I never would've believed the scenario we'd laid out here, but today, with the upsurge of live-feed suicides and homicides, it was, tragically, not that incomprehensible.

"I couldn't find any legislation that the senator is currently reviewing that appears to be directly related to the case," he said. "However, he has a pet project right now dealing with new technology in encryption and Internet privacy."

"Internet privacy?"

"I know—and then his son dies while live-streaming his suicide. He's on a committee that's examining the practicality of instituting quantum encryption capabilities in our military networks. With all that we know about this form of sending data, it's unhackable. There might be something there. I'm going to keep looking into it."

"Listen," I said, "I found evidence that a blogger and freelance journalist named Thomas Kewley from Baltimore took his own life. Based on my conversation with Calvin, Kewley was likely onto the Matchmaker when it happened."

"Hmm . . . Have you heard anything more from Werjonic?"

"No, not since we spoke at lunch. I tried calling him a little while ago, but he didn't pick up."

Ralph saw me straightening my tie instead of loosening it, which would've been more natural for me to do at this time of day.

He looked at me quizzically.

"Big date with Christie," I explained. "Welcoming her back to the city."

"Nice. When this is all over, maybe the four of us can get together—you, Christie, Brin, and me."

"Sounds good."

"Hey, you don't by any chance know where Sasha is, do you?"

"The last time I saw her was about an hour ago. She was working with Greer on the Selzucaine connection."

"Yeah. I wanted to speak with her about that. I pulled up a number of leads on who the major distributors are along the East Coast."

"Check in with Greer at his office. It's on the eighteenth floor. She's probably up there."

"Gotcha."

"By the way, you ever hear of Vidocq?" I asked.

"What's that, some yoga pose? Yogurt brand? Some sort of French cheese?"

"A French detective, actually. He lived about two hundred years ago. Calvin bought me a book of his memoirs. Calvin seemed to indicate that it has something to do with the case, but I'm not sure what that might be."

We left my office, and Ralph walked beside me toward the elevator bay.

"Hey," he said. "How well do you know Greer?"

"Why do you ask?"

"I don't know. A vibe."

"A vibe?"

"Okay, we'll call it a gut feeling. And not a good one."

"I'm not a big believer in gut feelings."

"I know."

"Did he do something to make you suspicious?"

"No. Nothing in particular."

"I don't know him extremely well, but he's a straight shooter. I trust him."

"Alright. That's enough for me."

We reached the elevators.

"Say hi to Christie for me."

"Will do. Keep me up to speed."

A nod.

"And let me know what you find out from Sasha," I added.

"I will."

++++

free

wonder

thinking losing spinning memory turning once again.

briskly fading go season's viewing sharply they blur

   now unfocused again . . .

The words tilted and jumbled through Timothy's head. All a mess. Nonsense.

Or maybe not.

He tried to make sense of them, tried to put them into sentences, but found it hard to focus, hard to concentrate.

Mental deterioration.

"No. No, that's not it."

Fear and madness and pain.

And madness.

And pain.

Stay on track, Timothy. Focus!

"But how, when there's a dead body in my bed?"

He took a deep breath and stared at the mirror. He hadn't wanted to come upstairs because of Julianne's corpse in his bedroom just down the hall, but this was where he kept the lotions and anti-itch creams.

And truthfully, part of him wanted to make sure she was still there, that she hadn't somehow moved from where he'd left her.

He saw that she had not. Not even a little.

Now, he stood naked in front of the mirror and squeezed some aloe vera gel onto his palm.

It felt cool and tingly to the touch as he slathered it across his arm. He also spread some on his stomach and over his legs where more sores had begun to appear. He probably used too much because it ended up being globby and gooey even after he spread it out, but it did calm down the itching a bit—at least enough for him to shift his attention to preparing for the book signing.

As he gazed at himself in the mirror, it struck him that he was deteriorating quickly. He hadn't realized how much scratching he'd been doing and how much the sores with those tiny black fibers in them had spread. That's what happens when the bugs get under the skin. They can spread anywhere.

"Alright, it's time," he said. "Get dressed, Timothy.

Get ready." He wasn't sure why he spoke the words aloud.

Focus!

Timothy steeled himself and then walked into the bedroom to get his clothes.

From research for his novels, he knew that corpses will typically give off a strong odor after twenty-four to thirty-six hours, but if the air is warm enough, it can start much sooner. So, when he brought her up here, he'd kept the window open and let the weather that had winter in its throat leak into the room. He didn't have perfume, but he did have some cologne, which he sprayed onto her wrists and cheeks as a security measure, a way to help. Just in case.

Thankfully, the bad odors had not yet come.

But he didn't sniff her closely because he knew they were on their way.

He found a black turtleneck long enough to cover the length of his arms and the scratches on his neck from when he was nervous before his fight with Julianne, and tugged it on.

You must not let anyone see. You must not let anyone know.

As he thought about the signing tonight, Julianne spoke to him from the bed: *"Read something about Emily. Something about the girl. Do that and I won't bother you anymore. Do that and I'll leave you alone."*

He didn't want to hear anything more from Julianne, didn't want to have her arguing with him, especially after he was away from the house and was in public, so he slipped out of the bedroom, left his novel on the table, grabbed his journal with the handwritten draft of what he was working on with Emily, and then hurried outside to catch the train that would take him into the heart of the city.

++++

Sasha MacIntyre climbed into the executive car.

She had on a body-hugging dress and wore a thigh holster with a 9mm Ruger LC9s. The options for a concealed carry with this outfit were limited, but that was alright. She preferred the thigh holster anyway because, even if she was patted down, most men who frisk women don't tuck their hands on the inside of her thighs when they check for a weapon. It's just too intimate of a gesture.

And that worked to her advantage.

She had a small tracking chip inside the heel of her left shoe.

Blake wasn't waiting for her in the backseat of the car, but one of his men was. She'd been hoping that maybe it would be Mannie, but instead, it was one of the goons who'd brought Aaron Jasper to Blake yesterday, right before he shot him in the forehead.

"I'll need your phone," the man said to her.

"My phone?"

"Rules are rules."

Somewhat hesitantly, she passed it to him. In return, he held out a sweating bottle of water.

"Thirsty?" he said.

"I'm good, thanks."

"Blake wanted to make sure you were taken care of. Have some water. It's good to stay hydrated. Right?"

She considered her options.

The tracking device would be enough for Greer to follow if by some chance the water was drugged and she went unconscious or Greer lost the car in traffic. So, she reassured herself that this time, at least, she would not be venturing into Blake's snake pit alone.

She accepted the water bottle, unscrewed the cap, and took a drink.

50

Christie turned sideways and looked at her profile in the mirror. "Well?" she asked her daughter.

"Honestly?"

"Honestly."

"He's not gonna be able to take his eyes off you."

For tonight, Christie had chosen the most elegant evening gown that she owned. Silky and the color of midnight.

"You don't think it's too much?"

"With that slash in the side of it, I don't think you have to worry about the dress being too *much*."

"I'm just wondering if—"

"No, yeah, I know. Seriously, Mom. You look great. Actually, you look hot, but it would just be too weird to say my mom looks hot so let's just stick with great."

"Thanks."

"Okay, so I heard this thing that in India they sometimes ask women: 'You're stuck in a castle and you can't leave. You get to choose—you can either have one dress and a mirror, or a thousand dresses and no mirror. Which would it be?'"

"I'd take the thousand dresses and then look at my re-

flection in the castle's silver candlesticks." Christie spritzed
a touch of perfume on her neck.

"Ha. That's cheating. You have to choose."

"Hmm. Then I think I'd go with the one dress and the
mirror. What does that say about me? Vanity?"

"I wouldn't read too much into it."

"You?"

"I'd take the thousand dresses, tie them together to
make a rope, and climb down from the castle tower to get
away."

"That sounds like cheating too."

Tessa shrugged.

Christie wanted to tell Pat about her diagnosis at dinner, but she was torn.

She felt the need to put everything on the table and
figure out what the next step should be; however, she also
wanted to simply enjoy tonight with no stress, no pressure,
not letting thoughts of death and grief edge in on their
time together.

And, of course, she didn't want to lose it and start crying at a fancy restaurant.

So, there was that.

In the end, she decided that it would be best to play it
by ear, see how things went and tell him only what she felt
led in the moment to say.

Led by who? By God?

Is he really guiding any of this at all?

"And you're going to that book signing?" she asked
Tessa.

"Yeah."

"It's a school night. I want you back by ten thirty."

A sigh. "In honor of your being home again, I'm not gonna argue, but give it time, and then I'll be back to my endearingly obstinate adolescent self again."

"Sounds like a plan."

Normally, Christie didn't wear much makeup or jewelry, but tonight she borrowed some of Tessa's mascara, then touched up her lipstick and found the turquoise teardrop necklace Pat had given her when they were engaged and slipped it on.

"What's the occasion anyway, Mom?"

"Going home."

"Don't you mean coming home?"

"Yes, sorry. Coming home."

Christie found her clutch purse and reminded her daughter to be safe.

"I will. It's just a book signing. No big deal."

"Yes. Okay."

Then Christie headed out the door to hail a cab.

++++

Unlike the gridlike streets surrounding it, Greenwich Village has narrow, winding roads.

Christie mentioned to me one time that she'd read that the Village had been quarantined from the rest of the city because of cholera outbreaks in the 1800s while road construction was happening all around it. Afterward, they'd never corrected things, never straightened the roads out, leaving those distinctive serpentine streets.

Death had caused this corner of the city to remain anomalous and unique.

While thinking about that, on the way to the restaurant, I swung by a florist to pick up a rose for my wife.

++++

The man who'd been watching Timothy Sabian through the hidden camera in the novelist's living room had planned to attend the book signing, but now some obligations at work were interfering with that plan.

He was also the one who'd shown up at the pier when Timothy was out there getting involved in some mischief by the trunk of his car.

Earlier in the day, through the video feed, he'd observed Timothy carrying Julianne's body up from the basement.

It gave him an idea for a climax that would both be memorable and wrap things up with a neat and permanent bow.

It was time for some closure.

Time to move on.

It was just a matter of finding exactly the right victim to end on before killing Timothy, the boy he had raised until that monumental night when Timothy called 911 and told the police what his father liked to do in their basement.

++++

After her mom left, Tessa doodled in the church bulletin she was using as a bookmark in the Timothy Sabian novel Patrick had bought for her.

She turned the bulletin over to the empty space that was left for taking sermon notes and jotted,

I wish that I could paint the spaces
    between the colors,

pronounce the silences
   between the words,
bridge the gaps
   between my thoughts.

I wish that I could touch the light
that threads its way through
   the ever-present
   rays of darkness
   all around me.

The waters of this moment
rush over my head.
I drink in the truth
and find that it tastes
   like tears
just as I suspected.

She slipped the bulletin back into the novel to mark her place, grabbed a quick bite for dinner, then, taking the book with her, she left for Timothy Sabian's signing at the Mystorium.

51

From my experience, there isn't necessarily a moment when you realize that it really is true love.

Sometimes it only occurs to you after the fact. After you kiss your woman, or you ease aside a trail of hair that has glanced down across her cheek, or you feel her take your hand and intertwine her fingers just so, in the way that only she does, and you realize, "I'm in love with this person. I am—and I have been for a while. I want to be with her forever."

However, sometimes it does happen on the spot. A wink or an unpretentious smile, a spur-of-the-moment decision to steal a kiss, or a slow dance that goes on just long enough to speak its own language. It's true love. Love at first sight. Yes, it happens. Yes, it does. It's not just for the fairy tales, it's for real-life lovers searching for real-life love.

For Christie and me, it was definitely attraction at first sight, and although it wasn't love right off the bat, that was not long in coming.

When I'm with her, somehow everything becomes more confusing and clearer at the same time. It's like I'm more confident but also more unsure of myself, both freer to be myself and more thankful to be entwined in someone else's life. It's tough to explain, but it's also the best feeling in the world.

I arrived at the restaurant about ten minutes early and told the hostess my name.

"We have you down for a table for two," the young woman told me. "We're getting it ready now. Would you like to wait here up front, or shall I take you back?"

"I can wait here." I showed her the rose. "Listen, if there's any way, could we get this to our server so he can deliver it to my wife when he brings out our meal?"

She accepted it to take to the back and smiled warmly. "You are such a romantic. Your wife is a lucky woman."

++++

Carrying the Timothy Sabian novel, Tessa entered the bookstore.

She'd been to the Mystorium so often that she could've probably worked here if she'd wanted to. She knew all the nooks and crannies of the sprawling, labyrinthine store and had even had to watch the cash register for Rebekah a few times when she went into the back room to get more cash or rolls of receipt paper.

Already, there were two dozen people or so packed into the largest space available. Rebekah was setting up folding chairs.

Tessa asked if she needed a hand.

"I should be good. I'm almost done. So, have you ever heard him speak before?"

"No. Actually, this is the first book signing I've ever been to."

"Oh, well, we've only had him here once before. If it's anything like last time, he'll probably read a little from his work in progress, do a Q and A, and then sign." Rebekah paused, and her eyes lit up slightly, but just enough for Tessa to notice. "It's really good to have him back."

A tiny smile. "Are you crushing on this guy?"

Rebekah cleared her throat. "Never."

"Uh-huh."

When Rebekah glanced at the pile of novels on the table up front, Tessa felt vaguely guilty that she hadn't purchased her book here. She started an apology: "I guess I shouldn't have brought this in. I should've bought one from you."

Rebekah waved that off. "Totally fine."

Tessa found a seat in the back and waited for Timothy Sabian to come in.

++++

Timothy emerged from the subway tunnel.

Do not scratch your arm, he reminded himself. *Just read a little bit about Emily, sign the books, and get back home.*

Social anxiety. Brain fog. Scattered thinking. All of it. It's happening to you. It's permanent.

"No," he told the voice. "We have a choice. We always have a choice. We can fight it. We can win."

From here, it was less than a five-minute walk to the bookstore.

++++

When Christie stepped out of the taxi, she took my breath away.

She wore an elegant black evening gown with a slit that revealed just enough of her willowy leg to be a distraction to me but yet still remain appropriate for a good conservative Baptist girl to wear in public.

Well, okay, maybe not that last part.

When she saw me walking out to meet her, she smiled demurely.

"You look stunning," I told her. "Every guy in this restaurant is going to be jealous of me."

She blushed. Shy with a touch of sly. "You look quite fetching yourself, Dr. Bowers."

"Thank you."

I took her hand to lead her inside.

"I told you I'd come up with a tongue twister for tonight," she said.

"Okay, do you have one?"

"Check test texts. Try it. Five times fast."

I started but fumbled after just two attempts. "That's a good one. You go."

She did it. No hesitation. Amazing.

"You've been practicing," I said.

"Maybe," she told me elusively.

I made a valiant attempt at the "extinct insects" twister I'd shared with her earlier in the day but managed to flub it up epically.

"You'll get there," she said.

Inside the restaurant, our server directed us to a table near the back, in a secluded corner away from the main dining area. Candlelight. Linen napkins. Elegant wine flutes. Way too many pieces of silverware for me to be able to use in a single meal. The whole deal.

I pulled the chair out for Christie, and she took a seat. "Was it hard to get a table here?" she asked.

"Not when you know the right people."

"Impressive. Mr. Connected."

"Just one of my many fine talents."

"Hmm. And is another one of them being humble?"

"Absolutely."

When the server brought the wine list, I wondered at first if they'd accidentally printed an extra zero after each of the prices. I said to Christie, "Whatever you want tonight, go for it. Let's make this special."

Our server's eyes lit up, and he directed her attention to the bottom of the list, which he definitely did not need to do. However, she didn't take his advice and chose one instead from the middle of the list, a 2006 Vina Cobos Marchiori Vineyard Malbec from Perdriel, Argentina.

"Bottle or glass?" the server, whose name tag read BEN-JAMIN, asked.

"Bottle," I said.

Benjamin gave a pleased nod, and as he returned to the kitchen, Christie said, "Are you sure?"

"We don't do this enough. Just the two of us. It's been too long. Now, tell me about your weekend."

52

The people milling around the Mystorium settled into their chairs.

The crowd had grown since Tessa had taken a seat, and Rebekah had run out of folding chairs. Tessa gave up her chair to a gray-haired lady who looked a little unsteady on her feet and kind of reminded her of Patrick's mom, whom she'd met a couple of months ago at the wedding.

"Are you sure, young lady?"

"Yeah. No problem. I promise."

As Tessa went to stand in the back, a man entered the bookstore, and she recognized him right away from the photo on the back flap of his book jacket as Timothy Sabian. He didn't look a ton older than her, though she knew from the author bio in the book that he was in his late twenties.

Okay, yeah, he was cute. Too old, probably. No—definitely too old. But still cute.

No wonder Rebekah had a thing for him.

The people in the audience smiled at him and whispered to each other as he passed.

"That's him," the woman two rows up from Tessa said admiringly to the man beside her.

Tessa wondered what it would be like to be famous like that, even in just a little corner of the world.

Probably flattering and annoying—both—at the same time.

You want the solace of privacy but can't find it, and your fame gets in the way of every friendship you have because you could never really know what the friendship is based on—a desire to *be* with you or to *be seen* with you.

Rebekah spoke briefly with Timothy, then led him to the table up front and welcomed everyone to the signing. "So, I'm super-excited that we have an *amazing* author with us tonight. I've read all of his books, and if you haven't read them, you're gonna love 'em. Seriously, they're fabulous. Timothy Sabian has written seven best-selling novels, all of which have appeared on the *New York Times* bestseller list. He's imaginative, provocative, brilliant, and knows how to send a chill down your spine, and I'm glad to introduce him to everybody here. Please give a big hand to Timothy Sabian."

++++

Sasha eased out of the executive car and looked around.

She felt slightly off center, somewhat unsteady on her feet, and guessed that her water had indeed been laced with something.

The sporadic exterior lights revealed that the property held five expansive greenhouses and what appeared to be an office building. Through the glass of the greenhouses, she could see that one of them was filled with mannequins.

What's going on here?

"Blake's waiting for you inside." Her driver pointed toward the office building. "You first."

He didn't pat her down. Didn't even bother.

She didn't see any sign that Greer had followed her.

Good. He was doing his job and staying out of sight.

++++

Our wine arrived.

In keeping with Christie's tradition, we ordered dessert first while we considered our entrée options. I chose the *Délices d'amande*, which the translation app on my phone told me was "almond delight." The menu described it as *Roasted almond mousse, whipped vanilla cream, shaved almond, and tuile*.

I didn't know what "tuile" was, but everything else sounded good, and I figured that at this price, whatever tuile was, it would fit in there with those other items in a tasty way.

Christie chose *La douce évasion*, the "sweet escape," which the menu told us was *Warm chocolate ganache, brandied cherries, and Tahitian vanilla ice cream*.

Benjamin looked a bit confused. "And you are saying that you wish for me to bring the dessert out *before* the main dish?"

"Yes. Please," Christie told him.

"And no appetizers?"

"If we have room we'll order them after our meal."

"Yes, of course." He spoke respectfully but was clearly curious about our backward ordering process. "As you wish."

After he left, I offered a toast. "To our future together."

Christie paused slightly, but then she smiled and tapped her wineglass against mine. "To our future together."

After we'd both taken a drink, I said, "Well?"

"Well?"

"The wine. What do you think?"

"I think it's worth the price."

I wasn't entirely convinced, but she was much more of a wine connoisseur than I was, so I took her word for it.

"Oh." She took out her phone. "I wanted to show you some pictures from the monastery."

She scrolled to them and was about to hand the phone across the table when she must have realized that it would be easier to describe the photos if she was seated next to me, because she scooted her chair around the edge of the table until she was by my side.

The first picture showed the inside of the church—a simple, vacant space with an area up front designated for the monks and another, farther back, for parishioners or those who might be worshipping with them.

"Did you join the monks in their chanting and prayer times?" I asked her.

"Not too much."

"Were they in Latin?"

"Sometimes, yes. But even when the words were in English I wasn't quite sure what to make of them. Everything seemed to be in a minor key, even when they were singing about the joy of the Lord. It was as if they were somberly going through words that should have elicited the exact opposite response. For me, there was a disconnect between the mood of the service and the words of Scripture."

"Interesting."

"I'm not trying to be too critical or judgmental. Some of it just didn't feel appropriate to me. I longed for more joy."

"I hear you."

The next photo showed a two-meter-high rock wall encircling a courtyard, and it brought to mind the paradox inherent in the ministry of these contemplative monks: they close themselves off from the world but then welcome the world in, one visitor at a time.

One by one, she explained each picture to me—the gardens and the statues, the Stations of the Cross, the meditation room, and the tranquil ponds across the road from the retreat center itself.

"I went to confession for the first time in my life," she told me.

"Confession? Really?" I couldn't think of a whole lot of sins that she might need to confess. "How did that go?"

"Good, I suppose." She hesitated a long time, and I had the sense that she had more to say, but she chose not to, and I didn't press her.

She returned her chair to the other side of the table. "Over the weekend, I was reading a book about memories and meditation, and it mentioned that people's clearest memories often revolve around the first time they did something, the last time they did it, or the most unique time. So, for example, we don't remember all of the thousands of times we've brushed our teeth, but most people would remember the last time they did, or a time when they were brushing their teeth and something unusual happened to interrupt them."

"Memory conflation," I said. "Yes. It often comes into play in eyewitness accounts and—"

She put her hand on mine. "Pat, let's not talk about work tonight."

"Oh. Right. Sorry. I just . . . It just came out."

"It's okay."

She didn't take her hand away, and that was fine by me.

"You were saying? Memories?"

"Something I want to do tonight. Something to share."

"What's that?"

"Think of the three most special memories you have of us being together."

"How do I choose only three?"

"Keep talking like that and you never know where this evening might lead."

I had some ideas. I liked them.

"I'll go first," she said. She lifted her hand to take a drink of wine. "The first time we met has to be on my list."

"Under the umbrella. In the cool April rain."

"Mm-hmm. My knees went weak when I first saw that scruffy face of yours."

"I had no idea the power of scruff."

"It's what was underneath—but the scruff didn't hurt. You let me take your arm, even though we didn't know each other."

"I remember."

She let out a slightly dreamy breath. "A woman likes a man with enough strength to make her feel safe. I like the strength in your arms, Pat."

"Thank you."

Benjamin brought our dessert and pleasantly asked if we were ready to order our meals. I told him we needed a little more time to decide.

After he left us, Christie told me it was my turn.

"Our first kiss," I said. "That night by the riverfront."

"Mmm. Yes. The taste of your lips. Shimmering city lights reflecting off the river. Very romantic."

"You have a good memory."

"It was a good kiss."

"Yes," I agreed. "It was."

"I was nervous."

"Nervous? Why?"

"I hadn't been dating much over the last few years," she told me. "Kissing much, either."

"You didn't seem out of practice to me."

"And once again, that was the right thing to say."

We both tried our desserts.

I realized that I would be content just ordering a couple more of these tuiles and calling it a night.

"What's memory number two?" I asked.

"This may sound strange, but it was the time I first introduced you to Tessa."

"Really?"

"She'd never had a dad involved in her life, and I'd never found a man who I thought would be good enough as a role model or a father figure to her. But then I found you. You're the two most important people in the world to me, and I was happy she didn't hate you."

"So was I."

"You know how she can be."

"Being opinionated is just part of her charm."

"Okay, now you. Number two."

"Our wedding."

Once we'd decided to get married, we hadn't waited long to do it. Neither of us could think of any reason to put it off—we didn't need to finish graduate school or find a job or move to a new part of the country. We were ready to tie the knot, and Christie pulled the planning for the wedding together faster than I'd ever seen anyone do, except, I suppose, for those who elope.

As far as the dance, we made a deal that Christie would choose two songs, and Tessa and Azaliya could work out the rest. So apart from two eighties love songs—"Desert Moon" by Dennis DeYoung and "Lovesong" by The Cure—we had a night of Russian dance tunes and screamer bands.

But, as Ralph's wife, Brineesha, pointed out, the goal of a wedding isn't to have everything go by without a hitch but to create memories that last a lifetime. "No one is going to forget seeing Ralph out there doing a Russian Cossack dance."

That was true.

Oh yes, that was very true.

Now, I said to Christie, "Over the years, I haven't always known the right thing to say, but the two easiest words I ever said were 'I do.'"

"Pat, you know how to make a woman feel loved."

There was an odd finality to her words that left me momentarily unsettled.

I felt her foot nudge against mine, and at first I wondered if she was simply repositioning her leg underneath the table, but by her smile, I knew it was more than that.

"Alright, what's your third one?" I asked.

"The night you proposed. Central Park. We'd been walking for almost an hour."

"Yes."

"I noticed that your shoe was untied, and when I pointed it out, you knelt down, pulled out the ring, and . . . You were so earnest when you proposed. Were you nervous?"

"Naw."

"Thought so." She took a delicate bite of her dessert. "I never asked, did you plan to have your shoe untied?"

"I'd read that scientists have discovered that the force of impact when a foot hits the ground causes the shoelace to stretch, which loosens the knot, and then when you swing your foot backward, the string relaxes because of the inertial force and loosens. They're studying it to understand how complex structures—such as DNA—fail when—"

"Eh-hem. You were doing so well with being a romantic."

"Ah. Right. Sorry."

"So, the shoelace?"

"Why do you think we walked around so long beforehand? I'd left it loose on purpose. I needed it to come all the way undone and for you to notice."

"Alright, Pat. What's your third memory?"

I entwined her fingers in mine. "The one that's unfolding here, tonight."

I saw the glint of a single tear sneak out of her right eye.

"You okay?" I said.

"I've never been more okay than I am right now."

++++

Timothy read to the silent, attentive crowd.

Emily was not sad that her father was gone. After what she had seen him do, she was glad he wasn't around. But she always wondered if he might return and find her.

And so, as she grew up and was shuffled from one foster family to another, she learned to sleep with her desk light on and her shades drawn, so that she wouldn't see the darkness staring in at her from outside the house.

She was caught between loving him and hating him. Everything she knew about right and wrong told her to hate him, but everything she knew about being a daughter told her to love him.

How do you sort through feelings like that, especially when you're a kid? How can you be expected to know right from wrong? How can you be certain you won't grow up to become just like the one who terrifies you the most?

And as Timothy went on from there, he wasn't sure how much he was reading Emily's story and how much he was recounting his own.

++++

We ordered our meals—Christie went with the pan-fried caramelized Chilean sea bass and I chose a medium-rare T-bone steak, a safe choice from a menu filled with dishes I couldn't pronounce and had no idea what they actually contained.

As we talked, time faded away into nothingness. Love is not just a gift of the heart; it also has a way of harnessing moments and allowing time to become subject to your lover's smile.

It made me feel like nothing could go wrong tonight and that nothing could ever sever the strong cord of love that held us together.

++++

As whatever drug Blake had given her kicked in, Sasha felt more and more bleary, as if the air around her were liquid and everything was beginning to move in slow motion.

Blake strode toward her and welcomed her with a kiss. "Hello, my dear."

The man in the car had taken her phone from her, but she knew Greer had been tracking her. He should be here any minute.

He should be here already.

"Listen, babe," she said to Blake. "I need to use the washroom."

"Of course. It's this way."

53

To Christie, the night was all she had hoped it would be. Now she watched as their server returned, carrying a single rose along with their entrées.

"This is from your thoughtful date," he told her, then asked if they needed anything else.

When she told him that she was good and Pat echoed the sentiment, Benjamin bowed slightly before stepping away.

She smelled the aromatic rose and then laid it softly on the table beside her plate. "That is so sweet of you, Pat."

"You mean the world to me. I don't slow down often enough to let you know that."

Tell him now. This is the perfect moment.

No! Don't ruin this. Let this night be something special. He told you it's one of his favorite memories. Don't turn it into one of his worst.

"What is it?" Pat gave her a concerned look. "Are you okay?"

Don't say it.

"Yes. I'm just a little overwhelmed. Tessa mentioned that you took her to church yesterday."

He tilted his head with curiosity as if to say, "That's quite a transition."

"Tell me about it," Christie said, then took a bite of her sea bass. "About church."

"Um. Well, the sermon was about casting our burdens onto Jesus."

"I understand it was Dr. Williams."

"Tessa again?"

"Yes."

"What's it like, though?" Pat asked. "Dr. Williams had a lot to say about the benefits, but I didn't really catch hold of how it's done."

"How?"

"A person lets Jesus carry his burdens. In theory, it sounds great, Elysian even, but in practice, I'm not sure I understand how it plays out, especially since Christ told his disciples that they had to take up their crosses to follow him. How do you do both at the same time? Let go of a burden and lift one up?"

Although Christie believed that sometimes God worked in mysterious and even ironic ways, the fact that he would lead Pat to ask her such a question—one that she herself needed an answer to—was almost too much.

"You look deep in thought," Pat said.

"Yeah, it's just . . . It's nothing. I'm not sure what to tell you. I think God wants us to bring him our cares and burdens, but"—she tapped the rose stem—"he's also saying that it won't be a bed of roses to follow his ways."

"All too often, this world turns on its saviors."

"Yes, it does."

"And their followers."

"In some cases. Yes," she agreed. "Even casting our

cares onto Jesus doesn't mean we won't feel pain. This is a fractured planet. Too much grief. Too much death."

"I can't argue with you about that."

++++

I waited.

Christie said nothing in reply. Both of us ate in silence for a few minutes, then found somewhat obligatory compliments for the meal, but it was like something significant had shifted, like an invisible wall had settled in between us.

I wondered if she'd taken my questions about Jesus the wrong way and if maybe I'd offended her. I was trying to come up with a way to address that when she said, "Did I ever tell you about the turtles struggling to get to shore?"

"The turtles?"

"When I was maybe eight years old, I loved turtles more than any other animal. For most of my friends it was dogs or kittens or ponies, but for me it was always turtles."

"I knew you liked them. I didn't know you liked them that much."

She nodded. "Well, one night I was watching a documentary on sea turtles and how hard it is for them to survive, to get safely to the waterline after they hatch on shore."

She paused.

"What happened?"

"The filmmakers showed a shoreline spread out with hundreds of sea turtle hatchlings. Seagulls were circling around them, I believe, or carrion birds of some kind. They were swooping down and snatching up the baby turtles as they tried to make their way to the water. I had a stuffed turtle with me that I'd been watching the documentary with, and I held my hand over his eyes so he wouldn't see, and I screamed, 'Why don't they stop them?!' 'Who?' my mother asked. 'The people filming it! Why don't they stop the birds and help the turtles!'"

"What'd she say?"

"She tried to reassure me, telling me that there were so many turtles that many of them were going to make it to the seashore, but then the man narrating the documentary started talking about all the dangers in the sea, including sharks that liked to eat baby turtles, and my mom shut off the television. I was crying and clinging to my stuffed turtle, and all I could think of was all those baby turtles getting eaten by the gulls or making it to the water and thinking they were finally going to be okay, that they were finally safe, and then getting gobbled up by a shark who was prowling that area of the beach, eating turtle after turtle after turtle."

"It must have been terrible to think those things as a little girl."

"I'll never forget how upset I was. Then, after I became a mother myself, when Tessa was little, I watched a documentary on global warming with her, and the filmmakers showed a polar bear cub stranded on an ice floe. She slid into the water to try to swim to the mainland. She struggled more and more to make it, until finally she disappeared beneath the water. Tessa gripped my arm and gasped. 'Did they help her?' I remembered the turtles, so I lied and reassured her. 'Yes. They wouldn't have let her get hurt.' 'Or drown?' 'Yes. Or drown. Once they turned off the cameras, they helped her find her mommy.' She nodded and said, 'Oh. Okay.'"

Since there was so much going on with the case today, I'd brought my phone along. Although it was silenced, I saw the screen light up with an incoming request from Calvin for a video chat.

I ignored it.

Christie continued. "She didn't stop holding my arm until the show was over and she went to her room to play, and I heard her reassuring her teddy bear, Francesca, 'They helped the baby find her mommy again.' I hope she doesn't remember me lying to her, but if she does, I hope she'll forgive me."

The cell went still.

"Sometimes a lie is a gift?" I ventured, trying to discern where she was going with this.

"Sometimes keeping the truth from someone can be a way to show them love."

"But the truth is always the greater gift," I said. "I mean, right?"

She silently stared at her wineglass.

"Is there something you're trying to tell me?" I asked at last. "Did I say something that hurt you?"

"No, you didn't. Not at all."

My phone's screen lit up.

Calvin again.

Maybe he found the Matchmaker.

"You can answer that, Pat," Christie said.

"I don't want it to distract us from tonight, from being together."

"I know. But it's okay. Take it."

"You're sure?"

"It's okay. Really."

I finger-swiped the screen to accept the call.

"Hello, my boy. I might have something for you."

"Yes?"

"The Matchmaker." He gave me an address in the Bronx.

"How did you find this out?"

"Targeted inquiry," he said, as if that explained everything. "He'll disappear if you bring a large police presence. We'll go in quietly. And we must be ready for anything."

"We? No, not we. Just me."

Silence.

"Calvin?"

I repeated his name again but then realized he'd ended the call.

I stared at the phone.

Get there and dissuade him.

"What is it?" Christie asked.

"I think I need to go. Is that alright?"

"Of course. I'd feel guilty if I even tried to keep you here. I'll bring your meal home."

"We can pick this conversation up later. Truth. Lies. Love. The greatest gift."

"Of course."

After kissing her good-bye, I left the restaurant.

++++

Christie watched him go.

She hadn't thought of the turtles or that polar bear cub in years, and now, the more she did, the more she realized that what Pat had said at first was probably true—sometimes a lie is a gift.

And her response felt true as well: Whether people forgive us or not, at times, keeping the truth from them might be the most powerful way to show our love for them.

Maybe Pat and Tessa didn't need to know about the cancer after all. Maybe silence about her condition would be the best way for her to extend her love to them. What right did she have to steal their happiness from them by telling them such tragic news? Silence was a gift she could give, a gift they deserved. Whether they eventually forgave her or not wasn't her main concern—whether or not she could serve them now, was.

++++

In the bathroom, Sasha put a finger down her throat and forced herself to vomit up whatever she'd been drugged with. Rinsing the taste of vomit out of her mouth was difficult, but she did the best she could before she left the restroom to meet with Blake again.

54

Timothy finished reading about Emily and, a bit self-consciously, accepted the applause of the audience at the bookstore.

They'd been entertained by Emily's struggles.

By her pain.

Of course they had. That was what they'd come here to listen to: artfully chronicled accounts of suffering.

In one of the paradoxes of art, people only want to read books about characters who go through the kind of troubles they themselves would never want to experience in real life. Nobody wants to read a story in which everything goes right, and nobody wants to live a life in which everything goes wrong.

It's the predicament of every author. No aspect of life is immune from being picked over for a plot point, a character quirk, a description, the seed of a scene. Pain is material. You become a voyeur on suffering and make a living by re-creating it for others.

And you cannot help but *feel* when you do that. You cannot help but identify with the pain the characters experience.

Now, as Timothy was thinking of Emily's suffering, he looked across the faces of the people in attendance and saw

Miranda Walsh, the young graduate student who'd disappeared six months ago on the night of his last book signing.

No. It can't be.

But there she stood—her blonde hair curling down and landing so gently on her shoulders, her clear innocent eyes, her gentle-shy smile. She was—

She's gone!

Yet there she was.

The woman he had cared about.

The woman he had loved.

And as she opened her mouth, her eyes rolled back and turned ghostly white. And then the dark blood began to seep from her slit throat, oozing down across her lemon-colored dress, leaving behind deep and terrifying stains that would never come out. The crimson evidence of a terrible death at the hands of a terrible man.

There she was.

And then she wasn't.

He blinked and blinked and she didn't return.

You're seeing things again, Timothy! You're losing it!

He tried to pretend that he hadn't just seen what he had, tried to pretend that everything was fine and he was still in control control control.

He scratched at the wretched bugs skittering underneath the turtleneck and across his arm.

Rebekah stood, enthusiastically thanked him for reading, and then announced that it was time for the Q and A.

"Anyone have any questions?" she asked brightly. "It's not every night you get to ask a world-famous novelist about his stories or how he comes up with them."

++++

"Was there something in my water?" Sasha said to Blake, pretending that she was still feeling woozy. "The water that guy in the car gave me?"

"Just something to help you relax."

"You drugged me?"

"It's not what you think."

"Oh really? Then tell me what's going on here."

"When someone lies, certain physiological changes come over her. I just gave you something that enhances those, that makes it easier for me to tell if you're holding something back from me. If you're not being honest."

Of course, as a DEA agent, she knew about drugs like that—ones that heighten pupil dilation, ectodermal response, heart rate, respiration. But as an escort, she needed to pretend that she wasn't familiar with what he was talking about.

"Why would you think I'm going to lie?"

"I have to be careful who I trust. There are consequences for betrayals. And the more intimate the betrayal, the more severe those consequences must inevitably be."

She leaned a hand against the wall to feign losing her balance. "I don't want you to take advantage of me."

"And I don't want you to take advantage of me." He placed her hand in his and slid two fingers down her wrist to check her pulse. "Your heart, it's racing."

"It must be what you gave me."

"Did you betray me, Sasha?"

"What are you talking about?"

"Did you tell someone about the condo? That I was using it?"

"Who would I tell about that?"

"And see, that's not a direct answer. That doesn't engender my trust in what you have to say."

She pulled away from him. "I want to leave."

"I'm afraid that's not possible at the moment. As you can see, your driver is gone. There's no car outside."

Where is backup? Where is Greer?

Blake approached her, and she swiftly drew her weapon. "Easy there, cowboy."

"Aren't you full of surprises."

"I want to leave."

"You can keep your gun out if it makes you feel safe."

"Actually, it does."

"Let me show you around the grounds."

"What? Why?"

"I want you to know what's going to happen here."

Why is he doing this? A stall? To set you up for an ambush?

"Don't try anything." She was still playing the role of an escort. "You don't drug a girl and then just pretend that everything is fine. Something's wrong with you."

"Please." He gestured toward the door.

Well, stalling would work to her advantage rather than his.

"After you," she said, keeping the Ruger carefully pointed at his head.

++++

To Tessa, so many of the questions people were asking Timothy Sabian seemed sophomoric and lame: "What's a typical day like for you?" "Did you always want to be a writer?" "Where do you get your ideas from?"

It was tiresome.

She wanted to ask him the opposite of that last one, actually: how he kept ideas at bay—which would probably be a lot more legit of a problem for an artist. The issue almost certainly wasn't one of coming up with ideas as much as knowing which ones to disregard. Wherever ideas come from, as a writer, sifting through them must be a lot tougher than coming up with them in the first place.

Finally, after the Q and A was over, people lined up to get their books signed, and Tessa accidentally-on-purpose found her way to the back of the line.

Although Timothy looked a bit ill-at-ease doing so, he took time to speak with each of the people as he signed the books they handed him. As a result, the line moved slowly, but it was a good kind of slow because it showed he cared about the fans who'd come to see him.

There were just two people in front of Tessa when Re-bekah snuck out from behind the register and came toward her, looking overwhelmed and tense. "Tessa, I'm out of ones. Why did everyone suddenly decide to pay in cash tonight? It's crazy. Could you go grab some more for me from the back room? That would be awesome."

"Oh. Yeah, sure. No problem."

Tessa passed through the aisle of books by authors Q–R and opened the door to the part-office, part-workroom, part-storage area in the back of the bookstore near the exit.

A waist-high pile of books on the left waited to be shelved. Ahead of her, a desk and scribble-covered wall calendar. To her right, a mini-fridge where Rebekah and the other two people who worked here kept their lunches and drinks.

Usually, Rebekah stored extra money in a shoebox on a

shelf above the desk, tucked behind a collection of books claiming to know who Jack the Ripper really was. It was the closest thing the Mystorium had to a safe.

Tessa opened the box and found it bereft of ones, with only a dozen or so fives and three twenties. She returned it to the shelf and repositioned the Ripperology books in front of it to keep it hidden.

She'd never known the staff to put money anywhere else, but maybe Rebekah had a new system in place.

Okay, where else would they keep their cash?

She started with the desk drawers. The first one, nothing. Just a few papers. The one below it, envelopes. She was about to close it when the door to the workroom opened, and she turned and found herself looking into the eyes of Timothy Sabian.

55

Timothy hadn't meant to startle the girl in the office, but by the way she gasped and by the look on her face, he must've really scared her.

He held up both hands in a disarming gesture. "Sorry, didn't mean to burst in on you like that. You must be Tessa."

She looked at him warily. "How do you know that?"

"Rebekah sent me. Told me she forgot to tell you where the money was." He did his best to smile in a reassuring way. "They moved it."

"Oh. Right."

He gestured toward the desk. "Do you mind?"

"Uh-uh."

He entered and stepped around her, letting the door close of its own accord behind him.

And that's when he noticed the ceramic Mystery Writers of America mug beside the computer monitor on the desk. It contained a clutch of pens and pencils. A highlighter. Two markers. And a letter opener—silver and sharp and capering there in the light.

He heard the voice tempt him to pick it up: *You're back here alone. You could take care of things. Take the money to Rebekah and no one would know. No one would find out.*

"Yes, they would," he muttered.

"Who would what?" Tessa said.

"No, I just . . . Never mind."

She suspects something. You can't let her leave now.

"I have to!" he exclaimed. "I'm not going to hurt anyone!"

Tessa edged closer to her purse, which she'd set on the office chair. "Why would you hurt anyone?"

"I'm sorry, no." He stumbled for the right thing to say. "I need to leave."

++++

Okay, at this point the guy was seriously weirding her out, but oddly enough, Tessa got the sense that he was more frightened than she was.

As she was sorting through whether to say something to him or just take off, she heard shouting coming from beyond the door in the main part of the bookstore.

"Where is he?" It was a woman's voice.

"Who?" Rebekah asked.

"Timothy Sabian."

Tessa edged the door open and peeked out. A desperate-looking, disheveled, middle-aged woman stood near Rebekah with her hand suspiciously stuffed into her purse.

From living with Patrick this long, Tessa had learned that a hidden hand is a bad sign since it might very well conceal a weapon—especially if it's in a situation when you would expect the hand to remain visible.

She's reaching for something. Pepper spray? A gun?

"He left already," Rebekah told her.

"No! I know he's here. He's supposed to be here!"

The woman started searching the store.

Something's really wrong with her. You need to get him out of here.

Tessa urgently asked Timothy, "Did you leave anything out there?"

"Just the journal I was reading from."

"I'll get it for you after you're gone." She took his hand. "Follow me." Quickly and quietly, she led him toward the back exit.

Behind them, she heard the woman shrieking, "He killed my daughter. He killed her! That detective told me his name. Where is he?"

Tessa threw the back door open, and she and Timothy escaped into the night.

"What was that all about back there?" She was filled with a disorienting rush of nerves and adrenaline. "What did she mean by that stuff about you killing her daughter?"

"I didn't. I swear."

"But you do know what she's talking about."

"A young lady disappeared after my last signing. That woman must think I had something to do with that. But I didn't. I wouldn't. I would never hurt anyone."

More shouts came from inside the bookstore.

"You should get out of here," Tessa told him.

Spur-of-the-momently, she slipped the church bulletin out of her book and scribbled her contact info on it, then handed it to him. "Drop me a note and tell me a snail mail address. I'll send your journal to you."

"You sure?"

"Yeah, now go."

Timothy tucked something into her palm, thanked her effusively, and then hastened off into the night.

Tessa looked down and found that he had given her a letter opener that she hadn't even seen him holding.

++++

"What are you planning to do with all these mannequins?" Sasha asked Blake.

She still had her gun out, but Blake hadn't made any move at her, and as far as she could tell, he still believed she was just an escort. Yes, perhaps an escort who'd given up the location of his condominium, but not an undercover agent.

"They're not just mannequins, Sasha. They're a way to spread a message."

"I don't understand."

"There are forces out there that have in mind to harm our country and destroy our way of life."

"Terrorists."

"That's right. I want to protect us. And sometimes sacrifices need to be made in the service of the greater good."

"So what are you going to do?"

"Make a statement that will open up the pathway to a safer, more prosperous future for us all."

++++

I parked down the block from the address Calvin had given me.

When I checked my messages, I saw that we'd received the cell records of the previous suicide victims. Although it might very well take hours to pore through them looking for connections to specific locations, I wondered if we could cut right to the chase.

I tried Agent Collins, but she'd left the office for the day, so I put a call through to Angela Knight in the Cyber division at Headquarters in D.C. I've worked with her in the past, she knows me, and she always comes through when I'm in a pinch. I filled her in, then told her the address Calvin had passed along. "See if you can pinpoint any incoming or outgoing calls from that location from the previous suicide victims. Add Thomas Kewley to the mix."

I gave her the info she would need.

"Let me plug that in. Stay on the line."

56

"Where's Mannie?" Sasha asked Blake.

"Temporarily indisposed."

"What does that mean?"

"I'm afraid he's otherwise engaged right now."

She saw movement out of the corner of her eye and realized that it was the man from the backseat of the executive car, the one who'd given her the water. He'd surreptitiously entered the greenhouse and was now coming her way.

"Sasha," Blake said, "do you have any idea how long I've known?"

"Known what?"

"That you're not who you say you are."

"No one is who they say they are."

"That may be true. But not many people are DEA agents."

"What are you talking about?"

"Why do you think Agent Greer hasn't shown up yet?"

"What?"

"Agent Greer. Your backup. The tracking device in your shoe."

How does he know? How could he possibly know about that? Unless—

Earlier, Greer had told her that he would contact her supervisor at the DEA once they had a location.

Blake got to one of them. He has to have. It's the only thing that makes sense.

Blake's goon came closer to her, and as she swung the gun in his direction, Blake went for the weapon. She was good at her job, but he was lightning quick. He struck the back of her hand with one of his, while also hitting the inside of her wrist with his other hand. This dialed the gun away from him, and then, with a quick twist of his wrist, he was able to disarm her and obtain her weapon.

He leveled it at her chest but did not fire.

"Sasha, the lies can stop now. There's no need for them anymore. It's time for your investigation, your deceit, to come to an end. You're the one who gave up the location of the condominium that was raided earlier today, aren't you?"

She said nothing but quietly assessed her situation, looking for a way to turn the tables on him.

"I'm going to give you a choice," he said.

"What choice is that?"

Blake commanded the man to lead her back to the office building, but when he approached her, she grabbed his arm, swept her leg forward, and took him down with a sideways reap. As big as he was, he hit the concrete hard, colliding with a satisfying thud.

She spun toward Blake, but he fired at the ground beside her foot.

She froze.

"That's enough of that. The next bullet will shatter your kneecap. Now, go on. Back to the office. There's something you need to see. It has to do with a friend of yours and a very important decision you're about to make."

57

It didn't take long for Angela to verify that I was on the right track.

"Yes," she said. "That location—it looks like three of your victims visited it within a week or so of their subsequent deaths. Kewley as well. What's located there?"

"I'm about to find out."

I exited the car and scanned the neighborhood but saw no sign of Calvin.

It was a crime-riddled area, and tension between the lower-income residents here and law enforcement had heightened over the last few years and resulted in fewer cops patrolling the streets since they didn't want to be the next star of an arrest video on YouTube. The ones who did come around typically just drove through and didn't get out of their cruisers unless absolutely necessary—and that only exacerbated the problem, resulting in even more crime.

And now, I had the wrong skin color to be in this gang-controlled neighborhood at this time of night.

But so did Calvin.

On the phone earlier, he'd said, "We must be ready for anything," and I couldn't imagine that he would have said that unless he was planning on being here somewhere.

I tried his number again to no avail and decided it was possible he'd beaten me here.

I started across the street toward the address the suicide victims had visited before they died—the same address Calvin had uncovered as the place to search for the Matchmaker.

++++

Inside the building, Blake directed Sasha to have a seat.

By then, his man had joined them and did not look happy to have been brought down by a woman her size.

Well, too bad.

Blake nodded to the guy, who walked to one of the file cabinets, opened the drawer, and produced a roll of duct tape, a plastic bag, and three zip-ties.

Sasha felt her heart begin jackhammering in her chest.

You need to get out of here. Now.

"We have an enthusiastic viewing audience tonight," Blake told her. "They're either going to be treated to a homicide or a suicide. I'll leave that up to you."

"I'm not going to kill anyone, if that's what you're thinking. Unless it's you. Then I might have to make an exception."

"I'm afraid it's not me that you need to be concerned about right now. It's Agent Greer." He showed her his phone's screen. "You're going to decide whether he lives or dies."

Agent Greer was tied to a chair, and Mannie was standing beside him holding a plastic bag and a duct tape roll of his own.

Blake said homicide or suicide.

Suicide?

No.

"I'm not going to kill myself."

"Let's do a practice run and see how all this works," Blake said. Then he spoke to Mannie through his cell. "Do it."

Mannie tugged the plastic bag over Greer's head as the restrained FBI agent tried futilely to lean out of the way. Then Mannie began to loop the duct tape around Greer's neck to secure the bag in place.

"No!" Sasha cried. "Stop it!"

Greer yanked at his bonds but couldn't get free. As he tried to breathe, the bag suctioned in against his mouth and nose, sealing off any air that might've been in the bag.

Buy time, Sasha. Anything to buy time!

"Take it off! Whatever you want, I'll do it! Don't kill him!"

"I don't believe you," Blake said.

You're watching him die. He's going to die!

"Believe me!"

Blake said into the phone, "Let him breathe."

Mannie tore the bag open, and Greer gasped, desperately drawing in as much air as he could.

"What do you want from me?" Sasha asked.

"It isn't just what I want. It's what they want." He wavered his phone at her, then glanced at the bottom of the screen. "There are nearly two thousand already."

He gestured toward the items that the man beside him was holding. "Put the bag over your head and then tape it in place around your neck, or you'll watch it happen to Agent Greer, and this time, we won't stop it. You do it; he lives. You refuse; he dies."

"How do I know you won't hurt him if I do what you're saying?"

"Trust, Sasha. I haven't lied to you yet. It's a big decision. I'll give you a few minutes to decide."

++++

I saw a drug deal going down on the corner across the street, and when the two men noticed me, one of them hurriedly stuffed something into his pocket and hustled off into the shadows.

Not my concern at the moment.

The other man glared at me, but I shifted my attention to the house.

In this neighborhood, I hadn't expected to see any single-family dwellings but found that the address in question was, in fact, a dilapidated two-story home.

As I crossed the street, four men who were sitting outside a nearby brownstone looked my way. One of them stood and called to me, but I ignored him and proceeded toward the house. Another tugged out his phone, tapped in a number, and started talking with someone while he continued to stare at me.

No lights were on in the house.

When I turned and glanced over my shoulder, I saw that the man who'd shouted to me from the stoop was briskly approaching me and was now only about ten meters away.

He called out angrily, "Whatcha doin' here?"

"I'm looking for a tall guy," I said to him. "Slim. White. Probably wearing a trench coat. Late sixties, early seventies. English accent."

He was quiet but stopped short about five meters from me.

"Have you seen anyone like that?"

"I think it's time for you to leave."

"I want to talk to the Matchmaker."

"Ain't no matchmaker 'round here."

"Is that so." I ventured out on a limb, but I remembered Vidocq's advice about obtaining the trust of those you're investigating by gaining their confidence and using subterfuge, and said, "I have an idea for a video he might be interested in."

"I don't know nothin' 'bout no videos." He started toward me again. "You need to get back in your car."

"Don't provoke me," I said. "I don't want anyone to get hurt. Keep your distance or you'll regret it."

He paused and stared at me, clearly trying to figure out what was going on here—was I stupid? Was I bluffing? Was I a cop?

He brushed his hand across the front of his jacket to show me his gun. When I didn't back away, he pulled it out, and I recognized it as a Taurus PT92. Higher-end than I would've guessed for a street thug to carry, but maybe he wasn't just a street thug.

Could this guy be the Matchmaker?

"This is cocked and locked," he told me. "You know what that means?"

From my experience, that was more a phrase a soldier rather than a gangster might use, and I wasn't certain *he* knew what it meant.

"It means it would be prudent for you to put it back beneath your belt."

"You threatening me? I'm the one with the gun!"

"I'm searching for my friend. If you can help me, help me. Otherwise, you're wasting my time."

"And the Matchmaker. You're lookin' for him too."

"That's right."

"Who told you 'bout the Matchmaker?"

Vidocq.

Think like Vidocq.

"Someone at work. Someone who's looking for some-thing unique and memorable."

"How memorable?"

"Memorable."

I was making this up as I went along, but it seemed to be working.

The guy glanced over his shoulder toward the porch where he and his buddies had been. It was empty now.

He came toward me, and I braced myself for a fight, but instead, he went to the door of the house, clicked it open, and gestured for me to go inside in front of him.

When I did, he followed close on my heels. "To the left and then down the stairs," he said tersely. "Go on."

The only available light in the darkened house was the thin, muted smear of it that seeped through the windows, but it was enough for me to find the stairwell.

Still no sign of Calvin.

Halfway down the stairs, I realized that the man with the Taurus wasn't following me anymore.

At the base of the staircase, I came to a steel-reinforced door.

I knocked and waited.

When the door finally opened, I was greeted by a man with no nose. The scarring told me it wasn't a birth defect. Somehow his nose had been removed—and based on the irregularities and jagged scars, it didn't look it'd been done by a surgeon.

The room had no overhead lights, but half a dozen computer screens emitted a bluish tinge that dimly illuminated the room. The sweet-stark smell of marijuana hung the air. The noseless man cocked his head and eyed me. Flame tattoos curled around his face, and he'd done body modification to create two nubby horns on his forehead. His four lip rings glinted in the blue light of the basement.

"I'm here to see the Matchmaker," I said.

"Why?"

"I represent someone who has an idea for something very special."

"Special, huh?"

"Yeah."

"You a cop?"

"I'm a federal agent."

He scoffed in a good-natured way. I couldn't tell if he believed me or not. In either case, he looked me up and down, assessing me, and, without another word, stepped aside.

I walked into the basement, and he closed the door behind me.

++++

"Well?" Blake said to Sasha. "What's it going to be—you or Agent Greer?"

Sasha considered all of her options. Blake was out of reach, so if she went for the gun, he and his men would undoubtedly kill both her and Greer. She had no idea where they were keeping Greer, so there was no way of getting to him even if she was able to overpower Blake—which she doubted she would be able to do.

You cannot let him die.

From what she'd seen earlier of Mannie and from all she knew about him, he at least seemed to have a conscience.

Then why is he helping Blake with this? Is he just going along to make it look like they're serious? Would he really go through with it and kill Greer?

She doubted it.

"You're bluffing," she said to Blake.

"I don't bluff."

In the end, even if Mannie wouldn't do it, that didn't mean that Blake's other men wouldn't kill Greer.

And her.

Her only hope was to trust that Greer had gotten word out about her location and that backup was coming.

"Time's up," Blake said.

The only chance she had at resolving this favorably was drawing things out as long as possible.

And that meant she would have to put the bag over her head.

"Alright." She held out her hand. "Give it to me."

58

In addition to the guy with no nose, there were three other men and one woman in the room.

All of them, apart from a man standing in the middle, who appeared to be calling the shots, were seated at computer keyboards. The guy who was on his feet was probably about my age but looked like he spent a lot more time at the snack machine than on the treadmill.

He turned and eyed me.

"Are you the Matchmaker?" I asked him.

"Who's asking?"

"My name is Patrick Bowers. I'm with the FBI."

He smirked slightly, and the man who'd greeted me at the door snickered.

"FBI, huh?"

"That's right."

He didn't bother to ask me for my ID but simply said, "We're not doing anything illegal here."

"Then you wouldn't mind if I invited some of my co-workers over to have a look around. We can all have a little—"

"It's a spectator sport. That's all."

"A spectator sport." I felt my temperature rising. "Watching people die?"

"Public executions have been popular all throughout human history, Agent Bowers. They're still held in eight countries today. There's nothing abnormal about wanting to watch others expire. It reminds us of our own mortality. Helps us treasure each precious moment that we have."

As long as he's talking, get as much out of him as you can.

"Have you had a tall Englishman down here? Dr. Werjonic?"

"You're our first visitor tonight, I'm afraid."

Maybe I shouldn't have believed him, but I did.

"What do you know about the Selzucaine?"

"Sometimes people want something to take the edge off when faced with a stressful and irreversible decision. That's all."

By his tone, I could tell this guy treated death as trite, and that didn't sit well with me. "I want to know about the man who was there when Jon Murray died."

"Everything we do is confidential."

"How much do I have to pay to be present when someone else dies?"

He was quiet.

I cursed. Couldn't help it.

"The man on the roof," I said. "The grandfather and the bleach. The mom who overdosed. Who was present when those people took their own lives?"

He shook his head. "This is a can of worms you do not want to open. You have no—"

Losing my temper, I grabbed him by the collar. "Who was there when they died?"

"Joe," the woman who was seated in front of one of the computers blurted, "it's happening. She's going to do it."

I looked at the screens throughout the room.

Every one of them contained the same image—Sasha MacIntyre, seated on a chair in a nondescript office. She had a plastic bag and a roll of duct tape in her hands.

I couldn't imagine this ending well. "Shut it down."

"We can't."

She'd tightened a zip-tie around her belt and then attached two more ties to it and threaded the free ends through the hole just far enough to get the loops started.

For her wrists. For when it happens. So she can't stop it once it's started.

"I said shut it down!"

"We have no way of contacting them." Joe didn't sound concerned for Sasha at all. "Look at the counter!" he exclaimed excitedly. "We're up to almost four thousand viewers!"

++++

Sasha took a deep breath, then drew the plastic bag over her head.

Through the transparent plastic, the world became crinkled and blurred. Wrinkles of reality folding in around her.

Backup is coming.

She reassured herself that they were going to get there in time.

But even if they don't, you can save Greer.

She kicked off her heels.

You might have to do this. You might actually have to go through with it.

++++

Behind me, I heard the noseless man exclaim, "Got another one back here."

I turned in his direction and saw that the door to the basement was open. Calvin appeared and locked his gaze onto Joe. "You're the man who convinced Thomas Kewley to kill himself."

"There isn't time for that now," I said to Calvin. I pointed to the computer screen where Sasha had pulled out a length of duct tape and was starting to wrap it around her neck to seal off the bottom of the bag. "We have to stop her."

++++

Sasha was still holding her breath when she finished with the tape.

She tore off the end and dropped the roll.

++++

"The person who paid to watch," I shouted to Joe, "tell him to stop her."

"It doesn't work like that."

I unpocketed my phone and hit redial to reach Angela at Cyber.

"Where is this online?" I asked Joe.

He said nothing, but the woman who was seated nearby said, "It's being run through a Krazle account."

"Give it to me."

I repeated what she told me to Angela, then added urgently, "We need to trace this now. Sasha wasn't suicidal. Someone's coercing her to do this. Find her. Stop this."

"I'm on it."

The noseless man made for the door, shoving Calvin aside as he fled. He limped heavily on his left leg, just as the man I'd chased into the subway station had done.

"No one else leaves this room." I pointed to the men. "Get on your knees. Calvin, call for backup."

"Right."

On the screen's counter, the number of viewers continued to grow.

++++

Although on one level she'd known it all along, now the seriousness of her situation overwhelmed Sasha in a gut-punch realization—she was going to die, or she was going to be responsible for Bill Greer dying.

As she slipped her left hand into its zip-tie loop, she prayed that Greer would be saved and that God would accept her soul even if she truly did end her own life by her own hand.

Your life for his.

Don't give up. Don't give in.

It was getting harder and harder to hold her breath.

A few more seconds and that would be it, then she would have to let out her air and try for more.

She tugged her left arm to the side, tightening the zip-tie around her wrist.

++++

Angela got back on the line with me. "I've got nothing," she said, taut desperation in her voice. I suspected she was seeing what I was seeing. "It'll take too long to trace."

I said to the woman at the keyboard, "If there's anything you can do for that woman, you need to do it now. She's not killing herself because she wants to. Someone is making this happen. Can you help her?"

She was quiet.

"Please."

She glanced at the screen. Sasha was passing her free hand through the second looped zip-tie. Once she tugged that one tight, she wouldn't be able to rip the bag away no matter how desperate she became.

Rather than answer me, the woman repositioned the keyboard and began typing furiously, entering code. Her screen shifted from the video of Sasha to a scrolling set of digits and numbers while all of the other screens showed Sasha yank her right wrist tight, securing the loop.

++++

Sasha couldn't hold her breath any longer.

She let out what was left of her air and tried to breathe in again, but the plastic bag suctioned in and sealed the air off, pressing up tightly against her lips.

++++

All at once, two of the men in the basement scrambled forward and went at Calvin, who was standing between them and the door. He spun with surprising agility and drove his foot down against the side of the man on his right's knee, and it crumpled, sending his assailant to the ground.

The other man tried to hold Calvin by the back of the head, but my friend threw an elbow at the man's nose, connecting hard enough to send him reeling backward.

I whipped out my SIG. "No one else moves!"

++++

Sasha found herself yanking frantically at the zip-ties, but she couldn't free herself.

Here it is. It's too late. This is happening now.

++++

Though I didn't want to watch, I needed to see if someone else was present or if something might appear on the screen that would give me a clue to where Sasha was, so I didn't turn away from the monitors.

"Hurry up!" I told the woman who was typing, the only chance we had at the moment to save Sasha. "We need to stop this now!"

The bag had steamed up from the moist air Sasha had exhaled, but the terrible mechanics of this means of death took over as she did her best to draw in more air, and each time she tried, the plastic closed up tightly over her nose and mouth.

++++

Sasha had grown up hearing that those who commit suicide go to hell, but she hoped that God would forgive her, would know her heart, would see that she was doing this only to save Greer, and she prayed that the Almighty would not hold it against her.

Backup wasn't coming.

"Greater love has no one than this . . ." She heard the scriptural words deep in her soul, echoing through the years from the time when she still went to church. "That he lays down his life for a friend."

This was how she was going to die.

Sasha kept her eyes open.

She wanted to view the world for as long as she could before it all went away.

++++

I watched Sasha become more frenzied in her attempts to breathe. As she instinctively yanked at her restrained wrists, the chair crashed sideways to the floor.

Whoever was recording her death zoomed in on her face.

The plastic bag did its job.

The duct tape sealed out the air she needed to survive.

It didn't take long.

After just a few more heart-wrenching seconds, Sasha MacIntyre stopped moving, stopped struggling, and lay limp and lifeless on the floor.

"No!" I cried, my voice reverberating starkly off the basement walls.

Sirens screamed down at us from the street outside.

Backup.

It was over.

But then it wasn't.

The electricity clicked off, and all of the monitors went black, sinking the basement into a thick, unforgiving darkness.

I still had my phone in my hand. I tapped the screen to wake it up, then used its light to see as best I could.

No one was coming at me, but the men were trying to escape.

I shouted for them to stay where they were but heard scuffling, and two of them headed toward the steps. The first man knocked Calvin to the ground, and then Joe kicked my friend twice in the abdomen as he rushed past. They were brutal, powerful kicks, and Calvin gasped harshly in pain.

This could easily turn into a bloodbath if I started shooting, and as far as I'd seen, no one down here was armed, so, swearing, I holstered my weapon, cuffed the remaining man, and ordered the woman not to leave her chair.

She sat there staring at her screen, muttering how she'd been too slow, how she shouldn't have let this happen.

And then, as I knelt beside Calvin to see how he was doing, I heard her begin to cry soft, tender tears for the woman she had just watched die.

59

NYPD stopped every one of the basement's occupants from escaping the neighborhood except for the noseless man, who'd slipped away before they arrived.

The officers took them all into the station. We would need to let our lawyers sort out what charges might be leveled against them. The physical assault against Calvin might be enough—might be all we could get.

Right now I wasn't concerned about any of that.

I was concerned about my friend making it through the night.

He wasn't recovering from being kicked while he was on the ground, and the EMTs loaded him onto a gurney to take him to the hospital.

"I'm riding along," I told them unequivocally and, after exchanging a glance with each other, the one in charge nodded. "Alright."

As we left, the ambulance's emergency siren sounding, I tried to process all that had just happened.

Calvin was injured.

Sasha was dead.

I'd witnessed her suffocate, and that was not a memory I would ever be able to erase or escape.

Somehow she'd been coerced into killing herself, and

thousands of people had clicked to the Matchmaker's Krazle account to watch her do it.

And someone had filmed it. Had zoomed in on her face to make sure the viewers got the best possible angle of her struggling to breathe.

I felt my fists tighten.

Right now, there wasn't anything I could do about what had happened, but I vowed that when the time came, I would do whatever was necessary to see justice done.

Calvin slipped into unconsciousness while we were still en route to the hospital.

The EMT beside me assessed his vitals and told me that he might have extensive internal injuries.

"As far as I know, he was only kicked twice," I said, as if pointing that out would somehow help my friend recover.

"Yes. Okay." But his voice was grim, and I realized that this might be even more serious than I'd thought.

I contacted Christie and told her that Calvin had been injured and that I was heading to the hospital with him. I couldn't think of any good reason at the moment to mention Sasha's death.

"I'm not sure when I'll be home," I told her. "I'll text you as soon as I know more."

++++

When Tessa walked through the front door, her mom asked concernedly how she was.

"Fine. Why?"

"I just wanted to make sure. How was the book signing?"

"Memorable."

"Did you get to meet the author?"

"Yeah. Briefly."

"And?"

"And?"

"Did he sign your book?"

"Well, actually, no."

"Why not?"

"Something came up."

Tessa tried to figure out exactly how much to tell her mom about secreting the novelist out the back door while the woman who'd burst into the bookstore shouted accusations about him killing her daughter.

Probably better not to get into all of that.

"The guy had to rush out before I could get the book signed. It's no big deal. Really."

"Alright."

"Where's Patrick?"

"With a friend who was injured tonight. They're on their way to the hospital."

"Is the guy okay?"

"I'm really not sure."

++++

At the emergency room entrance, the paramedics hurriedly transferred Calvin inside, and as I was following them, I got a call from Greer.

"Did you hear what happened to Sasha?" I asked.

"Yes," he replied heavily.

"Where are you?"

"On my way to the nearest precinct. A couple of NYPD uniforms picked me up." He spoke in a tight, strained voice. "Blake's men caught me. They were gonna kill me.

Mannie put a plastic bag over my head and cinched it tight. I thought I was a dead man. I swear to God, I thought my time had come. But then, a couple of seconds later—the longest couple seconds of my life—he ripped it open. Then he left me there in that chair. That's all I know. I waited, it was a little while, but then the officers showed up. I don't know how they found out where I was."

Mannie was going to kill him? That didn't seem right at all. From my experience with Mannie, when he had the chance to save lives, he did. As far as I knew, we had no evidence that he'd ever taken anyone's life.

"I'm glad you're alright," I told Greer.

"That makes two of us."

I saw an incoming call from Ralph and I told Greer I'd call him back.

Ralph explained that he'd spoken with both DeYoung and Angela. He knew about Sasha, but that wasn't why he'd called.

"Don't you find it a little convenient?" he said.

"Find what convenient?"

"The anonymous tip about Greer's location. The fact that he wasn't killed. And then he walks away from all this without a scratch?"

"What—you think he's involved somehow?"

"I wouldn't say that, but I think we need to make sure he wasn't."

I couldn't believe that Greer had anything to do with this or that his abduction had been faked.

"Think about it," Ralph said. "He plays the part of the victim so they can get Sasha to kill herself."

"That seems like a stretch to me. Let's see where the evidence takes us."

"Yeah," he replied soberly. "Let's do that."

++++

Back at his house, Timothy Sabian stood in front of the upstairs bathroom mirror.

Things were starting to pull apart at the seams. Miranda's mom was convinced he was the one responsible for her daughter's disappearance—for her death.

His life was a piece of cloth that was unraveling right before his eyes.

He flung his head forward and smashed it violently against the glass, shattering the mirror.

This has to end. This has to stop!

The only way for that to happen is getting rid of Julianne. Or getting rid of yourself.

He stared at his splintered reflection, at the unyielding cracks slicing up and through and across his face.

That's an option. That's always an option, Timothy. Don't forget. You can take care of what needs to be done here at any time.

The last time you used the letter opener against your throat you just didn't go deep enough. You can fix that. You can be free from the past. Next time, you can make sure you go as deep as you need to go.

Until then, he found the X-ACTO knife and went to work freeing the bugs that were trying to climb out of his left side.

60

Two broken ribs and a lacerated liver.

Even for someone much younger, the injuries would have been serious, but for someone Calvin's age, the lacerated liver could be life-threatening.

The doctors kept him in the ICU so they could monitor him more closely.

I tried to sort through where we were at.

Ralph suspected Greer of being complicit in Sasha's death.

It was unfathomable to me.

As I considered the possibility, it struck me again that she was dead. Unequivocally dead. Now and forever gone.

We still hadn't been able to track down where she'd been when she suffocated. We didn't have a body; we just had proof of what'd happened with a video that was watched by nearly six thousand people and downloaded hundreds of times before it was finally taken down.

I'd met Marcus Rockwell, Krazle's founder, last summer and had been impressed by him. Sharp. Clear-headed. Generous and unpretentious for a thirty-one-year-old billionaire.

The last I heard, just fourteen percent fewer people were doing online searches using Krazle than Google—

and things were trending in their direction. And as far as a social networking platform, Krazle was on its way to surpassing Facebook in the number of daily user interactions.

Though Jon Murray had streamed his suicide through 4chan, the others had all used Krazle.

If Marcus's platform was being used to post and share live-streamed suicides, I thought he would likely do all he could to stop that. I made a mental note to call him in the morning and see if we could have a little talk about what Krazle was and was not doing in this arena and how he could help shut this down.

The details about Greer's abduction and how he was overpowered were still murky—he'd been following an executive car that'd picked up Sasha. He stopped at a red light, and a person dressed as a vagrant walked up and started to clean his windows for a tip.

When Greer lowered his window to wave the man away, someone else leapt out of the shadows, and the two men overpowered Greer—somehow getting him out of his car. They restrained him and hooded him, then drove him to a warehouse where Mannie was waiting for them.

Ralph had a point.

It did look suspicious.

From what we could piece together, the men who took Greer hadn't necessarily intended to kill him but rather used his abduction to convince Sasha to take her own life. Since they left him alone afterward, it appeared that he hadn't been the primary target.

Once again, just like when I was at Jon Murray's funeral, I was forced to think about life and death.

Vapor.

Our lives appear for a little while and then, like mist, they vanish away.

No matter how hard we attempt to cling to life, we cannot. Time passes over us, and we're left behind, trying desperately to grab hold of something solid in its fleeting, amorphous shadow.

Sand in an hourglass, flying away—just like that image on James Leeson's gravestone. Or those words, "Remember death." Yes, this week, how could I forget it?

How do you let it register that a woman you spoke with earlier in the day is now dead and will never speak, never dream, never breathe again?

It's tempting to pretend that she'll somehow appear alive again, that death isn't really the end, but unless the afterlife exists, nothing awaits us beyond death's door, and there's really no lasting solace or anything solid to put your hope in.

Back in the sixties, Elisabeth Kübler-Ross outlined five stages of grief in her book *On Death and Dying:* Denial. Anger. Bargaining. Depression. Acceptance.

Because of the nature of my job, I tend to move past the denial stage pretty quickly. I just see too much death—so much more than most people—that I've learned to acknowledge its universal inevitability.

And so, tonight, I found myself leaping over denial and landing headfirst into anger.

Territory I was pretty familiar with.

Sometimes it seemed like I spent way too much of my life stuck in that stage rather than moving on, rather than finding closure, healing.

That last stage of true acceptance might be a worthy goal, but right now, I wanted the anger to remain fresh and tender in my heart. It was part of what served to keep me going in an investigation like this.

Over the years, I've found that anger is necessary, but it must reach an equilibrium: You need just enough but never too much. If you don't let it in, you become hollow; but if you let it take over, you become its slave.

When you see evil like what this case was exhibiting, you either become numb to it, or you have to find a way to put your rage on a leash. Then you need to be careful not to let it gnaw through whatever coping mechanism you're using to restrain it.

At last, at nearly midnight, the hospital staff assured me that Calvin was stable and that I could head home. "There's nothing you can do for him right now. Let him sleep," the doctor told me, "and get some rest yourself."

At home, I found Christie waiting up for me.

"You know how I'm not supposed to discuss anything related to my cases with you?" I said. "Well, tomorrow you'll hear about this on the news: We lost an agent. A DEA agent. We believe she was forced to kill herself. Her suicide was filmed and aired online."

Christie covered her mouth with her hand. "Oh, Pat."

"Yeah."

"I don't know what to say."

"I don't know that there is anything to say."

"How are you?"

"I'm okay. But pray for her family, will you? And for Calvin. And pray that I find the people I need to before anyone else gets hurt."

Gets killed, I thought, but let myself stick with the less telling phrase.

Dr. Williams's sermon came to mind, and the Scripture

verse he'd read to us about the Spirit making intercession "with groanings which cannot be uttered."

I could certainly identify with that right now. The soul-stifling language of pain—one that God must know all too well if he knows us at all.

"Listen," I said, "at the restaurant, I had the sense that there was something you were trying to tell me. We were talking about love and truth—if it's right to protect someone with a lie. We were going to pick up the conversation later, when we saw each other again."

++++

Christie took Pat's hand.

"None of that matters right now," she told him. "It's nothing. Not the turtles. Not the polar bear. They're just stories from my life, just stories to help you understand me better."

"What is it you need me to understand?"

She was quiet.

"You can trust me," he said, "Whatever it is, Christie, let me in."

"We don't need to talk about me tonight. I want to pray for your friend. And for the family of the woman who died."

++++

Sometimes there is no elaborate plan, no criminal mastermind who's always one step ahead of the authorities, who's playing a twisted game of Catch Me If You Can with the cops.

Sometimes there's just senseless pain and death, just tears and inexplicable evil. You want it to make sense, but it doesn't. You want morality to come out ahead, but instead you find only the merciless swipe of the Reaper's scythe and blood spraying in its wake.

And another corpse lying on the ground.

That was all I could think of, despite how hard I tried to join Christie in her earnest and heartfelt prayers.

STAGE V

Acceptance

Called off the house. Inside the parking garage.
"Help my lack of love." The man behind the curtain.

61

Tuesday, November 6
7:02 A.M.
7 hours left

It was November-cold for the first time this week.

An empty water bottle skittered across the street, rolling and spinning at the whim of the wind.

For now, freezing rain spattered sporadically onto my city, but it was predicted to turn to snow by early afternoon.

The rain dotted the car windows and the pavement like drops of chilled saliva falling from the mouth of a great, looming beast.

I'd intended to walk alone to clear my head, but Christie had insisted on coming along, and now she held my hand as we made our way in silence down the street.

I carried our umbrella in my other hand.

For us, since we'd met beneath it, this old umbrella had become a symbol of our love for each other. Today, I wished it would somehow offer us protection from death and grief and provide at least a momentary place of respite and solace, but all it did was dome the raindrops aside, leaving me feeling just as hollowed out by Sasha's death as I had been.

Something was up with Christie. I wasn't sure what, but there was definitely something she wasn't telling me and, although I didn't want to press the issue, I couldn't help but be concerned.

So that was on my mind.

As was the case.

As was Sasha.

I kept replaying what'd happened in the Matchmaker's lair, kept wondering if there was anything more I could have done to help Calvin or her, but I kept coming up empty.

From earth to earth. The words caught hold of me when I thought of Sasha. *Ashes to ashes. Dust to dust.*

Last year, while consulting on a case in which a victim was buried alive, I'd had to research that saying. I'd expected the phrase to come from somewhere in the Bible but found that there aren't any Scripture verses that mention "ashes to ashes."

In Genesis 3, there's a reference to mankind returning to the dust that we were taken from. The "earth to earth, ashes to ashes" part came from the *Book of Common Prayer*, first published in 1662.

It's one of those things that you hear and assume must be from Scripture somewhere, but it's just not there—like the saying that "God helps those who help themselves." That one's not biblical either. In fact, some people would say it's antithetical to Scripture's main teaching about salvation through faith—that heaven is a gift given despite our efforts, not because of them.

Assumptions: sometimes they don't just fail to lead us

to the truth, sometimes they lure us in the opposite direction altogether.

In life.

In religion.

In investigations.

And once an assumption gets rooted in your thinking, it becomes like a tenacious vine that is not easily removed.

The breeze was picking up, bowing the few tree branches that still held their leaves as it passed.

Apart from the noseless man, we had the Matchmaker and his crew in custody. However, though we'd stopped them for the time being, I wasn't naive enough to think that the live feeds of suicides were over.

Our society has turned a corner, and there will be no going back. I hated to even think about it, but based on the statistics, somewhere in our country this week, some troubled, lonely person would be positioning her camera and turning it on before placing a razor blade against her wrist or emptying a bottle of pills into her hand.

Another live-streamed suicide—a phrase that was heartbreakingly tragic in its irony.

Once a week.

Every week.

And the number continues to grow every year.

As Calvin had said to me yesterday, *"It is our world. I hasten not to judge it for I am a part of it."*

And so am I.

So are we all.

The rain became more steady and, in the escalating wind, it began to slant down at us in thin angles, slashing more than falling, the drops masquerading as wicked little liquid knives. A roll of unseasonable thunder sounded like laughter—not the light laughter of children, but the chortling of a man as he watches you, slit-eyed and hungry for what the night might bring.

"What are you thinking?" Christie asked me, her voice soft and nearly overwhelmed by the sound of the rain battering against the umbrella.

"That I'm fighting a losing battle."

After a few more steps, she said, "Inside of you or outside of you?"

"You do know me pretty well, don't you?"

Rather than pursue that, she changed the subject, which was fine by me. "It means a lot to Tessa that you're teaching her to drive."

"Of course."

"I want you to look at her as if she were your own daughter—I mean, as much as you can. After all, I don't know if we'll ever have kids of our own."

That came out of nowhere.

"We don't need to decide anything like that now, Christie. We've only been married a few months."

"I know. I'm just saying."

"Okay."

Kids. Wow. Yes, the subject had come up before, but I'd always deflected it, saying I was open to the idea but only when the time was right. The thought of bringing a child into this world was still a daunting one to me.

She went on. "I guess what I'm saying is, if anything ever happened to me, you'd be there for her?"

"Nothing's going to happen to you."

"I know. But if it did."

"I'd be here for her. Yes. Always."

She was silent.

"Are you alright?"

"Yes." She gave me a quick kiss, a silent confirmation of her confidence in me. "Are you heading to the Field Office this morning?"

"I'm going to swing by the hospital first, see how Calvin is doing."

"Let me know if he needs anything. I'd like to help if there's anything I can do."

Christie had never met Calvin and, although I would have liked to introduce them to each other, this might not be the best set of circumstances for that to happen.

"Thanks. I'll see."

All of my thoughts over the course of this last week concerning pain and God and the burdens we carry cycloned around inside me. My wife seemed so strong in her faith, so true to her beliefs. Finally, I said, "Christie, what does Christianity mean to you?"

"You mean when it's really lived out?"

"Yeah."

"It means treating everyone you meet as if they were worth dying for."

"Because Jesus taught that?"

"Yes. And because they are."

++++

Julianne's body was starting to stink, so last night Timothy had slept on the couch in his living room instead of the spare bedroom upstairs.

But now, when he awoke, it wasn't her body that he smelled.

It was coffee.

And then he heard the rattle of dishes.

Someone was in his kitchen.

No, you're hearing things. You're alone. No one else is here. No one else could be here.

Timothy still had Julianne's Beretta, and now he silently retrieved it and gripped it firmly as he started toward the kitchen.

"Hello?"

He'd never shot a gun before, but it couldn't be that difficult to use. Just point and squeeze the trigger.

Aim for the biggest target. Aim for the torso.

"Who's there?"

No reply.

The lady from last night? From the bookstore? Miranda's mom? Was that possible?

That woman really did think he had killed her daughter.

So did Julianne. She thought you killed Miranda too.

None of this made sense.

Maybe you did.

Timothy came to the far end of the living room and steeled himself.

Then stepped around the corner into the kitchen.

A man stood before him, early to mid fifties. He didn't appear at all fazed that Timothy was pointing a gun at him.

"Hello." He held a cup of coffee and now blew softly across the top of it. "My name is Blake Neeson. I thought it was time we had a little chat."

62

A scalp-prickling terror gripped Timothy.

After Julianne had given him the papers at the pier, he'd brought them home and found a reference to Blake Neeson in them. He wasn't certain, but from what it implied, Neeson was the one who'd dug up the information for her. An online search had told him that Neeson was on the FBI's Ten Most Wanted list.

"What are you doing here?" Timothy managed to say to him.

"You sent me a photo."

"A photo? What photo?"

"Of Julianne. And a message that you wanted to talk. I'm here. Let's talk. I want to know why you killed her."

"It wasn't me. I didn't send you anything."

Neeson took a sip of his coffee. "Do you want a cup? I made enough for both us."

"No. You need to leave."

"Timothy, do you know anything about coffee burns? Steaming coffee can cause second-degree—even third-degree—burns if enough of it is poured onto just the right spot. Especially if it happens slowly enough. It'll veritably melt the skin away."

"Please. I don't know how to help you."

"They never found your father, did they, Timothy?"

And then a thought. And with it, a chill. "You? Are you my dad?"

"No." Neeson laughed slightly. "No. I'm not."

Timothy wasn't sure if he should believe this man or not.

He'd been just a boy when his father disappeared, and the actual memories of him were difficult to separate from the fantasies he'd overlaid on them since his childhood—fabled dreams of a dad who was there for him, who loved him, who didn't hurt anyone. Not ever.

Though the voices that wouldn't let him alone told Timothy that he'd killed his dad, drowned him, he didn't believe them. His father might still be living out there somewhere.

"Do you know who he is?" he asked Neeson. "Do you know where my dad is?"

"No, I don't."

"Listen to me." Timothy lowered the gun slightly. "I don't know what you're talking about with messages and photos. I didn't send you anything. Now, you better leave, or I'm going to call the police."

"Well, then." Neeson held out his cell. "Go ahead. Call them. Tell them about Julianne."

Timothy didn't move.

"I didn't think so." He pocketed the phone. "Where is she, Timothy? What did you do with her body?"

"What?"

"Don't play games with me. I'm not in the mood, and I don't have time to waste. Where is Julianne Springman's body?"

Take him to the basement. The grave is already dug. Shoot

him and put him in there. Then cover him up. Bury him.
You can—

"No!" Timothy shouted. "I won't do it."

Neeson studied him, then said, "You really do hear them, don't you?"

"Hear who?"

"The voices. The ones you told Dr. Percival about."

Oh. So that's where he got the information.

Could Percival be your dad? Could he be the killer?

"What did he tell you?" Timothy said.

Neeson didn't answer him, just said, "Julianne is the one who gave you my email address, isn't she? Before you killed her."

"I just want you to leave."

"Show me Julianne, and I will."

Enough.

End this. Do it.

"She's upstairs." He pointed. "It's this way."

++++

Tessa rolled out of bed, yawning, and found a text from her mom:

Walking with Pat. We should be back before you leave for school. Luv you.—M

She yawned again, then rubbed at her eyes.

Serious eye scabs today.

Last night, she'd heard Patrick and her mom talking in the other room after they thought she was asleep. She couldn't hear everything, but something had happened at work with Patrick. Someone had died. She wasn't sure if it was the same person that her mom had told her Patrick was riding to the hospital with or not.

Tessa had figured that she would wait and see if they brought it up with her this morning.

There was a lot weighing on her.

What was that woman at the bookstore even talking about when she said Timothy had killed her daughter? Why would anyone say something like that—unless there was some kind of proof? Unless there was some sort of evidence?

Timothy had told her that a young woman disappeared after his previous signing. It shouldn't be that hard to verify that. It was just a matter of matching a date with a disappearance.

Last night, after ferreting Timothy out of the bookstore, Tessa had gone back in and retrieved his journal. Only after Rebekah had taken out her phone to call the cops did that frantic woman finally leave.

So now, Tessa had the journal and was waiting to hear from Timothy regarding how to get it back to him.

Then there was also the whole issue of her mom's return.

Yeah, of course, it was good to have her back home again, but there was something serious eating away at her. Tessa knew her well enough to tell that whatever was troubling her wasn't just the normal sort of stuff that wears on people.

She was anxious to find out what was up with her mom—anxious in both senses of the word.

Anxious in the worried sense.

And anxious in the urgent one.

After slumping into the shower to try to wake herself up, Tessa returned to her bedroom and gazed at Timothy's journal, the one he'd read at the Mystorium.

It felt slightly intrusive to have it—like holding someone else's phone or purse or something.

He was going to get his address to her so she could mail the journal to him, but until then . . .

You shouldn't read it. That's private.

But he read aloud from it last night, a voice countered. *It wasn't intrusive to hear him reading from it, was it?*

That's not the point.

Okay, too much to figure out right now. Tessa decided to decide later whether or not to read it, but she did know that she didn't want to leave it lying around.

It was definitely better to take it along with her to school than risk letting her mom find it here.

She stuffed it into her school backpack with her books.

++++

Blake stared at Julianne's body lying on Timothy Sabian's bed.

"I didn't kill her," Timothy declared. "I found her."

Blake wasn't exactly sure what to think. "And you brought her here?"

"She was in my basement."

"Not your car?"

"What?"

"You didn't kill her when she was in the trunk of your car? That's where she was in the photograph."

He held out his phone and showed Timothy the picture of her corpse from the email.

"I don't know anything about that photo."

"You tell me that you didn't kill her or send me her picture. Do you have access to the federal building in Manhattan? To the computers there?"

"I have no idea who sent that to you or how they might have taken that picture. No one else knew about . . ."

When he hesitated, Blake said, "What?"

"There was a man in a car who might have seen us together out by the riverfront."

"Tell me about this man."

"There's nothing to tell. I didn't get a good look at him. His car was some sort of sedan. But he had duct tape on his license plate. I noticed that."

"Duct tape."

"Yes. He saw me. He may have seen her. Maybe he's the one who killed her and left me the note that she was in my basement. He could've also been the one who sent you the photo."

The earnestness in the novelist's voice led Blake to believe that he was being truthful.

Well, in that case, it resolved one issue—someone in addition to Timothy might have known about Julianne— but it left the bigger question unanswered: who was behind the photograph?

"Alright," Blake said. "I want to look over your emails. The sent ones. If I don't find any evidence that you routed that photo to me, I'll leave. But if I find anything that leads me to think you emailed me that photograph of Miss Springman, we're returning to the kitchen, and I'm going to pour you some coffee, now, while it's still hot."

++++

At our apartment, Christie and I found Tessa ready for school.

Christie walked her outside on her way to work, and I grabbed my computer bag and laptop.

It all seemed so typical, so normal, a slap in the face at the harsh travesty of Sasha's death. Routine. Life goes on. In that mixed curse-and-blessing way, it has to. The metronomic movement of each day pulses past us, pressing us forward, on and on and on until we find death's unyielding grip has found us too.

Before taking off, I reviewed the work schedules of the staff on duty when Mannie escaped and saw that Thurman had been scheduled to work only half of the day. He might have even been on his way out when he was attacked. I wasn't sure what to make of that, if anything.

I began dictating my report of what'd happened last night at the Matchmaker's, then I left to go see Calvin, continuing my dictation on the drive to the hospital, thinking once more of the limping, noseless man and his escape into the night.

63

My friend was not doing well.

The doctors had placed him on a ventilator overnight, and when I arrived, they were removing it so that he could breathe on his own.

I stood in the hallway and spoke with a member of the medical team, out of earshot of Calvin.

"We're keeping an eye on his blood counts," she told me soberly. "We've done one CT scan, and we have him scheduled for another one later this morning to make sure there isn't active extravasation."

I'm no medical expert, but I'd been in this job long enough to know that extravasation meant fluid seeping from an organ.

"What happens if you find that?"

"Surgery," was all she said.

"Okay." I gave her my cell number. Calvin didn't have any family in the area and, although I believed he had grown children, I didn't think he was close to them. "Text me the results of the scan."

"I'll need his permission to do that," she replied. "Privacy issues."

Her associates finished with him, and she got Calvin's permission to keep me updated. Then, as she was leaving, I went into the room to speak with my friend.

Gaunt and sallow, he looked ten weary years older than he had yesterday when we met for lunch.

"Calvin, you're going to be okay," I told him reassuringly, as much for my benefit as for his.

"Things did not quite go to plan last night," he said, reminding me by the idiom that he was English. Then he added weakly, "Not as hale and hearty as I used to be, I'm afraid."

"You gave those two men a good thumping before the lights went out."

"Perhaps that'll teach them to pick on someone their own age."

I wasn't sure if Calvin would still be interested in giving us any input on the case, but I left the paperwork beside his bed for him to fill out if he chose to when he was feeling better.

The hum and murmur of hospital sounds floated around us—the soft blip of the machine monitoring Calvin's vitals, the hushed voices of nurses talking in the hallway, the relentless ticking of the clock on the wall beside the window as its hands made their way methodically around its face.

"Christie sends her thoughts and prayers," I told him. "She mentioned that she'd like to see you, if you're up for it."

"I would very much like to meet her. I still regret not

being able to attend your wedding." He grimaced as he repositioned himself on the bed. "So then, you have the Matchmaker in custody?"

I debated how much speculation to allow myself. "It's quite possible, yes. None of the people we picked up are talking, but I think there's enough to keep them on. We'll see what else we can come up with—besides the assault against you."

"I don't intend to press charges, Patrick."

"What? Why not?"

"Time. It is a precious commodity, my boy. With each passing year, that becomes more and more clear to me. I would rather not spend my life conferring with lawyers and appearing in court."

"It's not your life, Calvin. It's just some of your time."

"Time is life, my boy."

"Calvin, I—"

He shook his head with firm resolve.

Alright, you can sort all that out later.

I laid a hand softly on his arm. "Okay. I hear you."

"Good thing you aren't the one on this bed," he said.

"Why's that?"

"As I recall, you have a certain reticence towards being poked with needles."

"I don't prefer it. No."

"You don't prefer it to what?"

"Getting shot. Stabbed. Drowned. Things like that."

"Minor things."

"Right."

After taking a few breaths to regroup, he asked, "By the way, did you ever catch the young man who was bereft of his nose?"

"No. He got away."

"I see."

"Calvin, I've been thinking. We assumed that Joe from the basement was the Matchmaker, but what if someone else is the true puppet master?"

He contemplated that. "Mr. Noseless, for instance."

"Yes. He might very well have been much more than the doorman. He limped like the man I chased in the subway. No one from the basement will tell us anything about him. Also, someone killed the electricity down there after he left."

"That's not enough."

"No. Not yet."

Calvin smiled weakly. "It appears I taught you well."

"Assume nothing. Test everything—"

"And the truth will rear its head," he said, finishing the axiom for me.

We sat in silence for a few minutes and, despite the case's urgency, it felt like the right thing to do. Finally, he patted my hand. "You have work to do. This case will not solve itself while you sit here waiting for me to convalesce."

"I'll be back later to check on you."

"Tell your wife that I'm glad to have her visit anytime, if she desires."

"I will."

++++

Timothy let out a sigh of relief as Blake Neeson finally left.

Though he wasn't confident it would necessarily do a whole lot of good, he locked the door behind his unwelcome visitor, then leaned a grateful hand against the doorframe.

And then, scratching at his arm, he went to pour the nearly full pot of coffee down the drain.

++++

Tessa stood across the street from her high school, trying to decide if she was going to play hooky today or not.

She really wanted to know what Timothy had been talking about when he mentioned that woman going missing after his previous signing.

Although she was hoping to find out who that might have been, she knew that searching for the answer at school, either on her laptop or her phone—without getting caught—would be tricky, even for her.

But then again, it wasn't like she'd never bailed on her classes before.

What would another day of unexcused absences really matter?

She could see both sides—but with her mom being troubled lately, she decided that it would be best not to add to her stress. Plus, there was an English exam that she had but hadn't studied at all for. Better to pass it than get a zero. She could always slip out during lunchtime if she needed to.

Tessa crossed the street and entered the building just as the tardy bell was sounding.

++++

I paused in the hospital's lobby and texted Christie that Calvin was open to seeing her. Maybe you can come over during lunch? I wrote.

Then I perused the online case files to see if there'd

been any movement on things while I was visiting my friend.

According to the latest updates, the team was still looking for Julianne Springman's location.

Yesterday we'd started the search for her, and frustratingly, it was taking longer than we'd anticipated. She hadn't disclosed her new address to the Detroit Police Department when she left the force, and New York City can be a pretty big haystack to search through for a needle that isn't necessarily interested in being found.

When I saw that we had a history of her credit card usage over the past two months, I took a careful look at the times and locations of her purchases. People tend to make financial and logistical choices based on trying to save time and money, so their purchase patterns often reveal their understanding of and familiarity with their surroundings and movement spaces.

Functional cognitive mapping is one of the foundational principles of geoprofiling, and now I found a cluster of purchases that narrowed down a two-block possible point-of-origin region in Brooklyn.

I contacted DeYoung and told him to focus the search within those blocks, looking for places that'd been leased within the last three months. "Focus on one-bedrooms that were rented to a single female Caucasian."

"Consider it done. Where are you?"

"Still at Metro Medical. I was visiting Calvin."

"How is he?"

"Recovering. And oh, let's put some more resources into finding the guy without the nose who was at the Matchmaker's. He might be more important to all of this than we've been thinking. Maybe we don't have the Matchmaker in custody after all."

++++

Blake was on his way back to the greenhouse when he got the call.

Before he'd left the novelist's house, he'd told him, "I have people who specialize in taking care of situations like this, like the one you have here with this dead woman. I'll have them come by."

"Why are you helping me?" Sabian had asked him. "What do you want from me?"

"I want nothing from you. But her body, if it is discovered—and the way you're treating things, that's simply a matter of time—could eventually lead back to me. We will both benefit if the situation is satisfactorily re-solved. Other than that, we have nothing more to discuss."

Now, on the phone, he heard from Ibrahim.

"The canisters are here," the Syrian told him.

"Have the chemicals been mixed?"

"Reese was adamant that we not prepare the Tranadyl until the plane landed."

"I understand. Do it now. Then spray the mannequins down. They should be ready to ship five hours after that. Take all the necessary precautions. Hazmat suits. Use it all. Whatever you need."

A slight pause. "I thought that what we're using is inert on its own. It's only when you snort or shoot up Selzu-caine that's been tainted with it, that it—"

"Better to be safe in this instance than put anything—or anyone—at risk."

"Yes, sir. I understand. And then we will make a statement that will not soon be forgotten."

"That's right." Blake slipped into the role he was playing of the terrorist mastermind, Fayed Raabi'ah Bashir. "That's exactly right. One about depravity and holiness."

"Yes."

"Allahu Akbar," Blake said theatrically.

"Allahu Akbar," Ibrahim replied with genuine fanatical fervor.

From what Blake could tell, Ibrahim still believed he would be around to see the results of the shipments going out. And that naiveté played in Blake's favor.

After the call, he thought through the route his silent ladies would take after they left the greenhouse: boarding the two semis and, from there, embarking to cities all along the Eastern Seaboard.

By tomorrow at this time, the product would be on the streets and people around the world would once again fear the name of Fayed Raabi'ah Bashir.

++++

Hospitals in New York City faced the difficult task of providing enough parking for staff and patients while also keeping out people who were simply looking for a convenient place to park.

Today, the underground garage was about three-quarters full.

I heard from Ralph that the team had pinpointed a location for Julianne Springman in the area I'd suggested.

"Well, then," I said to him, battling spotty reception,

"let's head to her apartment and have a word with our old friend from Detroit."

Then my bars dwindled off and I walked toward my car in the tight-cornered, concrete cavern beneath the hospital.

64

Considering the severity of the allegations against Miss Springman, DeYoung hadn't wanted to take any chances and had sent an FBI SWAT team over to clear the apartment before Ralph and I entered it.

By the time we arrived, they were already on-site.

As the two of us waited somewhat impatiently for them to reconnoiter and breach the premises, Ralph notified me that Greer had been put on administrative leave for his actions in allowing Sasha to go out alone and not requesting backup when he should have.

I understood the administrative leave protocol all too well—I'd walked that path more than once myself—but still, it was unfortunate, especially since we could've really used Greer's help right now with the case.

"And we still don't know where Sasha's body is?" I asked.

"No. Greer said she had a tracking device with her, but when we tried to locate it, we got nothing. Blake and his men must have found it and either disabled it or destroyed it."

"Anything more on the people from the Matchmaker's basement?"

"Not yet. Collins and her team are analyzing their computers, but the files are encrypted, and it's not looking like it'll be an easy process getting into them."

"And the people we arrested aren't helping?"

"Not at all."

Last night I'd thought about contacting Marcus Rockwell, the CEO of Krazle, to find out if there was anything he could do to help us track down the Matchmaker through the use of that compromised Krazle account. Now, while we waited for SWAT to move in, felt like as good a time as any to give him a call.

It took a little work to track down his personal assistant, but when I told her who I was, she informed me that she would pass my contact information along to Mr. Rockwell and have him reach out to me "at his earliest convenience."

"Convenient or not, I need to speak with him as soon as possible."

"I'll let him know," she replied matter-of-factly and then, to my irritation, ended the call before I could reiterate how pressing this was.

I said to Ralph, "I mentioned this to DeYoung, but I want the team to focus on finding the guy who escaped from the basement before the electricity went out. He might be the actual Matchmaker."

"Maybe we've gotten ahead of ourselves."

"Yes. Maybe we have. Also, based on his limp and the interconnected nature of the rest of this case, I'm wondering if he might be the man I chased into the subway tunnel."

"You're not sure?"

"I'm trying to be careful with assumptions."

Apart from the subway cameras, which hadn't yielded anything, I tried to think of a way to verify if he was the same individual, but at the moment, I couldn't come up with anything definitive.

SWAT went in and, less than a minute later, called for us to enter.

"She's in the bedroom," Agent Raudsepp informed us grimly. "And she's not gonna get up. Ever."

Expecting to find Julianne Springman's body, Ralph and I entered the room, but it wasn't Julianne that we saw. Instead, Sasha MacIntyre's corpse lay on the bed.

Still clothed, missing only her shoes.

The plastic bag still cinched lethally over her head.

Even a cursory look around made it clear that she had not died here. The video of her suicide had been filmed in an office with different flooring and a desk in the background. There was nothing like that in this bedroom.

Obviously, she'd been moved, brought here to Julianne's apartment for reasons I couldn't even begin to imagine.

"Where does this leave us?" Ralph said quietly.

"Let's get NYPD to canvass the neighborhood. Maybe someone saw something that'll help us identify who brought her in here. CCTVs, personal cell phone videos—whatever we can get."

"These guys are good. I'm not holding my breath."

"Neither am I."

While we waited for the Evidence Response Team to

show up, Ralph and I took a careful look around the apartment, searching for any clues as to Julianne's whereabouts.

Nothing appeared unusual or all that revelatory: her clothes were arranged neatly in the closet, the dresser drawers hadn't been rifled through, the papers on her desk were all in order.

No calendar, date books, or daily organizers.

No notes on her fridge that gave anything away.

The computer needed a password, but I was no hacker, so that wasn't going to happen.

However, beside the keyboard lay a pile of printouts and articles about the novelist Timothy Sabian.

I flipped through them as Ralph came up with a well-worn copy of Sabian's novel *Cold Clay*.

"It looks like Julianne is a real fan of this guy," he said.

"That's the author that Tessa went to see last night." I had no idea what to make of that. "I think we should pay him a visit."

When the ERT showed up, we heard from DeYoung that the senator was going to be swinging by the Field Office at eleven to see about the progress of the investigation into his son's death. I still wasn't sure why he'd acted so strangely after I spoke with him at his house—calling the press conference and offering that reward.

Maybe it wasn't strange after all. Maybe it was just desperation.

Regardless of his reasons, now we had to deal with the ramifications.

It would be close, but eleven o'clock might just give us enough time.

I suggested to Ralph that we find out what we could from Mr. Sabian and then go have a chat with the senator.

"You read my mind, bro."

++++

Christie checked her messages and saw a text from Pat regarding the status of his friend Calvin Werjonic. Pat noted that Calvin would be glad to see her, if she had the chance to get over there.

He suggested she might swing by at lunch, and if she had a productive morning, that just might work.

If she could take an early lunch, depending on how the subway lines were running, she could probably make it to the hospital by noon.

65

When Timothy Sabian opened the door, Ralph and I identified ourselves as federal agents, and then, without missing a beat, Ralph said, "Mr. Sabian, do you mind if we come in?"

But even as he was asking the question, he was moving forward and, though Timothy didn't look very excited about us joining him inside the house, he appeared even less excited about getting on Ralph's bad side, and he mumbled, "I'd rath—um. Sure."

He stepped back, and we entered the living room.

The house smelled of disinfectant.

Ralph wrinkled up his nose. "Doing a little cleaning?"

"Cleaning?"

"Smells like a hospital in here."

"Oh. Yes. The bathroom. You have to take care of things every once in a while or they get out of hand."

"Right," Ralph replied slowly.

"Did you have a good book signing last night?" I said. I decided not to mention that my stepdaughter had been there.

Timothy eyed me carefully. "Yes . . . how did . . . ? How can I help you two gentlemen?"

"We're looking for a woman who might have attended it."

His face blanched. "Did something happen to her?"

"To who?" I said.

"The woman. The one at the signing."

"And which woman would that be?" Ralph asked.

"I didn't do anything. I swear. She just burst in and started yelling those things."

Ralph and I exchanged a look, and then I said, "What, exactly, did she yell?"

"That I hurt her daughter. But I didn't."

I eyed him quizzically. We had no knowledge that Julianne Springman had any children. "Her daughter?"

Ralph pulled out his phone and scrolled to a photo of Julianne, which he showed to Timothy. "Is this the woman who was yelling those things?"

When Timothy saw the photograph, he swallowed and almost imperceptibly edged away from us.

"Are you alright, Mr. Sabian?" I asked.

"Maybe you should go."

"Do you know this woman?" I pressed him. "From the book signing or not—have you ever seen her before?"

++++

Timothy heard the voice.

These men are here for a reason. Something led them here. Don't deny meeting Julianne or they'll know you're lying.

"I didn't know her well," he told them. "I just met her briefly. We spoke over the weekend. She told me about her website. She was looking for a partner. She wasn't at the signing, no."

How do you describe the sensation of bugs skittering across your skin? Think of a spider on your neck, then think of a dozen, then think of a thousand, but not just on your neck—scuttling all over you. The light touch of tiny feet, the running scurry of invisible bugs.

Tiny mandibles clawing at your skin. You have to dig those bugs out. You have to. You can't leave them alone or they'll multiply more and more and more.

But you can't dig them out now. No. Not when people are watching. Not when—

"A partner?" Agent Hawkins said, and Timothy was back in the moment, his drifting attention refocused again.

"Financial. Sometimes when people think you're rich or famous they come looking for you to invest in their pet projects or donate to their charities. It's amazing how many peculiar and necessitous people come out of the woodwork once there's a Wikipedia page about you."

++++

"May I use your washroom?" I said, in order to get an excuse to have a look around. Plain view doctrine would come into play, but as long as I was on my way to a bathroom and was simply looking around—range of sight—we would be alright.

"Oh . . . yes. Just down the hall."

As I walked toward the bathroom that I didn't really need to use, I heard Ralph follow up with Timothy. "You said it was a website. What kind of site is it?"

"It's a little troubling, actually. She would photograph dead babies in the arms of their mothers."

He said "would photograph," not "photographs." Past tense. What does he know?

While the young novelist explained that Julianne's site was set up to help mourning mothers cope with the loss of their children, I scrutinized the house, keeping an eye out for any sign that Julianne had been—or was still—here, but saw nothing.

When I came to the stairs leading to the second level, I noted that I was out of sight of Ralph and Timothy.

It might not be a bad idea to have a quick peek up there.

"And did you see her again after that?" Ralph was saying. "After she asked you to partner with her?"

I started up the stairs.

It smelled like Timothy had done most of his cleaning up here rather than in the bathroom on the first level.

When I reached the top of the stairs, I saw that the doors were all open at least a crack.

Excellent.

I began to peer into the rooms one by one, making my way down the hall.

++++

Timothy wasn't sure what to think.

He wanted these men to leave, yes, of course he did. But he also wanted them to know the truth and to finally have everything out in the open. And if it was true that he was a killer, then they should arrest him, stop him, keep him from hurting anyone else.

From killing.

From killing anyone.

Dead is dead is dead.

But then the desire for self-preservation kicked in and—

"Agent Hawkins." The voice came from upstairs, interrupting Timothy's thoughts. "Bring Mr. Sabian up here."

The big man beside him gestured for him to head to the stairs. "After you."

66

Ralph and Timothy appeared at the doorway, and I indicated the nightstand beside the bed in the master bedroom. "That's a nice Beretta you have there."

"Thank you."

"Do you use it to hunt with?" Ralph said, which was a bit of a strange question considering how hard it would be to hunt with that type of handgun, but I figured Ralph was trying to feel him out, see how familiar he was with guns.

"Target shoot, mainly."

"Really? Which range?"

"I . . . used to do it more before I moved to New York City. It's harder to find a good range here."

"But yet you keep your gun beside your bed. Is it loaded?"

"I don't . . . Yes."

"You don't what?" Ralph eyed him. "Do you have a permit for this handgun?"

"Yes . . . somewhere."

"Somewhere."

"Yes."

"So if we looked up the serial number, we'd find that it's a legally registered firearm under your name. I mean, you didn't borrow it from someone and just forget to return it?"

Timothy shook his head. "It's my gun. I'm sorry. I wish I could help you two more. I just don't know what to tell you."

"Your mirror in the bathroom is broken," I said, noting what I'd discovered before I invited them upstairs.

"Yes. I was careless. Slipped and hit my head."

He tipped his hair aside and showed us a bump high on his forehead.

I motioned toward the open window. "Airing things out?"

"The smell can be a lot. Of the cleaning agents."

"The rain is supposed to turn to snow later today."

Timothy walked over and closed the window authoritatively. "I'll keep that in mind. Thanks. Now if you don't mind, I need to get back to work."

Outside Sabian's house, I said to Ralph, "Well, what did you think of that?"

"He's a lying son of a . . . biscuit."

"Nice save there. Swearing off swearing, I mean."

"Thanks. That guy knows more than he's telling us. He's hiding something, and I want to know what it is. He referred to Julianne's website in the past tense."

"I noticed."

"I doubt that Beretta is even his. I should have checked the serial number before we left."

"Don't worry." I pulled out my phone. "I did—before I called you two up. Let's run it and see what we get."

++++

Timothy was just glad Blake's men had shown up when they did to take Julianne's body out. He didn't know where they might have taken it, and frankly, he didn't want to know.

That was over.

That part of his life was done.

At least with Julianne gone, she wasn't talking to him anymore. At least there was that.

Gone is gone is gone.

Dead is dead is dead is dead.

Yes.

Whatever else might be up in doubt, at least that much was true.

And the agents were gone. Thankfully thankfully thankfully that was taken care of too.

Now, he just needed to pick up where he'd left off before Julianne Springman tracked him down in the first place and turned his life inside out.

Writing. Surviving. Making the bugs go away.

And the first step in returning to normal was getting his journal with his notes about Emily back from that girl, Tessa, who'd helped him get out of the bookstore last night after Miranda's mom showed up.

++++

Tessa wasn't the best person in the world at checking her phone's screen without getting caught while she was in class, but she wasn't the worst either.

However, she still hadn't found out anything about who disappeared after Timothy Sabian's last signing.

While doing her best to avoid letting her teacher see her using her phone, she received a message from the very person who was foremost on her mind.

The novelist wrote to her:

Thank you for helping me make my escape last night. So very cloak and dagger.

Also, those words on the church bulletin: "The waters of this moment rush over my head. I drink in the truth and find that it tastes like tears just as I suspected."

Did you write that?

It's good.

I never got the chance to sign your book yesterday. The next time our paths cross, I will. If you're interested, that is.

Then he included a snail mail address in Ozone Park so she could send him the journal, but he also suggested that if she wanted to meet somewhere instead, if that was easier for her, and so that she wouldn't have to pay for postage, he would be glad to do that.

She messaged him back, Yeah, no problem. Thanks for saying that about the poem. Means a lot. And yeah, I'd love to have my book signed. What if I brought it by in person?

The reply was slow in coming, but it did come: That would be fine. I should be here all day.

Huh. It must not have registered with him that she had school. Maybe he thought she was older, in college or something. She tried to figure out if he was being flirty or forward or inappropriate, but in the end she decided that he was most likely just a little clueless and not very socially adept.

Okay, so she could visit him after lunch.

After she'd found out all she could about the missing woman that he claimed not to have killed.

++++

The Beretta was registered to Julianne Springman.

Another wrinkle in the case.

Or maybe things were finally starting to get smoothed out.

"What do you think?" Ralph said. "Go back in and have another talk with our friendly lying neighborhood novelist?"

"Let's look at what we know—Julianne was working with Dylan in Detroit. After his death, she moves here to New York City. Somewhere along the line she takes an interest in Sabian, visits him, and now she's missing and he has her gun."

"And Sasha's body is in her apartment."

"Yes."

We both considered the implications, but the connection between Julianne, Sasha, and Timothy remained elusive to me. The first two had ties to Blake, but how did Timothy fit into the mix?

"Alright," I said, "here's what I'm thinking—we stake out his place and hers. Let's see if she shows up at either location, and if he leaves his house, we'll have an undercover team follow him."

"Works for me. For now. But I don't like that he lied to us."

"I don't either."

"And that makes me angry." Ralph tightened his jaw.

"And you know how Buddhists say you're not supposed to lose your temper? That anger shows you haven't yet reached enlightenment? Well, that's me right now."

"But you're not a Buddhist."

"No, I am not. I'm something else."

I took the bait. "What are you?"

"A Ralphist."

"And what exactly are the tenets of Ralphism?"

"There's five of 'em. Courage. Honor. Justice. Action. Anger."

"Anger?"

"If you don't get angry about injustice, you won't act, and if you don't act, evil will win. Don't be a coward, treat people with honor, and do what's right regardless of whose feelings get hurt. The road to enlightenment is paved with well-directed anger, not denial."

Although he made some good points, I wasn't quite ready to become a Ralphist.

I checked the time and realized that if we were going to get to the Field Office for a sit-down with Senator Murray, we needed to get moving.

Ralph offered to stay here and keep an eye on Sabian's place until we could get a team on-site. "I'll hitch a ride with an NYPD car, meet up with you at the Field Office," he told me.

++++

Christie notified her boss, Brian Stokoe, that she was slipping out.

"A friend of the family is in the hospital. I'm going to swing by and see how he's doing, then grab lunch. I should be back around two or so, but I can stay later this afternoon to make up the time."

"That shouldn't be a problem. I just hope your friend is okay."

"Thank you, Mr. Stokoe. So do I."

++++

Timothy Sabian's father—the avid killer, the man who was watching him—shook his head in disbelief.

Throughout the morning, he'd been monitoring the video feed from his son's house, and there'd been an awful lot of activity there. First Blake Neeson, then the men who'd removed Julianne's body, and at last, two FBI agents: Agent Hawkins and Agent Bowers.

Yes, he knew them both.

And here they were, working so diligently to see justice done.

Too diligently, perhaps.

He'd been wondering how to wrap things up with Timothy in a satisfactory and climactic manner. Making the ending a little more personal for one of those two agents might just do the trick.

But it might also draw undue attention to himself and to the pastime he'd had for the last twenty years.

Originally, he'd planned on setting his son up for everything. Now, he decided that he should be prepared to disappear in case that fell through. He began making the arrangements, and then thought again of the end of the story.

Hawkins was from out of town, so if it was going to be a member of his family, that would be more difficult to pull off.

But Bowers was not. A little checking confirmed that he had a wife and stepdaughter here in the city.

Yes. Either of those two would work.

He put a call through to have Christie Ellis's phone traced.

67

In the wake of Sasha's death last night, a solemn heaviness weighed on everyone at the Field Office.

We gathered in DeYoung's conference room.

Word was, Senator Murray was on his way over but was running a little late and might not arrive until closer to eleven thirty.

"Let's see what we can cover before he gets here," De-Young said.

In addition to the assistant director and me, Thurman was there, as were three other agents who were working behind the scenes on the case. Apparently, with Greer on mandatory administrative leave, Thurman was being asked to play a bigger role in the investigation.

We took our seats.

"Alright." DeYoung's voice was heavy. "Before we get started, I want to offer a moment of silence for Agent Mac-Intyre. She didn't deserve this. It's up to us to finish what she started and bring Blake in."

++++

"Tessa, are you still with us?"

Tessa blinked and shifted her gaze to the front of the classroom. "What?"

"Perhaps you'd be more comfortable on a couch. Would you like me to have a couch brought in here for you?"

A few snickers from around the room.

She hadn't been dozing. She'd been deep in thought, but still, her teacher's question deserved a reply.

"No thanks. Your teaching is soporific enough. Oh wait, you went to a government school, didn't you? You probably don't know what that means. Soporific: sleep-inducing. It's from the Latin."

"I'm proud of my public-school education. And you should be thankful for yours."

"There's no such thing as a public school."

"Really?" He was smirking.

"'Public' simply means 'government-run.' It's just that it plays better to say 'public' instead. People don't like being reminded who's behind our failing education system—after all, we all know how efficient and effective government employees, like you, are at—"

"That's enough."

"Really? 'Cause I can keep going."

"In the hall, young lady." His eyes were ice. "I'll be out to speak with you in a moment."

She collected her things.

Oh well.

No, this wasn't her first time getting kicked out of class. She knew the routine: she was supposed to wait in the hallway and then talk with him, but today she didn't feel like doing either of those things, and she figured she could deal with the consequences for leaving school later.

Go to Sabian's place. Deliver the journal. Get your book signed. It works out better this way anyhow.

++++

Ralph was still en route, so I brought everyone up to speed on what we'd found out this morning at Julianne's place and at Sabian's house.

"Sabian lied about the gun?" Thurman said reflectively.

"Yes."

"Are you thinking he's working with Julianne?"

"He told Ralph that she contacted him because she was looking for a partner. When Ralph pressed him about that, Sabian claimed that she meant a financial one, but we already know that she visited Blake looking for someone to kill with. In either case, she's still missing, and Sabian has a clear connection to her."

"Which means he has a connection to Blake," DeYoung concluded.

"Yes. Also, he seemed to indicate by his word choice that he believed Julianne was no longer running her website."

"And we have surveillance on him—on Sabian, I mean?"

"Ralph set it up. There's a team stationed outside his place. They know to follow him wherever he goes. Ralph's on his way back here."

DeYoung nodded agreeably. "What else do we know?"

One of the agents I'd only been introduced to this morning said, "We've been investigating how they're getting the Selzucaine around the country. Looks like a trucking company called Transit Corp. I'm studying their routes and their drivers' backgrounds."

"Good."

I said, "Last summer when I was tracking Blake in Detroit, we pinpointed one of the shipping companies that was bringing the mannequins over from Russia. Let's take a look at connections between the two companies."

DeYoung checked his phone. "Yes, yes, yes. And this might be just what we're looking for. Reese—the chemist from Phoenix—is talking. He's scared, wants his family protected."

"What'd he have to say?" I asked.

"Well, he's at the Phoenix Field Office now. I'll see if we can get patched through for a conference call."

While we waited for his receptionist, Annalise, to set it up, he again addressed the question of how the Match-maker was getting the suicide victims to engage in such gruesome deaths.

"The Selzucaine?" one of the team members suggested.

"Maybe," I said. "But I'm not convinced that's the only thing involved. Earlier we were looking into who might benefit from the person's death, but what if it's not a person?"

"Not a person?" DeYoung said with some confusion. "Then who?"

"Or what. Something Sabian mentioned when we were at his place: charities. If the people who died made large donations to charities or nonprofits before their deaths or had anonymous gifts given in their names around the times of their deaths, then that might be a way to trace back who the observer was."

Thurman agreed to look into it.

Annalise returned and announced that everything was ready. DeYoung put the conference call on speakerphone and conferred briefly with the agent in charge in Phoenix, then Reese came on.

"They're going to be shipping out the drugs today," he told us.

"When?" I asked.

"They would have treated them when they arrived this morning. They'll send them out this afternoon. Based on everything I know, I'd say two o'clock your time, at the latest."

"Where are they now?" DeYoung said.

"I don't know."

"Can you find out?"

"No. They've always contacted me. I've never reached out to them."

"There's a first time for everything," Thurman interjected. "If you want immunity or witness protection for you and your family, we're going to need specifics."

There was a pause on the line.

"Are you still there, Mr. Reese?" I said.

"Yes," he replied. "I do have a number, but I'm not sure what'll happen if I call it. I need to know that my family will be safe first."

"The Bureau will do all that's necessary to protect you," DeYoung assured him. "But we need anything you have so we can move on it. And we need it now to stop those mannequins from being shipped out."

"Mannequins? What do you mean?"

"The drugs," DeYoung clarified.

"You said mannequins?"

"Yes."

I found it informative that Reese apparently wasn't aware of how the Selzucaine was being shipped.

"Before he makes the call," I said to DeYoung, "let's see if Cyber can trace the number or locate the other party when they pick up."

"Right." Then DeYoung directed his words to Reese

again. "We're the FBI. If we want someone to disappear, he'll disappear. We can give people a new start, erase the past. We have the resources—all we need is the motivation to use them to your advantage."

Then Reese told us about the Tranadyl and the effects it would have on anyone who snorted it while it was mixed with Selzucaine.

He confirmed that shipments of Selzucaine had been coming in for the last six months, so the supply chain was in place—all the distributors, the buyers—and now all they needed was for one final shipment to go out, one that was tainted and would enter the stream the same as the others had.

"Only this one isn't the same," he told us. "It'll get powdered, packaged, and sent out, and anyone who uses it will be snorting themselves into a coma or a casket."

We had to stop this.

We wrapped things up with him, with the agents in Phoenix waiting for word from Angela at Cyber before having him make the call to his contact, a man he knew only by the name Ibrahim.

Sasha had mentioned that name to us earlier as well. DeYoung assigned one of the new agents to find out all he could about any Ibrahims in Blake's network.

Reese had mentioned two o'clock, so we had a deadline, but we didn't have a location.

It was a start.

++++

Blake looked over his silent ladies, all treated and now drying in preparation for being shipped.

He'd never really liked the term "fall guy," but in this

case, it was probably the best description of the role Ibrahim was going to play.

The Brigade of the Prophet's Sword was an organization that the original Fayed Raabi'ah Bashir had founded nearly four years ago. Over time, numerous men had taken on the identity of the terrorist—Blake doing so himself after he removed his predecessor from the role with a blade to the throat.

The Brigade was responsible for over a dozen terrorist acts, including the bioweapons attack last summer in Detroit that had resulted in the CDC shutting down and quarantining a two-block section of the city.

Now, this week, the next attack would undoubtedly result in expanded efforts to quell the rise of extremism both domestically and, because of Ibrahim's ties to Syrian extremists, internationally.

The president had campaigned on the promise of being tough on terror, but once he was elected, things had shifted toward reductions in the military with a new strategy of using private security firms whenever possible in a bid to "trim excessive spending" and keep the military "lean and agile."

Which worked out perfectly for Blake.

Some people say they want to own a piece of the pie.

Blake didn't want a piece of the pie.

And he didn't want the whole thing.

He wanted to own the bakery.

And he was on his way to making that happen.

68

We waited while Reese tried Ibrahim's number, but no one picked up, and Angela wasn't able to trace the call or locate the man's cell. Apparently, but not surprisingly, whoever was using that number had either chosen a burner phone or was using high-level end-to-end encryption.

"To take us closer to Blake we need to nail down this novelist's relationship to Julianne Springman," DeYoung told us. Then he assigned Thurman the task of uncovering the connection. "Springman's a former cop. She wouldn't likely give up her gun to a stranger. Maybe they have a past together."

Senator Murray showed up, and while DeYoung went to speak with him for a few minutes, Ralph, who'd finally arrived, joined us.

"That was an interesting idea about looking into charities," Thurman observed to me. "What made you think of that?"

"Just trying to cover all the bases. Listen, you specialize in working with confidential informants. From your experience, do you think it's possible we could turn Mannie?"

"I suppose it is." He looked past me thoughtfully. "I really couldn't say without knowing more of his background. We'd need to find out what's motivating him first."

Motives. Great.

I recalled what Ralph had told me about the legislation on the senator's desk, and I considered the timing of what was happening in this case. "Quantum encryption research?"

"I'm not sure I know what that is."

"I'll forward you the files," Ralph said.

One of the other agents, a petite woman named Patricia, said to me, "After I got word about Sabian earlier this morning before the briefing, I started looking into his background. Turns out this novelist of ours has quite a past."

"In what way?" I asked.

"When he was a boy, his dad was suspected of five murders but disappeared. Timothy's mom was sent to prison for her involvement with the crimes, spent more than a decade behind bars, and then, only a couple weeks after she was released, she was found dead in a bathtub, wrists slit."

"That's enough to send anyone off the deep end," Thurman noted.

Patricia went on. "According to the files, Timothy was the one who made the original 911 call to the Cincinnati cops back when he was a kid. Turns out he saw what his dad was doing with a hammer to the people in their basement."

I tried to take all of that in. "And his dad was never found? Never arrested?"

She shook her head. "Nope."

"Post the notes to the online case files," Thurman said. "This might explain why Julianne contacted Sabian."

"Why's that?" she asked.

"Maybe he wasn't the partner she was looking for. Maybe it was his father."

DeYoung was still speaking with Senator Murray, so I decided to work in my office until they were done.

Though I wanted to ask the senator about the gambling debts and the Internet encryption legislation, perhaps the biggest question I needed answered was also the most obvious and the most potentially offensive: if he was the one who'd stood by and watched his son commit suicide.

It was probably out of the question that the senator was in some way involved, but I couldn't afford to discount any possibilities. As Calvin had noted earlier, if we assume nothing and test everything, eventually the truth will rear its head.

The suicides occurred in three different states, and it shouldn't be too difficult to compare the senator's travel schedule with the times and locations of the deaths to see if he could've possibly been present when those other people took their own lives.

It seemed self-evident to note this, but the observer would've had to travel to those locations and then leave by some means.

The man's face wasn't fully visible in any of the videos, but his frame matched and, based on the analysis that Angela was able to do regarding the left-handed mannerisms

I'd noted, there was a seventy-two percent probability that it was the same person.

However, back at my desk, it didn't take long to verify that the senator couldn't have been present at two of the suicides because of a public function that he was attending on the night of the first and a Senate vote that he made on the night of the second.

So, if it truly was the same observer at each site, the senator was in the clear.

Years ago, when I was tracking a serial killer in the Midwest, I'd studied flight records to see if we could pinpoint who'd traveled to and from the regions where the murders were occurring. In the end, the process had led me to a man named Richard Basque, a killer I eventually captured and who was still in prison.

Now, I wondered if I could apply the same strategy to this case.

Since one of the deaths was in Seattle and another was just outside of Miami, it was implausible that the observer could have driven from the first site to the second—the timing just didn't work.

That left flights.

Angela's computer, which she'd congenially named Lacey and treated like a coworker rather than simply a machine, could tackle a meta-analysis of the names of passengers who flew into and out of nearby airports on the days preceding and following the suicides. If we found a name appearing more than once, it might be a good indication that we were on the right track.

I contacted Angela and got her and Lacey looking into it.

A text message from DeYoung informed me that he would be bringing the senator up in a few minutes.

I decided to spend the time nailing down which questions to ask him—and how to do so tactfully.

Which was going to be a challenge, considering the topics I would be addressing.

69

Christie knocked lightly on the door to Dr. Calvin Werjonic's hospital room.

He enjoined her to come in, and she introduced herself. "Dr. Werjonic, I'm Christie Ellis, Pat's wife."

"Ah. Yes! Please. Have a seat."

Though he looked frail lying there in bed, he had a distinguished air about him.

"I brought you a card," she said somewhat awkwardly.

He accepted it, read it, then warmly thanked her and positioned it on the stand beside his bed next to a pile of paperwork that she noticed had his signature at the bottom.

"Patrick has told me so much about you," Calvin said, "about how thankful he is to have found you."

"I'm thankful too."

"I understand that fate brought you two together under an umbrella in April?"

"Well, yes . . . but I like to think it was more than fate."

"He mentioned that you're a spiritual person. So, part of a divine plan, perhaps? The two of you meeting the way you did?"

"I guess I just don't believe that there are such things as coincidences. Fate isn't a big enough explanation to me to account for the blessings that come into our lives."

But, Christie, what about the things that aren't blessings?
Who brings those into your life?

Is pain, is suffering part of the divine plan too?

"And in that belief," Calvin noted, "you share a common bond with your husband. He believes that apparent coincidences are simply clues to a deeper truth in an investigation, and you see that deeper truth at play as well—in all of life."

"I suppose so."

"Brilliant. Perhaps you're both right! And truth lies at the center of both perspectives, which I am always glad to see. When he was in my classes, I taught him the principle that truth is the greatest scalpel of all."

She wasn't exactly sure how they'd gotten to this philosophical point so soon in their conversation—talk of fate and truth and divine plans—but Calvin didn't appear to be someone who was much interested in small talk. "How is truth a scalpel?" she asked.

"Most of us layer on lie after lie until our hearts are thick with them. And nothing slices through misconceptions and distorted beliefs as effectively as the impartial blade of truth."

Christie thought of the Scripture verse in Hebrews that talks about how God's word is sharper than any two-edged sword and how it divides soul and spirit, judging the thoughts and intentions of the heart.

The Word of Truth.

The Sword of the Spirit.

The Scalpel of God.

Hmm.

"Yes," she told Calvin. "I believe that truth is a scalpel as well."

"I'm relieved that you two have based your relationship on such a blade." As he spoke, he winced, and it was clear that he was in a lot of pain. "It's been my experience over these many years that without truth at the nexus of a relationship, it stands little chance of weathering the storms of life that will inevitably come its way."

At that, she was quiet.

It was almost like he could read her inner struggle and that his words were laser-focused on her current situation and her dilemma of whether or not to be honest and tell her husband the truth about her cancer.

And about your faith struggles.

About your questions.

About your doubts.

You haven't told Pat anything about those either.

"Is it always best to tell the truth?" she asked Calvin. "Or is it better, at times, to keep it from someone for their well-being?"

"I would say, my dear, that truth is always a gift, no matter how hard it is to hear or to bear. To obfuscate it is to judge that something is greater than knowing the truth, and I can't think of any instance where that might be the case."

"Now you sound like Pat," she said.

A tiny smile. "He does have a few redeeming qualities."

++++

DeYoung and Senator Murray showed up at my office.

"You remember Agent Bowers?" DeYoung said by way of introduction.

"Yes." Senator Murray nodded. "Of course. Agent Bowers, how is your progress coming on the case?"

"Moving forward."

"If anyone can get the answers for you, it's Patrick," DeYoung told him confidently.

"I'm glad to hear that."

With that, DeYoung left us alone, and I said, "Senator, do you mind if I ask you a few questions?"

"Certainly. But may I ask you one first?"

"Yes, of course."

He peered down the hall earnestly. "Is there a place in this building that serves coffee? I've been on the move since I woke up and haven't had a chance to grab my morning cup."

If we were talking coffee that was drinkable, the cafeteria was out of the question.

"There's a kitchen down the hall. I can't guarantee that the coffee there will be fresh, but one of the agents here keeps a stash of organic, shade-grown whole beans in the freezer. We can grind our way to a good cup if we need to."

"Sounds like my kind of agent," he said.

I couldn't tell if he had guessed that I was that agent or not. "Mine too," I told him.

++++

Tessa tugged her coat up over her head to keep the freezing rain at least sort of at bay.

Umbrellas were one of those New-Yorky things she'd never quite gotten into since moving here from Minnesota with her mom when she was in fifth grade.

She stood outside the school debating where to go.

Two things to take care of.

Yes, she wanted to deliver the journal to Timothy Sabian, but first she needed to find out what was up with the woman disappearing after his last book signing.

So, go home and work on that, or do it at a restaurant or something?

Home was close.

Home was free.

Two for two.

Doing her best to stay out of the ever-deepening puddles, she left for their apartment.

70

The coffee—if you could call it that—that awaited us in the pot was cold, somehow gray, and in need of immediate disposal. It might have been sitting there for days.

Troubling.

I found the beans that I kept on hand and headed to the grinder.

"Senator, Mannie told me that he was watching Jon's funeral to see who you might talk to but that he wasn't able to confirm what he wanted to confirm. Do you know what he might've been referring to or who he might've been looking for?"

"No. I have no idea."

"Do you remember who you spoke with while you were there?"

"I don't know, exactly. I mean, well-wishers. Family. Friends. The media was on hand."

"What about someone named Jake Reese?"

"Yes. From Phoenix. He flew in."

"How do you know Mr. Reese?"

"He was on an advisory committee that we put together from the pharmaceutical industry. We met when the Senate was addressing the opioid epidemic."

"What about Marcus Rockwell?"

"Yes." He was slow in answering. "Now that I think about it. He was there."

I poured in the beans and dialed the knob toward a coarser grind, which provides a better cup of coffee than a finer one when you're using a drip percolator, then I punched the button and waited.

The machine whirred to life, and when it was done grinding the beans, I poured in enough filtered water for four cups, transferred the beans into the filter, then found the spray bottle in the cupboard and carefully spritzed a mist of water across the beans.

"What's that for?" the senator asked.

"Dampening them makes for a more uniform brewing experience. Adds to the flavor."

"You take this seriously."

"There's a lot at stake."

"A tasty cup of coffee."

"Exactly."

I closed the lid and started the coffeemaker. "You were saying that you spoke with Marcus Rockwell?"

"Yes. As you know, my son interned with him over the summer, but seeing him there did surprise me. We aren't what I would call close."

"Do you recall him saying anything out of the ordinary to you?"

The senator looked at me curiously. "Is he under investigation?"

"No. Not at all."

"Just that he was sorry for all that I was going through and sorry that the Internet had been used in this way."

"The Internet?"

"Yes. It was almost as if he was apologizing that

something he was so personally invested in would be implicated in any way with Jon's death. That struck me. I hadn't really thought of it again until just now, but yes. He seemed apologetic."

Interesting.

Ralph had mentioned legislation involving Internet privacy, and now I asked the senator about it. "What can you tell me about the bill that deals with quantum encryption? I understand it's in committee right now."

"What does this have to do with my son's death?"

"I'm really not sure."

The coffee began to percolate.

"The future of message transmission is through quantum encryption," he told me, "specifically what's referred to as high-dimensional quantum encryption, or 4D encryption. The data is sent on photons that each encode two bits of information: 00, 01, 10, or 11."

"Okay."

"In order to secure sensitive data, we're striving for a worldwide quantum encryption network that'll be able to send messages securely between earth and our satellites."

"We?"

"The government. The military. Our allies. Right now, the Chinese are at least two years ahead of us in the development of light-harnessing quantum key distribution, or QKD, and we can't afford to be left behind."

"I'm sorry. I'm not very familiar with all of this. What does that mean? Quantum key distribution?"

"Basically, it's using quantum states of light to provide decryption information. If someone tries to listen in on the transmission—that is, hack into it—the data will be altered, and this will immediately be obvious to the sender. Then, the actual message won't be sent."

I could see why this was important. Clearly, there was a lot hinging on it. And when you have something this high-stakes, it doesn't necessarily bring out the best in everyone.

In fact, the opposite would more likely be the case.

"Every week the Chinese are siphoning off millions of dollars' worth of corporate and military secrets," he told me. "If they're able to encrypt their information in a way that's unhackable and we're not, we would fall behind in ways that our country might never be able to recover from."

Enough coffee had brewed for a couple of cups. I poured one for each of us.

He tried his and gave me a satisfied smile. "Very nice."

"It's called Total Eclipse. The blend is from Leopard Forest roasters in South Carolina."

"I'll have to remember that. And a coarse grind."

"You noticed."

"Yes."

"That's very observant of you."

"I try to keep my eyes open. Sometimes it's easy to miss the things right in front of you."

"Of course." I wondered if there was something right in front of me that I was missing. "You were telling me about the encryption?"

"Adaptive optics technology is necessary for overcoming atmospheric turbulence, but that's just one hurdle that needs to be addressed. Thankfully, Marcus Rockwell is contributing resources to the fight. Consequently, that's the main reason that we know each other—his involvement in this area of research."

"And your son's internship."

"Yes."

"And the bill—would it benefit him? Marcus, I mean?"

"Sure. All of us will benefit if we can catch up with, or surpass, the Chinese."

With regard to the investigation, I tried to process what he'd told me.

Marcus Rockwell.

Jake Reese.

Senator Murray.

There were evidently threads connecting all the different people, and the more I looked at things, the more those threads all seemed to be intertwined around Jon's suicide.

Which brought us right back to the start.

"Senator, did someone pressure you to offer the twenty-thousand-dollar reward?"

He had his cup on the way to his mouth but paused with it halfway there. "What do you mean?"

"The money. Why did you go against our advice and offer it?"

"A friend encouraged me to do whatever was necessary to find out the truth surrounding my son's death. I just decided I needed to be more proactive in solving things."

"Which friend?"

"What is all this about?"

I debated whether or not to bring up the gambling debts that Greer had uncovered, and finally decided that I needed to get everything I could from the senator, even if some of the questions made him a little uncomfortable.

"In the course of our investigation," I said, "it came up that you owed some people some money."

"What are you talking about?"

"Gambling debts."

"Were you digging into my life?" Fire had crept into his voice. "Am I the one who's under investigation here? You can't possibly be serious."

"We're just looking for answers, Senator. It's possible that the people you owe money to might have been involved in some way in your son's death."

He was quiet.

"What can you tell me?" I said. "Anything at all might be helpful."

"Sports betting. It's not out of hand. I just got a little behind. It's all being sorted out. I can't imagine that it has anything to do with Jon's death."

If he has gambling debts, I thought, *then how does he have the cash on hand to offer a twenty-thousand-dollar reward?*

Maybe he isn't the one who's footing the bill.

"I'd like you to write up the details for our team," I told him. "Accounts, amounts, contacts, anyone involved who might have wanted to see you suffer or take retribution on you in any way."

"This is ludicrous."

"We're just trying to find out who might have convinced Jon to act the way he did. Sometimes if you threaten someone that a person cares about, you can get him to do something he would never otherwise do."

The senator didn't look happy, but at last he agreed. However, he told me unequivocally, "I don't appreciate you prying into my personal affairs."

Alright.

Well, here we go.

"Were you aware that your son was using illegal substances?"

"The Selzucaine in the tox screen?"

"Yes."

"My son was not a drug user."

Rather than argue, I simply said, "We need to find out who supplied him with the drug that was in his system the night he died."

The senator set down the coffee mug. "I don't know anything about that."

Mannie had told me that Jon was talking about his father when he said his final words, "This is for you." Mannie hadn't been forthcoming on how he knew that, but I believed he was telling me the truth, or at least what he believed to be true.

Even though I'd established that the senator couldn't have been present when the other suicides occurred, I still didn't know about the death of his son.

"Were you there, Senator?"

"What?"

"Behind the door, watching when Jon died."

"You're blaming *me*?"

"I'm not blaming you. I'm asking you."

He shook his head angrily. "I've done all I know to help you find the identity of that person, and I have to say I'm insulted that you would even ask me a question like that."

It wasn't lost on me that he hadn't given me an answer.

"Good day, Agent Bowers."

Before I could reply, he spun on his heels and left the kitchen.

Okay.

That went well.

After taking my mug back to my office, I found a message waiting for me from Angela that Lacey couldn't locate any matching names that corresponded to those dates and locations from air transportation involving any commercial airlines.

My immediate thought turned to private planes.

Someone who could afford to pay the Matchmaker for the opportunity to watch others die might not fly the way most of us do.

I called Angela. "Let's look at private aircraft. The observer traveled to those locations somehow, and I want to know who it was and how he got there."

71

While Christie was listening to Calvin recount anecdotes about Pat's time in graduate school, the doctors came by to wheel him out for his CT scan.

"Would you like me to stay?" Christie asked him.

"Ah, and see, here all of that talk about truth earlier gets put to the test. I would very much like for you to stay, but I do not want to intrude on your plans for the day."

"No intrusion whatsoever. I'll wait here."

"I'll see you in a few minutes, then."

++++

Tessa found what she was looking for.

Timing and location. Patrick would have been proud.

To be thorough, she'd analyzed the dates of Timothy Sabian's previous three book signings and compared each of them to news articles about missing persons. It'd taken a while because, in the case of Miranda Walsh, she wasn't listed as missing until three days afterward, when her college roommate finally called the cops. As it turned out, the last time anyone heard from her was a text she sent out right after the signing.

Tessa couldn't find the actual text message anywhere, but from what she could tell, it was to her friend informing her that she was going out with some guy.

This was just getting weirder and weirder.

Could it have been Timothy?

She gazed at the journal she'd recovered for him when that lady—who must have been Mrs. Walsh—came into the bookstore yelling those accusations.

When Timothy had read to them last night about a girl named Emily, he'd said it was from a work in progress.

It probably wasn't smart to read it now. It might be—

No. Of course you need to read it—especially if you're gonna return it to him. You need to know everything you can about his state of mind before you go meet him. What if it says something about Miranda?

Tessa picked up the journal and thumbed to the place where Timothy had stopped.

Then read:

When Emily grew, she visited a restaurant and watched as the other people entered and left, watched as they sat and ate or sat and read or just checked the messages on their phones.

And she wrote in her diary.

Here I am. all together with myself.

But there are others here also. Some are singing, some are silent, some are angry, others are trying to fall asleep.

And all the while the voices in my head are screaming at me, telling me what to do.

To turn off the world and turn on the light and blind myself, here in the midst of everyone.

And surprise them.

Shock them.

And finally elude their smiles and accusations.

Then really surprise them and turn the light on them. ha.

That would be funny.

To reveal their barren hearts.

!

Yes! it would be a fun game to try—turn on the light, leave it on, burn out their eyes and watch them scream and see if the voices take over when the screams subside, see if the voices enjoy blood—

Steamy and red on arctic snow.

Dark and spotty on the desert sand.

It's a game I wish to play.

I think I'll try it when the time is right and no one is looking.

But I'll wait until the voices quiet down long enough for me to find my inner light.

the hot, unyielding light that tastes so, so good.

Okay.

This guy was seriously losing it.

No, he's just a good writer. It's just what that girl, Emily, would be thinking.

Then why didn't he read that part last night?

He just didn't have time to.

Too many questions.

It left Tessa in a quandary. She could contact Timothy and see if he would meet her somewhere, or she could just let him know she was going to come by his place.

Go to his house. Take the journal and your book, just don't go inside.

Part curiosity.

Part adventurousness.

Okay, yeah, true, part teenage impetuosity—she decided she couldn't *not* go.

Who cares? It would be alright. She would just deliver the journal, get her book signed, and then be on her way again.

But, no, she would not enter his home.

++++

Timothy called his psychiatrist, Dr. Percival, to find out if he was the one who'd given the confidential information to Blake Neeson, but the call went to voicemail. Timothy did not leave a message.

He knew that Julianne had suspected him of killing Miranda Walsh, but he had no recollection of harming her, or Julianne, or anyone else.

So what'd happened to Miranda?

And who left that note in his kitchen telling him to check the basement?

When Neeson was there earlier, Timothy had wondered if he was perhaps his father, but Neeson had pretty much laughed off the idea.

Who else could have hurt those women? Who else *would* have?

Also, someone sent that picture of Julianne's body to Neeson, and from what Neeson had said, it originated in the federal building downtown.

His dad? Did his dad work there?

There's no way you could have sent that email. It proves someone else is doing this. Someone else is responsible for what happened to Miranda and Julianne.

The note left in the kitchen.

The email sent to Neeson.

Julianne's body.

But if your dad is out there, if he killed Julianne, how did he get that picture of her in the trunk of your car?

Then the revelation, something that seemed now to be so obvious, but maybe that's why he hadn't locked onto it earlier: *He was here. He was in the house.*

Hastily, Timothy began to search room by room for any clues as to who from the federal building might have been there, inside his home.

++++

Ralph and I made it a working lunch, grabbing sandwiches from the cafeteria.

We cross-checked everything we could dig up about the associates of the people who were arrested at the Matchmaker's place with the information of the ones who'd come forward and claimed to be at the senator's house on the night when Jon died.

One name matched: Duane Sheldrick.

An anonymous caller had contacted the senator's hotline with the name.

When I pulled up Sheldrick's driver's license photo, I

saw that he was indeed the man who'd opened the door when I went to see the Matchmaker. He was the one with the tattoos, and the horns, and no nose.

The guy who'd limped as he fled.

He also had priors in drug possession and intent to sell.

We contacted dispatch to get a car to his apartment.

"Ralph," I said, "if someone were to make online communication unhackable—I mean through this quantum encryption—would that be a good thing or a bad one?"

"Well, I know one thing: it'd sure make our job a lot harder tracking down the bad guys. Why? What are you thinking?"

"Blake's fingerprints are all over this case—I don't mean literally."

"Right."

"I wonder if that might be the connection to Jon Murray."

"I'm not sure I follow."

"Jon interned with Marcus Rockwell, who's helping spearhead this research. It can't just be a coincidence that the senator has legislation about this on his desk right now."

"I'm still not sure what that has to do with Blake."

"Neither am I, except that the person who watched Jon die might be more connected to Blake's network than we ever imagined."

++++

Timothy was finishing his sweep through the living room when he got the call.

"Hello?"

"You've been busy, Timothy."

"Who is this?"

"I'm the one the voices have been telling you about."

This isn't real.

Yes, yes, it is.

He stared at the phone's screen to make sure there really was an incoming call.

"There's nothing wrong with your phone," the man said.

Timothy froze.

The only way the man would say something like that was if he was watching him.

He's here. Someone is here!

No. Not possible. No one else was in the house. He would have seen him during his search.

A camera somewhere?

Maybe he'd hacked into the phone and was using the phone's camera.

Or maybe not.

It didn't sound like Dr. Percival, but maybe it was him. Maybe Timothy wasn't hearing his voice correctly because he didn't want to hear it.

No, you would know. It's not him.

"Who are you?" Timothy demanded.

"I'm the one you've always been afraid of, Timothy. I'm the one you turned in when you were a boy. The one with the hammer."

"Dad."

"It's been a long time."

But is he someone from your life? Is he someone you've seen but not recognized?

"Where are you?"

"I'll tell you soon enough. When the moment arrives, don't hesitate or more people will die. When they're gone you need to leave."

"When who's gone?"

No answer.

"Where do I need to go?"

Silence.

"Who's going to die?" he exclaimed.

But the line was dead.

He has a camera somewhere in here.

Yes, that's it. That's the only thing that makes sense.

Timothy tried calling the number back but got a message that the line had been disconnected.

Your dad is alive. He's the one.

He killed Mom. He's been killing people all along.

Timothy set down the phone and began tearing his living room apart, looking for whatever his father was using to watch him.

++++

Timothy's father received word from his sources that Christie Ellis, Patrick's wife, was at the Metro Medical Center.

He left to go see her.

So much to do to make this work. So many pieces in play.

It was time to start clearing the board.

++++

While Ralph and I were discussing whether or not to leave and visit one of Transit Corp's distribution centers to follow up on the possibility that they were working with

Blake to ship the Selzucaine, I received word that Calvin was going into surgery.

Apparently, the CT scan had revealed that the extravasation was extensive enough to require immediate attention.

While I was processing that, Marcus Rockwell returned my call from earlier.

"Agent Bowers, I was told you wanted to speak with me."

"Yes." I cut to the chase. "Marcus, someone has been live-streaming suicides through Krazle, and I want to know if there's anything you can do to help us verify the identity of the people involved—and also stop the live streams."

He let out a sigh. "This issue, this type of streaming, has created more headaches than anything else for us. It's too late to change things, of course—almost every online social networking service provides some type of live-streaming option. And, when that's the case, you're going to have people stream things that should never be broadcast to the world."

"How do you monitor things? Keep inappropriate content offline?"

"We've hired thousands of staff to keep tabs on things, and we're using advanced AI to identify postings that don't meet our usage standards of conduct, but there's no way to be everywhere at once, and in the end, the users will always be one step ahead of content monitors."

"You mean censors."

"We opt for a less incendiary term."

"Senator Murray mentioned that you're working in the area of quantum encryption."

"We all are—there's a lot riding on it. Listen, I'm not sure how I can help you except to assure you that we're doing all we can to stop abuses in the area of online content."

"What about the people involved in the filming? If I have a name, can you pull his profile?"

"Our usage agreement ensures people's privacy."

"If someone is influencing your users to take their own lives, then that's murder."

"Okay. I see where you're going." He was right with me. "A murder investigation would supersede our privacy agreement."

"Yes. It would."

After a moment, he said, "What's the name?"

"Duane Sheldrick. Get me everything you can on him and the profiles he's using."

"Let me see what I can do."

Before he hung up, he gave me his cell number so I could follow up with him directly.

Because of the two o'clock cutoff that Reese had brought up, I was anxious to see some progress on this thing, and sitting around the Field Office was just not going to cut it.

I needed to get moving.

I needed to act.

"Ride with me," I said to Ralph. "We'll drive up to the Transit Corp shipping warehouse, and then on the way back down we can see how Calvin's doing." I knew how much Ralph hated driving in the city, so I offered to take the wheel. "We'll work en route. At least this way we can accomplish something without just sitting here on our hands."

"I couldn't have put it better myself. At least not without swearing."

"Especially with the 'sitting on our hands' part."

"Right."

"Let's go."

72

Outside, the rain had turned to snow.

The meteorologists were calling for two to five inches of accumulation by the end of the day.

Having grown up in Wisconsin, I was used to driving in weather like this. However, in New York City when the first snow of the year comes, drivers are overly cautious, slowing down and clogging up the roads, making even more of a mess of traffic than usual.

And today, this heavy, wet snow would make the roads slushy and travel tricky—especially if the temperature continued to drop and the roads froze over.

As I drove, we got word that Reese had tried the phone number again but no one had answered. Also, no one was at Duane Sheldrick's apartment. We put out a BOLO for him. So far, Thurman had discovered that two of the suicide victims did indeed make sizable donations within a few days of their deaths. He was studying the files and would get us more details as soon as he could.

I was still waiting to hear from Angela about the private flights to Miami and Seattle.

"Ralph," I said. "Take a closer look at Blake's known associates, front companies, and past email accounts."

"Searching for what? Exactly?"

"Sheldrick's name. We need to establish if he's the Matchmaker or the Selzucaine dealer."

"Or both."

"Yes. Or both."

++++

"Reese has been trying to call me," Ibrahim told Blake.

"Have you picked up?"

"No, sir. Of course not."

Blake considered Ibrahim's words. He couldn't think of any legitimate reason for Reese to call Ibrahim at this time.

"Did you contact him first?"

"No. I swear."

Blake decided to have his men in Phoenix confirm that Reese was at work at Plixon Pharmaceuticals and not at a police station or the Bureau's Field Office. If Reese had been arrested or compromised, then the time frame needed to be moved up.

And if Reese was trying to reach Ibrahim, there was a loose end there that needed to be snipped off.

He excused Ibrahim, contacted his people in Arizona, and then called Mannie into the room.

"I want you and your men to clear out the office," he told him. "All the physical files. All the printouts. Everything."

"I understand. And the QKD research?"

"Put it on the thumb drives. And prepare the building like we discussed earlier."

"You want to burn it."

"Yes. To the ground."

With things moving in the direction they were, Blake realized it would probably be best to allow Ibrahim to take the blame for the Tranadyl posthumously.

Yes, he would make certain that the Syrian would be in the building when it turned to ash, but Mannie didn't need to know that. It would be better this way. Blake wanted no hesitation on the part of his associate.

In the building, yes. But alive or dead when the fire began?

Blake decided to wait and see.

He located his seven-inch KA-BAR 1217 fixed-blade knife in the office drawer. It would do the trick when the time came, if he needed it to. It was specifically designed for the very purpose he had in mind.

++++

Timothy found the camera.

It was near the television, and he couldn't figure out how his father might have planted it there—unless it was the guy who'd come in to fix the cable that one time . . .

In either case, it was the last straw.

The bugs. The visit by the Feds. His dad watching him. Everything was spinning out of control.

He destroyed the camera, found two X-ACTO knives—one for each hand—and headed to the bathroom.

++++

Tessa located Timothy Sabian's house and made her way through the falling snow toward it, quickening her steps as she did.

++++

Ralph and I were traveling north to leave the city when we received word from the team that was staking out Sabian's house.

Ralph put the call on speakerphone.

"There's someone walking up to his front door," the agent told us.

"Who?" I said.

"I don't know. A girl."

"A girl?" Ralph asked. "Not a woman? Not Julianne?"

"Looks to be an adolescent. She has a maroon backpack—you know, those book bags kids these days carry and—"

"Wait," I cut in. "A teenage girl with a maroon backpack?"

"Yeah. Why?"

A quiver in my heart. "What's she wearing?"

"Torn blue jeans. I don't know. A raincoat."

"What color?"

"Black."

That was enough for me.

"Get up there. Find out who she is."

"It'll blow our cover."

"Then blow it. I need you to find out if that's my stepdaughter."

A pause. "Your stepdaughter? Are you serious?"

"Get moving. Her name is Tessa Ellis. Find out if it's her."

++++

"Are you a member of his family?" the doctor asked Christie.

"I'm a friend."

"We had to take Mr. Werjonic into surgery. Will you be here?"

"Is he going to be okay?"

"An injury like this is difficult to assess without doing so visually."

"I realize that, but . . . what are his chances?"

"I'm not able to answer that right now, I'm afraid. We'll know more once he's in surgery. We'll need to do an exploratory laparotomy and see what it tells us."

"Yes, I should be here. Let me know what you find."

++++

As Tessa pressed the doorbell, out of the corner of her eye she saw two men approaching her. They were dressed in suits, and one of them called to her by name, shouting for her to stop.

Timothy opened the door, saw them, and immediately whisked her into the house.

When she glanced back, she noticed one of the men tug out his phone while the other started hurrying toward the porch, reaching toward his waist.

A gun?

Maybe.

"Who are they?" she gasped.

Timothy pointed. "Go hide in the garage. Hurry."

But she was curious who the men were and what they wanted, and she didn't think she'd be able to hear from the garage, so she hid behind the corner of the hallway and listened.

"Hello," Timothy said to them. "How can I help you men?"

"Who was that girl?"

"My niece," he replied. "Why were you chasing her?"

"We were told to find out if she . . ."

There was a long unexpected pause, as if he'd suddenly lost his train of thought, but then Tessa heard him talking to someone on the phone.

"Are you sure, sir? . . . Yes, but he said we should see if . . . Alright. But what about the girl? . . . I understand . . . Yes, sir."

Then the guy apologized to Timothy for troubling him, and Timothy closed the door.

Tessa returned to the living room. "What was all that about?"

"I don't know. But I don't think it's safe for you out there."

"Why wouldn't it be safe?"

"Without knowing what they want, I don't feel right about sending you back outside."

"So, what? I just stay in here?"

"Until I can sort this out."

She was about to argue but realized that she felt safer here, right now, than she did when she thought about going outside.

He scratched repeatedly at one arm and then the other.

Unsure what else to do, Tessa said, "Um . . . I brought the journal for you." She dug it out of her backpack and handed it to him.

"Thank you."

A weird silence stretched between them, but maybe it wasn't as weird as it could have been.

"And I have my book for you to sign."

She found the novel, and while she was looking for a pen, his phone rang.

"Yes," he told whoever was on the other end of the line. "They're gone . . . What do you mean . . . ? Okay. I'll be there."

He hung up.

"What is it?" Tessa asked.

"You can't stay here. I need you to come with me."

"What's going on?"

"There's someone I have to see. I'll bring you along, but you need to hide."

"Hide? Hide where?"

"In the backseat of my car. I'll cover you with a blanket. I need to get you out of here, and that's the only thing I can think of."

"I probably shouldn't go anywhere with you."

"I don't think it would be safe for you here. He might come."

"Who?"

Timothy was quiet.

"That woman who disappeared," Tessa said. "Miranda Walsh. Did you hurt her?"

"No." But he didn't answer right away.

She slung her hands to her hips. "You're gonna have to tell me more about what's going on here before I get in a car with you. Seriously. And it better be good."

"I think that Miranda is dead and that the man who killed her might be watching the house. I think you might be in danger."

"Then we should call the cops."

"No. He'll know."

"How?"

"Trust me. Listen, I trusted you the other night at the Mystorium when you helped me. Trust me now. I promise I'll protect you."

Timothy went upstairs and came back down with a handgun.

Tessa backed across the room. "What's that for?"

"You," he said, holding it out for her.

++++

When I didn't hear from the agents who were staking out Sabian's house, I called them back.

"Well?" I was navigating through traffic with one hand while holding the phone to my ear with the other. "What was the girl's name?"

"It was Sabian's niece," the guy said.

"Did you talk with her?"

"No. We were actually called off the house."

"Called off the house? What are you talking about? Who called you off the house?"

"Assistant Director DeYoung."

What? Why would he do that?

"Are you sure it was him?"

Silence.

"Well?"

"The call came from his number. The guy said it was him."

Numbers can be mimicked, piggy-backed—

"But could you tell for *sure*?"

"The call was grainy. No."

"Are you still there at the house?"

"We just left."

I smacked the steering wheel. "Get back there and see who she is."

"Now?"

"Yes, now!"

With all that was happening, I asked Ralph if he could take over driving and we made the switch.

Thoughts flew through my mind—mainly about Tessa, but also about the case. How was Sabian involved? Who was Jon's dealer? Did someone help Mannie escape when he managed to get out of the Field Office on Sunday? How did the quantum encryption fit into all this? I had the sense that everything was connected, but I still couldn't identify the through-line that tied it all together.

Or what it had to do with Tessa.

++++

Blake's men in Phoenix notified him that Reese was last seen leaving Plixon Pharmaceuticals' office with two FBI agents.

So, he was working with the Feds.

Alright.

"Load the semis," he told his men, "and get them on the road. We move on this now."

Earlier, he'd disabled the tracking device that Agent MacIntyre had brought with her in her shoe, but now that the Feds were onto Reese, he didn't want to take any chance that it might be able to be traced, so he directed Mannie, who was preparing for the fire, to destroy it.

++++

When my phone rang, I thought it would be the agent I'd just had on the line, but the screen told me it was Greer instead.

"Patrick, listen, something's wrong."

"Does this have to do with my stepdaughter?"

"Your stepdaughter? No. The tracking device that I gave to Sasha—it's come online."

"How do you know that? You're on leave."

"I've been keeping tabs on . . . Listen, that doesn't matter right now. What matters is that it's back online and I don't know who to trust. I think Blake might still have someone at the Bureau who's feeding him information."

I evaluated that.

Thurman was conveniently attacked by Mannie but was left unhurt.

He's the one who suggested that Julianne may have been looking for Timothy's father. His job at the Bureau is handling confidential informants . . .

He's also the one who located the charities.

What if . . . ?

"Where's the device?" I asked Greer.

"It's on the move just north of the line in Connecticut."

"On the move?"

"Yes. On I-95."

He told me the GPS location, and I punched it in.

"Hang on," I said. "Let me check something."

After putting him on hold, I contacted Transit Corp and had them send me the GPS locations of their trucks in the area.

Two were located on a property off a county road just a few miles from where the tracking device was currently traveling away from.

"When did that device come online again?" I asked Greer.

"About two minutes before I called you."

Timing.

Location.

A quick calculation—

Yeah, it worked for leaving the property.

A decoy?

I plugged the coordinates in and learned that it was the site of an old greenhouse complex that'd been closed down for several years.

Alright, but then why are there two semis there right now?

That's it.

I asked Greer if he had anything else, and he told me no but that he'd contact me if anything came up. "I'll get state police on the vehicle with the tracking device," I said to him. "Ralph and I will go to the greenhouse."

Then, I summed up the call to Ralph and directed him where to drive, but he scoffed with disbelief.

"What is it?" I asked.

"Greer again. Really? He just happened to know that? To come up with that? Why haven't we heard it through dispatch?"

"You still don't trust him?"

"No. I do not."

"What do you propose?"

It took him a moment to reply. "If he is involved with all this, I don't want to tip him off. We head to the greenhouse like you said, assess the situation, and call in backup as needed. But this time, I don't want another team on-site until I can eyeball things."

I called back the agent who'd been stationed outside Sabian's place. "Well?"

"We're at the door," the guy said, "but Sabian's not answering."

"Break it down."

"We're not authorized to—"

"You are now. Do it!"

I listened in as he identified himself as an FBI agent, then gave a verbal request for Sabian to open the door. After a short hesitation, I heard the splintering crash of the door being kicked in.

Anxiously, I waited while they searched the house. Finally, the agent told me, "The place is empty. There's no one here, and . . ."

"And what?" Fear overtook me. The worst kinds of fears a father might have.

"The car's gone from the garage. He got away."

"And the girl?"

"There's no sign of her."

73

I didn't know what to do.

We could turn the car around and head back to look for Sabian's vehicle, but from here that was much farther than the greenhouse. Besides, I didn't even know where to begin searching for it.

But then what about Tessa?

I texted her to call me, then contacted her school to see if she was in class. They told me they'd check with her teachers. Finally, I texted Christie to see if Tessa had been in touch with her.

++++

The Matchmaker parked behind the first greenhouse and then walked through the deepening snow to speak with Fayed Raabi'ah Bashir in the office.

++++

The principal from Tessa's high school called me back.

It turned out that she'd been kicked out of class this morning and hadn't been seen since. As her stepdad, I was shocked that the faculty hadn't informed me or Christie earlier that she was gone, but we could deal with that later.

Hassling with the school administration was the least of my concerns at the moment.

Christie texted that she hadn't heard from Tessa today. What is it? What's going on? she wrote.

I'm just trying to find Tessa.

She's at school.

No. She hasn't been there since this morning.

That brought a phone call from Christie instead of a text. "What is this? Tessa isn't at school?"

"I'm trying to locate her. I just want to make sure she's safe," I said honestly.

"I can't believe the school didn't contact me," she said, echoing my thoughts from a few moments earlier. "Where are you?"

"On the way to Connecticut checking on a lead. Are you still at the hospital?"

"Yes. They took Calvin in for surgery."

"I heard. Listen, I'm going to do all I can to find Tessa. If she contacts you, let me know right away, okay?"

"Yes." She jammed a paragraph of worry into that single word. "I'm calling the school."

After she was off the line, just as I'd done on Sunday afternoon, I contacted Collins to see if she could locate Tessa's cell, but the last location she could come up with was Timothy Sabian's house in Ozone Park.

He took her.

He's going to harm her.

++++

Christie tried the school, but the administrators had no idea where Tessa was, just that she wasn't on campus.

Becoming even more distressed, she called Candice, one of the girls Tessa had started hanging out with lately, but not surprisingly, since it was during school hours, Candice didn't pick up.

Praying that her daughter was okay, Christie stared out the window at the snow-cloaked skyline of this city of eight and a half million people, wondering where Tessa might be, wondering if she was safe, wondering how to find her.

The discussion with Dr. Werjonic came to mind, along with his declaration that truth is always a gift, no matter how hard it is to hear or to bear.

His words hit home.

Yes.

Christie couldn't even imagine how she might react if something bad had happened to her daughter, but despite that, she wanted to know, *needed to know* the truth.

Earlier, she'd thought that perhaps Tessa and Pat could one day forgive her for keeping the truth from them about her cancer diagnosis, but now she thought it'd be best not to give them anything they needed to forgive her for in the first place.

A lie isn't a gift. Truth is. And that's what you need to give to your husband and your daughter.

Although Christie still had questions about God, about his plan for her, about how much she actually trusted him, she decided that right now loving her family was more important than her personal faith struggles.

And the way to love them was to let them know about her condition.

Trust. Love.

Truth.

But first, she needed to locate her daughter and make sure that she was okay.

First, she needed to—

Someone knocked on the door, and she called for whoever it was to come in, anticipating that it would be a nurse or a doctor with news about how Calvin was doing.

Instead, a man she didn't recognize entered and introduced himself as Special Agent Bill Greer. "I'm with the FBI. Are you Christie Ellis?"

"Yes."

"I work with your husband." He showed her his creds.

"Okay," she said somewhat distractedly, still worrying about Tessa. "It's nice to meet you."

Pat hadn't mentioned Greer's name to her before, but there wasn't anything necessarily unusual about that. She didn't know too many of his Bureau coworkers.

"I was looking for Dr. Werjonic," Greer said.

"I'm afraid he's in surgery."

Agent Greer studied the room as if he were searching for something he might have misplaced. "Did you drive here?"

"What?"

"Did you drive?"

"No, I took the subway."

She was about to ask why that mattered, but before she could, he said, "I should probably take you to Pat."

"Does this have to do with Tessa?"

"Tessa," he said simply.

"My daughter."

"Ah, yes."

"Was she found?"

"Come with me. I'll fill you in on everything I know as soon as we're—"

Christie felt her throat tighten with fear for her daughter. "I'm not leaving until you tell me if you know where she is."

"We haven't confirmed her location, but Patrick needs to talk with you about it in person. We should hurry. There are some things happening with this case that have left us . . . well, unsure who to trust."

"What do you mean?"

"We think someone from the Bureau might've been in contact with Blake Neeson. An email was sent to him from one of the computers at the Field Office."

A chill. She knew that name all too well from Pat's search for the man. "Neeson?"

"Yes."

"Are you saying he took my daughter?"

"No. That's not it." Greer gestured toward the door, but it seemed like less of a request and more of a command.

"I should call Pat."

"Certainly, Ms. Ellis. I'll wait in the hall."

He immediately left the room.

She took out her phone but then realized that if there was anything untoward happening with this man, he wouldn't have encouraged her to call her husband.

She knew that Pat was following up on a lead, so rather than bother him, she simply texted that she was leaving the hospital and would see him soon. I'm with Agent Greer, she wrote, then joined the man in the hallway.

"How long have you been working with Pat?"

"Off and on with different task forces for a little over two years."

"I see."

"He's a good man."

"Yes, he is."

Together, they headed to the parking garage.

74

Ten minutes to the greenhouse.

Collins let us know that an unauthorized email, content unknown, had been sent to an email address previously associated with one of Blake's accounts. It originated from Greer's computer at the Field Office.

When I was about to call him, I saw a text from Christie that she was with him.

I tried her number first, then his, but neither picked up.

Ralph didn't trust Greer, hadn't from the start. He was also suspicious about him escaping after being abducted by Blake's men.

Was he involved in this?

But then why would he have contacted Blake? How would he have even known how to reach him? And was he really stupid enough to send a message to Blake from his own computer at the Field Office?

I doubted that. It was too obvious, too convenient.

But he knew about the tracking device.

My head was spinning.

Who else on this case could have gotten into Greer's computer?

Thurman?

Maybe, but he wouldn't have likely had the clearance. It'd need to be someone higher up.

Then another thought.

Patricia had said that when Timothy Sabian was a boy, he'd made the 911 call to the Cincinnati cops, so . . .

Did Thurman ever work in Cincinnati?

I didn't know.

Who could have accessed that computer?

Collins? Someone from her division?

No. Higher.

The agents at Sabian's place said that DeYoung had called them off the house.

Was that even possible?

They couldn't be sure it was his voice, but—

The assistant director was from Cincinnati.

No.

He knows how to make someone's past disappear.

Could he be Sabian's dad?

Don't assume. Verify.

I tried Christie again, but she didn't pick up.

I contacted hospital security and sent them to Calvin's room. "Hurry. I need you to see if my wife is there. And if Assistant Director DeYoung is with her."

++++

As a boy, Timothy had been instructed not to play with knives.

He knew that he would get in trouble with his mother if he did, but he wanted to find something that was sharp enough to hurt his dad if he ever needed to protect her.

His mom let him open up the envelopes that they got in the mail.

He used a special opener.

It cut through paper, tape, even heavy packaging if you pushed hard enough.

He'd kept it with him all the time when he was young.

Hidden, so she couldn't see.

Hidden, but close.

And he kept one close by him when he got older as well.

So, before he'd left the house with the girl he'd given the Beretta to, he'd grabbed the letter opener and tucked it into his jacket pocket.

Then he slipped an X-ACTO knife in another pocket, already thinking of how he might use it if he needed to.

++++

Blake tapped record and let Ibrahim babble on, creating the video that explained the reasons behind the tainted Selzucaine: "We will use the vile hunger of the infidels against them, as we allow them to destroy themselves. We are The Brigade of the Prophet's Sword."

He had a flag of the group draped beside him. Very emblematic. Very jihadist.

The Matchmaker stood by and watched the whole time.

Blake would post the footage after Ibrahim was dead, and then he'd deal with the Matchmaker. The Selzucaine needed a new distributor; he would take that over himself.

And once the quantum encryption research came through, everything would be set.

When they were done with the filming, Blake asked Mannie, "How are the preparations coming?"

"Almost ready. One truck is loaded. We're finishing with the other one now."

++++

As Christie and Agent Greer neared his car, a man called to them from a nearby row of vehicles. Somewhat overweight and unkempt, he looked vaguely familiar, and Christie had the sense that she'd met him before, but she couldn't recall his name.

"Bill?" he said, walking in their direction. "What are you doing here?"

"I came to see Dr. Werjonic."

The man looked at Christie curiously, and Greer said, "This is Patrick Bowers's wife, Christie Ellis."

The guy introduced himself as Assistant Director De-Young. "You can call me Peter," he told her, then he turned to Greer. "I came to visit Calvin myself and to pick up the paperwork that he was going to fill out regarding his help with the case. He called me earlier to tell me that it was ready."

"He's in surgery."

"I didn't know that. Is he going to be alright?"

"They're not sure. It's serious."

Greer glanced at Christie somewhat uneasily, then said to DeYoung, "Sir, could I speak with you in private for a moment?"

The assistant director looked confused but agreed.

They walked behind a nearby minivan, and Christie overheard DeYoung say, "Bill, you're on administrative leave."

Administrative leave? Christie thought. *Why didn't he mention that? Why didn't he—?*

Greer said something to him in reply, something that

she couldn't make out, and then the sound of a gunshot ripped through the parking garage, its staccato echo reverberating harshly off the concrete walls.

One of the men grunted heavily, and then there was the sound of a thick thud behind the minivan.

75

Christie gasped and stared in the direction of where the men had gone.

"Agent Greer?" Her voice didn't even seem to be coming from her. "Peter? Are you okay?"

She heard the shuffling of feet behind the minivan.

Heart hammering, she edged around the side of the vehicle to see what'd happened.

Agent Greer lay crumpled on the ground with Assistant Director DeYoung standing over him, holding a handgun.

"He tried to attack me," he muttered. He seemed dumbfounded by what had just happened. "He tried to kill me."

Christie stared at the growing stain of blood spreading across Agent Greer's chest.

"Is he . . . ?" She barely managed to say the words. "Is he dead?"

DeYoung bent and gently checked for a pulse.

"He's gone," he said softly.

"But this is a hospital. Maybe they can bring him back. Right? I mean, right?"

"Yes, yes, good idea." He nodded vigorously. "I'll go. I'll get someone. I'll get help. You stay here—hang on, I don't want you near the body. Wait in my car."

He rounded the minivan and unlocked a sedan near where she'd first seen him, then opened the backseat door on the driver's side for her.

"Are you sure?" she said.

"I don't want anyone to suspect you of anything. I'll be back in a minute with the paramedics."

Without really thinking, Christie climbed in.

He patted at his pockets. "My phone, my phone," he muttered. "May I use yours? I need to contact our team, tell them what's happened."

"Um, sure."

She doubted her cell would get very good reception in this underground garage, but she handed it over and he closed the door.

Only then did she notice that there was a plastic barrier between the front and back seats.

And no way to open the door from the inside.

++++

"I think it might be DeYoung," I told Ralph. I whipped through my reasoning as he pulled off the highway toward the county road that led to the west end of the greenhouse property.

I heard back from hospital security that no one was in Calvin's room.

"Check the entrances and exits," I said, trying to keep the fear out of my voice.

I felt helpless being here on the other side of the city, but if someone from the Field Office really had been in contact with Blake, then finding Blake might be the best way to locate Christie, and maybe even Tessa as well.

++++

"What are you doing?" Christie shouted through the car door, but the assistant director ignored her.

He walked to Agent Greer's body, retrieved the man's phone, then smashed both her phone and Greer's on the ground before returning to the car.

When he took his place behind the wheel, he said to Christie, "I'm sorry it had to come to this."

"What's going on?"

"It's about my son."

"Your son? You just shot Agent Greer!"

He didn't reply but instead started the engine.

She pounded on the barrier separating her from the front seat. "Hey!" she screamed. "Let me out of here!"

She thought of the advice she'd learned from Pat, advice on staying safe in dangerous neighborhoods: If you ever encounter someone intent on doing you harm, never get in a car with them. Never let them take you to another location.

Too late.

It's too—

But as worried as she might be about herself, she was even more distressed about her missing daughter.

The assistant director put on his siren and pulled out of the garage, leaving Agent Greer's body behind.

++++

I called DeYoung's office number and reached his receptionist, Annalise. She told me that he was at his desk.

"Check. Make sure."

A moment later she said quizzically, "No. Actually, he's

not here after all. And he left his cell phone by his computer."

++++

Christie watched as Assistant Director DeYoung, if the man really was who he claimed to be, called a number using a flip phone and said, "The place by the riverfront where you met with Julianne. Be there by two."

Hoping that whoever was on the other end of the line would hear her, Christie shouted for help, but DeYoung quickly hung up.

++++

Timothy couldn't be certain, but it sounded like someone had been yelling in the background, terrified cries before the line went dead.

++++

"Who was that?" Tessa asked Timothy from the backseat.

"My dad."

"Your dad?"

"Yes."

"Where are we going?"

"The waterfront. It'll be okay. I just need to take care of things with him, then you'll be safe and I'll drive you home."

Here she was, alone in this car with this guy she barely knew, and despite his assurances that he wasn't going to let anything happen to her, she didn't feel exactly reassured.

This was, basically, a perfect storm of not-goodness.

You have a gun.

Seriously? What are you going to do with that? It's not like you're actually gonna shoot someone!

Patrick might. Her mom might. They went target shooting sometimes at the range, but she'd never even shot a gun in her life.

Why doesn't Sabian just drop you off somewhere?

"You wrote that the truth tastes like tears," he said to her, drawing her out of her thoughts.

"What?"

"On that church bulletin you gave me. You wrote that the truth tastes like tears."

"Oh." Her stupid poem was the last thing on her mind. "Yeah."

"And that you wished you could touch the light that threads its way through the ever-present rays of darkness all around you."

"You have a good memory."

"Is that really how you feel? Lost in the darkness, reaching for the light?"

"Sometimes," she said. "Yeah. It is."

"Me too."

"What do you do when you feel like that?"

"I try to cut the darkness out of me."

"Does it work?"

"No. I don't think I've ever quite gone deep enough yet."

76

Ralph parked behind a small rise in a wooded glen just off the gravel road that skirted along the edge of the property.

While we were planning how to approach things, I heard from Metro Medical that Agent Greer's body had been found in their parking garage with a single GSW to the chest.

Two phones lay shattered beside him. One was his. Based on my description, it took security only a few seconds to confirm that the other was my wife's.

I stared out the window at the heavy snow, rapidly tapping my leg, deep in thought.

The news about Greer was shocking, but I had the sense that the full impact of what'd happened would come later. Right now, I needed to move forward, needed to do what I could for the living.

For my family.

For—

"What do you want to do?" Ralph asked. "Go back or go on?"

As much as I wanted to turn around and look for Christie and Tessa, I knew that there wasn't really anything I could do at the moment to find either of them.

You're here. Clear this property.

Find Blake.

I couldn't shake the thought that if we tracked down Blake Neeson we'd be on the way to finding my wife and stepdaughter.

"The hospital is too far across town," I said to Ralph. "Driving back wouldn't do us any good right now. Get NYPD on it. I'm wondering—if Christie's abduction has anything to do with Blake—if his men might bring her up here. Get someone on the hospital's security cameras. Let's find out what happened in that parking garage." Then I added soberly, "And if Assistant Director DeYoung really is the one who took her."

++++

Christie prayed for her daughter, that she would be found, that she would be safe, that she would be okay.

Don't hold my own doubts against me, Christie begged her Lord. *Please. Do what you want to me. Make me suffer. Take my life, but please spare my precious daughter.*

And God was silent.

Christie watched as the man who'd abducted her pulled to a stop beside the shoreline of the East River near an abandoned warehouse.

You need to get out of here.

Use whatever you have at your disposal.

Attack him where he's most vulnerable.

Neck, eyes, nose, ears, groin.

She had her apartment keys with her and now tightened her right hand around them with two keys protruding from her closed fist.

As soon as he opened that door she was going to rake those keys across his eyes.

++++

We got word that Sasha's tracking device was in an executive car that the Connecticut State Police had pulled over. They took the driver into custody. He had no ID and he wasn't talking.

Time to move.

The snowfall cut down on the visibility, but I could make out the ghostly outline of three greenhouse structures as well as an office building.

Based on the amount of land we were talking about, however, I suspected that there might very well be more greenhouses tucked back out of sight in the snow-shrouded day.

A metal mesh fence surrounded the property.

A semi was backed up to one of the greenhouses, and a man was loading mannequins into it. Another semi sat nearby, idling. There was a gray sedan parked maybe ten meters from the second truck.

"Looks like we're gonna need more cuffs," Ralph muttered.

We called for backup, but in this weather, the best we could hope for was a response time of eight to ten minutes. That wasn't going to help us if there were people here in immediate danger.

"Are you good to go for it, Pat?"

"I am. What's the plan?"

"We do this fast and clean. We'll see if anyone here knows where your wife and stepdaughter are. Start with the guy by the semi and move on from there."

The two of us made our way along the tree line to the fence.

++++

After Blake verified with Mannie that the building was set to go up in flames, he met with Ibrahim in the lower level. Once the building had burned down, it would collapse into the basement, where the authorities would eventually find the Syrian's charred body.

"There's one more thing I'm going to need from you," Blake said to him.

"What is that, Fayed?"

"Your hand."

"My hand?"

"Here." Blake slipped the KA-BAR's grip into Ibrahim's palm and then wrapped his own fingers around it to hold it securely. "Now would be the time to pray, to make peace with God."

"What?"

"A sacrifice. Just like with Abraham and his son. God is asking me to—"

"No, Fayed." Ibrahim started to tremble. "I'm not ready to—"

Ibrahim tried to pull away, but Blake swept the knife across the front of the man's neck. One long, steady swipe to slit his throat.

Like a lamb.

Like a lamb to the slaughter.

Afterward, as Blake was wiping off the blade on a handkerchief, the Matchmaker approached from the stairwell. "Is that how you treat your friends?"

"Yes."

"Then I'm not sure I want to be counted as one."

You're not, Blake thought. *And I have something even better planned for you.*

++++

Ralph went south at the semi. I buttonhooked around the other side.

Mentally, I clicked through what to do: *Assess the nature and severity of the threat. Take immediate action to protect innocent life. Quiet any threats through whatever means necessary.*

Two men wearing Transit Corp jackets were gagged and tied up back to back on the ground near one of the trucks.

The drivers?

If so, it just made our job a little easier. Fewer threats to address.

Ralph made it to the semi's open door while I glanced into the greenhouse, where half a dozen mannequins stood stoically beneath a sprinkler system. Wet, heavy snow was collecting on the glass ceiling above them.

"Hands where I can see them," I heard Ralph shout.

I rushed over to help and ended up close enough to see what happened next, to watch it all go down.

The man that Ralph was confronting made a fatal mistake. Instead of complying, he drew a handgun. Ralph commanded him to drop it, but the guy raised it toward Ralph's chest.

Ralph fired.

Three shots. Center mass.

Put him down.

Textbook.

Hot blood splattering across the snow.

While Ralph went to the body to secure the man's weapon, I gazed into the semi, which was loaded with crates and mannequins. I wasn't sure how much each of the silent ladies weighed, but I guessed that if they were all made of Selzucaine, with this many we could easily be talking tens of millions of dollars.

But this time, based on what Reese had told us, it wasn't about the street value; it was about the Tranadyl. As he'd put it, the addicts would be snorting their way "into a coma or a casket."

Movement in the truck. I leveled my gun. "Hands up!" Then I said to Ralph, "There's someone in here!"

Fifty meters to the east, I noticed smoke coming from the first-floor windows of the office building.

Ralph joined me near the back of the semi. "Come out!" He repositioned himself to get a more direct line of fire. "And let's see your hands!"

Suddenly, as if from nowhere, Mannie emerged from behind the crates, passed through the row of mannequins, and agilely leapt to the ground.

"Agent Hawkins," he said.

"Mannie."

I thought back to last summer, to the only fight I'd ever known Ralph to come away from without a clear victory— when these two had fought in Detroit. Since Mannie had managed to get away, Ralph considered it a lost fight.

I didn't know of anyone else who could go mano a mano with Ralph.

Or with Mannie.

The giant held up his hands as he faced me. "Remember at the Field Office when I told you that you'd do what needed to be done? Now's the time. He's inside the office."

"I've got this, Pat," Ralph said to me. "Clear the building. Go!"

I took off in a sprint toward the burning office complex.

++++

Christie tightened her grip on the keys.

Open the door. Come on, open the door.

But the man who'd taken her didn't free her. Instead, he drove to the top of a long sloping boat ramp that ended in the river. He angled the car to face the water, then cut off the ignition.

Oh.

Not good.

It might not be the cancer that killed her after all.

It might be the East River.

The old priest at the monastery had told her that obedience was the pathway to deeper love. She wasn't sure if her loving feelings for God would ever return, but she did know that if it was up to her to regain that love, she would fail.

Always fail.

If it relied on her, her obedience would never be enough.

She needed grace more than anything.

A grace that might not be easy to understand but that would give her the assurance that God loved her, despite how she had failed to love him.

A Scripture verse from Romans came to mind: "Nothing can separate us from the love of God."

Then, she heard more words in her soul, ones directed

at her situation: maybe not words straight from the Bible, but ones that seemed to come straight from the Lord.

Not doubts. Not anger. Not questions. Not fear.

Not life. Not death.

Nothing.

Not lack of love. Not cancer.

No. Nothing can separate you from my love.

A prayer wrenched from deep inside of her: *I do believe. Help my unbelief. I do love. Help my lack of love.*

The priest had said, "Perhaps it is not your body that is the most in need of healing."

I need you, God, she prayed. *More than ever before. If you don't heal my cancer, at least heal my heart.*

And something stronger than fate warmed her soul, comforted her spirit. The Truth, the Living Truth, the Love of God, welcomed her, and she let herself fall into her Savior's embrace.

Then Christie's abductor exited the car, and she got ready to defend herself, but he didn't open the door for her. Instead, he just stood in the falling snow holding a hammer in his hand, watching another car make its way along the river road toward them.

77

Keeping his gun on Mannie, Ralph held up his handcuffs. "In a minute, you're going to be wearing these."

"They can't hold me."

"Maybe not, but I can." Then Ralph had a thought. "It was you, wasn't it? You turned on that tracking device."

Mannie didn't respond.

"But why?"

"I needed you to find us here in time."

"And the anonymous call turning Duane Sheldrick in?"

"Yes."

"Whose side are you on?"

"It's not about whose side I'm on. It's about what I'm fighting for."

"And what is that?"

"Hope." Mannie reached down to an ankle sheath and removed a combat knife, then tossed it to the side.

"Kneel," Ralph ordered. "Hands behind your head."

Mannie knelt.

Slowly, Ralph walked toward the mountain-sized man to cuff him.

++++

The office was on a slope, and the closest door was on the lower level. I threw it open and—with a sense of both caution and urgency—entered.

The cat.

The mouse.

Which was which?

Which were we?

Although there was a hazy layer of smoke, I didn't see any flames down here in the basement.

"Hello?" I called. "Blake? Sheldrick?"

As I rounded a corner, I saw, at the far end of the room, a man seated on a chair facing away from me.

"Hands up," I ordered. "Now!"

He did not comply.

"Let me see your hands!"

Still, he didn't move.

I approached.

His hair was the wrong color for Blake or Sheldrick and, based on what we knew so far about who was involved in this case, I couldn't guess who it might be.

However, as I came closer, I realized his head was drooping forward at an impossibly sharp angle.

Then I caught sight of his face.

Middle Eastern descent.

Dead. Throat slit.

Ibrahim?

Maybe.

We'd figure that out later.

A flag with the emblem of The Brigade of the Prophet's

Sword hung nearby, and a video camera sat on a tripod beside it.

++++

Mannie waited until Ralph was right behind him, then spun and went for the gun.

As they both struggled for it, it went off, the bullet burying itself near their feet in the snow.

Ralph tugged to get free, but Mannie's strength was unstoppable. He wrenched the Glock away and tossed it far out of reach.

"Let's settle this like men," Mannie said.

"Alright."

"I should tell you, I've never lost a fight in my life."

"Sorry to be the one who's gonna break that streak."

Immediately, Mannie threw a punch, but Ralph blocked it. Mannie did the same when Ralph came at him with an uppercut. Then, after backing up to collect themselves, the two titans went at each other in the cascading snow.

++++

A voice behind me. Blake. "I've got a hostage here, Patrick. Do not turn around or he dies."

78

2:02 P.M.

I froze.

++++

Timothy turned off the car, made sure he had the X-ACTO knife and the letter opener, and stepped outside to face his father.

++++

Blake said to me, "Drop your gun. Kick it behind you. Do it now."

I hesitated.

"If you make me give you a countdown, Duane dies."

Slowly, I knelt, set down my SIG, and slid it backward toward where Blake's voice was coming from. Then I stood.

"You can face me now. No sudden moves."

I turned around.

He was holding a tactical knife to Duane Sheldrick's neck but now indicated for Duane to pick up the gun, and when he did, Blake stepped away.

Evidently, he hadn't been planning to kill his associate after all.

Imagine that.

"Do you know where my wife and stepdaughter are?" I asked emphatically.

Blake shook his head. "No, Patrick, I don't."

"Tell me the truth."

"I'm afraid I am."

"Duane?"

"No."

Then Blake exchanged weapons with Duane and said to him, "You've been waiting for this moment. Go on. He's all yours."

The noseless man stalked toward me with that stiff limp of his, and I whipped off my belt to use it to trap his arm and get that knife.

++++

Mannie grabbed the back door of the truck and swung it at Ralph, smacking him hard enough to knock him off his feet and send him tumbling backward, skidding across the ground.

Crouching, Ralph went in for a low tackle. Grappling was more his thing anyway—get Mannie down, throw on a sleeper hold, put him out.

++++

Tessa peered out from beneath the blanket she'd been hiding under, then gazed up from the backseat.

Timothy stood next to the driver's door.

Another car was at the top of a boat ramp nearby, and

a beefy, middle-aged man waited beside it. She couldn't remember ever seeing him before.

Someone was in the backseat of the other car, but from where Tessa sat, she couldn't tell who it was.

++++

I expected that Blake would either leave the burning office building or stand by to watch the fight, but instead, he crossed the room and headed up the stairs toward the heart of the blaze.

What is he doing? Why doesn't he take off?

"Put down that knife," I told Duane.

"I will when I'm done with it. When I'm done with you."

I snapped the belt taut between my hands to wrap that wrist once he came close enough. "You're the Matchmaker, aren't you?"

"Some people call me that." He jabbed the knife toward me but didn't fully commit. I held my ground.

"And the Selzucaine too?" I said. "Was that you as well?"

"All part of the bigger picture."

"Why did you come to the cemetery on Sunday night?"

"I thought I was going to meet him there."

"Meet who?"

"The donor."

"Who is it? Who's the donor?"

Duane scoffed. "You have no clue, do you? You have no idea how deep this goes."

Actually, I was starting to.

"The quantum encryption," I said. "It all goes back to that research. To Jon's internship."

Then he flattened out his smile, and I got the sense we were done chatting.

As he swept the blade toward my abdomen, I went to secure his arm, but he must've anticipated the move because he pulled back before I could get to him. He flicked the knife around into a military grip and lunged forward, but I managed to pivot to the side in time to evade him. I readied myself for him to come at me again but then Blake reappeared on the stairs.

"I changed my mind," he said to Duane. "You are my friend."

Then he shot him twice in the face and spun to return up the stairs.

And I raced after him.

++++

Timothy faced his father. "How many people have you killed?"

"The number doesn't matter."

There's a number for everyone.

"Yes, it does!"

His dad passed the hammer back and forth threateningly between his hands.

"Did you kill Mom?"

"Oh, yes."

"And Julianne? And Miranda?"

"I killed them all, Timothy. All the people around you who've been disappearing."

Timothy felt a tide of grief wash through him. "But why?"

"It's always been a part of me, and working for the FBI just made every death richer, purer, more satisfying."

What? The FBI?

But at least that explained a few things—like how he got the camera that was in the house and how he managed to locate Blake's email address.

"You're sick," Timothy said.

"Then I do not want to be well."

++++

Tessa craned her neck to see who was in the backseat of the other car but still couldn't make out the person's face.

Screw it. I'm not staying here.

Bringing the gun with her, she climbed out and headed through the blowing snow toward the other vehicle.

++++

Timothy had an idea.

Morgellons. The bugs. Mental deterioration.

"You know about my condition?" he said to his father.

"Yes. *You're* the one who's sick."

He may have watched you in the living room but he hasn't watched you cut.

Timothy Sabian tugged off his shirt.

++++

Tessa could see that the novelist's chest and stomach were laced with scars and open sores. His arms were crisscrossed with more wounds.

Though her mom would've said she was taking the Lord's name in vain, she still found herself whispering, "Oh my God."

As he stood there shirtless in the snowstorm, Timothy produced an X-ACTO knife from his pocket.

"Help me make them go away," he said to the man. As Timothy walked forward, he drew the blade across his skin, leaving red, leaking streaks behind. "They just won't go away. They're getting worse."

"Put down the knife." The guy sounded rattled. It didn't look like he'd noticed her yet.

"I just want to be free of the bugs." Timothy passed the blade to his left hand and went to work on his right arm. "Always crawling. Always here. Always always always."

"Stop it!"

"I have to get them out."

++++

Tessa was scared watching him and wanted him to stop, but when she edged closer, she finally saw who was trapped in the backseat of that car.

A woman.

A woman she definitely knew.

Her mom.

79

Tessa rushed forward. "Mom?"

Her mother stared dumbstruck at her, then tried frantically to get out of the backseat, beating on and then kicking uselessly at the window.

"Get back!" Timothy warned Tessa.

"Ah," the other man said. "This is even more perfect than I could have planned."

He leaned into the car and clicked on the ignition, then stood back and faced Timothy. "In one of your books, you wrote about a woman drowning. Now you get to see what it looks like in real life."

He moved behind the trunk and leaned hard against the bumper.

As the car began to roll forward down the ramp toward the river, Tessa realized that he must have stuck it in neutral.

As fast as she could, she darted toward the car to try to somehow stop it before it took her mom into the East River.

++++

Thick, wandering tendrils of smoke were filling the room, making it hard to breathe. Images from earlier in the week returned to me: *Mist. Our lives are only a vapor, and then they're gone. A brief moment, and then they're over.*

I didn't see Blake, but I did recognize this as the room where Sasha had died.

Braids of fire were snaking up the wall and across the ceiling. More flames crept toward me on the floor. The heat, in sharp contrast to the weather outside, singed my skin and forced me to stay back by the doorway.

"Blake? Are you here?"

No reply.

The room was empty.

Though he might've gotten away, four more doors lined the hallway.

Clear the rooms. Make sure no one else is in the building.

++++

At first, Tessa thought she might be able to get in front of the car, but it was moving too fast.

That would be stupid. They'd both die.

She went for the backseat door, but it was locked.

They were halfway down the boat ramp on that icy pavement, slick with snow. Barely keeping her balance, she snagged the driver's door, threw it open, and scrambled inside.

"Tessa, get out of the car!" her mom shouted. "Now! Hurry!"

"I can do this."

Tessa punched the brake with her foot, and as she did, the car began to skid sideways, sliding to the right.

Steer where you veer, she thought, something Patrick had taught her: *"It won't seem to make sense, but steer into the skid."*

She cranked the wheel to the right and then slammed the car into park, but on the frozen ramp and with its forward momentum, the car continued to plummet—now sideways—toward the water.

"Unlock the back door," her mom said, "so you can get me out!"

Tessa searched for the unlock button, but it was some sort of cop car, and she was missing something. "I don't know how," she yelled. "I can't find it!"

"It's okay. You just need to go."

"I'm not leaving you."

The car hit the water, and the current, fueled by the furious wind, grabbed hold of it.

"Get out, Tessa!"

"Wait." She had an idea. "Hang on, I've got a gun."

"A gun?" But then, almost immediately, Tessa's mom tracked with her. "Get it to me. Slide it under the seat. Quick."

Tessa tucked the gun under the driver's seat and shoved it back to her mom.

The car continued to sink into the dark river.

"Tessa, go! You have to. *Now!*"

She didn't want to leave until she was sure her mom was alright, but she also knew that if she didn't get to safety now, she might lose her chance.

She wrenched the door open and managed to slip out, but water poured into the car.

After dropping into waist-deep water, Tessa struggled to get her footing. By the time she did, half of the car had already been swallowed by the river.

++++

In the final room, I found Blake.

He was standing near a computer monitor, jamming thumb drives into his pocket.

He aimed my gun at me.

"You had the chance to shoot me earlier," I said. "You're not going to kill me. Put it down."

++++

Christie positioned herself on her back, took aim at the window, and fired the Beretta, but the glass did not explode. The window must have been reinforced somehow. Cracks emanated from the point where the bullet had struck the glass. She tried kicking it.

It held.

Another shot. Then another. Finally, the glass was weakened enough for her to kick it from the doorframe.

++++

Tessa watched her mom emerge from the window, almost as if she were being born anew, as the East River engulfed the car.

Her mom sank out of sight. "Mom!" Tessa splashed over to help her get to shore.

It was hard to keep her balance in the current, but at last both of them were on their way back to the bank. "I'm okay, Tessa. You did it. You saved me."

Somehow, her mom had managed to keep the gun with her when she got out of the car, which was now gone, under the water.

"Get behind me," she said unequivocally.

Tessa did.

"Do not move, Peter!" her mother shouted to the man who'd left that car in neutral and started it rolling toward the water.

But he ignored her warning. "I'll be with you two in a minute. First you get to watch my son die."

The evil in the guy's voice left Tessa feeling dirty just hearing it. She couldn't even comprehend how lost he was.

All at once, he ran straight toward Timothy, hammer raised high, and Tessa thought her mom really was going to shoot him to protect the novelist, but Timothy stepped forward and ended up in the line of fire. He flicked his right hand out of his jacket pocket and raised something shiny and metal.

++++

As his dad was about to bring the hammer down at his skull, Timothy drove the letter opener into the murderer's neck, and he made sure that it went deep enough to do the trick.

To get the darkness out.

80

I was right—for some reason Blake must not have been interested in shooting me today because he slipped the gun under his belt, grabbed a desktop printer, yanked the cord from the wall, and threw the printer at me.

From where I was standing, I couldn't get completely out of the way, but I was able to turn and raise my left arm in time to absorb most of the impact.

Last summer, I'd fought Blake's brother, whom he'd trained in hand-to-hand combat and martial arts.

Dylan was good.

I anticipated that Blake would be better.

He angled toward me, leapt and spun, and kicked me hard in the gut. The force of impact knocked the wind out of me. As I was struggling to draw more air in, he came at me with his right hand chambered for a high punch. When I went to block it, I realized too late that he was faking the punch, and he landed a blow with his other fist directly where he'd kicked me. I coughed and fought to stay on my feet.

Advice from Ralph on fighting: *Find a weakness and exploit it. Find pain and capitalize on it.*

Yeah, Blake knew what he was doing.

I shoved him backward, but the desk was behind him, and he didn't stumble far.

I went to tackle him, but he pivoted as I did, using my momentum to carry us both toward the window.

The glass shattered at impact and we flew outside, fell nearly two meters, and crashed heavily to the ground.

I landed on my back, shaken, Blake on top of me.

He pushed himself to his feet and dashed toward the nearest greenhouse. It took me a second to catch my breath, but as soon as I had it, I was on my feet as well and after him.

++++

Mannie was a grappler too and managed to get Ralph in a rear choke hold.

Ralph turned his head and dropped his chin to keep his airway open and to break the choke. He jammed his jaw into the crook of Mannie's elbow, shrugged his shoulders up, then clenched his teeth to tighten his neck and buy himself a little more time before passing out.

If someone grabs you around the neck from behind, you attack him at his weakest point—his fingers are within your reach. Bend them backward and break them. It took snapping four of Mannie's fingers before Ralph broke the choke.

They both rose.

Mannie's fractured fingers were splayed to the side at odd and irregular angles.

Ralph circled right to reduce his adversary's right arm attack.

It was difficult for him to keep his balance on the snowy ground, but he had an idea, launched himself at Mannie, and wrestled him back toward the open doors of the semi.

++++

Unlike the first greenhouse I'd peered into—the one with the mannequins—this one was overgrown with untended plants. The dried brown stalks reached tenaciously toward the ceiling.

Blake appeared at the end of the aisle. "Have you figured it out yet, Patrick? How it all fits together?"

I thought of the flag that'd been near the man whose throat was slit. "You treated the mannequins with Tranadyl. Once they get shipped out and people start dying, who'll be to blame? I think you want it to be you. You want it to be the Brigade."

"Go on. Why?"

"I don't care why, Blake. I don't care about your motives. I'm just here to bring you in."

"What about the backlash of the deaths?"

"It'll result in heightened antiterrorist campaigns." Then I had it. "Ah. Arms sales. You're playing both sides. But how does ending the Selzucaine shipments benefit you?"

"You're close, Patrick, but you're not quite there yet."

"Quantum encryption, Krazle's CEO, and the legislation Senator Murray is working on. It's all connected. That closer?"

Blake didn't reply.

"Where is Julianne Springman?"

"Gone."

"Gone?"

"Dead." He raised the gun and I prepared to dive to the side, but then he said, "You know what? For old times' sake, let's make this interesting. What do you say? We'll see who can get to your SIG first. One of us will walk out of here alive. One of us will join Julianne."

He slid the gun directly between us in the middle of the greenhouse.

Without a word, I flew forward.

And so did he.

81

I slid in, feet first like a baseball player sliding into the bag.

I was able to snag the gun, but Blake leapt on top of me as I did, and before I could aim it at him, he shoved me brutally to the concrete floor.

With his left hand, he pinned down my right wrist, then, straddling me, he grabbed my throat with his free hand and leaned forward, squeezing, choking me.

I tried to draw in a breath.

Nothing.

The day became a dizzy smear of darkness and bleary, drifting pain.

I attempted to aim the gun at him, but the angle wasn't right, not with him holding down my wrist.

But it was right to aim at something else.

Find a weakness.

Exploit it.

Okay, I will.

I fired up at the glass ceiling, then squeezed my eyes shut and turned my head to the side to protect my face from what was about to happen.

I sent four shots through the glass, and as the bullets exited the ceiling, a burst of fragmented glass shards rained down over us in a deadly shower.

Opening my eyes, I saw shock sweep over Blake's face and I was able to roll out from under him.

He stood and turned just enough for me to see the hand-sized glass daggers that'd augured into his back and neck. He lurched toward me, and I directed the gun at his chest. "That's close enough. Do not move."

But he took another step, his foot landing on the snow-covered pieces of glass. He lost his balance, his feet flew out from under him, and he fell backward, landing solidly and unforgivingly on his back.

Driving those glass shards all the way in.

I went to his side. "Who's the donor, Blake? Who's the one paying to watch people die?"

He grimaced and then said, "Leeson."

"I know about the grave. Who is the donor?"

He opened his mouth but no words came out.

"The 4D encryption, is that it?" I said. "The quantum research?"

Blake smiled faintly and squeezed my hand, then drew in two long, labored breaths and gazed past me at the snow lashing down at us through the shattered ceiling.

Then he stopped moving, and when I felt for a pulse, I found none.

Gone.

I checked myself to see if the glass had found me.

Three pieces had embedded into my left leg, but it wasn't enough to worry about at the moment. Not life-threatening.

After retrieving the thumb drives from Blake's pocket, I hurried outside, SIG drawn, to see how Ralph was doing with Mannie.

I found my friend standing beside the back of the truck.

Mannie was nowhere in sight.

"Did he get away?" I asked.

"Not quite." Ralph patted the truck.

"He's in there?"

"Oh yeah."

I holstered my weapon. "How are you going to get him out?"

"I haven't really thought that part through yet. Blake?"

"No longer a threat. You alright?"

"Yeah. You?"

"I'm okay."

He was staring at the glass sticking out of my leg.

"Oh, that," I said. "I'll be fine."

For a moment I considered prying the glass out, but I had the sense that it would bleed quite a bit and I didn't want to deal with that right now.

What did Blake mean by mentioning Leeson's name?

Wait.

I'd been making an assumption this whole time—that the man I'd chased into the subway was the only one to show up at the cemetery. But Duane had told me that he went there to meet the donor. Someone else could've easily come by while I was in the tunnel and either found the graveyard empty or noticed the CSI team and left.

We could tackle all that in a minute.

The sirens told me that backup was close. Well, with a big enough team, we could address how to get Mannie out of this truck.

My thoughts returned to Christie and Tessa, and I pounded against the side of the semi, then shouted, "Mannie, do you know where my wife and stepdaughter are?"

"No," came the hollow, metallic reply. "Duane?"

"Dead."

"Good," the rumbling voice responded, and once again I was reminded of Mannie's confusing allegiances.

Then, harsh smashing sounds came from inside the truck, drowning out anything else Mannie might have been saying. He was either trying to bust his way out or he was destroying the mannequins Ralph had sealed him in there with.

Well, we would find out soon enough.

Two police cruisers arrived.

I told Ralph what I was thinking regarding the graveyard, and he contacted the team to get exterior security camera footage from surrounding businesses to see if someone else might've been there.

I tried dispatch to find out if there was any news on Christie and Tessa, but they put me on hold.

While I was waiting for a reply, a call came in from a number I didn't recognize.

"Hello?"

"Pat. It's me." Christie's voice was tense and tight.

"Christie!" I exclaimed. "Are you okay?"

"Yes. Tessa's here with me. We're fine. I promise. A little chilled—not a good day for a swim."

"A swim?"

"Can you come?"

"Absolutely. Where are you?"

"The paramedics want to take us in, get us checked out for hypothermia and shock."

"Christie, what happened?"

"I'll tell you when I see you. I'm calling from Timothy Sabian's phone. Use this number if you need to reach me."

Sabian's phone?

"You're sure you're okay?" I said.

"Yes. Can you meet us at the hospital? The closest one is Metro Medical. That's where they want to take us."

"I'll be there as soon as I can."

"I don't want you to worry, but there's something important I need to talk with you about, and it's something I need to tell you in person. Alright?"

"Um. Sure," I said, but after hearing her say that, I couldn't help but worry. "I'm on my way."

It was now quiet inside the truck, and I could only guess what Mannie was preparing to do.

I left while Ralph and three other officers were gathering around the back of the semi in preparation to open its doors.

82

I wished Christie would have told me more about what was wrong or what she wanted to talk with me about, but I trusted her.

Still, obviously, I was concerned.

The drive gave me a chance to think some things through.

Leeson's grave. Ten o'clock. The donor.

Mannie's the one who told you to be there at ten. When he was fleeing the Field Office, he attacked Thurman, grabbing his wallet.

Or . . .

Mannie's body size and ethnicity didn't work for him to be the one observing the suicides.

Jon's internship . . . The quantum encryption research . . . Duane said you had no idea how deep this goes . . .

Earlier, Marcus Rockwell had given me his cell number. Now, I called it.

"Marcus, this is Agent Bowers. Did you find anything out about Duane?"

"I confirmed that he was the one behind the postings. We shut down his account, and we're tracking all of his contacts."

If I was thinking in the right direction, I needed to have a longer conversation with Mr. Rockwell.

"I need to see you, Marcus."

"What is it?"

"Can you meet me at the Jacob K. Javits Federal Building?"

"When?"

"As soon as possible. I have one other thing I need to take care of first."

"I can probably make it in an hour or so. Will that work?"

I wasn't sure, but I said yes.

"What is this concerning?" he asked.

"I just need to resolve a few questions regarding the postings."

Then I called Senator Murray, and he agreed to meet me at the Field Office as well.

Okay, let's see how this goes.

On my way to the hospital, I got word that Calvin had pulled through surgery alright. Then I heard from Angela that she and Lacey had come up with a match on the search for flight plans from private jets near the sites of the suicides in Seattle and Miami. "You're not going to believe this," she said, "but I have a name."

"Marcus Rockwell," I said.

Silence on the line, then: "How did you know that?"

"Let's just call it a lucky guess."

I reached Thurman to find out if he had more information about the donations to the charities and learned that the amount varied for the different victims, but it averaged a hundred thousand dollars.

So, that's what it costs these days to stand by and watch someone take his or her life.

++++

Since their clothes were soaking wet, the hospital provided both Christie and her daughter with a set of scrubs to wear.

She could have told Tessa about her cancer while they waited for Pat, but, just as she'd decided while she was at the monastery, she still felt that he needed to be the first to know.

++++

I parked and hastened into the hospital, recalling Christie's stories about the sea turtle hatchlings and the baby polar bear.

She'd been preparing to tell me something else, had put it off, and I had the sense that I was finally going to find out the significance of those two television-watching experiences all those years apart.

I made my way through the emergency room waiting area to the exam room where the nurse at admitting told me my family would be.

The death of those animals and the lies told to protect the innocent.

What did that have to do with us?

It was probably good that I was here in the emergency room wing, since I still hadn't removed the glass from my leg. We could take care of that in due time. Right now, I needed to see Christie.

Both my wife and stepdaughter were seated on an exam bed with blankets wrapped around their shoulders. They'd changed out of whatever clothes they'd been wearing and had on scrubs.

Before I could even greet her, Christie pointed to my leg.

"Pat," she said with amazing calm, "there's glass sticking out of you."

"I know. I'll be alright."

"That's seriously gross," Tessa said. "I think I'm gonna be sick."

I turned to the side so she wouldn't have to look at the glass.

"You need to get that taken care of," Christie urged me.

"I will in a second. I just wanted to make sure you two are okay."

They told me the story of what'd happened with Timothy Sabian and his father, who, in truth, really had been Assistant Director DeYoung.

It was hard to wrap my mind around, but all that would get sorted out eventually.

Christie was proud of her daughter for leaping into the car to save her, and Tessa was proud of her mom for shooting her way out of the sinking vehicle. I was proud of them both.

When they were done giving me the details, Christie asked Tessa if she could wait in the next room over for a few minutes. "I need to talk with Pat alone."

"Yeah, okay." Then Tessa said to me, "I'll tell the doctors to bring in a bone saw."

"I don't think they'll need to amputate, Raven."

"Whatever."

Once she was gone, Christie said, "She likes it when you call her that."

"When I call her . . . ?"

"Raven."

"Oh. Right."

An awkward silence.

Christie asked me to have a seat, and I pulled up the rolling chair, positioning myself with my injured leg straightened out to keep the pressure off where it was hurting.

"You had something you needed to tell me?" I asked without even trying to hide how anxious I was feeling.

"Pat, remember when I visited the doctor last week?"

"Sure." I felt a deep tremor of worry. "What is it?"

"What I have to say, it's about the test results."

"Go on."

"They were positive."

"What kind of tests, Christie? What does that mean? What's going on?"

"I love you, Pat."

Under these circumstances, those four words did not reassure me at all. "Christie, what tests? What did the doctor tell you?"

"I have breast cancer. It's serious. It's aggressive." A pause, and then she added, "The prognosis. It isn't good."

I felt like I was caught on a dizzy, spinning midway ride and there was no place to get my footing, nothing solid to stand on or hold on to.

I wanted to tell her not to be scared, not to worry, that everything was going to be okay, but all that came out was, "We'll work through this, okay? We'll do it together."

"Yes."

I took her hand. "And that's why you went to the monastery?"

She nodded. "I needed a chance to think things through." She touched away a tear. "I wasn't sure if I should tell you."

"Why wouldn't you have told me?"

"To protect you. But then Dr. Werjonic mentioned that truth is always a gift, no matter how hard it is to hear or to bear."

Yeah, that sounded like him.

And, at least in this case, I believed he was right.

Then I drew my wife close and I hugged her. And neither of us said a word.

83

It took me longer than I'd anticipated when I first told Marcus and the senator that I'd meet them in an hour, but when I informed them that I was in the emergency room, they both agreed to wait as long as necessary at the Field Office.

While I got my leg taken care of, Christie and I spoke more in-depth about what she knew and what we could do regarding her treatment options. Tessa kept coming back into the room, and Christie kept telling her it would be just a few more minutes.

Earlier, when I'd heard that Greer was dead, I'd realized that the deeper shock of what'd happened would hit me later, and I felt the same way now with Christie's news—the facts were there, out in the open, but all of the implications hadn't hit me yet.

But they would soon enough.

Finally, Christie told her daughter.

Tessa listened in silence, then said, "Well, we'll fight it, right? I mean, chemo or whatever? You'll be okay. I know you'll be okay."

"Yes," Christie said. "We'll fight it."

"And you'll be okay."

"And we'll be okay. We all will."

Honestly, I didn't want to think about the investigation. I just wanted to think about my wife, just wanted to be there for her now. But she told me that she needed to spend some time with Tessa, and I arranged for a car to take them back to our apartment while I prepared to tie up the loose ends of the case.

I checked in on Calvin before leaving the hospital. He was sleeping, and I didn't wake him but trusted the doctors when they told me that he was going to be alright.

Thank God.

At least there was one bit of good news.

On my drive to the Field Office, I heard from Ralph that the team had been able to corral Mannie into one of the police cars, and they were transferring him to the nearest precinct.

"Be careful," I told him. "After escaping from the FBI Field Office, getting out of a local police station might just be a cakewalk for him."

"I hear you. I'm not leaving his side until he's locked up tight. By the way, you know those sounds we heard coming from inside the truck?"

"Yes."

"He busted up a bunch of the mannequins and laid out the limbs and heads."

"What?"

"Some sort of design on the floor of the semi. Filled half the truck."

"The limbs and heads in a pattern?"

"Yeah."

Or a code.

"Send me a picture of it."

"We're en route."

"There are officers on-site, right? Call them. I need to see what Mannie left in there. If I'm right, it might be a message."

"For who?"

"Me."

Thurman met me in the lobby. "The senator and Rockwell are waiting upstairs," he said.

"Walk with me. Tell me everything you know about the charities and the donations."

As we rode the elevator, he filled me in on what he'd discovered.

In the first two instances, the donations had been made before the deaths to nonprofits that the victims supported and that were doing research that would benefit a sick relative—cancer research in one case, AIDS research in another. In the third instance, the donation to a hospital was sent after the suicide.

It seemed extraordinary to me that the money alone would've motivated the victims to take their own lives, but their visits to the Matchmaker's website indicated that they might've already had suicidal ideation and Thurman speculated that the money ended up just being the tipping point the victims needed.

Motives. What a tangled mess they were. I was just glad it wasn't my job to make sense of them.

"And Jon Murray? Was it the gambling debts?"

"His dad's bookie has connections to Sheldrick."

Why didn't that surprise me.

"How much money are we talking about?"

"Almost a quarter of a million dollars. Enough to torpedo his career if it became public knowledge."

The senator had assured me that his debt wasn't significant, that it was under control.

"All paid off?" I said to Thurman.

"In full. Anonymously, three hours before Jon's death."

We came to the conference room, excused the agent who'd been waiting there with Rockwell and the senator, and, knowing that I'd been at the hospital, they asked if I was okay.

"Yes," I told them. "I'm fine."

The blood on my pants might not have inspired too much confidence in what I was saying, but they left it at that.

There he was: Marcus Rockwell, the billionaire. Blonde. Wearing black skinny jeans, canvas tennis shoes, and a stylish sweater. My eyes were on his Chuck Taylor All-Stars—the same type of shoe that'd left sole impressions outside the window at Senator Murray's house.

"Now, how can we help you?" the senator asked.

Normally, I would have cared more about propriety, but half an hour ago my wife had told me she was dying of cancer, I wanted to get back to see her, and right now I didn't really care if I stepped on anyone's toes.

"Marcus," I said, "where were you on Sunday night at ten o'clock?"

"What?"

"Sunday night. We're checking the subway and the security cameras of the businesses surrounding Trinity Church Cemetery. Will we find you on them?"

He must have anticipated that we would be successful in our search because he said, "There's nothing illegal about visiting a graveyard."

"And you've been on some recent trips, I understand, to Seattle and Miami?"

He eyed me.

"What's going on here?" Senator Murray asked.

"Marcus," I said, "tell the senator where you were on the night his son died."

Senator Murray looked at me, then at Marcus, and then back at me. "Are you saying he's the one who was in my house, watching?"

"Why don't you ask him?" Thurman suggested angrily.

Marcus gave us a cold and unforgiving glare.

"Did you know Thomas Kewley?" I said to him.

"If you're accusing me of something, just come out and say it."

"Wait," the senator cut in, agitated. "I want to know if you were in my house."

Marcus gave him no reply.

"What do you do when you have tens of billions of dollars?" Thurman muttered. "When you have everything you could ever want? You expand your horizons." Then he pounded the table and said to Marcus, "Who gave the victims the ideas for the ways they died? Was that part of the deal? The more creative, the bigger the donation?"

"I didn't commit any crime." Marcus turned to the senator. "Your son loved you. That's why he did it. Because of your debts."

"My debts?"

"I paid them off."

Horrified, Senator Murray rose to his feet. "You could have saved Jon, but you didn't?"

"He did it for you. I did it for you."

The senator was quick.

Before Thurman or I could stop him, he rushed Marcus and landed two solid blows to his face.

It took both of us to pull him off the tech mogul.

"I didn't break any laws," Marcus protested, holding his broken nose. "I just watched the suicides. Just like thousands of other people did online."

"Actually," I said, "since you donated the money before two of the suicides, you influenced the victims—especially since they were on Selzucaine when they died. Those donations will be considered coercive to get the people to harm themselves. So will the money to the bookie. That turns them into homicides, not suicides."

"That'll never hold up in court. My lawyers will have a field day with this."

"Maybe," I acknowledged. "But maybe not."

If nothing else, the trial would be enough to finish Marcus's career. Perhaps it would even bring down Krazle.

Two other agents who'd heard the scuffle showed up at the door, and Thurman and I handed Rockwell off to them. "Arrest him," I told them. "Take him away."

"On what charge?"

"Murder, for starters. We'll move on from there."

I knew that none of this would bring back Senator Murray's son or any of the other victims, and all I could say to him was how sorry I was.

"I can't believe it was him," he said softly. "So, he met Jon during the internship, and then what? Somehow found out about my gambling and targeted him?"

"That's what it looks like, yes."

We located one of the staff psychologists to speak with the senator, to comfort him, then the photo came through from an officer at the greenhouse property, the image of the inside of the semi, and I saw the code Mannie had left for me with the snapped-off limbs and heads of the mannequins:

$$\sqsubset \sqcap \sqsupset \sqcap \sqcap \sqcap \sqcap \sqcap$$

I recalled the tic-tac-toe grid and mentally decoded the cipher: FIND HOPE.

I processed that.

Find hope?

Oh.

His wife's name was Hope.

Is it possible that—?

"You good?" Thurman asked me.

"What?" I said distractedly. "Yeah."

He noticed that I was staring at the image on my phone. "What's that?"

"Mannie destroyed the mannequins in the truck and left the body parts in this pattern."

"Is that the same code he used at the Field Office?"

"It is."

"Does it mean something to you?"

"I think it means his wife is alive." Then it hit me, how this was all tied together, how Mannie had managed to escape from the Field Office. Thurman was only scheduled to work half the day on Sunday. *Timing and location.* "But you knew that already, didn't you?"

"What are you talking about?"

"You're a good actor, Thurman, I'll give you that."

Just like Vidocq.

"An actor?"

"After Mannie got your wallet. You shed a tear for your wife and kids who were never in any danger. That's why

Mannie gave us a ninety-minute window—you were scheduled to work only half of the day, and he needed you there to help him escape."

Thurman quietly appraised me.

"How long have you been his handler?" I said.

"You're basing all this on my work schedule? How could that even matter?"

"Everything matters. It was no coincidence that you were right there at that key intersection in the hallway or that you sent me in the wrong direction. You helped him. And Hope, his wife, she's alive?"

"Yes," he said at last.

"Where is she?"

"A black site in Djibouti."

"You're holding her just to get him to help you?"

"It's not like that. She's not a prisoner. We're protecting her."

"Can she leave?"

"You're missing the point here, Patrick. It's—"

"Can she?"

Silence, and then, "You need to look at the big picture, what's best for everyone."

My anger was tightening. "When were you planning to reunite them?"

"When we had what we needed on the other people in Blake's network and on the quantum encryption research. There's a lot at stake here. We have to get this right. If the Chinese beat us to developing the network, we might not get a second chance."

"Are you going to get the two of them into witness protection?"

"We'll have to see. It'll depend on how much intel

Mannie is able to provide about the other players overseas." Thurman shook his head. "I don't even know how many laws he broke this week."

"I don't even know how many laws *you* broke this week." Thurman might have had the best intentions, but keeping an innocent woman imprisoned and helping Mannie escape were not his calls to make. "It's time to make this right."

He studied me. "Are you going to turn me in?"

"You free his wife, you do the right thing with witness protection, and I won't have a reason to."

"That can be arranged."

"And then you resign. You're finished at the Bureau."

"And if I don't quit?"

"I'm guessing prison. But that'll all depend on which of those laws we end up addressing. Now, you need to go tell Mannie that Hope is safe—and that you're going to let him see her."

On a normal day, I might have felt more satisfaction from wrapping up something like this, but today, all I could think of was Christie and the news she'd told me while we were at the hospital.

While Thurman went to speak with his confidential informant, I went home to see my wife.

84

Over the next several months, Christie and I had many conversations about life and God and death and hope.

Some days were better than others.

"How can you love a God who would do this to you?" I asked her one night in a moment of anger.

"Sometimes, Pat, I think you want a God small enough to be able to tell him what to do."

"No," I said. "I want a God big enough so that I don't have to."

A touch of silence. "I used to think the same thing."

"What changed your mind?"

"I realized that his love wasn't something I'd ever be able to understand, but if I was going to believe in him in the good times, then I needed to believe in him in the hard times too. Otherwise I was just using him."

"If he's small enough to understand, he wouldn't be big enough to worship," I said.

"Something like that. Yes."

++++

Timothy Sabian would have been glad to go to prison for killing his father if it meant protecting others from violence, but both the girl and her mom who were present there at the riverfront that day testified that he'd killed his dad in self-defense.

In his heart of hearts, he wasn't certain that it was *solely* in self-defense, but he was at least sure that he'd done it in the service of justice, and maybe that was enough.

For Miranda.

For Mom.

For all the others.

Were the bugs still bothering him?

Yes.

Some problems are not so easily solved.

But he had answers now, and a certain peace about who he was: a novelist with a felicitously overactive imagination.

He wasn't sure what his next book would be about, but he did know that he was going to finish Emily's story, and he was going to give her a happy ending.

++++

Studying Blake's computer files that were on the thumb drives I'd found on his body gave us what we needed regarding capturing the men in Phoenix who'd abducted Jake Reese's son.

The drives also contained Marcus Rockwell's findings on overcoming atmospheric turbulence to help establish the worldwide quantum encryption network.

It would be hyperbolic to say that whoever cracked that type of encryption first would rule the world, but it wasn't exaggerating to say that they would be able to control the world's secrets.

With that technology, Blake could've sent and received essentially unhackable communications with any terrorist group worldwide. He could have expanded his operations exponentially.

Now, the findings he'd gotten from Marcus could be put to much better use.

Calvin recovered, and it didn't take long for him and Christie to become friends. We found out he'd battled cancer himself a decade ago, something I hadn't even been aware of, and his encouragement meant a lot to her.

Thurman managed to wangle a lucrative severance package, which he accepted. Apart from hearing that he and his family were fine, I hadn't been in touch with him.

Mannie dropped out of sight, but he sent me a Christmas card with the coded message that he had Hope once again. I heard rumors that he was working with the Bureau. Though I couldn't be positive, I had confidence that he'd turned and was ready to give up the secrets that Blake had kept so dear while he was alive.

Senator Murray came clean about his gambling addiction, agreed to counseling, and it looked like his constituency was willing to forgive him, which I was glad to see. He was healing from the loss of his son—he told me that having resolution about what'd happened was the first step to moving on. And that was always a good thing.

And Marcus Rockwell?

He went on trial for four counts of second-degree murder.

It looked like the wheels of justice, although slow to turn, were at least moving in the right direction.

++++

To Tessa, the days seemed to last forever, but the weeks seemed to fly by.

She read a lot. She sat with her mom a lot. Sometimes she skipped school and just walked around New York City, thinking about what it would be like to live without the one person who'd always loved her.

Patrick tried to help. She could tell he was doing his best. One day, he gave her a book by a French detective.

"It's his memoirs," he said. "A friend of mine bought it for me. I want you to have it."

She eyed it. "Is it any good?"

"It's interesting. It's not always easy to tell what's fact and what's fiction in it."

"Sorta like life?"

"Maybe, yeah."

"I don't want to take it from you."

"It's okay, really. I've read it. And with your interest in solving mysteries, I thought you'd enjoy it. You're more of a bibliophile than I am, anyway. It's yours."

He took her out driving more. Sometimes they talked when he did. Mostly they were quiet, but it wasn't a lonely sort of quiet. It was more like the kind you have when you're with a friend.

++++

For Christie, seeing Pat with Tessa was enough to take away some of the sting of what was happening.

They were going to be okay.

As long as they were there for each other, things were going to be alright.

In the final days, Pat made up more tongue twisters for her—one every day, and she relished all of them—even if they weren't all that tough to say.

He never could seem to get them right.

It made her smile.

The two of them tried to add to their list of favorite memories, and the top three continued to change as each day passed.

85

With February came her death.

At first, you don't believe it.

You think that at any moment she'll suddenly material-ize, walking in from the other room, carrying a load of laundry that needs to be done, and she'll smile in that quiet, flirty way of hers and say, *Hey, you. What are you up to?*

But no.

She doesn't appear.

She's gone.

The death of your true love brings the cruelest of all miseries because it cannot be healed, not ever. Not really. Time might loosen its grip, but nothing can untwine the love that you have for that person when she passes away.

Passes away.

Dies.

I wanted a resurrection, something to remind me of her grace and beauty. But no resurrection came.

I cried deep and long. That's how all of this ended. That's what happened when the cancer won.

The first few weeks were the hardest.

I found a handwritten poem tucked in her Bible. I

didn't know when she might've penned it, but it was worn and crumpled and it looked like something she might have spent a good deal of time with.

> I bow and I rise, a child of the skies,
>   with glory and grace in my soul.
> A broken disguise, a sudden surprise,
>   a heart fully, finally whole.
> A secret that grows, a shadow that knows
>   where grace and mystery dwell.
> A heaven that glows, a Savior who rose
>   and tumbled the towers of hell.

After reading it, I went for a long walk carrying the umbrella that we'd met underneath, once upon a time.

It wasn't raining, and I didn't care.

++++

Tessa wasn't normally a ring wearer, but she wore one now—the ring her mom had given to her, the wedding band that Patrick had bought for her.

When her mom first asked her to take it, Tessa had told her there was no way she wanted it, but her mother had said, "Why would I want to get buried wearing this? I want you to have it."

"Don't even talk like that. You're not gonna be buried for a long time. You're gonna be alright."

"Humor me. Wear it, please. It doesn't fit me anymore, anyhow. It's too big now."

Tessa wore the ring on her right hand's ring finger. Sometimes, she ran her thumb along the edge of it just to feel something solid, real, lasting, that had been her mom's. She wasn't sure how long she was going to wear it, but she knew she was going to keep it until the day she died.

++++

Every week after her death, Tessa and I went to Christie's grave. The first two times we didn't really say anything, but on the third trip, Tessa asked me quietly if I believed in heaven.

"That's a hard question."

"No. It's an easy one. All you need to do is answer it."

I wasn't sure how to put this. "I believe in justice, and for that there must be a hell. And I believe in mercy."

"And for that there must be a heaven."

"Yes."

"So you do?"

"Well, I can't prove that heaven is real, but—"

"I didn't ask you to prove it."

"I know, but—"

"Do you *believe*?"

"Yes. I'd say that I do."

"Mom did too."

"I know." Silence. "And you?"

She shrugged. "If I didn't, I don't know how I could ever have any kind of hope."

I was quiet.

"So Mom's there now. She's not gone. Not forever."

"That's right."

The air was warm, but winter's grip was still on the city. Spring hadn't yet been able to overcome it.

"What happens now?" Tessa asked.

We move on, I thought. *We pick up the pieces and we do the best we can to make things work.*

"I'm not sure, Raven."

"Will you be there for me?"

"Of course."

"'Cause—not that I would ever need to—but I mean, if I ever *did* need someone to talk to, or whatever. Someday, I mean."

"I'll be here. I promise."

"Okay."

A long pause, then she said, "I miss her so bad."

"So do I."

"I hate pain." Her voice was soft and broken. "It's almost as bad as not feeling anything at all." She leaned her head against my shoulder, and I put my arm around her and held her as she cried.

Memento mori.

Remember death.

No, I have a better idea.

Let's remember life.

Moments, so brief, so precious.

Mist.

A vapor that so quickly passes us by.

I didn't know if Tessa would pull away. I half expected her to, but she didn't. Instead, she wrapped her arms around me, and I felt the warmth of her fingers as she squeezed my hand ever so slightly.

It was hardly enough to notice.

But it was enough to matter.

It was enough for now.

And I would hold her again if she needed me to, and I would do it every day after that until forever.

Because I love her.

And she's my daughter now.

And I'm her dad.

ACKNOWLEDGMENTS

Special thanks to Matt McCrory, Ashley Schwartz, Dr. Todd Huhn, Dr. J. P. Abner, Tom Colgan, Chris Grall, Grace House, Dan Conaway, Dr. Saad Al-Khatib, Dr. Kenneth E. Ferslew, Chanley Cox, Trinity Huhn, Liesl Huhn, and Sonya Haskins.